OF BLOOD AND ROSES

SAMANTHA ZIEGLER

ISBN: 979-8-9879534-2-6

Cover design: Cedric Daniel A. Vitangcol | @designsby.ced

For my father.

You have always been the rock of our family, and that has never been more apparent than this past year.

Thank you.

Kiza has done it again! Created a phenomenal playlist, that is. Listen to it on Spotify while you read!

CLIFFGUARD

SASKIA RIVER

ASTERIAL MOUNTAINS

PRESTOWNE

BENDSWORTH

TO ZUBIR'S

Rhodan

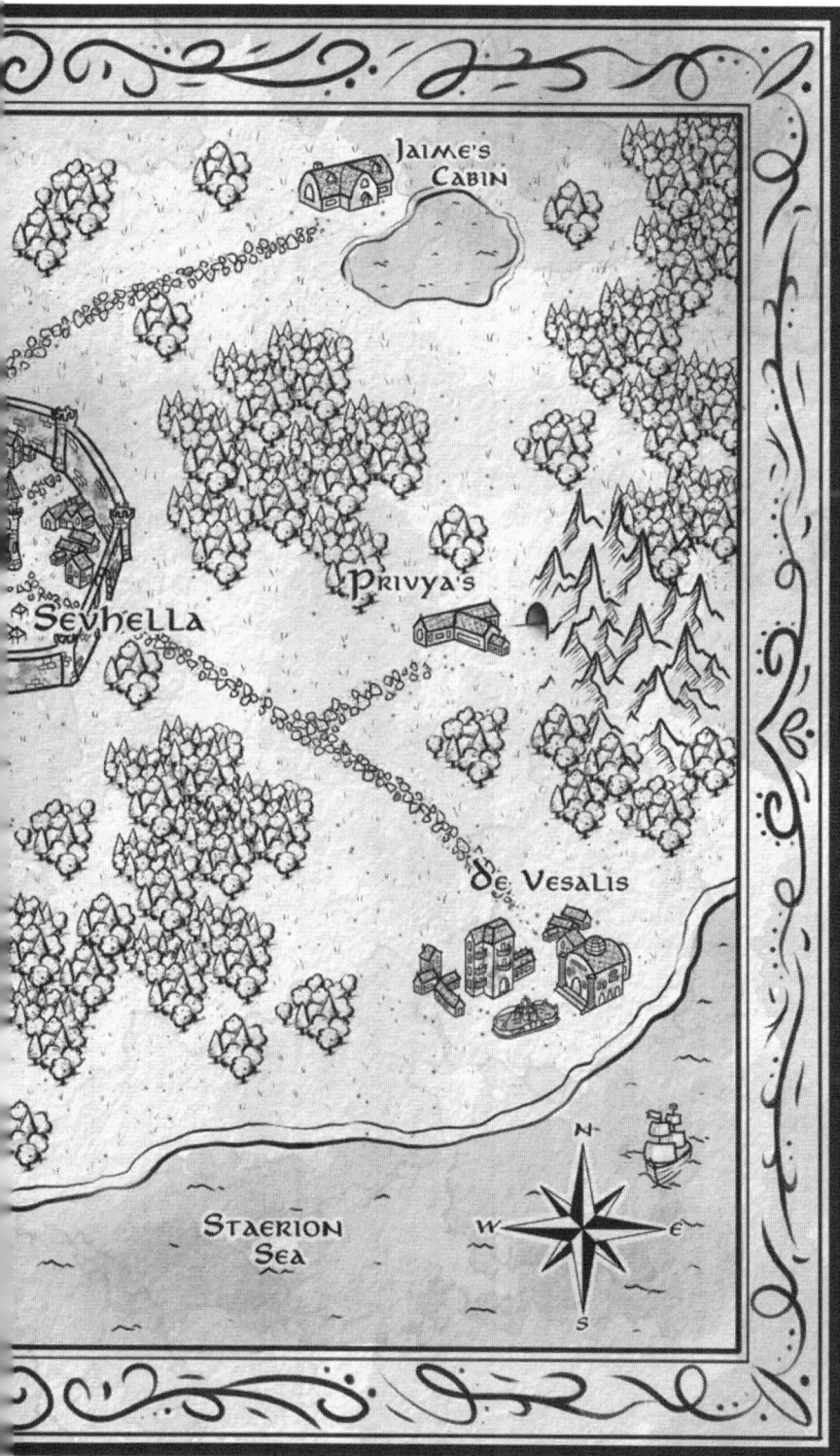

JAIME'S CABIN

SEVHELLA

PRIVYA'S

DE VESALIS

STAERION SEA

N
W   E
S

PROLOGUE

E lyse collapsed onto the cobblestone in a bloody heap, blue smoke dissipating around her. An arrow protruded from her arm—an arrow fired by Killian. Her vision blurred, light and dark crashing together. She squeezed her eyes shut as she dragged herself toward the hazy structure before her. She had lost so much blood. Her magic was nearly depleted. Yet she managed to raise her uninjured arm and rap meager knocks on the door.

She didn't know if the city street was empty, or if a passerby might spot her, bleeding and sobbing. She didn't care. She had lost her home, her business, and the respect of the man she cared for. And she was going to lose her life if someone didn't help her soon.

The door opened soundlessly—or perhaps her hearing was starting to fade. Dark shapes moved before her, ebbing in and out of reality. Shoes, she realized. Pointed, black shoes, and layered skirts sweeping across the floor.

"Elyse!" She barely heard a woman's gasp. Then, a moment later, "Fetch the master!"

Elyse didn't know if she groaned or screamed as the woman hauled her over the threshold. All she knew was that every movement was excruciating. Cobblestone was replaced by cool tile, and Elyse splayed herself against its embrace. Part of her wanted to give up, to let it all end here on this cold, hard floor. Surely death would be favorable to this.

She focused on the way the ceramic felt against her cheek, ignoring the woman's comforting words.

"It's all right, dear. It's all going to be fine."

If Elyse weren't utterly broken, she might have laughed. Nothing would be all right, not after today. She was a criminal on the run, and Killian would never stop searching for her. She'd seen it in his face—his absolute devastation.

No, it would not be all right.

Just before Elyse closed her eyes and let darkness overtake her pain, the woman's promising whisper met her ears.

"Don't worry. Master Jaime will be here soon."

CHAPTER 1

— • —

KILLIAN

The arrow hurdled toward Elyse as she stopped and flung her hand toward the ground, smashing a blue potion on the forest floor. Blue smoke erupted around her, and in the blink of an eye, Elyse and the arrow both disappeared.

The same dream—the same nightmare—haunted Killian every night for two damn months. He awoke each morning, gasping and drenched in sweat, the memory fresh in his mind.

He sat up straight in bed, his breaths ragged, and tried to calm his frantic mind. He'd spent so much of his childhood sleeping in this same bed, waking night after night from terrifying dreams of his siblings' deaths. That pain had finally faded, only to be replaced by a different sort of aching—one that he could only blame himself for.

His fingers trailed absentmindedly over the scar on his chest. If hearts could scar the same way skin did, what would his heart look like? Would it be worse than the pale flesh that marred his chest? Elyse had shattered his faith in himself, in humanity even. She had broken him so thoroughly, fracturing his life into little more than fury and numbness.

He'd been a well-respected lieutenant in the Royal Guard, and now he was reduced to nothing more than a grown man living with his mother. Mrs. Southwick told him every day that things would turn around, that he wasn't disgraced, and that he would find his way. But he heard the whispers behind his back on the rare occasions he ventured out into the city.

"That's Lieutenant Southwick, the one who was tricked by that murderous witch."

"Don't you mean *former* lieutenant?"

"What would his father say?"

Indeed, Killian had wondered that same thing himself. For once, he was glad for his father's passing. He didn't know how he could have faced him if he were still alive.

It wasn't that Edwin Southwick was an unkind man. He would have patted Killian's shoulder and consoled him, perhaps even offered him a story about a mistake he had made in his youth. He would have told Killian to pull himself up, dust himself off, and get on with life. But it wasn't anything his father would have said or done that would have been so unbearable. Merely being in his presence would have driven Killian to insanity. His father had been so proud the day Killian joined the guard, following in his footsteps. To have been dishonorably released from service, though—he wouldn't have been able to look his father in the eyes.

And the worst part of it all was that he had nothing to show for himself. Even after two months of searching, he didn't know where Elyse was or if she was even alive. Had his arrow pierced her? Surely it must have, or else it wouldn't have disappeared in the smoke—right? And if the arrow had pierced her, then where? Was it a superficial wound that could easily be patched? Or had he killed the woman who betrayed him?

The woman you fell in love with, echoed the voice in the back of his mind.

"Killian! Breakfast!" His mother's voice called from downstairs, wrenching him from the same circular thoughts that tormented him day in and day out.

Killian rolled over and glared out the window. From this angle, he couldn't see anything except for a bright, sunny sky and the occasional bird flittering by. He could hear children laughing and playing, though. Their happiness mocked him.

It wasn't too long ago that his mother's home had been filled with children's laughter. Georgie, the boy she'd taken in after Killian found him mixed up with the wrong crowd, had made several friends around the neighborhood. At one time, Killian had enjoyed mentoring Georgie, acting as an older brother to him. But after Elyse's failed arrest, he'd hardly had time for the boy.

The arrangement was never meant to be permanent though. And now that Georgie had been taken in by a kind family a few streets over, Killian and his mother were alone again.

"Killian!" Mrs. Southwick called up the stairs, the sweetness slipping away in her tone.

"Coming," he murmured as he rolled out of bed.

The small bedroom was mostly bare, its only furniture a narrow bed, a chest of drawers, and a small table. None of it matched, and though his childhood bedroom hadn't been used in over a decade, each piece was well worn. Killian's mother had never been one to throw anything out. "Each piece tells a story," she would say.

Normally he loved his mother's eccentricities, but lately he had failed to see the joy in them.

Killian pulled a tunic over his head and slid on a pair of trousers—both gray and neatly pressed. He kept the bedroom just as clean as he had his quarters at the palace, tidiness ingrained in him long ago.

"Killian!" Mrs. Southwick hollered as he laced up his boots. "Your breakfast is getting cold!"

He could imagine his mother standing over a hearty breakfast, hand on her hip.

"I'll be down in a second," he half called, half groaned.

Killian paused and regarded the map of Rhodan that lay atop the small table. The ragged parchment was spotted with tiny blue dots, each gently illuminated and pulsating softly. His eyes instantly shot to the capital, located in the center of the map. Nothing appeared amiss. As always, his reaction was a combination of relief and disappointment. He sighed before he yanked open his bedroom door and trudged down the stairs.

Sure enough, Mrs. Southwick stood beside a table full of eggs, fruit, bread, and sausage, with one hand on her wide hips, the other holding a glass of milk. Sweat gathered on her dark skin, though the true heat of summer was only just beginning. Contrary to Killian's beliefs, she didn't seem bothered. A cheery smile was on her face.

She passed him the milk and gave him a quick peck on the cheek before Killian seated himself at the small feast.

"Eat your fill," she ordered in her motherly tone. "Today is going to be a good day—I can feel it."

Killian made a noncommittal grunt as he forked a sausage and took a hearty bite.

"It is," his mother insisted. She seated herself in the chair beside him but didn't touch any of the food.

"You say that every day, Mum," Killian protested. "You make all this food, but you hardly eat any of it. It'll be a good day when you help yourself to your fill."

Killian's mother opened her mouth, likely to object, but a knock at the door interrupted.

"I'll get it," Mrs. Southwick said as she hoisted herself from the chair and bustled her way toward the front door. "You get yourself some of those eggs," she called over her shoulder. "Sunny side up, just the way you like!"

Killian scooped two eggs onto his plate but didn't bother to tell his mother, for the hundredth time, that he preferred his eggs scrambled.

Mrs. Southwick swung the front door open, and sunlight illuminated the entire room. Killian let out another grunt at that. He blinked a few times against the brightness, and the silhouette in the doorway started to take shape. A short boy stood on the threshold, a scroll of parchment in his hand.

"A letter, ma'am," he said cheerily up at Mrs. Southwick, his mop of brown hair shaking as he went. When he smiled, Killian noticed he was missing one of his front teeth. "It's for Miffter Sowfwifck," the boy proclaimed through his lisp.

Clearly, this young man didn't know who Killian was, or else he wouldn't be so merry.

"Thank you, dear," Mrs. Southwick said as she took the parchment from the boy. "Would you like some breakfast?" She pointed her thumb over her shoulder to where Killian sat at the table.

"No fanks, ma'am. I've got a whole bundle of letters to deliver." He patted his hip, where a satchel bursting with parchment rested.

As Killian's mother bid the boy farewell and crossed the room with the letter in hand, Killian wondered who it could be from. Perhaps it was some official business from the Royal Guard regarding his dismissal, or an update on Elyse's whereabouts. No, certainly not that. He had been searching for her rigorously these past two months—if not more than the entire Guard had. He would know if she had been found.

Mrs. Southwick handed him the letter as she sat down beside him, and he tore open the seal immediately.

"Honestly, Killian. Can't you finish your breakfast first?" she scolded him. "Sometimes I don't know who raised you."

But Killian was in no mood to tease his mother back, or even huff at her comments. He held his breath and gave his entire focus over to the few words scrawled on the parchment.

Noon. Today. 453 W Abernathy.

That was all it said, but it was enough.

His appetite disappeared immediately, replaced by anticipation. He'd waited so long for this meeting, and now everything else seemed trivial.

"Thanks, Mum," Killian said, the chair scraping across the floor as he stood up.

Mrs. Southwick began to protest, but Killian kissed her on the cheek.

"I'll be back this afternoon," he told her. He tried his best to school his features into nonchalance, but Mrs. Southwick didn't seem convinced.

"Where are you going?" she called after him as he marched toward the door. "What did the letter say?"

Killian paused before the front door, his hand landing lightly on the handle. He turned back to his mother, who sat at the table with her mouth open, a crease between her brows. Killian knew she'd worried over him these past few months, and that he'd done nothing to quell her anxieties. If anything, hiding away in his room and disappearing into the forest for hours at a time had only made things worse.

He sighed as his heart sank. Killian was all she had left, and he had been lost in his own world, obsessing over Elyse. He would have to do better by her. But for now, he could tell her a little white lie, couldn't he? If only to make her feel better?

He forced a smile on his face and softened his eyes. "It's about a job," he said with false cheer. The lie made him nauseous, but he couldn't very well tell her the truth.

Mrs. Southwick's entire countenance changed as her face lit up and her shoulders relaxed. "A job? Where?"

Her excitement ate at him.

Killian held up a hand to stop her. "Mum, I promise I'll tell you all about it later, but for now, I want to take a walk and clear my head." He said the words gently, then added sincerely, "I love you."

A smile rippled across his mother's face, genuine and pure. "I love you too—even if you are a pain in my behind."

Killian chuckled as he grabbed his cloak, then turned back to the door and flung it open. For the first time in months, he marched into the street with a spring in his step as hope fluttered in his heart.

CHAPTER 2

— • —

ELYSE

The morning was quiet—just as quiet as it had been these past few months. Elyse stared out the enormous window of the country estate, taking in the picturesque lake that spanned the landscape. She blew on her tea, which she held cupped between both hands, and then took a small sip, savoring the bitter yet familiar taste of citronascia.

These peaceful moments were all that kept her sane. Every morning, she lay in bed until the sun fully illuminated her chambers, then she padded down to the kitchen, steeped her tea, and stared out the window.

She realized several weeks earlier that she never looked to the sky to determine the weather. No, she looked to the lake. Some days, the water was nearly blinding, and she had to blink away the glaring sunshine. Other days, the lake's surface was calmer, reflecting the clouds that strolled lazily overhead. And still other mornings, the waters were dark, churning in anticipation of a storm.

For a moment, Elyse would take it all in, rejoicing in the mild weather, or lamenting a stormy day. Then realization would set in, gripping her in its cold, bony hand. Realization that the weather had no bearing on Elyse or her plans for the day. She was to be cooped up in this house for the foreseeable future. And then she would sigh and retire to her chambers, or the library, or one of the other lavish but impersonal rooms. Her heart sank.

The country estate was far more glamorous than her small cottage, but that was little consolation after two months of solitude. At least at her cottage, she would be surrounded by her own things—things that reminded her of her childhood and her mother. Things that brought her joy: her favorite blanket, even if it was faded and worn; her spell book, with its folded corners marking her favorite spells, and notes in the margin; and her obstacle course, where she could immerse herself in training for hours.

She tried not to think about what had happened to all of her belongings. There was no point in fretting over things out of her control—at least, no more than she already did.

Every time she closed her eyes, the same face drifted into her mind. Killian's expression of anger and hurt played over and over, endlessly breaking her heart.

No matter how much time passed, it still felt fresh, like a wound that refused to heal. It had been two months since Killian tried to arrest her for murdering King Cyril. Since she had magicked herself to Jaime's doorstep, bleeding and desperate. Since she had nearly died trying to escape the only man she'd ever trusted.

She'd collapsed into darkness, giving in to the pain. For hours, or perhaps days, she had seen nothing but Killian's face, the cold stare and tight jaw and utter pain in his eyes. When she awoke, groggy from a drug-induced stupor, she had been alarmed to find herself in an unknown bed, blinking at an unknown ceiling. She'd been even more alarmed to hear a man's voice speak gently to her.

"You're awake."

Jaime Lindgren, her former lover.

Reality had flooded Elyse like waves crashing over a broken levee, threatening to send her back into an oblivion that hovered between nightmare and denial. But Jaime brought her a glass of water and sat patiently while she slowly caught her breath, giving her the space to collect herself. He ran his hand through his blond hair, glancing anxiously at her as if she might fall back asleep. Finally, Elyse set the empty glass down, and Jaime began to explain everything.

"You were in a bad way," he'd said softly, and Elyse had to look away. Too much concern filled his gaze, reminding her of others she'd hurt. "You had an arrow in your arm, and a poorly healed wound on your wrist. It looked like..."

His words trailed off. It looked like exactly what had happened: she had cut off her own hand to escape the magic-suppressing shackles, then hastily reattached it. Heat seared her cheeks, and she chanced a glance at Jaime. His light skin was even paler than usual, his blue eyes rimmed with dark circles, and his expression conveyed horror.

"I brought you here, to one of my properties outside the capital," he continued after a moment. "No one knows you're here, and well..." He rubbed the back of his neck, smiling sheepishly. "This estate isn't exactly titled in my name. One of the perks of the trade," he'd chuckled.

Jaime had made quite a fortune for himself, traveling and collecting magical artifacts and knowledge. Elyse didn't know the details, aside from some of the adventures he'd recounted for her, but she wasn't surprised to hear he had made some off-the-books purchases.

Then Jaime reached out his hand and laid it atop hers. It was warm and soothing, a feeling that Elyse didn't deserve.

"You're safe here," he'd said, and Elyse couldn't hold it together anymore.

She'd wept, her body racked with sobs, and Jaime had just held her, stroking her hair as she cried.

She told him everything. She couldn't stop herself as the words, ripe with self-loathing, spilled from her lips. Her voice was raspy, serrated from disuse, as she told him of Lazarus, and how he had been controlling her for years. She told him about the disease, how it had taken her mother, and how Killian had given her a cure. And finally, she told him of how she had been ordered by Lazarus to kill King Cyril, and how Killian had found out.

She'd expected Jaime to cast her out, to sic the Royal Guard on her, or to at least scream at her for being so reckless. Any of that would have made sense to her. Instead, he gave her a sympathetic look, one that made her heart swell with both pain and comfort, and told her it was all right.

Elyse didn't know how to react, so she simply cried more. She certainly didn't deserve his kindness or his understanding, and yet it was the only thing keeping her from clawing out her own heart. And she was so tired—not just from the blood loss, but emotionally. She'd forgotten how draining it was to be heedlessly honest, and so she had wept against his chest until she fell asleep.

When she awoke sometime later, it had not been to Jaime's blue eyes or fair hair, but to a note.

Elyse,

I had to step out and attend to some things. I will be back soon.

Do not go outside, and do not use more than simple magic. The Royal Guard is searching for you.

Rest, and remember, things will get better.

Yours always,

Jaime

That first day, Elyse barely moved from the bed. She'd drifted in and out of sleep, wishing her dreams would offer some escape. But of course, that hadn't been the case.

True to his word, Jaime returned a few days later to check on her. Since then, he had stopped by the estate a handful of times, but never for more than an hour or two.

"It will be suspicious if I'm gone for too long, since the Guard knows that we're acquainted," he'd explained. Apparently, they had come and questioned him on multiple occasions, and he had seen members of the Guard in plainclothes following him about town. "But don't worry," he assured her. "I've taken the precautions to make sure you're safe."

Elyse didn't know what those precautions were, and she couldn't bring herself to care. Truthfully, she couldn't bring herself to feel much of anything. She spent her days in a numb sort of daze, aimlessly wandering the many rooms of the estate, or sleeping the day away, not even bothering to eat more than a few morsels. Her appetite had abandoned her along with her happiness.

"You just need a hobby," Jaime tried to encourage her. "Something to pour yourself into."

Each time he came to the estate, he brought her a new distraction: pencils for sketching, a beautiful leather-bound journal, paints and brushes. He'd even brought an upright piano for her, along with several instructional books, but Elyse hadn't played a single note.

For a fleeting moment, she considered that today, a day when the waters of the lake reflected a crystal blue sky, she might attempt to play. The feeling was soon extinguished, though, as apathy washed over her.

She wasn't left in her dread for long. A rap at the door reverberated through the country home, meeting her ears.

Two quick knocks, three heavy pounds, and two quick ones again.

Jaime was here.

Elyse padded down the hallway lined with paintings of hills and valleys she had never seen. Her feet didn't feel quite as heavy as they had a moment ago; at least when Jaime was around, life was more tolerable. She found herself wondering what sort of activity he had brought her this time.

As she entered the foyer, she saw Jaime standing tall, a basket hanging from the crook of his elbow. He looked healthy, a slight glow to his skin as if he had been enjoying the summer weather, and his gold hair seemed brighter.

A warm smile graced his lips, his blue eyes bright. "I have a surprise for you."

Elyse merely regarded the basket, waiting for his latest offer at a distraction. She was surprised when he added, "How would you like to have a picnic?"

Elyse froze, though her heart raced at his words. "Outside?" she asked, almost afraid to know the answer. He had forbidden her from stepping foot outside the house, for her own safety. She longed to envelop herself in fresh air, to feel the warmth of the sun on her skin, but she didn't dare get her hopes up.

"Yes," he said, his grin widening. "I think, with me around to protect you, you should be able to get away from here for an hour or so."

Elyse didn't know what to say. Her heart pounded in her chest as Jaime extended his free arm to her. A faint smile graced her lips as she took his arm and followed him out the door.

CHAPTER 3

— · —

KILLIAN

Killian clutched the letter in his hand as he stalked through the quiet street. He'd been casually meandering around the block for the past hour or so, gathering his bearings. His palms were drenched in sweat as the appointed time neared, and not just because of the summer heat. The sky was nearly cloudless, a sunny glow cast over the city, but Killian couldn't shake the eerie feeling that chilled his spine. He knew he was walking into unfriendly territory, but it was a risk he had to take. He'd sought out this meeting for a month, and prayed it would be exactly what he needed after so many dead ends.

The address appeared to be an abandoned bakery, its sign half torn away, and the windows boarded up. It was in no worse shape than many of the other buildings on the block, including the businesses that were still open. Others milled about the street, their hoods pulled low to hide their faces, but they paid him no mind. In this part of town, it seemed the people kept to themselves.

Killian eyed each passerby, studying them with a decade's worth of training. He imagined what sort of devious plans brought them to this neighborhood. A few months ago, he would have turned up his nose at them. Now he was one of them.

All the while he waited, his excitement grew. This was it—exactly the break he needed. It was the same feeling, the same weightlessness and goose-pimpled skin he would get before interrogating a suspect, knowing damn well he had them dead to rights. Yet there was an underlying tone to it, one he couldn't identify.

Finally, it was time. He walked briskly, his cloak flowing behind him. As he pulled the door open, it emitted a loud *creeeeak*. He looked over both shoulders before tearing across the threshold.

The inside of the building looked exactly as he had imagined. Dust covered nearly every surface, tattered signs lined the walls, and a rodent scurried behind the counter. Perhaps at one point it had been a quaint family bakery where people could socialize and buy little cakes, but now it was downright depressing.

Though there appeared to be no threats, Killian stood tall, his hands ready to cast a shield, his dagger poised at his hip.

"Hello?" he called out.

A door behind the counter swung open, and a grisly man stepped through. He appeared to be in his forties—or perhaps time hadn't been kind to him. Despite the heat, the man wore a leather jerkin. Stringy brown hair reached to his shoulders, and a scruffy beard coated his face. "You must be Killian." His voice was as haggard as his countenance.

Two more men emerged through the doorway, similarly dressed in leathers. They weren't as stocky as the first man, but they carried themselves with a formidable air as they marched into place on either side of him. Seeing the way they stood together, their silent but palpable camaraderie tugged at something in Killian's chest that he didn't want to acknowledge.

He kept his voice even as he replied, "And you must be Siamus."

Siamus's chin lifted ever so slightly in affirmation, a glimmer of pride shining in his dark, cunning gaze. His pride was fitting. He hadn't become the leader of Rhodan's Bastards—the most ruthless and powerful mercenary group in the kingdom—through incompetence. The legends surrounding the man were astounding bordering on absurd. Even if only a fraction of the stories were true, he was still a force to be reckoned with. For a moment, Killian wondered how Elyse would fare against him, both in combat and conversation. Their arrogance would be well met.

"You said you have a job for us?" Siamus asked in that gruff voice that dripped with apathy.

Killian took a few sauntering steps toward the wall and leaned against it, reveling in the way Siamus's lackeys tracked his every movement. "I want you to find someone and bring them to me—alive."

Siamus's face remained impassive. "Kidnapping ain't exactly a job for the Bastards."

It was true. A mere kidnapping would be far too bland for their normal capers. The Bastards were more accustomed to robbing high-profile merchants or terrorizing bar patrons. But this was no mere kidnapping.

Killian let a small smile play across his lips. "But you don't even know who the target is."

"I'm listening," Siamus grunted.

Killian's smile grew a hair wider. "Elyse Crenshaw."

He realized it was the first time he'd said her name aloud since she'd disappeared. It tasted like filth against his tongue.

The only reaction Siamus gave was a tiny twitch of his mustache, but the other two men exchanged quick glances. That told Killian enough. They would take the job.

"Have you heard of her?" Killian asked, feigning casual ignorance.

"Aye," Siamus conceded. "You'd be pressed to find a wielder in Rhodan who hasn't heard of her." He widened his stance and crossed his arms over his broad chest as he added, "She's untouchable."

Killian's ribs seemed to tighten, knitting together at Siamus's words. He would never be able to fathom Elyse's infamy.

"Are you saying you can't do the job?" Killian goaded.

Siamus's eyes narrowed. "Careful," he warned. "I'm saying it'll cost you."

"I don't care about the price," Killian drawled. "Just get it done."

Siamus nodded. "Half a million gold," he said. "Half now, half upon delivery."

Killian had to rein in his surprise. He knew that their cost was high, but damn—Elyse really did hold a reputation.

No matter, though. He could get it done.

"And we'll need something to track her by—a hair or something," Siamus added.

Killian frowned. He'd tried using Elyse's hair and other personal belongings to wield tracking spells, but with no success. He supposed the Bastards had their own methods.

He stood up straight and crossed the dusty floor in three lazy strides, trying to conceal his excitement. Finally, after two months of fruitless searching, after countless spellbooks, after so many sleepless nights, this felt like progress. So why was his hand so heavy as he lifted it toward Siamus? Why was his voice raw as he uttered his agreement?

Siamus hesitated for a moment, long enough that Killian thought he'd said something to offend the leader. The dusty air floated around them as they stared one another down, their cooperation hanging in the balance between them.

Then he took Killian's hand in his own massive, scarred hand and shook it—and the deal was made.

CHAPTER 4

— : —

ELYSE

There was nothing like fresh fucking air.

Sure, Elyse had opened the windows before and let a summer breeze caress her. She'd even been out of the house twice—with Jaime's blessing, of course—to perform her full moon rituals. But feeling the seductive warmth of sunshine and being surrounded by nature, watching the birds soar overhead and inhaling nothing but pure, fresh air... For a moment she could forget that she was a wanted murderer.

She sat on the edge of a blanket with her bare feet nestled in the grass. Jaime had led them to a spot near the lake, and the rhythmic lapping of the water against the shore was soothing. He'd spread out a few snacks as well—cheeses, crackers, pastries—but Elyse hadn't touched any of them. For now, she just wanted to bask in the outdoors.

Jaime lay beside her, his face lifted to the sky. His golden hair hung loose around his shoulders, shimmering in the sunlight. His pale, flawless skin and his sharp blue eyes fit the landscape perfectly, like a painting brought to life.

"Nothing from Lazarus?" he asked gently, as if scared she might run at the inquiry.

Elyse didn't answer right away, instead staring off at the shoreline, watching the waters swell and recede, swell and recede. Two full moons had passed while she'd stayed at Jaime's cottage, and she hadn't performed the ritual for either of them. She'd stayed awake the whole night the first time, sitting up in bed with her knees to her chest as she awaited Lazarus's condemnation. It hadn't come.

She'd been certain that he would find a way to torment her, just as he had when she'd refused to kill Kelia, the young girl whose death had changed everything. Then, he'd somehow infiltrated her mind, besieging her with visions of how he would punish her if she didn't obey. Surely, she'd thought, he would do the same—or worse. But the night had passed and the sun had risen without so much as a hint of Lazarus's wrath.

Elyse's shock had captivated her for the better part of a week. She'd been scared, of course—downright terrified if she were being honest. And yet, she couldn't shake the feeling of disappointment. Part of her had sat in that bed, loathing the plush mattress and the silk sheets, eager for Lazarus's judgment. It would have been a reprieve to bear someone else's affliction for once, instead of her own. She would have welcomed it.

By the time the second full moon shone in the sky, her anxiety had ebbed. If Lazarus was angry at her for abandoning her duties, he wouldn't have waited a full month to retaliate. She didn't understand why he no longer seemed to care about her obligations, and she didn't wish to dwell on it for long. She'd never understood his motivations. She didn't have the energy to start caring now.

Jaime continued to gaze at her, awaiting her answer. Finally, she managed a shrug.

He nodded, his posture nonchalant, but his blue eyes confessed his concern. Elyse looked away.

She knew she should try harder, if only for his sake. He had done so much for her. Not only had he saved her life, he'd kept her hidden from the Guard. He made certain she was well cared for and tried to help her stay sane. The gifts and activities he brought her were thoughtful, and he came to see her as often as he could. She was lucky to have him, yet she just couldn't bring herself to *care*.

She sighed and stretched her toes deeper into the grass, trying to ground herself in something familiar. "How's business?"

She felt him tense a little beside her as if he hadn't expected her to speak. "Business is... excellent," he said, somewhat timidly, like he was hesitant to admit his good fortune in light of her own pitiful situation. "I'm actually going to be gone for a few weeks, acquiring some new artifacts. That's why I wanted to do something special today."

Elyse glanced at Jaime as a knot formed in her stomach. She hadn't realized that some part of her looked forward to his visits until she was faced with a prolonged absence. Dread crawled up her spine. She would be left with nothing but her own company for weeks.

Jaime gave her a sympathetic smile as he touched her hand. "You'll be all right," he encouraged. "You're strong."

Without thinking about it, Elyse curled her fingers around Jaime's hand. Devil's blaze, it had been so long since she'd had any sort of contact with another person, and her chest seized. She let his touch anchor her. Jaime squeezed her hand in return, and Elyse thought her heart might stop from the pure comfort it gave her.

They sat together like that for a long moment, simply holding hands. Elyse's mind was a pendulum, swinging between resolution that she would be fine on her own and utter panic at her future's uncertainty. Was this her life now? Hiding away in the countryside, alone and nearly catatonic? Craving the company of a man she saw sporadically? Even if she did take up a hobby, what was the point? Art and music—they were all meant to be shared, appreciated collectively. She detested the idea of drawing or writing or learning piano if there was no one else to validate it. Perhaps that made her selfish, or simply human. But she had been someone before all this. She'd had a reputation as a proficient businesswoman and a ruthlessly powerful witch. And it hurt so badly to have *nothing* to show for herself.

21

She was getting carried away. Nothing had to be decided now. There were still options to pursue. She could escape to another kingdom and build a new life there. She just needed to take a little time and figure out what she wanted, and then she could form a plan. She was, after all, one of the most cunning and capable women in all of Rhodan. She could do this.

She looked to Jaime, her confidence growing. With his help, she could do this.

"Thank you," Elyse murmured, unsure why she was saying it. "For everything." She let out a long breath, trying to banish the anxiety from her body.

Jaime gave her a warm but crooked smile. "I have a confession to make."

Elyse tilted her head, a little nervous but curious nonetheless.

"As wretched as the circumstances are, I'm secretly a little glad," he said. His blue eyes seemed to penetrate Elyse as he continued. "I'm glad you felt like you could come to me, and I'm glad to be able to spend this time with you."

She wasn't sure what to say. Some part of her, buried deep beneath her melancholy, was perhaps glad for their reuniting as well. But it was nearly out of reach, shrouded by self-loathing and guilt.

Jaime cleared his throat and continued, somewhat sheepishly. "I felt horrid that I went so long without reaching out to you when I got back."

Elyse recalled the night she'd run into him at Taverne De Lac. She'd thought he was away traveling the continent, and when she found out he'd been back for six months, she'd felt slighted. She wasn't used to being carelessly tossed aside, certainly not by men who seemed entranced by her, and she had resented him for it.

Jaime rubbed at the back of his neck with his free hand. "I meant to reach out right away, but I got busy with a trade as soon as I came back. And then weeks passed and I felt ashamed that I hadn't gotten in touch with you, though I still wanted to. I was scared you'd be upset, or maybe you wouldn't even want to see me. And so I kept putting it off, which only made me feel more ashamed, and..."

He was rambling. He was always so collected, always swaggering, and now he was stringing his sentences along like he couldn't help the way they poured out. The tiniest hint of a smile tugged at Elyse's lips.

"I can say wholeheartedly that all is forgiven," she said, and she meant it. It seemed such a silly thing to hold over him in light of how much he'd done for her these past months.

His face split into a grin, and his gaze traveled away, toward the lake.

"I'm glad you got to spend some time out here," he mused. "I'm sorry that you'll be cooped up for so long."

Elyse followed his gaze out to the lake. It was so much more breathtaking up close. Feeling the breeze and seeing the tranquil movement of the water was incomparable to merely watching it from a faraway window. She sighed and sat up straight, pulling her hand away from Jaime's.

"Perhaps I could just—" she began, but he cut her off abruptly.

"No. The safest place for you is inside the house. That's where the wards are." She didn't look at him, but she could feel the heat of his stare. "The Guard is using all sorts of tactics to track you down. It's too risky."

Elyse nodded. As much as it pained her, she knew he was right. She glanced up at the house and steeled herself to be locked up once again. At least in a few weeks there would be another full moon, and she could get out then.

CHAPTER 5

— • —

KILLIAN

Sweat trickled from Killian's dark curls, down his temple and his hard jawline. It dripped from his chin to his mangled pectoral, where the flesh was pocked and discolored, and down his chiseled abdomen that heaved with every ragged breath. He stood with his hands resting on top of his head, gulping down the humid air.

He'd pushed himself hard today—had needed to. The meeting with Siamus had left him with a lingering exhilaration that he needed to expend. He'd gone to the place he always went when he felt overstimulated—Elyse's obstacle course.

The Guard stayed posted outside her shoppe, keeping an eye out for Elyse, but they had paid little mind to the training course in the woods behind the cottage. Killian could come and go as he pleased, free to use the course without anyone even noticing.

What seemed like a lifetime ago, Elyse had shown him how to, for lack of a better word, *communicate* with the course, tailoring it to different skill levels and emphases. It had been designed to mimic actual, multi-person combat. The burlap-sack dummies could be activated to shoot stones or stunning spells at a moving target, and they could shield themselves as well. It was truly a brilliant combination of both traditional and magical engineering, reminding Killian every day just what level of cunning he was up against.

He'd come a long way since his initial days of training, when he'd had to put all his focus into creating a tiny shield. Now he could duck and dive through obstacles, shield himself, and shoot hexes at the dummies. Sometimes his spells even hit them.

He was especially proud of his performance today. He had moved with intention and lethal elegance fueled by adrenaline, and he'd hit one of the dummies square in its chest three times in a row.

While the course was essentially perfect, there was one way in which it lacked. Training alone meant no one to celebrate with. He missed the brotherhood of the Guard and sharing an ale with his fellow soldiers after a hard day's training. He missed it like he missed his siblings and his father.

He heard a faint rustling—barely audible over his own panting—and turned toward the sound. Manny, his best friend and former second-in-command, strolled through the trees toward him. He wore his black military jerkin, the sight of which sent a pang through Killian.

He looked flustered. His sandy-blond hair was pulled back into a bun, but the edges along his hairline curled into wisps from the humidity. Sweat gathered on his brow, and his cheeks were reddened from the sun. He smiled at Killian, offering him a wave, but the smile was forced, not the genuine one he almost always donned.

"I figured I'd find you here," Manny called as he stepped through the obstacle course and into the center of the fighting pit. "I stopped by your mother's place, but she said you weren't home. Mentioned something about a job?"

Killian sensed a full conversation coming, so he dropped to the sandy floor and perched his elbows on his knees. He toyed with the strip of leather on his wrist—the one threaded with a crystal. The crystal given to him by Elyse that allowed him to channel his magic.

"There is no job," he said finally.

Manny sighed. "I was afraid of that." He sat down beside Killian without any of his usual grace. His broad shoulders wilted as he dropped his forehead to his palm.

"You're going to give that woman a heart condition," he groaned.

Now it was Killian's turn to sigh. "I know." He leaned back, digging the heels of his hand into the sand and glimpsing up at the brilliant blue sky. The sky always seemed richer after training. "It'll be the last lie I tell her. I promise."

Manny harrumphed at that, and the silence settled between them.

Killian had debated telling his friend about hiring the Bastards to track down Elyse. He expected Manny would only scold him for it, reminding him for the thousandth time that he needed to let the Guard handle it, and that he should find a way to move on. Manny didn't seem to understand that Killian would never move on, perhaps not even after Elyse was caught.

And yet other times Manny would look at him with nothing but brotherly sympathy in his eyes, as he did now. His faith in Killian felt misplaced. It made him shift, driving his boots into the sand.

"Is there a reason you came to find me?" he asked.

Manny gave him a one-sided grin. "I've got the day off tomorrow. Thought you and I could get a pint tonight. Or six."

Killian didn't return his smile. "Not tonight."

Tonight he had things to do. He'd promised Siamus he would get him a quarter million in gold, which meant he had to—quite literally—dig it up.

After Elyse's escape, her shoppe had been infested with guards. By daylight, they crowded into the cottage, tearing apart the shelves in search of any evidence they could find. But at night, they posted only a handful of guards to keep a lookout.

Killian had watched from the woods for several days, waiting for his opportunity. It had finally come on the fourth night when he recognized one of the guards on duty. Andrew had been in Killian's regiment for years. Killian had trained him from a rascally teen to a respectable adult, and he hoped the soldier still held him in high esteem, even after all that had happened.

Killian waited until Andrew was alone, then approached him from behind and clamped a hand over his mouth.

"You ought to know better than that, soldier," Killian taunted him, letting just enough humor into his voice to let Andrew know he meant him no harm. "I'm going to uncover your mouth now. And you're not going to shout, right?"

Andrew had nodded his head vigorously, and Killian released him. The young soldier immediately turned and grasped Killian's forearm.

"Sir," he breathed out. But it was of pure habit. Killian no longer held such a title.

"It's good to see you, Andrew," Killian had said, letting a genuine smile play at his lips.

"You too, sir. But—" Andrew cast a glance over each shoulder. "What are you doing here?"

Killian kept his voice low but commanding. "I need to get into the shoppe and have a look around. I might be able to spot something the Guard missed."

Even in the faint moonlight, Killian could see the way Andrew's face paled. He hadn't needed to say *why* he might have an additional intuition; the implication was there. He had known Elyse intimately.

"All right," Andrew ceded. "But be quick—and quiet."

Killian had smirked. "Who do you think you're talking to?"

Andrew had helped him sneak into the cottage unnoticed, and from there he had snatched up as many spellbooks and personal items as he could carry—including the enormous ledger that held all the shoppe's data on sales and inventory.

He'd spent the next few days riffling through the accumulation. He tried every spell he could find to track Elyse down, but they'd all proven ineffective. Wherever she was, simple tracking measures wouldn't work.

He'd spent most of the time looking through a small notebook. It seemed Elyse had scribbled random thoughts on the parchment, and she'd used the same code as the one in the ledger, the code he'd deciphered to discover she was King Cyril's assassin. So he'd gotten to work, unraveling each passage. Some were meaningful, others appeared to be nothing more than simple to-do lists. The page that stood out to him the most was the one that seemed to be some sort of coordinates.

As soon as he'd gotten the chance, Killian had gone into the forest behind the cottage, following the directions of the coordinates. There didn't appear to be anything special about the areas that had been jotted down, but Killian hadn't expected to find anything obvious. So, he'd returned the next day with a shovel and gotten to work.

After perhaps an hour, the shovel's head struck something hard. With renewed vigor, Killian unearthed the object—a metal chest.

The chest was large but surprisingly light. Killian's heart had nearly beat out of his chest as he hoisted it from the ground with ease and undid the latch. He almost fell over backward when he lifted the lid to find gold coins—so many of them, they threatened to spill over the sides.

He lost track of time as he counted the coins. One hundred, two hundred, three hundred... They never seemed to end. Finally, he set the last gold coin in a pile beside the others.

Five hundred thousand.

A half million in gold.

He'd just sat there completely bewildered, gold scattered around him. Elyse was rich—disgustingly so. She had never complained about money, but she hadn't flaunted her wealth either. Her clothes had been simple, her home small. And yet she had a fortune stashed in the woods.

Realization dawned on him that this might not be the only cache. He'd quickly dumped most of the coin back into the chest—pocketing a small sum for himself—and then dug a new hole a hundred yards away. He marked down the new coordinates in the notebook, then made for the next set in Elyse's journal.

Sure enough, he'd found two more chests, each filled with roughly half a million in gold. And each one he carefully reburied somewhere else in the woods.

Killian hadn't told anyone about the gold, not even Manny. He saw no reason to. And perhaps a small part of him felt bad for taking some of it. Stealing was stealing, even if it was from a wanted criminal.

Yet Killian felt no qualms about using that money to pay the Bastards for her bounty. No, that was just poetic justice.

"Are you all right?" Manny asked, breaking Killian from his daze.

Killian shook his head clear of thoughts of gold and bounties. "I'm great actually," he said, allowing a tiny smile to sneak through. "I'll go to the tavern another night—soon. I promise."

Manny nodded, smiling weakly, but Killian didn't miss the skepticism in his friend's gaze.

CHAPTER 6

— · —

ELYSE

E lyse's fingers thrummed on the table like a tiny quartet. She slouched in the oversized dining chair, her thoughts a universe away from the finery surrounding her.

It'd been three days since her picnic with Jaime. Since he'd abandoned her.

Not abandoned, she corrected, though the word plucked a resonant chord in her chest.

She'd told herself she would be fine, that she would take up some activities and that the weeks of his absence would be over before she knew it. She believed her trip outdoors had been enough to satiate her for a while, and another visit from Jaime would give her something to look forward to.

That was, of course, naivety.

Approximately nineteen hours later, she'd become thoroughly agitated. She paraded the halls of the house, scrambling from room to room, desperate for something to appease her. Nothing had. She missed the days when she had been lethargic, content to languish in bed all day. Now she had an unexplainable, ravenous energy that hummed through her veins.

She'd finally calmed down enough to sit at the dining room table and attempt to simply *think*. A simple plan was all she needed. A long-term solution to her problems. Yet her mind kept doling out the same ill-conceived advice again and again.

Leave, demanded the voice in her head. *Jaime will never know. Just get out for a few hours.*

But even if she did leave—which of course, she would never do—where would she go?

Killian's face appeared in her mind again and again, sometimes smiling, sometimes brooding, sometimes with that painful look of betrayal and agony. Seeing him, though, was utterly out of the question.

But what about someone else? What about Sera?

Elyse perked up at the idea, sitting a little straighter in her chair, her fingers ceasing their thrumming, before uncertainty bled into her thoughts.

Would Sera even want to see me?

Did I ruin things between her and Manny?

The notion that her oldest and most beloved friend might betray her made Elyse sick, her palms sweating as a knot solidified in her stomach. Yet the most nauseating thing about it was that she wouldn't blame her friend for it; it was what she deserved after lying for so many years and reeling her into chaos.

Still, something nagged at Elyse, ensuring her that Sera was a loyal friend. Certainty overpowered doubt, and Elyse stood abruptly, her decision made.

By the time she gathered a few vials of transportation potion, traveled outside the wards of the country home, and magicked herself to Sera's apartment building, her confidence waned. She stood on the thirteenth-floor landing, facing the strands of iridescent beads that served as Sera's front door, one hand raised in a fist, ready to knock on the door jamb. Her knees buckled beneath her, and she couldn't bring herself to knock. Just as she was about to turn and bolt down the twelve flights of steps, she heard a stirring in the apartment.

"Please, come in," Sera called in her endearing lilt. Elyse didn't know if Sera had heard her in the hallway, or if she had simply known someone was present, but she didn't care. That voice, so welcoming and pure, was her undoing. She strode into the apartment, sending beads clattering into one another, and stopped just inside the threshold.

Sera sat on a ledge by the open window, a book in her hand. Her vibrant purple eyes lifted to Elyse, and the entire room seemed to still, as if the walls themselves were holding their breath.

"Elyse," she uttered, her expression unreadable.

Elyse's mind turned to mush, incapable of coherence, yet she managed a feeble "Hi."

And then Sera was tossing the book to the floor and running toward Elyse, her silken dress flowing behind her. She wrapped her arms around Elyse in a fierce embrace that was inexplicable for someone so thin, and Elyse hugged her back. Hell's fire, Elyse didn't even mind that she had a face full of Sera's long hair or that she was fairly certain Sera was bruising her ribs—there was nowhere else she would rather be.

She hadn't even realized she was crying until the two women pulled apart from one another, and Elyse stood back to observe her friend through her tear-blurred vision. She let out a nervous laugh as she wiped her eyes, and Sera did the same.

Sera was just as beautiful as Elyse remembered, perhaps more so. Her black hair contrasted lovingly with her fair skin, and her pastel silk dress clung to her frame adoringly. She took hold of Elyse's hand and, with her typical grace, pulled her to the settee.

As she sank onto the familiar cushions, Elyse let out a long exhale. It was funny how emotions seemed to have a way of smothering themselves until they were allowed to release. And now that she had emancipated an ounce of feelings, they assaulted her all at once. Her heart pounded with gratitude.

"I didn't know if you'd want to see me," she blubbered.

"Elyse," Sera sighed, so much emotion in only two syllables. "Of course I'd want to see you."

"You don't hate me?" Elyse choked out. Her chin wobbled as she stared at her friend.

Sera gave Elyse's hand a squeeze. "You did something terrible, and you lied about it. But..." She paused and shook her head. "I know your soul, Elyse, in a way that only someone with my gifts can. I know you have a true heart. Whatever your reasons were, I trust that they were good. I just want to understand."

Elyse didn't know what to say, so she stared at her lap. She wanted to thank her friend, to tell her she was undeserving of her kindness. Yet all Sera wanted was an explanation, and Elyse wasn't sure that she could give it to her.

When she'd told Jaime, she'd been an emotional wreck, still reeling from the way her world had collapsed so suddenly. Since then, she'd been able to restore her walls, creating the barrier she'd hid behind for so many years. She wasn't sure how to break out of that sanctuary again.

She took a deep breath. She owed it to Sera; it was the absolute least she could do for her friend.

She started at the beginning, explaining how she and her mother were enslaved to a demon named Lazarus. At first, she faltered through her words, waiting for Sera to rebuke her. But the more she explained, the faster her words flowed, until she was professing every detail.

Sera listened intently with tears in her eyes. She held Elyse's hand the whole time, even as she described her first kill. When Elyse told of how she took her own life ten times to try and get out of murdering a young woman, Sera's expression mirrored her own grief. And when she described killing King Cyril, and how she despised herself for every moment she had fallen deeper in love with Killian, Sera rubbed her back in soothing strokes.

As difficult as it was to relive each moment, the solidarity she felt from Sera gave her the strength she needed. By the time she was finished, she felt the tiniest bit better, like a fraction of a weight had been lifted. They sat together, holding one another, until Elyse's breathing slowly returned to normal, and she had no more tears left to cry.

Sera relaxed against the settee. "I had no idea," she breathed. "I wish you would have told me. I could have shared your burden."

Elyse immediately shook her head. It felt liberating to tell Sera the secrets she'd held for so long, but it hadn't been easy. And even now, there were still secrets that she held back. She couldn't bring herself to talk about how Lazarus might be her father, and that she was too terrified to learn the truth—that she might be half-demon.

"No, I—thank you. That's kind of you to say, but... I already involved you more than I wish I had. You lied for me, Sera. You were my alibi—you could have been thrown in jail. And Manny—"

Sera held up her free hand, cutting off Elyse's rambling.

"Manny and I are fine," she stressed. "Great, actually. He understands why I lied—he would have done the same for Killian."

Hearing his name sent shivers down Elyse's spine.

"And Killian," she began timidly. "Do you know how he is?"

Sera glanced away, and Elyse's heart lurched. "He's... Well, he's torn up—as is to be expected. I haven't seen him personally—I don't think he wants to be around me—but Manny tells me he spends most of his time..." She paused and glanced back at Elyse. "...searching for you."

Elyse only nodded. There wasn't much she could say.

Sera finally pulled her hand away and patted Elyse's leg. "But I'm glad you're here," she said, plastering a smile on her face. "I say we get utterly drunk, just like old times."

Elyse laughed as cherished memories flooded her mind. "Remember when we started a brawl at the Black Cat?"

"Yes," Sera laughed. "Remember when we were bored and drunk and decided to switch bodies?"

"Yes," Elyse snorted, recalling the way she had felt so ridiculous in Sera's lanky form. "Remember when we challenged those guards to see who could finish a cask of ale first?"

"Gods, I was sick for days after that," Sera lamented. "And that's why I don't drink ale anymore. But, lucky for us, I have a bottle of wine in the cabinet."

She began to stand when she abruptly fell back onto the settee and pressed her hand to her temple. Her face was pinched, her eyes closed, and she let out a groan.

Elyse rushed to keep her friend from falling forward. "Sera? What's wrong?"

But Sera was unable to say anything coherent. She groaned again, squeezing her eyes tighter, her already pale skin drained of any remaining color.

"Sera?" Worry invaded Elyse's chest, eradicating any solace she'd gained over the last hour. As she squeezed Sera's hand, trying to provide some form of comfort, a helplessness flowed from her racing heart through her veins.

And just like that, it was over. Sera blinked her eyes open and let out a long, shaky exhale. The pain she'd felt a moment earlier seemed to vanish, though her face was still ashen, her eyes distant.

Elyse frowned, her concern lingering. "What was that? Are you all right?"

Sera nodded and exhaled again as color slowly returned to her cheeks. "Yes, I'm fine. It's just—I've been having these... visions."

"Visions?" Elyse repeated. She'd never seen anything like that before—not from Sera or any other clairvoyants. "Is that normal? It looked excruciating."

Sera gently rubbed at her temple. "They are quite painful. Would you mind steeping some tea for me?"

"Of course," Elyse said as she quickly moved to the kitchen and grabbed the kettle. With one eye still on Sera, she asked, "Have you had visions before?"

Sera shook her head, then winced at the motion. "No—I mean yes, I've had this same vision a few times over the past week. But until then, I'd never experienced anything like it."

Elyse noted a faint apprehension in her friend's voice, one that was stark against her usual cheeriness. After a moment's hesitation she asked, "What did you see?"

Sera fidgeted with her hands in her lap, avoiding Elyse's wary gaze. "It's... awful," she said softly.

Elyse turned and gave Sera her full attention.

Sera's voice was quiet, haunted even. "People screaming, bodies falling to the ground. And so much fire."

The dread that had abated now wholly returned to Elyse. She stared at Sera, who stared back at her with a look of pure torment.

Elyse knew enough about visions to understand that seeing fire and death was bad—very, *very* bad. But why was Sera experiencing them all of a sudden? Sometimes visions were related to the seer, yet other times they were inexplicably random.

"What do you think it means?" was all she could manage to ask.

Sera pulled her knees to her chest and wrapped her long arms around the silky fabric of her skirts. Her voice was barely more than a murmur. "Nothing good, I'm certain."

Elyse abandoned the kettle and strode to her friend. "If you keep seeing the same thing, maybe it hasn't happened yet," she said, forcing hope into her voice. "Maybe we can prevent it."

Sera bit her lip, her beautiful purple eyes void of their usual light. "I thought of that, but I don't even know where to begin."

Elyse had no idea where to begin either, but something tugged at her. She felt reinvigorated, like fate had taken her by the shoulders and shaken her from her languid state. This could give her purpose, something to do in her vast free time. She would probably have to sneak out of Jaime's property again, but it would be worth it if it meant stopping something horrendous from happening. She would worry about Jaime, and her own safety, later. For now, she needed information.

"Tell me everything," she demanded, kneeling before the settee.

So Sera did.

CHAPTER 7

— • —

KILLIAN

Killian lay with the map in his hands, the soft mattress beneath him as a single candle brought a dim light to his room. He turned onto his side to view the map better, taking in each color-coded dot with the utmost attention. The blue dots, as small as pinpricks, were the most numerous. They spread across the entire parchment like thousands of glittering stars.

Using a spell he found in one of Elyse's books, Killian had enchanted the map to show every encounter of magic across the kingdom. Each blue dot represented an instance of minor magic—perhaps an incantation whispered over a potion or a simple levitation spell. The green lights, which were slightly larger than the blue, were the next most common, sparkling like the tiniest emeralds known to man. Wherever green shimmered was a slightly more complex spell, like transportation potions hauling someone from one place to another. There were just a few amber circles that radiated across the kingdom, representing more serious magic. They were especially common at night, when tavern brawls ran rampant, and teenagers summoned spirits.

Killian had spent weeks tracking down each of the yellow-orange dots that surrounded the capital, investigating for any signs of Elyse, but after so many dead-ends, he'd lost hope in the map's ability to lead him to her whereabouts. Still, each night and a good part of each day, he studied the map. Sometimes as he dozed off, he would imagine the person behind each dot.

Scorned lovers taking revenge on their cheating partners. Overwhelmed housewives enchanting their dishes to wash themselves. Courtesans using spells to enhance their appearances.

But now he was too unsettled to play his little game. He'd been that way ever since he'd met with Siamus, as if he expected a letter from the mercenary at any moment. Surely the Bastards worked quickly—had they really not found her yet?

"Untouchable," Siamus had called Elyse. And perhaps that was truer than Killian wanted it to be.

Or perhaps she is dead.

No, that wasn't the case. Somehow, somewhere deep in Killian's soul, he knew that she was alive. He could never be rid of her that easily.

He told himself that he wanted her to be alive purely so he could see the despair on her face as she stared down the gallows—not because he needed some sort of personal reconciliation with her. And yet every time he saw a silver-haired woman or caught the scent of jasmine, his heart gave a little leap.

Restless, Killian rolled over in bed. He hated the way his mind was so erratic, swinging from one extreme to the next, never content to be in the moment. He'd thought that getting the Bastards involved would help him feel more at ease, like some of his burden had been lifted. But it only seemed to rattle him more.

He let out a heavy breath. Perhaps he should take Manny up on his next offer to head to the tavern together. A night out would be good for him, and maybe he'd even—

All thoughts ceased immediately as the map began to glow brighter, so bright he had to squint against the light.

A few inches west of the capital, a deep, ruddy orange was spreading. Killian watched as it slowly expanded, like ink seeping into parchment.

When it seemed to reach its full size, it was nearly the width of a silver coin.

"What—" he breathed. He'd never seen anything like this—didn't even know that this level of magic was possible.

The orange dot continued to burn on the map. It seemed to pulsate, casting Killian's bedroom in a daunting, flickering light.

His heart hammered against his ribs, painfully so. This—this was what he'd been hoping for. He knew, without a doubt, that this was *her* doing.

A town name had been scrawled on the map just along the edge of the orange glow—*Prestowne*.

Without a second thought, he grabbed his weapons, scribbled a note to his mother, and was out the door.

CHAPTER 8

— · —

ELYSE

The library was one of the more impressive rooms in the country estate, with nearly two thousand books if her estimates were correct. It certainly wasn't the largest personal library she'd ever seen, but it held an excellent selection of spellbooks, history books, and novels, and the tufted armchairs and floor-to-ceiling windows made it especially charming.

Elyse sat at the long table in the library with her head propped on her elbow, a hoard of books spread before her. The sun had set many hours earlier, and she now read by the flickering light of a candelabra, its tapers burning low. Most of the books she'd selected were histories of Rhodan, though she'd also chosen a few studies of clairvoyance and visions. So far, nothing she'd come across shed any light on Sera's visions, and her ambition was waning. She yawned freely as she flipped another page.

Sera hadn't been able to give her much to go off. She'd said the images were so quick and often dark that she could barely make anything out. Most of the people were fair skinned, and they ranged in all ages—teenagers, the elderly, mothers cowering with their children. Their homes appeared small and simple, not like the elegant stone townhouses of the capital, and their clothes were often plain. The most significant piece of information she'd shared was that she'd caught a glimpse of a statue of three figures. She'd been more focused on the panicked faces of the scurrying townsfolk than the actual statues, so she couldn't recall many details.

"I think they were statues of people, but I can't be sure," she'd said.

But Elyse had been hopeful. She suspected she was dealing with a smaller town, based on the architecture and clothing Sera described. And the skin color would also help eliminate many towns, as people living outside the capital tended to cluster in groups of similar heritage. And surely the statues would be easy to identify—how many towns could possibly have a three-figured statue?

Yet half a day and countless books later, Elyse was no closer to finding any mention of such a town.

Her research into visions had proven just as fruitless. There were numerous reasons why a seer might have visions, including catastrophic events, personal traumas, or even diet. The visions could be past, present, or future, and they may be real or simply subject to interpretation.

Still, Elyse couldn't shake the idea that the visions were some sort of warning. Sera's anguish had been too intense to merely dismiss this as poor diet. Something about the fire and bodies dropping to the floor had sent an unforgettable shiver up her spine.

Despite all this, Elyse could hardly concentrate. The words on the pages were garbled nonsense, and she simply looked at the drawings—if there were any. There were statues of maidens, of warriors, of dogs and children and even a particularly bizarre statue of a horse with a duck's head and a bat's wings...

But no three-figured statues.

She glanced out at the stillness of the night and considered wandering down the hall to her dim bedchamber. *Just get through the end of this book*, she told herself. There had to be at least a hundred pages left. She let out a groan before stretching and yawning again.

Flip, flip, flip, she went through each page, her vision blurring. When she turned to a page with a sketch of a statue of three females, she took no notice, flipping idly to the next page.

She blinked, then blinked again. Her heart thrummed loudly, each beat waking her more and more. She sat up a little straighter, held her breath, and turned back the page.

The right side of the page was dedicated to a sketch of the statue: three women stood in a circle with their hands upraised: one elderly, one middle-aged, one barely pubescent. *The matriarchs of Prestowne*, read the caption beneath the drawing. *Mary Preston, her daughter Emilia Preston, and her granddaughter Alivya Preston.*

This had to be the statue from the visions. Pages upon pages and pages, and there hadn't been anything else. Elyse was convinced it was the only statue like it in the entire kingdom.

She shoved the book aside and snatched up the nearest atlas, flipping violently through the pages until she found what she was looking for: a map of Rhodan. With her finger sliding across the pages, she scoured every city and town on the map until finally she found Prestowne. It sat just west of the capital, about twenty miles away.

Renewed energy coursed through Elyse, setting her skin ablaze as she formed a plan. She hadn't been to Prestowne before, so she couldn't magick there, but... Her finger trailed south along the page, where a circle marked another town—Bendsworth. She'd been there many summers ago with her mother. If she magicked herself to that town, she could walk the ten or so miles to Prestowne and be there by dawn.

Elyse stood, grabbed the book on statues and the atlas, and hurried down the hall to her bedchamber. She packed a bag with supplies for a few days and a handful of transportation potions. As she went to tie off the bundle, she paused. Guilt trickled into her stomach. She was abandoning Jaime's requests. He'd done everything for her and asked nothing of her in return. Yet there she was, ready to throw it in his face.

Elyse blew out a breath and knotted her bag. She would have plenty of time to ponder her actions on the walk from Bendsworth to Prestowne—and to develop her plan. As she clamored out the door of the estate and paced to the edge of the wards, she didn't even look back.

CHAPTER 9

—·—

KILLIAN

The trees rose high on either side of Killian as he rode the dirt path from the capital to Prestowne. When he looked behind him, he could barely make out the first rays of sun peaking through the summer foliage. He was making good time, thanks to the mare he'd "borrowed."

He felt some shame about taking the horse without the stable owner's permission, but no one would have lent him a horse in the middle of the night. He'd left more than the horse's worth in silver for the stable hand, and a note that he'd have her returned in a few days at the most.

The pinto mare seemed to match Killian's enthusiasm. She had obediently followed him out of the stall without any trouble, patiently letting him saddle and bridle her. And as soon as they'd hit the cobblestone streets of the capital, she'd taken off at a gallop, as if she'd been born for the mission.

They'd slowed as they exited the gates of the capital, but still maintained a steady pace. The mare, who Killian took to calling Lady Midnight, eagerly obeyed each tug of the reins and kick of his heels. If he weren't so anxious about what he faced in Prestowne, he might have found the ride relaxing.

Instead, dread ate at him. Whatever produced that level of intense magic couldn't be good. He felt foolish for not reaching out to Manny for backup, but it was too late now. This was his mess, and he wouldn't ask anyone else to clean it up for him.

Prestowne couldn't be far off. He kept his eyes peeled, searching for anything suspicious. But above all, he searched for signs of *her*.

How would he react when he saw her? He assured himself he would remain steadfast in his commitment to bring her to justice. If anything, two months of ruminating over his failure had only hardened his heart more.

Lady Midnight came to an abrupt stop, shaking her head ferociously. Killian dug his heels into her sides and kissed her forward, but the mare turned to the side, trying to hike back up the path.

"Woah, girl!" Killian shouted. Lady Midnight bucked, and he had to hold tight to avoid flying out of the saddle. He let her take them a few paces back up the road, and she settled noticeably, though she still seemed rattled as she snorted in disapproval.

Again Killian tried to coax her to the west, but she refused to budge. What in the gods' names had gotten into her? Perhaps a snake had spooked her, or some other creature. She'd been mild-mannered the entire journey, but it seemed he might be endangering himself by pushing her forward.

Based on his calculations, he couldn't be far from Prestowne, maybe a mile at most. Reluctantly, he decided to tie Lady Midnight to a tree and make the rest of the trek on foot.

Once he started walking, he was grateful for the exercise to help relieve his agitation. But the relief was short-lived. The closer he came to Prestowne, the more nervous he grew, and he fidgeted ceaselessly with the hilt of his dagger. He knew danger lay ahead, he just didn't know how much.

Killian lifted his gaze to the treetops. The western sky should have been brighter, given that the sun had half crested the eastern horizon, but nothing but black sky could be seen between the tree limbs. The short hairs along the back of his neck prickled, but he kept moving onward.

When the trees finally parted, opening to show the road to Prestowne, he understood the darkness. Pillars of black smoke suffocated the sky as they rippled from nearly every building in the village. Woe punched into his gut as his knees buckled beneath him.

He was too late.

CHAPTER 10

— • —

KILLIAN

The town was silent save for the smoldering crackle of dwindling fires and Killian's panicked motions. He hurried from one half-scorched building to another, praying to find someone alive, but all he found was corpse after corpse sprawled on the floor, their flesh seared. The stench was unbearable. The smoke mingled with the scent of the charred bodies, and he vomited up his guts more than once. Yet the smell was nothing compared to the eerily visceral doom that had settled over the town, thickening the air and sending a permanent chill up Killian's spine.

He didn't know how many buildings he searched before he gave up, accepting that he would find the same haunting tale in every house, tavern, and business. His head spun, each blink bringing the image of another body. They were too badly burned to discern who was male or female, old or young, but his traitorous imagination could fill in the gaps.

A mother.

A wife.

A son.

A brother.

The image of his own siblings' bodies resurfaced in his mind, the details fresh from the horrors around him. His knees buckled. He wasn't getting enough air. He felt as if he would scream if he didn't get out of this wretched place now.

He collapsed in the middle of the corpse-lined street, his heart thundering as panic tightened its fist around his lungs. A thousand thoughts roared through his head at once, but none of them were coherent.

He was too late. Hundreds were dead, and he could do nothing about it.

The worst part of it all was the fear that Elyse had something to do with it.

He had to breathe. He had to calm down. He had to stop losing his gods' damned mind.

He forced his breaths from shallow, heaving pants to slower, more controlled inhales and exhales. The barrage in his mind was still frantic, but it quieted some, enough that he could try and think rationally. He was a former soldier, trained to handle a myriad of situations, and though he had never expected to see anything so monstrous, so vile as this, he could still use that training. He rolled off his knees and sat on the ground, forcing his chest to expand with air as he tried to make sense of it all.

What had he seen? What was he still seeing all around him?

He started with the fire, how nearly every building in town was scorched, but none of them had burned to the ground. That meant numerous small fires. There were no strange odors, and from what he had seen of the burn patterns, it didn't appear that any sort of accelerant had been used.

Setting that many fires in such a short span of time would take at least a dozen people. What motivation would they have shared? Or was it possible one person had created this whole devastation on their own?

Killian's heart seized.

The orange glow.

That's what he had seen on the map. His senses had been too overwhelmed for his brain to piece it together until that moment.

He still had a hundred questions, but he was able to grasp at a theory. As he sat there, thinking through everything logically, a numbness enveloped him—a sort of compartmentalization that allowed him to distance himself from the deaths. It felt inhuman, but it was a necessary coping mechanism that kept him from fleeing the scene.

He stood and went to lean against the sole remaining wall of a nearby home as his mind wandered toward the victims. Soot stained his clothes, flaking away into dust on the breeze, but his thoughts were centered on one thing. He had seen fires and burned corpses before—nothing close to this level, of course—but it wasn't just the scale of the destruction that seemed off. Something was different here.

In the Guard, he had been sent to investigate several fires, and the victims usually fell into the same pattern. Often they slouched on the floor near a barricaded door or window, like they had been trying to escape to their last breath. Or they huddled together, hands and bodies permanently entwined from the intense heat, as they accepted their fate. Occasionally, a body would be found among the remnants of their bed, having slept through the fire and died of suffocation.

His mind flickered to the half-charred bodies strewn about him, heaped along the street. Why had they simply stopped in the middle of the town? How did the fire even reach them out here? And what were so many people doing out of their homes at night?

Even the bodies inside were scattered, almost none in beds or near exits or clinging to their loved ones. Pandemonium had clearly roused the entire town from whatever sleep it had been enjoying. It was as if the citizens had been running about, panicked, and then just... dropped dead.

His stomach recoiled more at the thought, but he forced himself to stay calm. This was bad. Epically bad. Genocide on a supernatural level.

Killian shook his head. He had left home fully believing that Elyse was behind everything, but now that he had seen firsthand the horrors cast on the town... He balled his hands into fists as he tried to remind himself that she was ruthless, a liar, and a murderer, and yet he just couldn't bring himself to believe that she was capable of something this utterly evil.

But if not Elyse, then who?

A crunching of boots on gravel forced Killian from his thoughts. It was fully daylight now, and he scoured the streets but saw no one. Dread seized his chest, the footsteps haunting in a city full of the dead.

A woman's figure emerged into the intersection, not fifty yards away. She stopped, her countenance still aside from the satchel she grasped in one hand, which swayed by her knees. Her green cloak was too vibrant around so much death, as was the bright, silvery hair that spilled from her hood.

At first, Killian thought he was imagining her, that by thinking of the witch he had somehow tricked his mind into hallucinating her. Because that seemed the only reasonable explanation for why Elyse stood before him.

Her skin was so pale, stark white against her dark eyes, which took in the town with confusion, perhaps even abhorrence. Her breaths were shallow, a rapid rise and fall of her cloaked shoulders.

Killian stood still, watching her, his hands trembling with rage. He watched as she took one slow, careful step, then another. He watched as those obsidian eyes scanned the buildings, the corpses, and finally landed on him.

Her entire body tensed. The air went taut between them as Killian planned his move. Even the plumes of dark smoke seemed to cease their billowing, instead watching the chaos about to unfurl. For a moment, the whole world hung by a string—a string of tangled feelings frayed by deceit.

And then she ran.

Chapter 11

— · —

Elyse

Before Elyse knew what she was doing, her feet were carrying her down the abandoned street, kicking up gravel in their wake. She didn't understand why she had run—why she was still running, instead of magicking herself away. She felt the weight of the transportation potion in her pocket as she pumped her arms wildly, propelling her down the road, but it was as if her hands refused to obey, not letting her reach into her pocket and grab the simple potion.

She had been so overwhelmed by the corpses, by the smell of seared flesh, by the utter stillness of the town, that she had been completely caught off guard to see someone slouched against a building. It had taken her a moment to realize she was looking at another living person, and then the true depth of realization had hit her as she saw the umber skin, broad shoulders, and that unforgettable scowl. There had been nothing but cold hatred in his eyes.

It had been torturous to find that she was too late, that Sera's visions had come true mere hours before. But to run into Killian, here of all places… It was ludicrous. Her panic tripled as she sprinted through the streets, and she dropped her satchel to run faster.

She could hear him chasing after her. "Stop!" he bellowed. A single warning before a zooming white light blew past her—a stunning spell.

51

As she shielded herself, she chanced a glance over her shoulder to see him forty, maybe thirty yards behind her, running furiously and gaining on her. Devil's horns, he was fast. Another flare of white blazed by her, followed quickly by a purple ball of fire that hit her shield and dissolved.

Fuck. She was certain she hadn't taught him that hex. It was clear he'd been practicing as another spell deflected off her shield.

Sweat dripped down her neck as she raced onward. Her heart pounded, her fear exacerbated by the heat of smoldering fires, the taste of ash that coated her tongue. She spared another glance back at Killian to find his expression livid—just as it was in all of her dreams. Her chest tightened at the sight, but she couldn't stop to think about the pain she'd caused him, not as he sent another curse her way.

The street wasn't very long, and buildings rose directly ahead of her. She slipped down a side street, sliding in the gravel but recovering quickly. Killian skidded after her.

Transport away! she demanded of herself, but she couldn't do it. She had to talk to Killian and explain her side of things. She had to make things right—or at least better.

But he clearly wasn't in a talking mood. He sent another hex her way, then sent a flash of green light ahead of her. The light hit the ground and jutted upward, forming a wall nearly eight feet tall that spanned the width of the street. By instinct alone, Elyse flicked her hand and levitated herself over the wall. She landed hard, kicking off the ground as fast as she could. When she looked back, Killian was scaling the top of the wall and hurdling himself over it. Had he managed that climb without magic? She wouldn't be surprised.

She couldn't keep running. Killian was faster than her, and he would inevitably catch up to her. She refused to send any hexes back at him—he wasn't her true enemy.

At the end of the street, a building loomed ahead of her with a bell tower jutting into the sky—a church. Its wooden exterior was scorched, but it appeared mostly intact. It would have to do.

Killian sent more hurdles and hexes at her, but Elyse dodged them easily. She passed a tall statue of three females—*the* statue—she realized. The one from Sera's visions. But she didn't have time to linger or compare it to the picture in the book. Instead, she bound up the stairs of the church, flung the double doors open, and tried to escape Killian's wrath.

Even inside, the air was heavy, laden with ash. Three massive iron chandeliers hung from high rafters, with dozens of candles that illuminated the rows of benches in a flickering glow. All traces of prayerful solace had been desecrated.

In the center of the aisle, a man lay splayed on the floor, his robes spread around him, drenched in blood. His ashen face was frozen in anguish. For a moment, Elyse forgot about Killian as she sprinted toward the body. She let her shield down and grabbed the man's blood-covered wrist, but no pulse greeted her fingers.

Peculiar symbols drawn in blood surrounded the priest's body. Elyse squinted, trying to study them in the dim light, but she heard Killian's footsteps. She looked up to see him cresting the stairs, and she flicked her hands to slam the doors shut. With another quick twist of her wrist, the benches slid across the floor to barricade the door. It wouldn't keep Killian out for long, but she needed whatever time she could get to analyze the scene.

Boom came the sound of Killian's body slamming into the doors. "Elyse!" he screamed, but she blocked him out.

Her heart raced as she looked back toward the symbols. There were six of them, forming a hexagonal shape around the priest's lifeless form. Familiarity scratched at Elyse's mind as she wiped sweat from her brow with the back of her hand. She had seen these symbols before but couldn't pin down where. The feeling nagged at her, pleading to be remembered.

Boom, boom, boom! Each time Killian's body or magic slammed against the doors, the sound reverberated through the sanctuary, shaking the mighty chandeliers. Elyse rose and strode toward the barricade of benches. She compelled her voice to sound strong yet calm, pleading yet demanding as she called, "Killian?"

The pounding at the door stopped.

"Killian, please listen," Elyse shouted. "I can explain everything. I don't know what's happened here, but—"

The tiniest shiver blew its cold breath up her spine—an eerie warning. She threw up her hands defensively, forming a shield of hard air around herself, just as the doors and the benches burst apart in a vehement explosion.

CHAPTER 12

KILLIAN

Anger and hatred fueled Killian as he tore down the street after Elyse, sending blasts of power her way. The zeal of combat surged through him, entrancing him. He was finally able to put his training to use—and against her of all people. His spells were sharp and strong, his aim mostly true, but no matter what he sent her way, Elyse dodged or shielded it artfully.

Now she had locked herself inside the half-scorched remains of a church, leaving Killian outside, pounding on the doors. He couldn't let her slip through his fingers again. Last time, he had been weak. He had hesitated, shown mercy. But the last two months had wiped out any dregs of sympathy he might have felt for the witch.

Killian threw his shoulder into the doors, but they didn't budge. Whatever she had done would require magic to break through.

"Killian?" he heard her call from the other side.

He ignored her as he balled his hands into fists. How dare she speak his name. Before the day was through, he would make sure that treacherous mouth of hers would never utter another word again.

He took a few steps back and paced along the steps lining the church doorway. There was a spell he could use—a hex that he'd tried once before. He'd blown the hay-stuffed training mannequin into a million pieces, a satisfying yet formidable feat. Killian squared up to the doors and lifted his hands.

"*Desidrio!*" he shouted as he thrust his hands toward the doors.

Smoky white light shot from his palms and assaulted the double doors before detonating into a bright cloud. The whole building shook. He couldn't see the damage behind the cloud, but he heard the doors ripping from their hinges and the clatter of debris. Then all was silent again.

Killian didn't wait long before stepping into the slowly dissipating fog and crossing the threshold into the church. He needed to see Elyse—to make her suffer the way he had, the way King Cyril had, the way Queen Andrielle had suffered through her grief. Yet just before he emerged from the haze, his heart gave a small lurch. He imagined Elyse lying dead on the cold floor, and with the image came a fleeting anguish.

Shattered planks of wood littered the stone floor. In the center of the room, standing with her shoulders back, was Elyse. Her silvery hair shimmered in the light of the candles that somehow still illuminated the vast space, giving her an almost angelic appearance. Killian scoured her for cuts or blood, but found nothing. As his eyes roved from her face down her body, and then to the floor, he realized why. The floor around her was clean, creating a perfect circle free from shards of wood and debris. She had shielded herself.

She gazed back at him through the ash-tinted haze, and time seemed to pause. Killian didn't know what to do, what to say. He had imagined this moment, coming face to face with Elyse, every night for the past two months. He'd recited countless speeches on morality, on betrayal and justice, but they all escaped him as he stared into her obsidian eyes.

Elyse opened her mouth slowly, as if she, too, was contemplating what to say, but Killian snapped at her.

"Don't."

Hurt twisted her features. Killian didn't care.

"There is nothing—*nothing*—you can say to make me forgive you, to make me understand." He shook his head but kept his eyes narrowed on her, and took a step forward. "Killing King Cyril was bad enough, but now I find you here? What did you do?" His voice was merciless, his anger overtaking him like an infection.

Elyse's brows furrowed, her voice straining. "I didn't do anything," she stressed, taking a step toward him. "Killian, this is bigger than me—bigger than us."

Killian barely heard her. She had shifted slightly, allowing him to see past her, over her shoulder. A figure lay among the rubble—a lifeless figure. On instinct, he shoved past Elyse, who let him push her aside. In three strides, he stood over the body, taking in the man's pale, bloodied form. The body lay in a supine position, its arms tucked against its sides, like it had been placed there deliberately. Like a sacrifice.

"Killian, we need to—"

Killian turned on Elyse, his sharp movement cutting her off abruptly. We? *We?* There was no "we." She was wanted for the murder of his king. She had lied to him and deceived him. She had kissed him and made love to him, and now she had slaughtered an entire town with her witchcraft.

"You're an abomination!" he screamed as he thrust his hands toward her, sending a stunning spell directly at her chest.

Eyes wide, Elyse barely managed to flick her hand and form a shield in time to block it. The white light dissipated against her shield, but Killian sent another, then another, pouring every bit of his power into each spell. His entire body shook with rage as he moved closer to her, sweat trickling down his temple.

Elyse kept her shield up but moved back several paces. "Killian, please!" she cried in between blasts, but her voice only fueled his hatred more.

It was clear the stunning spells weren't going to cut it. Killian started throwing out any and every hex he knew. Blasts of fire, water, air, poison, magic arrows—but even as the memory of his last arrow piercing through her sent a jolt to his heart, nothing penetrated her shield. Everything either glanced off the iridescent wall of air or dissolved away on contact.

Elyse was hardly breaking a sweat. She seemed more frazzled than worn down as she kept shouting at him.

"Please!" she screamed, her voice cracking. "Killian, please *listen to me!*"

But he couldn't back down, not when she had taken so much from him.

No matter what he sent her way, Elyse only defended herself. She never retaliated. It only infuriated him more.

"Fight!" he bellowed. He'd backed her into a corner, where she stood, arms raised protectively, her expression imploring. He needed her to fight back. He needed her to show her true colors, once and for all.

"I won't," she answered, her voice drenched in resolve.

"*Fight!*" Killian growled louder, practically begging her as he sent a flaming spiral at her. It grazed the shield and hit the wall behind her, igniting the wood immediately. Elyse waved her hand and doused the fire, lowering her shield for only a fraction of a moment.

If that's what it took, Killian would burn the whole fucking place down.

Again and again he projected fire at her, each flame catching on the wooden walls of the church. Again and again, Elyse lowered her shield just long enough to smother the flames—quicker than the blink of an eye.

It was reckless, and Killian knew it. Every time she looked at him, all he could see was the trust she'd destroyed. Every pleading look she sent him clawed at his heart, tore at his lungs. With a final bellow, he hurled his hands at her, flinging destruction her way.

The same smoky white light he'd used to blow open the doors now raced toward Elyse, but instead of dissolving into her shield, it bounced off of it, refracting upward in a blinding haze. The entire ceiling disappeared, obscured by the smoky light, but the sound of the roof exploding was deafening.

Then something—something enormous and black—appeared from the fog. One of the massive iron chandeliers was hurtling down from the obliterated ceiling, headed straight toward him.

"Killian!" Elyse's scream was terror-filled, horrible and bloodcurdling. Before he could even move, she rammed her body into him, knocking him to the stone floor. His breath escaped him. Elyse's body covered his as he closed his eyes and prayed for a swift death.

At the last moment, Elyse projected a shield around them. The chandelier crashed into it with a thunderous clang. The iron monstrosity ricocheted off the shield, rolled a few yards, then settled onto the floor with another loud *boom*—though Killian could hardly hear it over the pounding of his own heart.

He stared up at the mist, which crept toward the sky through the giant hole in the roof. He tried to steady his breathing but choked against the ash floating through the air. He had lost control completely, and it had almost cost him his life.

And Elyse—she had saved him.

Bile rose in his throat as he realized she still lay atop him, protecting his body with her own. She must have realized it too, because she quickly rolled away.

"Are you okay?" she asked through panting breaths.

Killian couldn't bring himself to answer. He was drenched in sweat, his head was throbbing. He was completely exhausted, but he wasn't hurt. After everything he had said to her, after he'd chosen sheer, chaotic violence, she had saved him, and now she was asking if he was okay?

It made him physically ill that she had shown any shred of decency. A voice screamed in the back of his mind that he should hear her out. He raised his gaze to meet hers, taking in the soft curves of her face. Yet all he saw was his own shattered heart.

"Empty your pockets," he demanded.

Elyse's eyes went wide as she stared back at him. Confusion changed to hurt before she reached into her cloak pocket and pulled out two blue vials of transportation potion. Hesitantly, she extended them toward him. Killian swiped them from her. He transferred the vials into his own pocket and gritted his teeth.

"You have a ten-minute head start—not one second more," he warned. It was a small gratitude for saving his life, and the only one he would offer her.

Elyse's face remained grave. Her lips parted as if to speak, but she pursed them tightly and nodded.

Killian looked down. He couldn't bear to watch her leave, to watch his enemy escape once more, even if it was by his choosing. "You're wasting time," he said, his voice breaking as he forced out the words.

Elyse was nearly silent as she stood and moved toward the door. Killian told himself not to look, but he did anyway. Elyse was silhouetted in the doorway, sunshine pouring in around her. If he hadn't known better, he never would have guessed at the devastation on the street just outside.

She paused on the threshold, and for a moment she was just a figure, beautiful and fierce against the daylight, before she descended the stairs and left him there, alone.

Chapter 13

Killian

It had been three days since the destruction of Prestowne. Three days of being interviewed by the Royal Guard, of scouring the surrounding area for Elyse, of searching through spellbooks for answers. And it had all been for not.

When Killian had first magicked Manny to the town, he was forced to relive his initial horror through his friend's eyes. Manny, too, had keeled over and emptied the contents of his stomach. The summer heat had not been kind to the decaying bodies.

It had been just the two of them for a long while as they awaited the rest of the Guard to arrive by horseback. After touring the town and taking note of the devastation, Manny had stopped Killian in the street.

"Sera has been having visions," he confided, "of an entire town dropping dead, with fire blazing all around." There was heartbreak in his eyes as he shook his head, staring at the devastation around him. "It must be related."

That was how, three days later, Killian found himself climbing the twelve flights of stairs to Sera's apartment. At first, he had been resistant to the idea of talking to Sera. He hated her presence; it only reminded him of Elyse. He hated that she had lied to protect Elyse—even if she hadn't known the full extent of her actions. Besides, what good could possibly come from asking her about her visions? He held little belief that it would prove beneficial.

But after three days of spinning his wheels and getting nowhere, logic had beat out his emotional reservations. It would do no harm to talk to Sera, or at least, that's what he hoped.

As he mounted the final stairs and made his way toward the curtain of beads that served as the entrance to her apartment, he still held his doubts. Something gnawed at him, pestering him. His head ached dully, which didn't seem to bode well.

When they entered the apartment, Sera first greeted Manny with a kiss. Then she pounced on Killian, pulling him into a tight hug before he even had the opportunity to resist.

"It's good to see you," she said with bright eyes. She took his hand in both of hers, holding it there for a moment while she smiled at him.

Sera had always been a bit flamboyant for Killian's taste, but she had a sort of charismatic warmth that was infectious. Despite the knot in his stomach, he found himself half-smiling back at her. That was the best he could offer, given the circumstances.

They sat at the round wooden table in the center of the kitchen, the same one where Sera had read their fortunes a few months earlier. "The Fool," Sera had deemed him that day. He felt heat creep into the back of his neck as he realized, with disdain, just how accurate her reading had been.

Manny reached toward Sera and laid his hand atop hers. "Are you ready?" he asked gently.

Sera gave a nod, a gesture more solemn than any Killian had seen from her. He understood her reservation. Seeing the aftermath at Prestowne had been harrowing enough; he couldn't imagine watching it happen over and over again.

Sera bravely recounted her visions. There had been four but they were mostly the same. People dropping dead in their homes, in the streets. Chaos as families tried to flee or find one another. Fire scorching everything. The picture it painted only renewed Killian's vehemence.

"Do you have any idea who might have done this?" Killian asked, and Sera flinched. He realized he might have spoken harshly, and forced himself to soften his expression. Sera wasn't the enemy.

She shook her head, pain in her eyes. "No—but it had to have been someone very powerful."

Someone very powerful indeed. Killian swallowed, then asked in a low voice, "And do you have any idea why Elyse was there?"

He held his breath, waiting for Sera's surprise—either feigned or real. He was certain she would deny knowledge of Elyse's whereabouts.

Sera smiled, but not her usual lovely smile. It was awkward and timid, somehow both bashful and proud.

"I know exactly why Elyse was there." She sent Manny a sideways glance as she bit her lip. "She... She came to visit me the day before."

"She *what*?" Killian exclaimed. The chair scraped against the floor as he stood, staring at Sera in disbelief. He could feel the heat rising to his cheeks. Manny merely shook his head, the same shock coating his features, only less enraged.

Sera raised her chin. "She came by the day before, and I told her about the visions." Sera's voice was remarkably confident, as if she hadn't harbored a fugitive. "She wanted to know all about them—to help. I told her the only clue I had—about a statue of three figures. She must have figured out where the town was and gone to investigate."

"Sera," Manny sighed.

But Killian couldn't speak. He couldn't even think, he was so angry. Red tinged his vision, painting Sera's bright apartment in shades of scarlet and vermillion. He'd known—he'd *fucking known*—that Sera couldn't be trusted. What had she unraveled by sharing her visions with Elyse?

"You should have told us," Manny said in a voice that was firm but not unkind.

"So you could lecture me?" Sera quipped, cocking a defiant brow.

But Killian leaned across the table. "Where is she?" he blurted out. His fingernails dug into the grains of wood beneath them. He gritted his teeth as he glared at her, waiting for an answer.

Both Sera and Manny looked taken aback by the aggression in his tone. Why wasn't Manny more angry? And why was Sera acting like this wasn't a massive act of treason?

"*Where is she?*" he growled again, his voice low and coated with anger.

"Well..." Sera said quietly, and something stirred in Killian's ribs.

The moment before Sera's eyes flickered toward her bedroom, the moment before Killian heard the soft click of boots, he sensed her presence. She was there. She was in the fucking apartment.

His back was to the bedroom door. He turned slowly, rotating his torso with control despite the savage chaos brewing within him. Elyse stood there, looking down at him in his chair, her chin held high, her expression stoic. Killian could feel his rage heating his blood, but he didn't move or speak. Neither did Elyse. They just stared at each other for a long, long moment, tension pulling and pushing around them.

He hated how much he'd thought of her since seeing her in Prestowne. Hated that she hadn't fought back, that she'd saved his life, that she'd pleaded with him to listen to her. He hated that she was breathing, and that she somehow managed to take his breath away. The endless confusion overwhelmed him, seizing his heart and clouding his mind.

And then his eyes fell to her hands, to the silver shackles that bound her wrists.

Killian nodded toward the cuffs. "What's this?" he asked, his voice coming out weaker than he meant it to.

"A sign of good faith," Elyse answered boldly, lifting her chin an inch higher.

If she was affected by his presence, she didn't show it. Her voice was calm and even, her face neutral yet confident. It unnerved Killian to his core.

"The shackles are magic-suppressing," Sera added. "Elyse is here to make a bargain, nothing more."

He remained unconvinced. "What's to stop me from taking her down to the palace dungeons right now?" he asked, speaking about her as if she weren't standing before him, brimming with arrogance.

"You won't," Elyse answered. She took a small step toward him. "You won't because you know that just by being here, I'm taking a great risk, and that I wouldn't do so without a damn good reason."

Killian scoffed. "Your 'reasons' are just manipulation," he jeered. Even so, what she said resonated with him. The last time he'd seen her in shackles, when he tried to arrest her for King Cyril's murder, she'd cut off and reattached her own hand just to avoid capture. He could still see the scars from where she'd done so, peeking out behind the silver metal on her wrists. If she'd gone to such lengths to escape arrest, why risk her freedom by presenting herself bound and impotent?

She had spun so many lies. She'd tricked him into believing she proclaimed her innocence under the influence of truth serum, yet she had been immune to the potion's effects all along. She'd convinced him that she cared for him, even though she lied to him for weeks.

How could this be anything but a trick now?

"Just hear her out," Sera said—a command, not a plea. "And to make sure you're on your best behavior..." She held up a strip of leather with a pink crystal fastened to it—Killian's crystal.

His hand shot immediately to his wrist where the leather bracelet should have been, but of course, it wasn't there. Sera must have stolen it from him when he first arrived.

Vulnerability trickled into his veins. He'd only had the crystal for a few months, but he felt paralyzed without it. Since when had he become so attached to magic? The realization sickened him.

"My love," Manny began, pinching the bridge of his nose with his fingers. "This is all so reckless—stupid even—but I must say, I'm impressed with your sleight of hand."

Sera gave Manny a sly smile as she batted her lashes.

"This isn't funny," Killian spat, his chest heaving. "She is a murderer!" he added, throwing his finger in her direction.

He thought he saw Elyse flinch. Good.

Manny turned toward him and stared at him for a few seconds, seeming to gather his thoughts. "She is a murderer, and I want to see her punished for it. I do," he said with sincerity. "But I saw the aftermath at Prestowne, and I want justice for those people as well. If Elyse can offer any insight, then I'd like to hear it."

Everything about this was wrong, so wrong. How could Manny stand to be in the same room as Elyse? Killian's head was pounding, his muscles begging him to attack, attack, *attack!*

"How do we know she won't lie to us? That she won't lead us astray like she did with Royce?" He swallowed and added, "How do we know she didn't cause the destruction at Prestowne herself?"

The words tasted foul coming out of his mouth. He knew somehow, deep down, that she was incapable of that kind of slaughter.

"We don't know," Manny answered. "I might not trust her, but I trust Sera."

Killian didn't reply. He bit his tongue as a myriad of insults came to mind.

"Sit," Sera said to Elyse, taking Killian's silence for acquiescence.

Elyse seemed careful to keep her eyes on anything but Killian. She slowly moved toward the empty chair between Killian and Manny and lowered herself into it, resting her shackled hands in her lap.

This close up, Killian could see how pale she was, her skin nearly translucent. Her cheekbones were more pronounced than he remembered, and dark circles lined her eyes. Her lips quivered almost imperceptibly—a hint at the turmoil within.

He wanted nothing more than to storm out of the room, to throw her "bargain" in her face. Yet something within him wouldn't let him leave. His feet were heavy, his boots leaden. No matter how much he told himself Elyse was about to spew nothing but lies, some sick form of masochism kept him rooted in his chair. He told himself it was curiosity, but his dubious heart laughed at that.

Finally, he exhaled and crossed his arms. "This had better be good."

CHAPTER 14

— • —

ELYSE

It was nearly impossible for Elyse to stay calm as she sat beside Killian. For the last three days, she had thought of nothing else but the hateful looks he had given her and the loathsome words he'd spat at her.

That, and the endless corpses that had filled Prestowne.

As she sat at the table, she reminded herself that those innocent lives were the reason she was there. She had to be strong for them—had to get answers for them. Something strange and powerful was brewing in Rhodan, and she needed to stop it before any more lives were taken—even if it meant asking Killian for help.

Even if it meant her sacrificing her freedom.

She could feel Killian's eyes on her, but she couldn't bring herself to meet his stare. It had been difficult enough to hold his gaze when she had been standing across the room, but she had managed to keep her composure. Now, sitting this close to him, she could feel the disgust radiating off him, like a fire that burned too hot.

She lifted her eyes toward Sera instead, who gave her an encouraging nod. Thank the stars for Sera, whose faith in her remained unwavering, even when Elyse didn't quite believe in herself. She let out an exhale and chanced a glance at Manny. His gaze was far from warm, but there was a glimmer of something there—perhaps curiosity.

She could do this. She could lay out her plan and convince them to help her. Surely they would see reason.

With one more exhale, Elyse finally mustered the courage to speak.

"I think the slaughter at Prestowne is somehow demonic," she began, forcing her voice to sound confident.

Sera's brows crinkled with concern, and Manny's eyes widened.

"A demon?" Killian asked, his voice raw with skepticism.

"Yes," Elyse said, trying to ignore his disdain. "The man at the church—I think he was a priest. There were symbols written in blood around his body." She paused and shook her head as the unwelcome memory assaulted her. "I didn't recognize them at first, but I think the symbols were in a demonic language."

"You... read 'demon'?" Manny asked slowly.

"No, but I've seen symbols like that before in spellbooks. Symbols for summoning demons, speaking to them, making sacrifices to them—"

Killian huffed, cutting her off. "So what? Prestowne was just..." He made a vague gesture with his hands. "One giant sacrifice?"

"No. Maybe," Elyse said, confusion welling in her throat. "I don't know."

This had been a bad idea. Why did she ever think Killian would listen to her?

She sighed, trying her best to ignore his shaking head. "I don't know much, but I'm certain it's related to a demon. And I don't know about you, but I don't ever want to see that many innocent people killed again."

The room fell silent. No doubt Manny and Killian were also imagining the carnage they'd witnessed, Sera replaying the visions in her mind. Elyse had meant what she said. Prestowne would haunt her for the rest of her life, however long that was.

It was Manny who finally broke the silence. "We will certainly look into any connections with demons," he began. He threaded his fingers through his fair curls, pulling the long strands away from his eyes. "But

Elyse, why meet with us just to tell us? You could have sent a letter or passed the information through Sera."

"Because it's not enough," she said, her voice quivering slightly. "Whatever this is, it's bigger than me, it's bigger than the Royal Guard. I think..." She paused, steeling herself and focusing her gaze on Killian. "I think if we're going to figure this out, we're going to have to work together."

Killian's nostrils flared but he didn't make a sound. He held her stare, throwing as much intensity at her as he could, but she refused to back down.

"If you think I'd so much as *consider* working with you," he began, each word piercing and whetted, "then you're even fucking crazier than I thought."

The blow hurt, her heart capsizing. She'd expected such a reaction. Still, it made her feel small. She forced herself to match his intensity as she studied his face. Devil's hooves, he was just as handsome as she remembered, which made it harder to see the guilt she harbored manifested in his features. His full, decadent lips were pulled into a tight line, unwilling to speak further on the matter. His impeccable jawline fluttered as he ground his teeth. He'd meant every word he said, that he would never work with her.

That was why she'd give him the one thing he wanted.

"What if I agree to turn myself in?" she said calmly.

Killian blinked, then blinked again. Manny looked between the two of them, waiting for Killian to respond.

"Right now?" he asked. He spoke softly but Elyse swore she could hear the subtle elation. "You'd let me walk you down to the palace and turn you in for treason *right now*?"

"No," Elyse said, then quickly added, "but if you help me find whoever is responsible for Prestowne, I swear I'll turn myself in."

Killian opened his mouth to say something, but Elyse wasn't done. "I'll swear it with a blood oath."

Sera looked down at her lap. She had tried to talk Elyse out of offering to turn herself in, insisting that there had to be another way. But Elyse knew it was the only way she could entice them to agree. It was the best chance they had at finding the killer.

Killian still remained silent. Elyse took in his expression, the calculating look in his golden eyes, and wondered what he was thinking. She wanted so badly to reach out and touch him. His usually clean-shaven face was stubbled, and she wished she could feel it, could press her cheek against his the way she used to. But that would be unfair. She knew she'd made his life hell, had broken him so badly that he might be beyond repair, that seeing her hanged might never be enough for him. But she needed him to understand that whatever pain she had caused him was nothing compared to the chaos that would ensue if someone was using demonic powers to slaughter entire cities.

When Killian spoke, his voice was so quiet it was nearly a whisper. "What would be the terms of this blood oath?"

Elyse sighed with relief—yet at the same time her stomach clenched. She realized that part of her had been hoping Killian wouldn't agree, that she would be free from having to face the consequences of killing King Cyril. That had been a stupid fantasy.

"I will agree to turn myself in," Elyse said, sounding more resolute than she felt, "and in exchange, you will help me look for whoever is responsible—for one year."

"One year?" Killian shouted.

Even Manny gaped at her. "Our original agreement to find King Cyril's killer had only been a week," he pointed out.

Elyse smiled a tiny bit. She couldn't help herself. "Maybe you should have driven a harder bargain."

Killian snorted, a sound that undoubtedly meant something along the lines of, "As if it would have mattered."

"Whoever is behind this is extremely powerful—and dangerous," Elyse pressed. "It might not be so easy to track him down."

"Or her," Killian corrected with a sneer.

"Or her," Elyse conceded. "But I'm not going to turn myself over to certain death without giving everything I have to find whoever is responsible. I won't."

For once Killian had no retort. Perhaps he knew her stubbornness. Or perhaps he could relate to her words.

"Is there any way to break a blood oath?" Manny asked. "Any way to get out of it?"

Sera shook her head. "It's a powerful binding spell. Only death can undo the magic."

Manny glanced at Killian, his expression uncertain. But Killian was staring at Elyse with an icy countenance. She held her breath, waiting for an answer.

"One month," Killian said finally, then before Elyse could argue he added, "as a trial period."

Truthfully, it was the best Elyse could have hoped for. She nodded her agreement, even as a subtle terror rose in her throat. She swallowed it down, ignoring the goose pimples that now prickled her arms.

"And," he continued, "you must swear not to harm myself or anyone in the Royal Guard."

Elyse's lips parted, a protest on her tongue. She had no qualms with promising not to harm Killian or Manny, but what if another situation arose where she needed to protect herself? She didn't like the uncertainty of it.

Killian's face was stony, though. There wasn't any sense in arguing.

"Okay," she agreed.

"And," Killian said, stressing the single word, "you won't be able to lie."

Elyse swallowed as hundreds of secrets flew through her mind. It wasn't that she made a particular habit of lying, but the thought of being unable to tell a lie—even a little white one—felt suffocating. It would leave her open to so much vulnerability. What if she was forced to tell them about Kelia, the young girl she had been manipulated into murdering? Or what if they asked questions about her father? She didn't want them to know the possibility that she had been sired by a demon.

But if agreeing not to lie got her what she needed, what the people of Prestowne deserved, she would do it. She gave Killian a nod.

"Anything else to add?" Killian asked. He looked at Manny, who appeared surprised that any of this was happening. Elyse didn't know who he was surprised by—Killian, Elyse, or both.

When Manny didn't have anything to add, Killian sat up in his chair, leaning his elbows on the table. "So how do we make this blood pact?"

"We'll write out the terms of the contract and sign it with our blood," Elyse explained. She nodded to Sera, who went to find parchment, ink, and a quill.

Elyse noticed a silent conversation pass between Manny and Killian. It was nearly imperceptible—a slight tilt of the head, a slow blink. Their discussion seemed to be something along the lines of "Are you sure you want to do this?" and "Absolutely." Manny leaned back in his chair and crossed his arms, warily accepting his friend's decision.

Sera returned and splayed her gathered tools atop the table. No one spoke as she smoothed out the parchment and uncorked the bottle of ink. Elyse spared a quick glance toward Killian, but he watched Sera with an icy resolution that made her shiver.

Sera dipped the quill into the ink, her hand trembling. Elyse's heart felt suddenly heavy. She hadn't considered how difficult this would be for Sera, having to watch her closest friend sign her freedom away in an irreversible pact. But before she could say or do anything to comfort Sera, Manny reached out and gently took the quill from her still-shaking hand and slid the parchment in front of himself.

"Right," he sighed, and he began to write down the date.

Elyse breathed slowly as he wrote out the contract, savoring each inhale and exhale. After all, her breaths were numbered. One month was all she had to either catch the killer or convince Killian to extend the contract. No matter what, she would end up at the gallows. It was just a matter of when.

Though, the gallows might not be the end for her. Lazarus had brought her back from the dead before. Would he do so again? It was a strange thought. She had faced death many times, and yet there she was, living. She felt invincible and yet utterly mortal.

Manny finished writing and passed the parchment to Elyse. As her eyes roved over the words that sealed her fate, she forced her face to stay neutral. Killian, on the other hand, looked deviously satisfied as he read over the contract. He unceremoniously pulled out his knife and slid it across his hand, then dipped the quill in his blood and signed. When he was finished, he held the knife toward Elyse, a challenge simmering in his eyes.

Her gaze traveled from the knife, glistening with blood, to the cut on his hand. "I can show you how to heal that," she said, pointing to Killian's fresh wound.

His returning stare was cold. "Just sign," he said firmly, extending the hilt of the knife in her direction.

The weight of the chains was heavy as Elyse reached out her hands to take the knife. As she grasped the hilt, her finger grazed Killian's, and he instantly recoiled, fisting his hand against his chest. Elyse couldn't help the hurt that flooded her features. Despite herself, despite knowing exactly how disgusted Killian's stare would be, she couldn't stop herself from meeting his eyes.

But instead of finding anger or revulsion, his eyes were soft—pensive even. He looked away before she could decipher his emotions.

With a shaky breath, Elyse slid the knife across her left hand. Blood seeped from the wound—the twin to Killian's. The moment she scrawled the final letter and lifted the quill from the parchment, her whole body tingled as the magic of the oath settled over her.

Killian must have felt it too, because he shuddered, his face pinching.

It was done.

No one looked at each other, as if they had just done something foul. Tension brewed in the air, a mixture of fear and regret, with an undercurrent of hope.

"I'll get some bandages," Sera said, breaking the silence and excusing herself from the table.

Manny sighed. "So where do we begin?"

Elyse held her bloodied hand out to Sera, who began tending to her cut. "Well," she said once the wound was covered. "The place where I'm staying has an extensive library. We could start there."

Sera brought Killian a roll of fabric to bandage his hand, along with the small leather bracelet sporting the pink crystal.

"You can have this back now." She said it with an impish smile, though the levity didn't quite reach her eyes.

Killian let the bracelet lay on the table while he began bandaging his hand.

"I see you're still using the pink one," Elyse observed aloud. She had been surprised to see that he still had the crystal she had given him, especially since she'd chosen pink as a joke.

Killian didn't deign a response.

One month suddenly felt like an immense amount of time.

CHAPTER 15

— • —

KILLIAN

K illian strolled up the path to the country estate where Elyse stayed, Sera following behind him. Neither of them spoke to one another—Sera must have sensed that Killian wanted nothing to do with her company. He wished Manny was joining them, but his friend had been too busy with guard duties to attend. Still, Killian supposed that having Sera around was better than spending the day alone with Elyse.

It was now the third time he'd been to the enormous home, yet every time he saw it, he felt his anger renew. Over the past few months, he'd pictured Elyse many times. He'd always imagined her hiding out in shady inns, stealing to get by and traveling only by the cover of night. In reality, she had been living like a princess in a prim and spacious cottage.

The house was settled on top of a hill, sunshine pouring in through its tall windows. Pristine grass stretched in every direction, and rows of perfectly manicured tulips lined the walkway, yet Killian had never seen any groundskeepers. Perhaps the whole bloody place was enchanted to look immaculate. It belonged to someone named Jaime, and Killian wondered what sort of woman this "Jaime" was. Was she a witch like Elyse? Or more of a connoisseur of magic, like Royce? Either way, she was housing a wanted felon, and that made her an idiot in Killian's book.

He approached the massive mahogany door and performed the special knock Elyse had shown them on their first visit—the one that would let

76

them pass through the wards and signal to Elyse that she had friendly company. He couldn't tell if he imagined it, but he swore he felt a stirring in the air as he finished the last knock.

Moments later, Elyse swung the heavy door open. She smiled meekly up at Killian, but he brushed past her into the lavish foyer, down the hall adorned with expensive paintings, and into the library.

He could hardly keep from rolling his eyes upon entering the room, which was the size of his mother's entire house. The shelves were so tall that some of them required ladders to reach the higher levels, and every surface was covered in books. The only wall that wasn't obscured by shelves boasted an enormous map of the Kingdom of Rhodan, so pompous and gaudy that it made Killian snort.

He knew he should be grateful for the size of the library, and for having access to it, but did it have to be so damn lavish? It only served as a reminder that Elyse had won and was doing just fine. Better than fine, even.

He settled himself in the corner as Sera and Elyse entered the library. They were discussing something in hushed voices, but Killian paid them no mind. He had gotten good at tuning them out over the last few days.

He dove into the book at the top of the pile he'd set aside for himself—*An Extensive History of Western Rhodan*. They'd divided up certain areas of research to be more efficient, and Killian had agreed to look into Prestowne's history to see if there was anything relevant to the attack. Meanwhile, Elyse read through books on the demonic language to see if she could decipher the symbols that had surrounded the priest's body, and Sera looked up spells that involved genocide and fire.

Hours passed as they each worked in silence, occasionally reading a passage aloud to the group to get their thoughts. So far, nothing significant had come up in their search, but they earmarked a dozen or so pages to come back to just in case—probably more out of wishful thinking than actual merit. Time passed slowly, especially as the texts were incredibly dry, and Killian often found himself daydreaming about being out on the obstacle course behind Elyse's shoppe.

He had been proud of the way he'd fought against her in Prestowne, even if he hadn't been able to get any spells past her shield. His magic had been powerful, fueled by his emotions, and he had been mostly accurate. The duel only made him want to train harder, and he had spent hours each night since honing his spellwork. If it ever came down to a battle between him and Elyse again, he wanted to be sure he wouldn't lose.

He realized he must have been staring at Elyse, because she looked at him with furrowed brows. He shook his head and refocused his eyes on his book, but he could feel that she still watched him for a moment longer.

"I'll go make us some lunch," Sera announced suddenly as she stood up from her chair.

Elyse scooted back in her seat. "I'll come with—" she began, but Sera cut her off.

"Don't be silly," she said, waving her hand. "I can handle it on my own." Then she fled from the room before anyone could protest.

The library instantly felt entirely too small, as if all the books were pressing in on Killian, shoving him toward Elyse. He was acutely aware of her presence, the sound of her breathing like a horse snorting, loud and gusty. And it was so damned hot! The sun was practically roasting them alive through the grand floor-to-ceiling window. He tugged at the collar of his tunic, trying to get comfortable, but to no avail.

He tried to focus on reading, but his mind traveled. He wished that Sera would hurry back. He was in the middle of reading the same sentence for the fourth time when Elyse finally spoke up.

"How's your mum?" she asked quietly.

His hand flinched reflexively, his thumb and forefinger tightening around the page they gripped. "Fine," he answered without looking up from his book.

Elyse was quiet, and Killian thought that was the end of it. He started to read the sentence for the fifth time when she added, "And Georgie?"

Killian stared down at the book in his lap. He hadn't seen George in weeks, not since the boy moved in with his new family. He'd heard from his mother that he was doing well, that he got along great with his three new sisters and that he was excited for school to start. His expression soured as he realized, with a pang of guilt, that he should have gone to visit Georgie by now.

Elyse stared at Killian, one eyebrow raised as she awaited an answer. He shrugged and repeated, "Fine."

Before Elyse could ask any follow up questions, Sera returned with a platter of open-faced sandwiches. Killian stood to grab one of the sandwiches and planned to take it back to his armchair to eat it, but Sera shot him a stern look.

"Eat at the table with us, like a gentleman," she demanded.

Killian's nostrils flared. He was going to comment that they didn't deserve any sort of chivalry, having lied to and manipulated him, but he was nothing if not a gentleman, even to those who didn't deserve it. So he sat.

No one spoke at first as they each tucked in to their sandwiches. It was strange how sitting around doing nothing but reading could work up such an appetite. Then Sera had to ruin the silence.

"Have you found anything?" she asked Elyse.

Elyse, having just taken a bite of sandwich, simply shook her head.

"Me neither," Sera sighed.

Elyse swallowed and said, "You should take tomorrow off from researching. You have a business to run after all."

Killian had wondered about that. They'd worked late into the night that past two days, leaving no time for Sera to see clients.

"No, this is much more important," Sera said lightly, though her throat bobbed.

Elyse took another bite. This time, she didn't wait to swallow as she insisted, mouth full of food, "Really, Sera. We'd understand if you needed a day, or even two."

"No," Sera answered, her voice too low to be casual. "I'm fine, really." Her expression was serious, distant even. Something seemed to shift within her. She set her sandwich back on the plate and stared at it, her lip quivering slightly.

Elyse set her own sandwich down and focused all her attention on her friend. "Sera..." she began.

It was all the prodding Sera needed. Tears brimmed in her purple eyes, and her voice was barely a whisper. "I could have stopped it. I should have done more."

"Oh, Sera," Elyse crooned. In a second she was at Sera's side, wrapping her arms around her friend.

Killian watched, feeling like an intruder. He wasn't sure what to do. He wasn't especially fond of the idea of consoling Sera, but the sadness in her eyes called out to him. He had felt the same way upon arriving at Prestowne, like it was somehow his fault. If he had gotten there faster, if he had notified the Guard, would anyone have been saved?

A sob racked Sera's body, and Killian's hand twitched. His instinct was to reach out to her and place a comforting hand on her shoulder, but he didn't. Would she even want his comfort? Or would it be... unwanted? Taken as condescending? He kept to himself.

Elyse laid a hand on Sera's cheek and turned her face toward her. "Look at me," she demanded, stern but soft. "This is not your fault."

Sera choked on a sob, but Elyse continued.

"You didn't know if the visions were past or future—or if they were nothing at all." She paused, taking a deep breath, then said bravely, "The truth is, even if you had known the visions would come true, even if you had figured out where to go, who knows if we could've stopped it?"

From the angle where he sat, Killian couldn't see Elyse's face, but he could hear the sorrow in her voice. "It's true," he added quietly. "We still don't know how it happened. I doubt we would have been able to prevent their deaths."

Sera nodded solemnly as she wiped a tear from her cheek. "You're probably right," she agreed.

"Of course we are," Elyse said, smiling. "You aren't the only one who gets to be right all the time."

That earned a laugh from Sera, and Killian looked away. He hated that Elyse could be this way—kind and funny and wise. It was so much easier to think of her as cold and devious.

Knock-knock. Knock. Knock. Knock. Knock-knock.

Killian, Sera, and Elyse all looked at each other with wide eyes as someone rapped at the front door—someone who knew the secret code.

"Manny?" Elyse asked, but Sera shook her head.

"I don't think so," she answered hesitantly. "He said he'd be busy all day."

"Maybe it's Jaime," Elyse said as the sound of the front door opening echoed down the hallway.

Killian groaned internally. He wasn't particularly in the mood to meet anyone new, especially not the woman who had harbored Elyse for two months. He would almost prefer the visitor be a violent burglar.

"Elyse?" called a man's voice. "Elyse!" the voice came again, this time panicked.

Killian frowned. Why was a man entering the house looking for Elyse? "In the library!" Elyse called back.

Killian looked to her, assessing her reaction. She didn't appear alarmed, so she must know whoever was walking down the hallway toward them. Still, the slight purse of her lips meant she was worried about something.

A golden-haired man appeared in the doorframe, his bright blue eyes searching the room and landing on Elyse. "You're okay," he breathed, taking a step toward her—but then he must have noticed she wasn't alone because he froze, his brows furrowing. "Madam Sera? And..." His words trailed off as he beheld Killian.

The two men sized each other up. This man—intruder—whoever he was—was tall and lean, a bit of muscle to him, but not a warrior like Killian. His blond hair was disheveled, as if he'd been tearing his hand through it, but his clothes were elegant and pristine.

"This is Killian," Elyse said quietly, gesturing to him. "Killian, this is Jaime. He owns the place."

"Elyse—" Jaime pulled her by the elbow, violently spinning her toward him. Something lurched deep inside Killian. He expected Elyse to snatch her arm from Jaime's grip, but she did nothing as he began to lecture her.

"You let Killian, of all people, through the wards? Are you mad?" he hissed in a whisper, exasperation vibrating through him, but Killian could hardly pay attention to the conversation.

Jaime was a *man*.

Killian tried to recall every instance where Elyse or Sera had mentioned Jaime, confident that they had referred to him as a woman, but now that he thought about it, perhaps they had never used any pronouns. Perhaps Killian had merely assumed Jaime was a woman's name.

He remembered it then. Ages ago, when Elyse was training him on the obstacle course, she'd referred to her former lover. "Jaime and I were close for a while, and it was fun," she'd said.

Heat seared the back of his neck as he watched them, taking in the way they stood so close to one another. Their chests practically touched as they discussed Elyse's actions in hushed tones. Something hardened in Killian's stomach. Had they rekindled their romance? Had Jaime welcomed Elyse into his home—into his bed—taking advantage of her situation? Or worse, had Elyse seduced him?

He told himself that it didn't matter whose house Elyse lived in, whether it belonged to her handsome ex, an old woman, or a baboon. In fact, Jaime could have her if he wanted her. She was nothing but trouble.

"I know, I'm sorry." Elyse sounded genuinely apologetic. "I wouldn't have invited them here if it wasn't important. Something's happened—"

"Something *has* happened," Jaime interrupted in a dagger-sharp voice. "An entire town was slaughtered and burned down. Nobody knows what happened, and I just—I came here as soon as I heard. I had to make sure you were okay."

How nice, Killian thought, barely hiding his sneer. Jaime had dropped everything and come running back to his fancy house to check on the witch. It was nice to know Killian wasn't the only one she had managed to wrap around her little finger.

Jaime seemed more agitated than relieved. His eyes only left Elyse to flit toward Killian, darkening with anger at every glance.

Elyse must have noticed it too. "Killian. Sera," she whispered. "I think we're finished for today."

Twenty minutes ago, Killian had been desperate to leave their company. Now his feet felt heavy, weighed down by the tension in the air. He studied their posture, the way Jaime's hand touched Elyse's elbow in a claiming sort of way, and the supplication in Elyse's shoulders. Something about leaving her alone with the blond man felt wrong.

Sera gave him a look that said it was time to go, so Killian stood and moved slowly toward the door. Elyse met his eyes, and Killian felt he should say something, but not a damn word came to his mind. She was a fighter. If it wasn't safe here, she could handle herself. Not that it mattered to him anyway.

He nodded at Elyse, and she returned the nod, subtle and slow. He replayed that nod in his mind, as simple and bare as it was, as he walked down the hall and out the door.

CHAPTER 16

— • —

ELYSE

Jaime waited until Killian's and Sera's footsteps retreated down the hallway and the door closed behind them. Then he unloaded on Elyse.

"That was incredibly stupid," he snapped at her. He looked furious, yet somehow still beautiful, like a god reigning terror. "Sera alone is dangerous enough, but you actually invited the lieutenant?" He spat the word with such disdain. "Was it not *his* arrow that I tore from your arm when you were bleeding on my doorstep?"

Guilt trickled its way into Elyse's heart. She had to look away. "Former lieutenant," she corrected quietly. "And he can't harm me now. I'm protected."

"Protected?" Jaime repeated, sounding skeptical. "Staying here, laying low, keeping behind the wards—those are your protections."

Elyse shook her head. "I know." She kept her voice low and even, trying her best not to sound resentful. "Please don't be angry. I'll explain everything."

She gestured for him to sit at the table, begging with her expression for him to obey. He did, and she sat beside him, looking him right in the eyes. Ire still pulsated through him, fueling her guilt, but she steadied herself and explained how she had visited Sera and gone to Prestowne.

"You were there?" Jaime asked, both befuddled and angry. "Elyse, what were you thinking? You could have been caught or killed."

"I was thinking," she began, her voice growing bolder as the images of Prestowne assaulted her. "I was thinking that I was going crazy here. I was thinking about Sera's vision and that maybe I could stop it. I was thinking that someone had to do something."

Jaime stared back at her, apparently at a loss for words. Elyse knew he wasn't going to like the next part of her story, so she pried the words from her mouth.

"That is why I asked Sera to arrange a meeting with Killian and Manny, and I swore a blood oath that if they agreed to work with me to find whoever is responsible for Prestowne, I would turn myself in as King Cyril's murderer."

"You did what?" Jaime sprang from his chair and began pacing the library, his gait restless. He never took his eyes off Elyse as betrayal and confusion all cut into his expression. "Elyse, why? You're just giving up? This is a death sentence!"

"I know," she replied, an edge in her voice—an edge that hid her fear.

"You can't do this," he commanded, violently shaking his head.

"It's already done." Elyse could no longer hold his gaze. She looked away, but in a flash Jaime was kneeling before her, touching her chin and pulling her face to meet his stare.

"Then we'll run away, right now. We'll go to another kingdom and leave all this behind."

Elyse searched those watery blue eyes and found nothing but sincerity. He meant it, every word. He would run away with her. He would forsake everyone who had died at Prestowne.

"I can't," she croaked, fighting back her trepidation. "Not just because of the blood oath." Tears threatened to spill, but she stared at the ceiling, willing them to vanish. After a deep breath, she looked back at Jaime. "I can't live with all these deaths hanging over my head, the lies I told Killian. I'm ready to face the consequences. And if I can do something good before then, by avenging those who died and making sure no one else gets hurt, then..." She paused, swallowing down the emotions that swelled in her chest. "Then I think that is worth dying for."

She looked straight at him and let her brave facade slip away, revealing the fear beneath. She knew what lay ahead of her, but she would not be swayed.

Jaime said nothing, instead taking one of Elyse's fidgeting hands in his. He let his gaze fall as he traced his thumb along her finger, and a sigh escaped his lips.

"Every day for the past two months, my greatest fear has been that you will find yourself in trouble, and I will be unable to save you," he said, his voice low and gravelly. "And now, it seems, that day has come, and by your own choosing."

Elyse slowly freed her hand from his. She bit the inside of her cheek, unsure how to reply. Didn't he understand? She didn't want to be saved. She wanted to take control of her life.

"I don't need you to save me," she answered, trying her best to smother the discomfort that brewed inside her. She didn't blame him for caring for her, especially after she'd nearly died in his foyer, but the way he spoke made her sound weak, defenseless. "If you want to help me, then work with us. Help us avenge the families that died in Prestowne."

His eyes, narrowed and unblinking, bore into her. He bit his lower lip, as if fighting back an objection. Elyse's expression didn't change. She needed him to understand that her decision was made.

"Okay," he agreed, and something within Elyse relaxed.

Jaime pulled her into a hug, just as he had many times before. She let him hold her, his arms wrapped protectively around her, one last time. She could give him that.

CHAPTER 17

— • —

KILLIAN

The question tore at Killian, clawing its way up his throat, but he kept it at bay for as long as he could. He waited until after he and Sera magicked away from the estate and back into the city, right up until Sera lay an alabaster hand on the door to her building.

"How do we know we can trust Jaime?" he blurted out, breathless.

Sera turned back to Killian, a knowing look in her eyes. They hadn't said one word to each other, and he realized that she had been waiting for this moment.

"You were content to be in his house reading his books until now," she crooned. "What changed? Do his good looks concern you?"

"Don't be ridiculous," Killian snapped. Jaime's looks had nothing to do with this. There was something off about him. Clearly he cared for Elyse—he had stuck his neck out for her and made sure she was cared for. Yet something about his poorly concealed ire left Killian feeling unsettled.

Sera sighed and took a step toward Killian. "I trust that Elyse is safe with him."

It wasn't quite the answer Killian was looking for, but he supposed it would have to do. "I'll see you tomorrow," he said gruffly before turning and stalking down the street.

He decided he was going to visit Georgie. Sera's apartment wasn't far from his neighborhood, and the sky was cloudy enough that the temperature was mild, so he opted to walk. He barely noticed the other citizens on the crowded streets, too far entrenched in his own thoughts to pay them any attention. One of which was Jaime.

If Jaime had found out about Prestowne, then how long until the rest of Rhodan knew about the slaughter? How would they react? Would there be outright panic?

And how had Jaime found out? The Royal Guard had done their best to keep the devastation under wraps, but of course families would have to be notified and the local economy would be affected. Did Jaime know someone affiliated with the town? Or was he somehow connected to the deaths?

Elyse clearly wasn't thinking straight. Jaime had waltzed in and bombarded her with a lecture, placing his hands on her like he owned her. And Elyse had *let* him. Were her feelings for Jaime—past or present—clouding her judgment? Why else would she be blind to his menacing undertones?

"Killian!"

A boy's cry shook Killian's wandering mind, halting all his thoughts. Georgie was barreling down the street toward him, a grin splitting his bright face. Though Georgie was only half Killian's size, the boy collided with him with so much force that it nearly knocked the wind out of Killian.

"Hi, Georgie," he wheezed, returning his fierce hug.

"Is mum with you?" Georgie asked as he released Killian. He had taken to referring to Killian's mother as his own, a sentiment that warmed Killian's heart.

"Not today," he replied, "but I'll tell her you'd like to see her soon. What are you doing out here?" He gestured to the street around them, which was several blocks from Georgie's new home.

"I was going to the cobbler to see about some new shoes—I already grew out of the ones you bought me!" Georgie announced with pride.

Killian took a step back to appraise him. He was long and lanky, and at least an inch taller than Killian remembered him being. His gangly limbs hung awkwardly by his side, his hands nearly reaching to his knees. He looked healthy, a rosy color to his cheeks, which were framed by overlong brown curls.

"At this rate, you'll be taller than me in two winters' time," Killian commented as he and the boy began walking together down the street.

"You think?" Georgie asked. "I'll definitely be taller than Manny."

He said it so simply that Killian couldn't help but burst with laughter. Georgie beamed up at him, clearly pleased with himself for making Killian smile.

"Yes, I reckon you'll be taller than Manny," Killian agreed, still grinning.

They meandered down the narrow streets lined with tightly packed houses, the same streets where Killian and his brother Joe had played as children. It stirred both nostalgia and sorrow in his heart as he listened to Georgie's rambling. He'd once shared the same enthusiasm for such simple things—racing down the alleyways behind the rows of houses; getting sweets from the nearby bakery; and even terrorizing Old Man Parkins, who still lived in the gray house on the corner.

"Have you caught Miss Elyse yet?" Georgie asked, eyes wide and curious.

Killian's sentimental mood was swiftly erased. Georgie had called her "Miss Elyse." Not "Elyse, the king's murderer," but "Miss Elyse," someone he knew and had respected.

"No," Killian said with a grimace, leaving it at that. He wasn't about to explain the parameters of their blood pact to a twelve-year-old.

Georgie's voice was more hesitant as he asked, "But you're going to catch her, right?"

"Of course," Killian replied simply. He lifted an eyebrow and jestingly added, "You don't believe in me?"

Georgie smiled weakly, uncertainty in his eyes. "It's just... What will happen to her?"

Killian cleared his throat to buy himself a moment. Georgie wasn't exactly naive; he had lost his parents and been working in a black market potions operation when Killian found him. Still, telling a boy that someone he knew personally would be put to death for treason and murder was not a light subject. "Well," he said finally. "She will be punished."

"Will she die?"

Killian nodded. "More than likely, yes."

Georgie was silent for a moment, his brows furrowed as he contemplated it. "But why?"

"Well, she did something bad—"

"I did something bad," Georgie interrupted. "And I wasn't punished."

"Making illegitimate potions isn't as bad as killing a king. Besides, you're a child."

"I'm not a child!" Georgie replied indignantly. "Mum says I'm a handsome young man."

Killian smiled even as he sighed. "You're still a lot younger than Elyse."

Georgie nodded his head. "I suppose," he wondered aloud. "But Pete and the others didn't get punished."

"No, they didn't," Killian affirmed. It was true. Pete and the other crew members had been set free on probation according to a deal Killian struck with them. "But what Pete did isn't as bad as what Elyse did," he pointed out.

"It could have been," Georgie said with some shame. "Mum set me down and told me why it was wrong to make those potions—how people could have been hurt if we didn't make them just right."

Killian bit the inside of his cheek. He had no doubt that his mother had firmly but lovingly explained the consequences of fooling around with magic. Had she explained to Georgie that she had personally been affected by a seller of defunct magical wares? That she had lost two children to such an atrocity?

His throat had gone dry, the pain of his own loss overtaking him. He didn't know what to say, so Georgie filled the silence.

"Maybe Miss Elyse didn't know," he suggested, his eyes blooming with optimism. "Or maybe someone made her do it." He shook his head and spoke in a serious voice, as if pondering the problems of the whole kingdom. "Sometimes good people just do bad things."

Well if that wasn't the damn truth. Except, Elyse wasn't a good person. A good person wouldn't have upended his whole world the way she had. Yet his mind wandered back to the moment Elyse shared with Sera earlier, when she had assuaged Sera's guilt and assured her that she was not to blame for Prestowne.

"That's my house right there! With the yellow shutters!" Georgie pointed down the road to a bungalow where three little girls played on the porch. "Come on," he cried earnestly, shooting Killian a frenzied look. "I want you to meet my sisters."

"All right," Killian agreed, pushing aside thoughts of Elyse and treason and Prestowne. "Race you there? On your mark, get set—"

Before Killian could even say "Go," Georgie was sprinting down the street, leaving Killian laughing and jogging after him.

CHAPTER 18

— • —

ELYSE

E lyse looked up from her book to once again find Jaime glaring at Killian. She was grateful that Jaime had agreed to help them, and especially thankful that he'd allowed Sera and Killian back into his home. His obvious hostility, on the other hand, was exhausting. She kicked him under the table, stirring him from his trance, and gave him a stern look. Jaime returned the look, raising his eyebrows as if to silently say, "I allowed him in my home, but I don't have to be nice to him." Elyse rolled her eyes and returned to her reading.

It had been like that all day, each of them researching in a silent, tension-filled room. It didn't help that it had been an especially warm day. Even now, hours after the sun had set, heat seemed to linger inside the library, trapped by the endless books and enormous window.

Apparently, Jaime was on edge too. The next time she looked up, he was back to glaring at Killian. She kicked him again, a little harder this time, and gave a pointed look at the book he was supposed to be reading.

If Killian noticed Jaime's aversion to him, he didn't show it. He hadn't made a sound all day as he sat in the armchair in the corner, flipping through one book after another and paying no mind to any of the fugitive-harborers in the room.

She allowed herself to stare at him for one long moment. To her surprise, she felt like picking up the sketchbook Jaime had given her and actually using it. Killian looked so picturesque, sitting in the chair, the candlelight illuminating one side of his face. The lighting made his already sharp jawline appear even more cutting, the shadows adding a sense of mystery to him. She wanted to capture the scene on paper, to have a piece of him with her.

The thought made her cheeks heat—which was intolerable in the stuffy room. She fanned herself as she turned another page and scanned the prose for anything worthwhile. After flipping through dozens of books on demonic language, she still hadn't come across any of the symbols she'd seen in the church. They clearly weren't common, a realization that had only made her grow more concerned about the level of power they were up against.

She leaned back in her chair and glanced toward Sera, who bit her lip as she read. Sera, bless her soul, had tried several times to ease the tension throughout the day, making light comments about the weather or asking Jaime about his business. Each attempt at conversation had been quickly shot down by either Jaime or Killian, and apparently Sera had given up, resigning herself to read silently instead.

A hopelessness washed over Elyse as she slouched lower. They had been researching endlessly for four, perhaps five, days—they all blurred together in her mind. They hadn't found a single passage that was helpful, and she felt no closer to getting answers. When she'd made the deal with Killian, she'd been so confident that the four of them working together would be a sort of prodigious collaboration. Now they had an additional ally and nothing to show for themselves.

She sighed, and to her surprise, it was Killian who looked up at her. He didn't move—only his eyes glanced in her direction—but their gazes met. She must have looked dejected because he gave her a small, almost imperceptible nod of encouragement.

The moment was over quickly.

"I think I've got something," Sera said quietly. Her eyes were still glued to the page, but there was something in her voice that made everyone's heads snap her way. "Listen to this: 'The entire town must be sacrificed, sparing no one—not women, nor children. No less than one hundred deaths are required for the sacrifice to be successful.'"

Chills licked their way up Elyse's back, all heat she'd previously felt replaced by icy shivers.

Sera swallowed and continued, her voice uneven. "'The priest is to be killed first, his blood used to draw the symbols that will summon evil to the town.'"

"Does it show the symbols?" Killian asked, but Elyse was already moving to stand beside Sera. She looked over her shoulder at the symbols inked on the page. They matched the ones she had seen on the floor of the church, drawn in a hexagon around the priest's body. She nodded to him, unable to speak.

This had to be the spell used at Prestowne, the answers they sought. Yet reading it on the page, seeing the instructions that had been used to slaughter so many people, it didn't give Elyse any of the satisfaction she desired. She leaned against the table, steadying herself, trying to grasp the situation.

"It goes on to talk about how the town's buildings will ignite, fire will blanket the town, and the citizens will just... drop dead," Sera said, growing quieter with every word.

"That's definitely it," Killian declared. He sounded so calm, but Elyse looked over at him and saw her own dread reflected on his face.

"What is the spell for?" Jaime asked. He was the only one who hadn't gone pale; he was also the only one who hadn't seen the destruction at Prestowne, the only one who was able to think rationally without seeing the faces of those who had fallen. Elyse's mind was flooded with images of bodies strewn across a street, a priest's mutilated corpse, and hundreds of homes incinerated.

Sera turned back a page before she answered. "It's a series of instructions on how to..." She paused and glanced at Elyse. Something unrecognizable passed in her expression before she said, "How to make a demon corporeal."

Elyse's stomach fell to her feet. She had to sit. Why would anyone want to make a demon corporeal? She had seen firsthand the devastation a demon could cause with its body locked away in hell. To give a demon life, a body to freely roam the earth—it would be utter chaos. There would be no limit to the death and desolation they could cause.

She took a deep breath in through her nose then pushed it out through her mouth. This was a good thing—it meant they had some sort of direction. They would find whoever was trying to bring a demon to life and stop them before they could. However, her head was swimming, unable to stop imagining what sort of horrible future awaited them should they fail.

"I think we should stop for today," Sera said, looking out the window to the half moon that shone above the distant treetops.

Jaime opened his mouth to speak, but Sera cut him off. "It's getting late and we've hardly eaten all day. Let's get some rest and face this with fresh eyes tomorrow."

It seemed counterintuitive to stop when Elyse had so many questions, when her body craved more answers, yet relief filled her at Sera's words. Perhaps a good night's sleep would help them attack this better in the morning.

Everyone else seemed to reach the same conclusion as they nodded their heads in unison. "I'll walk you out," Elyse said, surprising herself with her ability to remember her manners. Perhaps she was acting on instinct, her body taking over for her frazzled mind.

Sera and Killian gathered up their few things, and Sera wished Jaime a good night. Killian didn't say anything, instead stalking out of the library with furrowed brows. Elyse ached to hear his thoughts, to ask what he was thinking, but she couldn't bring herself to speak to him.

When they reached the front door, Sera hesitated on the threshold for a moment, then abruptly pulled Elyse in for a tight hug.

"Read the entire passage," she whispered in Elyse's ear. Her heart hammered through her chest so powerfully that Elyse could feel it. "Alone," she added, her voice nearly inaudible.

Sera pulled away, and Elyse tried to hold her wrist, to ask her what she meant, but Sera was too quick. Without a backward glance, she hurried out the door and down the walkway.

CHAPTER 19

— · —

ELYSE

E lyse was restless as she and Jaime sat in the dining room to share a late dinner. She barely touched her food before retiring to her bedroom. For nearly two hours, she paced the room, circling the canopy bed and wringing her hands together, still stunned by what they had discovered. Why had Sera insisted that Elyse review the passage on her own? Thousands of possible reasons plagued her mind, but none of them made any sense.

She wished Jaime would go to bed already.

Finally, she heard him pad down the hallway and close the door to his bedchamber. By the light of a single candle, Elyse tiptoed barefoot down to the library, ignoring the wicked shadows cast by the candle's flickering flame.

The book lay on the table, exactly where Sera had left it. With trembling hands, Elyse set the candlestick on the table and seated herself in the high-backed chair. Faint moonlight trickled in through the window, and Elyse had to strain her eyes to see the haunting words scrawled across the pages.

She let out a slow exhale and then began.

Demons and Corporeality, read the heading. It was written in capital letters, expertly drawn and flourished, harrowing and beautiful at the same time.

The first step was to make contact with the demon. The book listed specific instructions on how to summon the demon's spirit and communicate with it across dimensions. Bile rose in Elyse's throat as she read through the directions—directions she herself had followed.

Dig up the body of a deceased man and remove its skull. Place the skull into a cauldron of boiling water, adding witch's salt and a drop of your own blood. Repeat the following incantation three times...

Elyse didn't have to complete the passage to know what would happen. She had performed this very spell herself long ago, as a means to communicate with Lazarus. When the skull was removed from the water, it would be black and act as an apparatus to communicate with creatures from hell. It was a common enough spell—a party trick used by teenagers who wanted to dabble in the occult. Everyone she knew had tried summoning a demon at some point in their life, either out of desperation or curiosity. It shouldn't have bothered Elyse to see the spell written out, yet she couldn't help but shudder knowing the instructions that followed.

She read on, wary of what she might find.

Each of the following steps must be conducted precisely and in order, should you wish to extract a demon from hell and provide a vessel for them to roam the earth.

Elyse scanned the pages, her eyes flitting over the dozens of complex rituals that would eventually lead to a demon taking human form.

Burn the body of a deceased orphan... Poison a whore with anoraxium... Fornicate with a possessed woman...

One horrid act after another, all listing out the specific parameters needed for the spell to be deemed a success. Each was just as vile as the next, and they melded together in Elyse's mind until she came across one particular set of instructions.

Murder a sleeping monarch using a blood-letting spell.

Elyse froze, the air in her lungs vanishing. She read the sentence again, then a third time, as a sobering understanding settled over her.

She had murdered a sleeping monarch using a blood-letting spell.

She had murdered King Cyril in his bedchamber, conducting the most grotesque spell she'd ever encountered, forcing his blood to multiply and spill from every orifice until he drowned in it.

She had unknowingly, at Lazarus's demand, been helping him become corporeal.

Nausea overtook her, and she gripped the table until her knuckles were white. Devil's horns, she had always wondered how Lazarus chose the tasks she was to perform, and now she understood. He was using her to take over a body—to walk on this earth. Her chest rose and fell, heaving air in and out of her lungs. Her mind was unable to grasp anything—anything other than the fact that she was responsible for this. She was fucking responsible for Prestowne and so many other deaths, and—

"Elyse?"

Her head snapped to the doorway to see Jaime's faintly illuminated silhouette. She hadn't heard him leave his bedroom.

She knew she should reply, or somehow acknowledge his presence, and yet words, logic, courtesy, all of it evaded her. She could only see the destruction she had caused, could only hear the black skull's cruel laughter echoing in her mind.

Jaime stepped forward, concern marring his face. "What are you doing in here?"

Elyse swallowed and forced her voice to sound calm. "I was just reading," she answered, hoping she successfully hid the guilt that raged inside her.

"You should be asleep," Jaime said quietly.

He moved toward her, and with each step, Elyse compelled her nerves to settle. She couldn't think about what she'd just read—not until she was alone and able to completely unravel. As she drove the images of Prestowne and King Cyril from her mind, she tried to think of something calmer. She imagined the feel of lush grass between her toes, the soft scent of rain, the rush of power she felt when she used her magic.

Jaime stopped just before her, moonlight illuminating half his face. One blue eye sparkled as the other remained cast in darkness. "I went to check on you, but you weren't in bed."

Elyse felt an immediate sense of invasion, like a warm, unwelcomed breath on her neck. "You checked on me?" She knotted her brows, not bothering to hide her annoyance.

"Of course," Jaime replied simply, as if it weren't strange at all. "We learned something critical today. I wanted to make sure you were able to get some rest."

Elyse shook her head. She wanted him to go away, to leave her to read so she could figure out exactly how involved she was in this nightmare—and how to fix it. Yet the way he spoke to her, like she was a child breaking curfew, it unnerved her more than she could bear.

"I don't need you to check on me," she said firmly. "I'm an adult. I can take care of myself."

"Oh really?" Jaime challenged. "You haven't exactly made the best decisions lately." He spoke calmly, as if laying out a rational train of thought, which only infuriated Elyse more.

"Really," she told him, snapping the book shut, "I'm grateful for everything you've done for me, and for helping us now, but I do not need a nursemaid."

"I'm not being your nursemaid, Elyse," Jaime stated. "I'm simply looking out for your well-being."

Elyse ground her teeth. She wished he would stoop to her level, would say something horrible or raise his voice so that she could tear his head off. She had so much built-up anger, so much hatred for this world and nowhere to direct it—nowhere but at herself.

She closed her eyes and lay her hands flat on the table, trying to force her mind to still.

"You're clearly upset," Jaime said. "You'll feel better in the morning."

Elyse's nostrils flared as she glared at Jaime. "Don't tell me what to do."

"I didn't tell you to do anything," he pointed out—a truth, but only technically. "The book will still be there in the morning."

Her natural instinct was to dig her heels in harder, or perhaps even fling the book at him. He might be right, though. She was pissed off, ashamed, not thinking right. No good would come from her poring over the book all night and stealing tomorrow's energy. Perhaps she should take a sleeping potion and face this in the morning when she would have Sera there to help her.

Besides, Jaime's alliance was a bridge she couldn't afford to burn. She couldn't let him win though. Not completely, anyway.

She stared at him for a moment longer, not wanting to be the first to break eye contact. Finally, she rose from her chair and strode across the library, her shoulder knocking into his as she sauntered past him and into the hallway.

CHAPTER 20

— · —

KILLIAN

Killian was glad that Manny was joining them today. Maybe with Manny around, Jaime would have someone else to glare at for a change. As soon as they walked into the library, though, it was apparent that Killian was still the target of Jaime's irritation. The asshole shot him a scathing look as he stood in the corner, arms crossed, his sole purpose to murder Killian with his eyes. Killian merely ignored him and seated himself beside Manny at the table.

Sera sat on the other side of Manny, next to Elyse. The two were engaged in a silent conversation, communicating something with subtle expressions. Killian wondered if it had something to do with why Sera was being unusually squirrelly. She had avoided looking at him after they left the estate the day before, and had hurried inside her building after a hasty goodbye—not that Killian had minded. It was simply peculiar.

"So you found something yesterday?" Manny asked, breaking the silence.

"Where's the book?" Killian asked as he looked around. He had expected it to be on the table, but he realized that all the books they'd reviewed were now reshelved.

Slowly, Elyse lifted a book from her lap and set it on the table. "It's here," she said quietly. She kept one hand on the cover, as if protecting it.

"Sera said that whoever is responsible for Prestowne is trying to—" Manny paused for a moment and shook his head, as if trying to wrap his mind around it. "—trying to bring a demon to life?" He rubbed the back of his neck as he met each of their eyes, like he was waiting for one of them to confess the whole thing was a joke.

Elyse nodded but remained silent. She seemed so shaken, her face paler than usual. Killian glanced toward Jaime, hoping to gain some sort of insight into what was going on with Elyse. Jaime's face remained plastered in a scowl.

"So what does that mean for us?" Killian asked. He'd mulled over the information most of the night as he lay awake in bed. A week ago, he hadn't even known that demons existed, and now one was terrorizing his kingdom. His thoughts had darkened as he pondered the nightmares a demon would unleash, and how he, of all people, had managed to get involved in such a crucible.

"We should see what the next ritual is," Elyse said wearily. She stared down at the book, her eyes shadowed and heavy. "If we can learn what their next move is, maybe we can find them. Maybe we can stop them."

She opened the book with slow, deliberate movements, as if it took great effort to do so. As her eyes passed over the words, her jaw clenched.

"What is it?" Jaime asked from his position against the wall.

Killian's nostrils flared at Jaime's tone—at his nonchalant stance. He seemed to care more about lording his library over them than he did about actually finding the person responsible for everything.

Elyse looked up, terror in her onyx eyes, her mouth slightly ajar. "The next ritual is the final one," she explained. "The one that will give the demon a vessel."

"Shit," Manny murmured.

Shit was an understatement.

"Well how do we stop it?" Killian asked, trying to remain logical.

Elyse bowed her head and read aloud. "*The final ritual will require angel's blood, the eternal rose, and a willing vessel. On the summer solstice, the vessel must mix the angel's blood with his own, covering the eternal rose. Just as the last light of day disappears, the vessel will burn the rose. Then the demon will be freed from hell and inhabit the vessel, strengthened by the rose's power."*

Summer solstice? Killian did a quick calculation. The summer solstice was only seven days away.

"So we have a week," Sera uttered, voicing Killian's thoughts. She looked to Elyse, who gave a somber nod.

"Angel's blood?" Manny asked incredulously. "Angels are real?"

Jaime gave him a pitying look. "You have no problem accepting that demons are real, but angels are hard to believe?"

Manny didn't bother responding to Jaime's rhetorical question.

"What is the eternal rose?" Killian asked.

Elyse, Sera, and Jaime all exchanged looks with one another. "You really don't know?" Jaime scoffed.

Manny and Killian both shook their heads in reply.

Jaime finally left his place against the wall and joined them at the table, seating himself beside Elyse. "It's a very powerful, very valuable artifact," he explained, as if it were common knowledge. Though, to wielders of magic, Killian supposed it was common knowledge.

"I didn't think it actually existed," Sera uttered. She stared distantly at a bookshelf, her purple eyes glazed in trepidation.

Manny gave Sera a troubled look. "What does it do?"

"No one really knows," Jaime answered, a mixture of concern and awe in his voice. "There are so many legends, all of them conflicting. Some say it gives the wielder immortality, others say it amplifies a sorcerer's power tenfold." He shrugged and crossed his arms again as quiet dread fell over them.

Killian stared at the book as he let the words sink in. The legends may not agree on the specifics of the eternal rose, but if the book before them recited instructions on how to obliterate an entire town, he had no doubt the rose was capable of helping a demon infest a human's body. And if that body became immortal? He let out a defeated breath and leaned back in his chair.

Elyse still didn't speak. Her lips were drawn together in a tight, unsettled line. Killian studied her, wishing he could know what was on her mind.

"Elyse, you used to sell magical relics," he pointed out. "Did you ever come across any information on the rose?"

Elyse looked at him so intensely that for a moment, Killian thought he had said something to offend her. Her dark eyes bore into him with a force that he couldn't read, and he struggled not to shift in his chair.

Then he realized it was the first time he'd spoken to her directly since forming the blood pact. Her expression was so convoluted, a mixture of shame and gratitude and apprehension, that he didn't know how to react.

"No," Elyse said after a beat, shaking her head. "I never bothered caring about it." She turned toward Jaime expectantly. "This seems like something in your domain."

Perhaps Killian was imagining the smug look on Jaime's face, or perhaps it was actually there. "I know someone who claims to have seen it," he said, leaning back in his chair. "I can leave today and be back in a few days, but..." As he trailed off, he leveled his gaze on Killian. "While I'm gone, no one is to visit the estate," he said firmly, then turned his attention to Elyse. "And you are to stay inside."

Elyse tightened her jaw ever so slightly before she nodded. "Of course," she said—so meekly that Killian furrowed his brows. What had happened to the strong witch who didn't take orders from anyone?

Killian sat up in his chair. "A few days is too long. Summer solstice is in one week—we can't afford that much time."

Jaime blatantly rolled his eyes. "Actually, you can't afford for me to sit around here and read books," he answered with a sneer.

Killian hated how successfully Jaime's condescending gaze taunted him. He had been the youngest lieutenant in the Royal Guard, and an expert investigator. He had faced down ruthless criminals. He had clashed swords with merciless warriors. And now he was forced to sit in a library and read.

"I agree with Killian," Sera said, strength returning to her voice. "Do you think you can get answers by tomorrow?"

Jaime's eyes flashed toward Sera, then Elyse, as his charming smile slid across his features. "I'll do everything I can," he said in a disgustingly saccharine voice.

Killian tried not to gag.

"Fine," he said, biting his tongue to keep from saying anything else. He didn't give two shits whose house they were in. If Jaime thought he was going to come in and take over their investigation, he was sorely mistaken. Killian didn't entirely trust him, but until Jaime gave him a solid reason to retaliate, he would keep his snide comments to himself.

Begrudgingly, he faced Jaime. "Do you have any literature on the rose?"

Jaime sighed and looked at the rows and rows of shelves that surrounded them. "There's probably some books in here that might give us some insight on its power," he mused. "You should take as many books as you can and research it while I'm gone."

Killian groaned internally. He wanted to point out that it would just be easier for them to come back to the estate and read in the library, but he didn't bother. He hated being here anyway.

It took them an hour to go through the books and select any that seemed relevant—books on demons, rituals, magical artifacts, corporeality, anything that might give them some sort of edge. Elyse kept the biggest tomes for herself while Killian, Sera, and Manny each took four or five books to review at home. They agreed that they would all meet back at the estate the next afternoon, when Jaime expected to return.

Killian stumbled awkwardly out of the library with an armful of books. Manny followed behind him as Sera said goodbye to Elyse, who already had her nose buried in one of the books. To Killian's surprise, Jaime hurried past them in the hallway, eagerly racing toward the front door.

"Let me walk you out," he said. He pulled the door open while they waited patiently—or as patiently as they could with sixty pounds of books in their arms—for Sera to catch up.

"Be safe," Sera called to Jaime as she sidled out the door.

"Thank you," Jaime said, then nodded to Manny as he crossed the threshold.

Killian was just about to step out when Jaime placed a hand on his shoulder.

"Killian, a word?" he smiled at him, though there was something icy in his eyes.

Manny took a step toward them, but Killian brushed his friend off. "Go ahead. I'll just be a moment."

Jaime partially shut the door, shielding Manny and Sera from view, and the smile abruptly dropped from his face.

"I don't like you," Jaime snarled in a low voice so Elyse wouldn't hear down the hallway.

Killian was so caught off guard, he couldn't help but let out a breathy laugh. "Well, we're on the same page then," he replied coolly.

Jaime's eyes narrowed on him as his lips curled into a grimace. "If you even think about hurting Elyse, I will end you so fucking fast."

Killian cocked his head and shifted the weight of the books in his arms. "Did Elyse not tell you about the blood pact?" he asked. Was he unaware that they were magically prohibited from causing one another harm?

"I know all about the blood pact," Jaime snapped back.

He took a step closer to Killian, but Killian didn't back down. He was a few inches taller than Jaime, and he stood a little straighter just to emphasize it.

Jaime continued anyway. "If you think you're really going to throw Elyse in prison when this is all over, think again. I'm going to find a way to get her out of this *arrangement.*"

Killian's mild amusement had quickly faded and been replaced by aggravation. He put on his most intimidating expression, the one he had honed through hundreds of interrogations, and leaned closer to Jaime until their faces were mere inches from one another.

"Try me," he growled. "She made her decision. She'd rather turn herself in and face what she's done than spend anymore time locked up here as your prisoner."

Jaime's eye twitched, and Killian knew he had struck a nerve. He returned Jaime's glare for a moment longer before turning and shoving his way out the door.

Manny gawked at Killian as he strode past him down the walkway. "Everything all right?"

"Everything's fine," Killian said, not bothering to slow down.

CHAPTER 21

— ∗ —

ELYSE

Time seemed to drag on as Elyse waited for Jaime's return. The sun crawled across the sky, beating in through the window, its angles shifting in languid motions. Elyse pored over the books she had designated for herself, finishing them all by the afternoon. She'd scoured the shelves for anything else that might help them, but they'd already done a good job of picking out anything relevant. Maybe Manny was having better luck going through the royal library at the palace.

As the sun ducked behind the trees, Elyse was surprised to hear a knock at the front door. She knew from the cadence of the knock that her visitor was friendly, but she still opened the door nervously.

Sera stood on the porch, looking as extravagant as ever in a lilac sundress that complemented her purple eyes. "Screw Jaime," she said with a smile. "I thought you might want to talk privately."

Elyse had never been more grateful for her friend. She was about to invite Sera in when the seer gestured with her chin.

"Let's take a walk?"

Grinning, Elyse darted out the door, not bothering to put on any shoes. She wanted to feel the grass beneath her bare feet, just as she had done so many times in the forest around her cottage. She wanted to feel *normal*, even if it was only for an evening.

They made their way to the back of the estate and down the hill toward the lake. Wind rippled across the water, more vigorously than usual. A storm was brewing, but for now the skies were clear.

"So are my suspicions correct?" Sera asked as the women trailed arm-in-arm beside the lake. "Was King Cyril's death one of the rituals needed to bring the demon to life?"

Elyse nodded, unable to confirm it aloud. Hearing Sera say the words was troubling enough. How could she have been stupid enough to let Lazarus manipulate her? She had thought of nothing else since. She should have fought harder to defy his orders—should have outright refused, whatever the consequences.

"You know you're not to blame, right?" Sera stated, as if the facts were plain. "You didn't know what Lazarus was planning. You tried to disobey him before. The punishment would've been worse than the action itself."

Elyse shook her head. "I can't help but think that if I hadn't killed King Cyril, then maybe all those people in Prestowne might still be alive."

That was the worst part of it. The book made it clear that the rituals had to be conducted in order. If she had found some way to stall or even prevent King Cyril's death, then the massacre at Prestowne never would have happened.

Sera pulled Elyse to an abrupt stop. "You can't think like that. You are *bound* to him, Elyse. There's no escaping his commands."

Elyse couldn't bring herself to meet her friend's eyes. It was true, she was bound to Lazarus—perhaps even in ways she didn't want to consider. Elyse never had a choice in the matter, having been born into his servitude. But her mother... Her mother had sold her own soul to Lazarus.

Maybe that was the true source of all Elyse's anguish. Deep down, Elyse knew that everything started with her mother. All of the deaths, all of the pain, every single full moon ritual was because of her and her desperation. If her mother had never made that deal, then Killian would still be in the Royal Guard, and she wouldn't have shattered his world.

But part of her knew that Sera was right. There was no point in thinking about what might have been. Besides, Lazarus had other servants to do his bidding. Even if she hadn't killed King Cyril, someone else would have, and Prestowne would have inevitably followed.

Elyse slowly started walking again, Sera by her side. They stayed quiet as Elyse watched the water lap up against the rocky shoreline, letting its rhythm soothe her.

"You should tell them, you know," Sera murmured. "Killian and Manny—you should tell them that you're personally connected to this."

Elyse looked at Sera like she was mad. "I can't—They'd never understand."

Sera's reply was much calmer. "I assure you Manny will understand. And I think Killian is more sympathetic than you give him credit for."

Elyse bit her lip as she considered. Killian had been aloof during their time researching—not that being standoffish was a far reach from his normal self. Still, he'd been amicable enough, not trying to antagonize her. The last time she'd seen him, he'd even addressed her directly—a simple action that had made butterflies stir in her stomach. But what would he think if he knew it wasn't just any demon responsible for Prestowne, but *her* demon. What if he knew that Elyse lay awake at night worrying that Lazarus was her father, and that she was part demon? There was no way in hell's seven circles that Killian would understand any of that.

"I'll think about it," she told Sera quietly, eager to be done with the conversation.

They finished the rest of the walk in silence as the wind picked up, stirring the waters of the lake. By the time Sera said goodbye and disappeared from the lawn in a puff of blue smoke, the first rain drops had started to fall.

Elyse was once again alone.

The house seemed darker than usual as rain pelted against the windows, or perhaps it was just Elyse's shadowy mood. She lit a taper and carried it down the hall, passing by the library. She couldn't bring herself to look at any more books. Her tired eyes begged her to crawl into bed, but sleep felt like a comfort she didn't deserve.

Restless, her feet carried her into the sitting room, where she stored all the gifts Jaime brought her. Her fingers traced the keys of the piano, but the smooth ivory did not call to her. Neither did the paints, their rich colors too bright and luxurious. She chose the sketch pad with its striking leather cover, splaying it open and savoring the subtle feel of the spine bending in her hands. Her eyes searched for a tool, holding her breath until she found just the right one: a charcoal pencil, its tip blunt and black.

With a fervor she hadn't felt in a long time, Elyse sat on the divan, curled up beneath a blanket, and drew.

CHAPTER 22

— · —

KILLIAN

If Killian had known it was going to rain, he would have run his errand earlier. The sun had shone bright all day in the cloudless sky, yet as soon as he stepped out the door, the wind picked up. A drizzle started not ten minutes later.

Maybe this is a sign, he told himself. He had been putting off sending this correspondence for a week now, and the sudden downpour didn't bode well. He hurried down one street after another, trying to duck beneath awnings when he could, and taking care to make sure the letter in his pocket stayed dry.

The letter was addressed to Siamus and consisted of three sentences: *Please be advised that I am no longer in need of your services. You are free from all obligations effective immediately. I ask that you confirm your understanding at your earliest convenience.*

Of course, it would have been much easier if he could simply drop off the letter at the postal office and have it delivered, but that was not how the Bastards worked. Instead, he was forced to travel halfway across the city, give the letter to a bartender at a seedy tavern, and trust that this stranger would deliver it to the appropriate person.

Even though he no longer needed help locating Elyse, it somehow felt wrong calling off the Bastards. Her betrayal clawed at him, reminding him that he couldn't trust her, blood oath or not. She had deceived him once—who was to say she wouldn't do it again? Terminating his agreement with the Bastards seemed almost reckless, like he was putting more faith in Elyse than she deserved.

Thunder rumbled as pedestrians escaped the storm. Killian picked up his pace, taking care to avoid the puddles accruing in the street. Mud caked his boots, but he hardly noticed. He was too engrossed in a single thought: the words he'd spat at Jaime earlier.

"She'd rather turn herself in and face what she's done than spend anymore time locked up here as your prisoner."

At the time he'd merely said it out of anger, a way to draw blood verbally. He hadn't given much thought to the insult's fidelity before delivering it, but now he wondered. Was there a truth to his words?

Elyse appeared to be a wholly different person than the one he'd known before. Killian had contributed it to deceit, to being rattled by Prestowne, to never really having known her in the first place. There were a hundred possible explanations for her sudden meekness, but there was one that he had refused to consider: that she actually felt regret.

Maybe it was true. Maybe she did wish to atone. Maybe she felt out of control. As lavish as the country estate was, it would be like a prison to Elyse. She'd lost her home, her business, her freedom. Perhaps signing the blood pact was a way to take control of her life again, even if it meant giving it up.

Or perhaps it's all part of some elaborate scheme, he thought as lightning crackled above.

Time would tell. For now, he would send the letter to Siamus, and hope that it was the right decision.

CHAPTER 23

— · —

KILLIAN

The next day, Killian knocked at the mahogany door a third time, the special rhythm reverberating against the wood. Still, no one answered, and he, Manny, and Sera exchanged concerned looks. There was no reason to panic—at least not yet. Elyse had probably overslept. That didn't stop Killian's mind from imagining one disastrous scenario after another.

"Should we just go in?" Manny asked, sounding unsure.

"No," Killian blurted out. There was a chance that Jaime and Elyse weren't answering because they were otherwise occupied, and that was the last thing he wanted to walk in on. "Besides, it's probably locked—"

Before the entire sentence was out of his mouth, Sera reached out and grasped the handle. The door opened easily, admitting them into the foyer.

"Elyse?" Sera called out as she entered. Her sweet voice echoed eerily down the hall. "I'll check her bedroom and see if she's still sleeping."

"I'll check the library," Manny said.

They both disappeared down the hall, leaving Killian alone.

"I guess I'll check the rest of the house," he mumbled to himself. He hadn't ventured any farther than the library before, but he let his feet lead him and prayed he wouldn't find something terrible.

"Elyse?" he called tentatively. He recalled that she wasn't a morning person, and though she was prohibited from hurting him, he still didn't feel like getting an earful for rousing her too aggressively.

He rounded a corner and found himself in the kitchen. His first thought was that his mother would love this kitchen, with its massive butcher block counter and enormous hearth. His second thought was that there were no signs that anyone had been there recently—no kettle hanging over the fire, no dishes laid out to dry.

An archway led to another room, so Killian headed there, finding himself in a sitting room with several plush chairs and divans spread about. In the corner, Elyse lay snuggled atop one of the divans. She was fast asleep, her mouth hanging open.

Relief flooded Killian. Elyse was okay—and not entangled with Jaime. He was about to call her name to wake her when he spotted several papers littering the floor.

Stepping closer to get a better view, Killian saw that they were drawings. Faces sketched in deep charcoal stared back at him—faces he immediately recognized. The first one he noticed was Sera, her soft features unmistakable. Beside that was Manny, sporting his classic look with his hair tied back in a knot. And there, laying just beside his feet, was Killian's own face.

There were others, too—King Cyril, Queen Andrielle, Royce, Tanner Wills, and a young girl with curly hair that Killian didn't recognize. He furrowed his brows as he studied each one. The drawings were amateurish, the lines crude and lacking confidence, yet there was an obvious pain behind each stroke.

Elyse must have sensed his presence because she stirred, blinking awake. She looked perplexed for a moment, then seemed to realize where she was.

"Elyse," Killian breathed, still entranced by the drawings. He'd never known her to have an artistic side, and he certainly hadn't expected her to express herself on paper. "What are these?"

Her face paled, and for a moment Killian thought she might be ill. Then he realized she was physically incapable of lying to him, no matter how inconsequential that lie might be.

"They're... the people I hurt," she croaked.

Killian looked at the drawings again, studying each face. His own memories assaulted him as he recalled Queen Andrielle's grief over losing her husband, and Tanner Will's severed head lying in a box on his desk. Elyse might not have hurt them directly, but all the suffering and violence could be traced back to her.

When he glanced up at Elyse, he was surprised to see her staring intently at him, a cacophony of emotions in her expression.

"Why?" he asked. Perhaps it was cruel for him to pester her when she was forced to tell the truth, but he couldn't seem to grasp what lay before him.

Anguish, pure and visceral, filled her eyes. "Because they haunt me," she whispered.

Killian's breath froze in his lungs. Her words were so raw that they shocked him, pinning him in place. This was not a manipulation. This was unadulterated pain, private sorrows scrawled on paper, meant for her eyes only.

She was miserable, plagued by her past just as much as Killian was. All this time, he'd thought her incapable of anything more than selfishness and cruelty, but the evidence at his feet contradicted that. Elyse lamented her actions, at least on some level.

Good, he thought. She ought to feel remorse. The drawings represented only a fraction of the lives she'd upended. And if she wished to atone by turning herself in, by avenging those lost at Prestowne, then it was the least she could do.

Even so, a trickle of sympathy slipped through his ribs, touching his heart.

Elyse looked away, her eyes trailing down to her lap. Killian followed her gaze to the sketchbook that lay open on the blanket. There was another face there, but this one was different. The eyes were black pits, as if Elyse had scribbled furiously. The lines weren't as distinguished, drawn and redrawn again.

"Who is that?" Killian wondered aloud.

Elyse didn't look up. "That's my mother."

Killian looked at the drawing again, stunned by the answer. Had she wronged her mother as well? Or was there something deeper at play? He wasn't sure how to respond, so he just stared until a voice called over his shoulder.

"Oh, there you are."

Sera sounded relieved, at least until she sensed the tension in the room. "Is everything all right?" she asked warily.

"Yes," Killian answered quickly. He cleared his throat and added, "Elyse was asleep."

Elyse looked up at where Sera stood in the archway. "Sorry," she murmured, smiling weakly.

"Don't worry about it," Sera said lightly. "Jaime isn't here yet, so you have time to get ready." If she noticed the drawings on the floor, she made no mention of them.

Killian lingered for a moment. For reasons he couldn't explain, he felt like he should say something to Elyse, some sort of consolation or understanding, but his mind was utterly void of words. He met her eyes once more before hurrying from the room.

He found Manny in the library, seated at the large table. "Did you find her?" Manny asked.

Killian could only nod. He was fixated on the drawings, the faces parading through his mind. *Because they haunt me*, Elyse had said.

How many times had he imagined her laughing at his misfortune, reveling in the chaos she had left in her wake? How many times had he pictured the moment when she would be sentenced to death, and the misery on her face. He never would have dreamed that she was already living in that misery.

Sera joined them a moment later, followed shortly after by Elyse. Her hair was brushed and she had put her stoic facade back in place, concealing the vulnerability he'd just witnessed.

The rest of the group speculated as to where Jaime might be while Killian remained entrenched in his own thoughts. Occasionally he glanced at Elyse, but she seemed to be avoiding his gaze.

Finally, Jaime arrived. He swooped casually into the room, one hand brushing through his blond hair.

"Oh good, you're all here," he said, as if they hadn't been sitting around waiting for him.

Killian snapped out of his trance and glared up at Jaime. "I don't know how you were raised," he began sternly, "but where I'm from, we apologize for keeping people waiting."

For once, Jaime appeared rattled. From the corner of his eye, Killian saw Manny suppressing a grin. Elyse looked embarrassed, though it was unclear whether she was embarrassed for Jaime's tardiness or Killian's blunt statement. Meanwhile, Sera seemed flat-out amused.

"I'm... sorry?" Jaime said, though it was one of those apologies that sounded more like a question than a statement. "I'd expect you'd be a little kinder to me after I spent the whole night busting my ass to get answers," he continued as he seated himself at the foot of the table.

"Did you find anything?" Elyse asked eagerly.

"Yes," Jaime answered with a sigh. "There is a private auction tomorrow, and one of the items is rumored to be the eternal rose."

Everyone exchanged excited looks with one another. Tomorrow? It seemed too good to be true, though Killian hoped it was just a torrent of much-needed luck.

"Do you think it's the real thing?" Elyse asked.

Jaime shrugged slowly. "I think so. My sources are usually correct."

"Well, it sounds like a good enough lead," Manny cut in. "So why do you sound so disappointed?"

Jaime leaned forward, resting his elbows on the table. Defeat washed over his features. "Because the auction is in De Vesalis."

Killian grit his teeth. De Vesalis, a coastal city along the far southern border of Rhodan, was known for its debauchery. "The City of Vice," it was called, as gambling, prostitution, and heavy drinking were its main attractions. And, of course, it was a two-day journey.

"We could ride all day and night and still not make it," Sera said, shaking her head. "Unless—"

"Has anyone been there before?" Killian finished her thought.

Everyone shook their heads, their faces despondent. Transportation potions would do them no good if none of them had traveled there before.

"What about..." Killian began, standing and striding toward the enormous map of Rhodan that hung on the wall. He pointed to Sevhella, in the center of Rhodan, then trailed his finger southwest toward the Staerion Sea. "Privya's clinic is more than halfway to De Vesalis," he mused, gesturing his hand between the general area of Privya's clinic and the coast.

Elyse stood as well and neared the map, her dark eyes alight with a plan. "We could magick there, and then it would just be a day's travel to De Vesalis."

She flashed a smile at Killian, her pink lips signaling her pride for him. His stomach fluttered at the warm sentiment, a reminder of what had been, and he smiled back before catching himself.

He turned abruptly toward the group. "We can use today to prepare and be there by tonight, ready to ride out in the morning."

"Wait," Jaime started, his brows knitted. "We don't all need to go. Elyse and I will—"

"No," Killian cut him off firmly. "Absolutely not."

Jaime's face twisted into a snarl, but before he could speak, Sera chimed in.

"I agree with Killian. We don't know what we could be getting into. Whoever is trying to resurrect the demon could very well be at the auction. We should at least all be in the same city."

Manny nodded. "So we'll go to the auction, buy the eternal rose, and then—"

"Oh, n-n-n-no," Jaime said with a cynical laugh. "The starting bid on the rose is expected to be ten million gold pieces, so unless any of you are secretly extremely wealthy…" He trailed off, looking around the room at each of them.

Ten million gold? Even with Elyse's secret horde of coin, they weren't even close to having that amount.

Hopelessness washed over the room. They were so close, the rose within their grasp, and yet still unattainable.

"We'll steal it," Elyse stated, quiet yet bold. She looked toward Manny expectantly.

Manny stared back at her, his expression incredulous. "You want to steal a magical artifact valued at over ten million gold pieces?"

"I don't really see any other choice," Elyse replied, casually raising her shoulders in a shrug.

Killian hated that he agreed with her, but she was right. Their hands were tied, and stealing the rose was their best option of keeping it safe from sinister intentions.

Manny sighed, but his lips quirked into a smile. "I suppose you want me to be the one to steal it?" he asked, a bit of pride simmering beneath his petulant tone.

"Of course," Sera answered, her grin mirroring Manny's. "But you don't know anything about magical artifacts. Elyse should go with you to the auction."

Elyse looked just as surprised to hear this suggestion as Killian felt. Her shock turned contemplative as she bit her lip. "It will probably be warded as well. You'll need help to steal it, and Sera's right. If you're going to an auction for high-value magical objects, you'll be expected to know a thing or two about them."

The thought of sending his best friend alone on a mission with *her* made Killian's insides twist. Manny was capable of taking care of himself, but Elyse was ruthless, and he still didn't entirely trust her. Still, Elyse was his best choice for a partner in this crime, and he took consolation in remembering that she was magically incapable of harming him or anyone else in the Guard.

"Wait," Jaime blurted out, standing from his chair. "I should be the one going. It's because of *my* connections that we know about this auction at all."

"And we're grateful for that," Sera replied diplomatically. "But..."

"It's not necessary," Killian stated. "Elyse and Manny will go together, pose as buyers for something else, and steal the rose." Before Jaime could say anything else, Killian turned to face Elyse. "I assume you can change your appearances?"

Elyse nodded. "No problem."

"And you're confident you can break down whatever wards might be protecting the rose?" he pressed.

She laughed, short and haughty, a bit of that arrogant witch he had known shining through. "I've never encountered a ward I couldn't defeat."

A smile began to pull at his lips, but this time, he managed to suppress it. "It's decided then," he said. He shot a triumphant glance toward Jaime before looking back at Elyse. "You'll need to look the part, though, which means fine clothing for the auction. And we'll need a replica, something to swap with the real rose."

Elyse looked more like herself than Killian had seen over the last week as a wicked grin split her face. "Consider it done."

CHAPTER 24

— · —

ELYSE

Despite a day full of frantic preparations for the journey to Privya's, everyone seemed to be brimming with energy. Elyse had barely had a moment to think between creating a replica of the rose, brewing a potion for changing their appearances, popping down to Privya's clinic to let her know about their stay, and trying on several exquisite gowns that Sera had procured for her. All the while, she and Manny had been refining their backstory as a married couple, Mr. and Mrs. Nottingfeld. Finally, by the time the sun was setting, they were ready to leave.

Elyse, Sera, Manny, Killian, and Jaime all stood together on the lawn, their bags slung across their backs. "Hold hands," Elyse instructed as she slid her own hand into Jaime's. Jaime clasped her hand back, then offered his free hand to Sera. She took it and smiled as she grasped on to Manny, who looked to Killian with hesitation.

"Does it hurt?" Manny asked, wincing a bit. He had never traveled by transportation potion before.

"Like hell," Killian replied with a devilish grin. He took Manny's free hand and nodded to Elyse.

They were ready.

Elyse threw down the vial of blue liquid and closed her eyes, picturing the clinic clearly in her mind. She felt Jaime's grip tighten, and then everything disappeared as they were cast into the void. They fell and flew through nothingness for a split second until their feet crashed onto gravel.

Before Elyse could open her eyes, something came barreling into her. She stumbled back a few steps as her eyes flew open to find a mess of auburn hair tickling her face.

"Elyse!" Corin squealed as she hugged Elyse tighter.

"Hi, Corin," Elyse managed to wheeze through compressed lungs.

As always, Corin's presence helped subdue Elyse's anxieties. There was something about her bold hopefulness that made it impossible to be anything but happy around her. That rosy personality had led to a fast friendship when Elyse stayed at Privya's clinic to heal her widow's decay. It was a bond that continued as Elyse returned to the clinic several times since, working to train Corin and others in self-defense.

Corin finally let go of her and stepped back, her freckled face bright with excitement. "It's so good to see you!" she cried. Then her eyes darted to Killian. "And you too!" She beamed as she wrapped Killian in a hug.

"Always a pleasure to see you, Corin," Killian said warmly. His golden eyes twinkled as he gave Corin a sincere smile.

"What are you doing here?" Elyse asked, still a bit rattled. "I thought you were off looking for more springs?"

Just before Elyse had been forced to flee, Corin left on an expedition. She was supposed to be searching for more healing springs, like the one tucked in the cave behind Privya's clinic. The hope was to find more so that they could offer healing services to people all across the kingdom.

"We found one!" Corin declared. "We just got back a few days ago."

"We?" Elyse wondered aloud. She thought Corin had been traveling alone.

Corin flashed a grin over her shoulder, and Elyse followed her gaze. Standing before the large wooden building was a thin brunette woman. She smiled at them with a wide grin, showing off nearly every tooth Elyse had regrown—every tooth she lost during her wretched servitude as a courtesan.

"Nina," Elyse breathed. Nina was no longer the timid and fragile girl she'd been when she first came to Privya's. No, she was a healthy, beautiful young lady, and it left Elyse speechless.

"Hi, Elyse," Nina said sweetly. Then, to Elyse's surprise, she stepped forward and wrapped one arm around Corin's waist. Corin leaned into Nina's touch, resting her head on Nina's shoulder.

Well, that was unexpected. Unexpected—but delightful. Elyse's heart sang as she took in the way the two seemed so comfortable together, so at peace. It was a small comfort to know that even if she and Killian hadn't worked out, at least they had inspired love in someone else.

"Everyone, this is Corin and Nina. They help Privya at the clinic," she said to the group. Then she pointed one at a time down the line. "This is Sera, Manny, and Jaime."

Sera curtsied and Jaime waved, but Manny barely managed a nod. His face had a green hue to it, and he was holding on to Sera to steady himself. Apparently traveling by potion didn't agree with him.

Corin invited them inside the clinic, and one by one they proceeded into the large front room that served as a dining and sitting area. The cozy armchairs and cheery walls instilled a sense of comfort in Elyse, quelling some of the homesickness she'd felt these past few months.

"Go ahead into the kitchen and help yourself to tea and leftovers," Corin offered, gesturing to a door on the back wall.

The others made their way over, following Corin's instructions, but as Elyse stepped toward the back of the room, Corin gently grabbed her wrist.

"Privya wants to speak with you." She nodded her head toward the small room that served as Privya's examination room.

Elyse thanked Corin and crossed the main room, wondering what Privya would want to discuss. Warily, she opened the door to find Privya sitting at her desk, reviewing some notes.

"Come in," the healer called without looking up.

Elyse stepped inside and shut the door behind her, looking around the room as she waited for Privya to finish up. It was just as she remembered, endless books and vials lining the shelves along the walls, and a table in the center of the room for conducting examinations. There were no trinkets, no paintings, only items that served to conduct healing. To some, it might have seemed cold, but Elyse knew it was a reflection of Privya's passion for medicine, and that gave the room its own unique pleasance.

"Have a seat," Privya ordered in that steady voice of hers. She spun around on her stool to face Elyse, her expression unreadable. Her face was remarkably tan now that summer was fully upon them, and her black hair had more gray and white strands than it had only a few months ago.

Privya was one of the few people in the world that Elyse would never question. She sat on the edge of the table without a word, waiting for the healer's lead.

"How are you?" Privya asked. She gave Elyse a penetrating gaze, the sort of dignified look that only she could pull off.

"I'm good," Elyse said with a shrug. Instinctively, she touched her hand to her arm where the rash of widow's decay used to be. "The disease hasn't returned," she said.

Privya shook her head. "That's not what I mean."

Elyse lifted her chin, refusing to let her guilty conscience weigh it down. Privya knew she was an enemy of the kingdom. She knew she had been hiding for months. It must've taken its toll on Elyse's health. Of course the healer wouldn't turn a blind eye.

"Your aura is…" She gestured vaguely at Elyse's body. "…unwell. You are not taking care of yourself."

Elyse could feel her cheeks heating. She despised talking about herself—especially her problems. And as much as she cherished Privya, she still disliked the subtle condescension. "If you already knew I wasn't well, then why did you ask?" she deflected.

126

A ghost of a smile graced Privya's lips. "Because it is easier to ask 'How are you?' than to tell you flat out that you're depressed and on a path of self-destruction."

Elyse shifted on the table, unsure how to respond. Privya sighed and touched her fingers to the bridge of her nose. She wasn't wrong. To say Elyse was depressed was putting it mildly. And a path of self-destruction? She was already there, knocking on self-destruction's door.

When Privya looked up, there was a clarity in her eyes that pulled at Elyse.

"My father was a healer," she began. "He taught me how to read and care for others—not just their bodies, but their souls as well. There was one lesson that he made clear to me at a very young age." Privya raised her brows slightly, emphasizing her next words. "You cannot win every battle, but that does not mean you should ever give up on yourself."

A knot formed in Elyse's stomach. Her first instinct was to snap back at Privya, to explain that she hadn't given up on herself. But she forced herself to remain silent and consider. Wasn't promising to turn herself in the very definition of giving up on herself?

"I'm just trying to do what's right," she said finally, sounding meeker than she wanted to. She was doing whatever she could to ensure she left this world a better place. Wasn't that worth something?

Privya nodded. "Sometimes we convince ourselves that being a martyr is what's best, when in reality, it's simply easier than dealing with our problems."

Elyse swallowed. Was that what she was doing? Was she giving in to a death wish that had hung over her for years? She shook her head and looked at her hands, which were folded in her lap. Even if that was what she was doing—giving up on herself—it didn't matter. It was too late. She had signed away her life with the blood oath.

"Oftentimes," Privya continued, "there are answers to the questions we face. We just have to decide to look for them."

Elyse raised her head to look at the healer. It was not the first time she had felt that Privya could read her thoughts, and she wondered if somehow Privya was aware of the blood pact—and if she knew how to sever it. "Do you know something that could help me?" she asked.

Privya's face remained stoic. "I am merely passing along philosophical advice."

Elyse felt her heart sink, though she hadn't even realized it had been lifted with hope. Of course that's all it was—advice. No one knew how to sever a blood oath. Elyse's fate was sealed.

"Come on," Privya beckoned, extending a hand to Elyse. "I'd like to meet your friends."

Laughter greeted them as they meandered into the kitchen. It was a large room, but with so many people, and so many excited conversations, the space felt crowded. Everyone bumped elbows as they helped themselves to a late supper, and Elyse navigated through the chaos to introduce Privya to each of her friends.

After heartily welcoming Manny, Sera, and Jaime into her home, Privya made her way to Killian. Elyse slipped into the background, leaving Privya and Killian to catch up privately. Still, she couldn't help but glance at them several times, despising just how handsome Killian was when he let himself smile.

When everyone's plates were filled, they paraded back into the dining room. The tables were small, but the group divided seamlessly. Corin and Jaime, it seemed, had been raised in the same part of Sevhella. They chatted together amicably while Privya graciously let Sera ask endless questions about healing. That left Manny and Killian to sit with Nina, who described her adventures with Corin as they searched for healing springs.

Deciding not to intrude on the other conversations, Elyse sat beside Nina. She listened intently as Nina recounted their journey, peppering in details about how she and Corin had fallen in love along the way.

"I never thought I would see so much of the kingdom," she concluded, breathless from her own story. "And I never thought I'd find someone who makes me feel worthy of love." She glanced at Corin, who was now engaged in a conversation with Sera. When she turned back, she met Elyse's gaze with watery eyes. "Thank you," she said sincerely, and moved her gaze toward Killian. "Both of you. I still can't believe how incredibly generous the two of you are."

"You're very welcome, Nina," Killian said, but his voice sounded tight. He flashed a half-hearted smile before asking Nina to tell them more about the springs they found.

After supper, Privya came and stood by Elyse's chair. "Shall I open a bottle of wine?"

There was nothing Elyse wanted more than to sip on a delicious red wine while chatting with her friends, but sleep seemed the more logical choice. Before she could open her mouth to decline, Killian answered for her.

"That sounds lovely," he declared. He gave Elyse a pointed look, one that she couldn't decipher. Was he angry about something?

"Is that a good idea?" she asked in a low voice. "We need to be up at sunrise."

Killian scoffed, but it was Privya who protested loudest.

"I've read many books about quests and adventures, and in every single one, the heroes always drink the night before a momentous occasion." She smirked knowingly as she sauntered away.

Manny leaned toward Killian and asked in a hushed voice, "Do you think she reads the sexy books too? The ones where people... you know..." He waggled his eyebrows suggestively.

From across the room, Privya stopped and turned to face him. Manny's face turned vermillion as he realized she'd heard him, and Elyse felt her own cheeks heat, embarrassed on his behalf. Everyone held their breath, waiting for Privya's retort.

But her pursed lips slowly turned up at the corners until she was smiling broadly. "Yes, Manny. *Especially* the sexy books."

CHAPTER 25

— · —

KILLIAN

Hours later, after several glasses of dry wine that made easy conversation flow even freer, everyone made their way to their rooms. Killian heard the quiet rustling in the adjacent bedrooms turn to silence as their inhabitants fell asleep, but sleep was far from his grasp.

He wandered down the stairs, his feet carrying him through the main room and back to the kitchen. He didn't know what he was doing. He just knew he couldn't sleep, and the confines of his room were driving him mad.

As much as he missed seeing Privya and the others, it was too strange being at the clinic with Elyse. They treated her like a dignitary, as if she hadn't done anything wrong. It made him sick—and restless. His irritation had grown all evening as he watched Elyse laugh and smile. It almost felt as if she were mocking him, rubbing his nose in her felicity.

Privya's was supposed to be a safe place, where people could heal and grow. Elyse had stolen that from him. Now every inch of the clinic reminded him of happier times, when he and Elyse had worked together to build others up.

He sighed as he poured himself a cup of water and sat at the counter, but he didn't touch the glass. His mind was elsewhere. Tomorrow, Elyse and Manny were going to steal an expensive and rare magical artifact. Part of him still couldn't fathom what had become of his life. Another part of him enjoyed all the adventure and challenge. And a third part hated himself for finding joy in it all.

The soft patter of bare feet on hardwood signaled someone's approach, and the kitchen door swung open to admit Elyse. She looked like a ghost, her pale hair and simple white nightgown a whispering shimmer in the night. Killian glanced away quickly. Even in the faint moonlight, he could see just how thin the fabric of her chemise was. It did little to hide the gentle curves of her hips, nor the soft shape of her breasts.

"Oh," she said, pausing on the threshold as she noticed Killian. "I was just getting some water."

Killian didn't deign to acknowledge her explanation, instead keeping his attention trained straight ahead. He'd endured enough of her presence tonight to last him a lifetime.

She rounded the counter and poured herself a cup, then drank deeply. When she had finished, she topped off the cup again, and stood at the counter, holding it. He still wasn't looking at her, but he could feel her glancing his way every few seconds. Finally, she downed the rest of her water and set the cup on the ledge.

"You'll be up half the night to relieve yourself if you keep that up," Killian said dryly.

From the corner of his eye, he saw her shrug. "I don't sleep well anyway," she replied, sounding resigned.

"Oh?" he quipped. "I figured you slept just fine at night."

He didn't know why he said it. He hadn't intended to pick a fight with her, but the frustration of the evening had worn down his self-control.

Before he could open his mouth to apologize, she crossed the space between them and stabbed her finger toward his face. "*Do not* claim to know me," she spat.

Killian blinked, a smirk playing at his lips. He'd been wondering how long it would take her to snap. She'd been so apologetic, a shell of the fierce witch he knew her to be, and he had known it would only be a matter of time before she grew tired of playing nice. Perhaps being here had set her on edge as well.

He held her intense gaze, pouring his own simmering aggression into his stare. "And whose fault is that?" he drawled back at her.

Her brows drew together, her jaw dropping, as if in disbelief that Killian had the audacity to challenge her. Her expression morphed to one of pure hatred, and something stirred in Killian's core as he watched her rage unfold.

"Whose fault is that?" she repeated. "I've been begging you to hear me out, and you have refused to listen again and again." There was no pain in her voice, just sheer anger.

"Can you blame me?" Killian demanded. She acted as if she was entitled to the opportunity to explain herself, but what she had done was far beyond deserving of basic courtesies.

Elyse shook her head, staring at Killian with pure incredulity. She moved to push past him, but he grabbed her arm and spun her toward him.

"I asked you a question," he growled. Their faces were close, nearly touching. He could feel her ire radiating from her, burning the space between them. "I trusted you. I gave you everything. And you betrayed me."

His voice cracked, and he hated himself for it. In a perfect world, he never would have let his anger rise to the surface. He would have been cold but composed. But their world was far from perfect. It was gritty, full of pain and hatred. And beneath all of that—longing.

He stared down at her, waiting for her answer, trying to ignore the way she gazed up at him through her lashes.

"Don't," she choked out, half a demand, half a plea.

Killian ignored her petition. "You want so badly to explain yourself? Then tell me this." He stooped lower so she could see the fury in his eyes. "Tell me how you live with yourself."

She said nothing. The moonlight faded, casting them in shadow. There was nothing but the cicadas humming outside, Killian's pounding heart, and the tension between their bodies, taut and explosive.

"Tell me," he commanded into the dark.

The moonlight returned slowly, illuminating the tears brimming in Elyse's eyes.

"I tried to fight it," she whispered, her voice breaking. "I never meant for things to go that far." She took a step closer, lifting her chin higher. She was so close to him, the fabrics of their clothes clung together. "You have every right to hate me, Killian."

Hearing his name on her lips... It didn't have the effect he thought it would. It flustered him, but not with anger. He didn't want to tell her to keep his name out of her mouth—he wanted to hear her say it again and again.

All wit abandoned him, his bitterness melting. Beneath the words she'd spoken lay a tacit truth: she hated herself as well. The evidence was in the strain of her voice, in the slope of her shoulders. It was in the way her dark eyes glimmered with shame. And despite everything that had torn them apart, something deep inside of Killian yearned to take that pain away.

She stared up at him, mouth slightly parted. He knew he should step away, that he should run before he did something regrettable.

She pressed even closer—so close that he could feel her peaked nipples against his chest. "I have spent my entire life doing what I'm supposed to," she rasped. "But for the first time, when I was with you, I felt like I was doing what I wanted, like I was in control." She paused, her lip trembling, her entire body going tense as if she made her last stand. "I'll be damned if it wasn't the best and worst decision I've ever made."

A lifetime passed as they stared at one another, possibilities and tragedies coursing between them. It wasn't an apology, not even close. It wasn't even a real explanation. But those words, *the best and worst decision I've ever made*, rang truer than he cared to admit. Because even now, even after everything he had lost, he couldn't say with certainty that he would take any of it back.

Slowly, Killian lowered his chin, drawing strength as he vanquished the space that separated them. Just before their lips met, they paused. Their breath mingled, stirring with anticipation. One last consideration before they plummeted over that edge together.

As soon as he tasted her, all logic was swept away. He grasped at her waist with one hand, the other tangling itself in her hair. Elyse let out a gasp as she clutched at his shirt, a quiet plea for more.

If more was what she wanted, then that's what he would give her.

He spun her around and hoisted her up, setting her roughly on the countertop. Her legs spread eagerly, inviting him to fill the space between them. He obliged, grabbing her hips and pulling her against him, evoking another gasp.

They moved together so easily, their bodies remembering one another like lyrics of an old song. He had denied himself this for so long, which only made her touch that much more tantalizing. She reached down and stroked the length of him, and he groaned his approval. Elyse seemed to delight in that, pulling her lips away from his to stare into his eyes as she plunged her hand into his trousers and wrapped her fingers around him.

Fuck. He felt dizzy and clear headed at the same time. He kissed her again, slipping his tongue into her mouth, and she returned the motion.

Their hands groped each other, pulling at the fabric that separated their skin. He needed to feel her, all of her.

As if sensing his thoughts, Elyse purred in his ear, "I need you."

That was all she had to say. Killian tore her nightgown up over her hips, exposing her wet skin. He took a moment to stare at it, marveling at its beauty. Gods he had missed this.

He kissed her again, their mouths devouring one another, as he slid a hand over her entrance. She moaned against his lips, sending shivers coursing through his body.

"Say my name," he commanded, teasing her with slow movements.

"Killian," she gasped.

Again, that flurry in his stomach. He could listen to her pleading for him for the rest of his life, never leaving this room. He slid one finger inside her, provoking another moan, and he couldn't help but smirk. He savored the way she felt, the way her hips bucked in rhythm with his hand, begging for more.

When he couldn't take it anymore, he freed himself from his trousers. He was practically trembling with anticipation as he guided himself inside her. As he slowly pushed deeper, Elyse wrapped her hands around his neck. Their lips met again as their bodies pressed together, eliminating any space between them.

"Killian," Elyse breathed, her voice a seductive caress.

He buried himself deeper as he pulled her closer, his hands steady on her hips. Their passion was visceral, filling the room, making Killian's knees weak. He thrust faster as pure lust overtook him, empowered by every gasp Elyse emitted.

"Yes," she moaned, her nails driving into his shoulders.

He moved faster, deeper, giving her everything he had. Her breaths quickened, the pitch of her gasps growing higher and higher as she neared her climax. Killian buried his hand in her hair, tugging at the nape of her neck and forcing her to look up at him.

"I want to see the look in your eyes," he growled. "I want to see you at your most vulnerable, and know that I was your undoing."

Elyse let out a whimper, but she nodded her head obediently. Their eyes were locked as Killian continued to thrust. With his free hand, he gripped her thigh and lifted it off the counter, allowing himself to plunge another inch deeper.

Elyse cried so loudly, Killian thought she might wake the whole clinic. But it didn't stop him from going deeper. His own climax was within reach, but he needed her to go first. He needed to see the ecstasy in her eyes as she toppled over that edge.

Her breathing grew ragged, as if she was choking on her own pleasure.

"That's it," he coaxed, and her legs began to tremble.

He knew the moment she reached her pinnacle. Her eyes darkened beneath her furrowed brows, and her back arched, pressing him closer. She bit her lip, stifling the sounds of exhilaration that he yearned to hear. Still, the euphoria on her face was intoxicating.

Killian wasn't long for this world after that. With a few final thrusts, he met his end, his body shaking as he held her tight. He pressed his forehead to hers as he let exhaustion and satisfaction consume him.

Elyse still gripped his shirt, as if never wanting to let him go. They stayed together like that, their panting breaths mingling like an erotic symphony. Killian untangled himself from her hair, his hand moving down her back. He couldn't let go of her completely—not yet.

What had they just done? His mind screamed at him that this was a mistake. So why did it feel like such a damn good decision?

Even now, even after the culmination of their desire, he still didn't want it to end. Something about holding her, being so close to her... It felt...

"Ahem."

Someone else was in the room.

Killian slipped himself out of her and pulled his trousers up around his waist while Elyse immediately leapt off the counter, tugging her nightgown down around her. He whirled to find Manny standing in the doorway, a look of unadulterated disapproval on his face.

Without uttering a word, Elyse shoved past Manny, hurrying from the kitchen. He heard her frantic footsteps as she raced up the stairs.

Manny just crossed his arms as he stared into Killian, judgment pouring from him. Beneath his disdain, though, there was an ounce of pleading. "Don't do this," his expression seemed to beg, his heart breaking for his friend.

Killian stood there, his arousal completely vanished. He knew it had been stupid of him to do anything with Elyse, yet he couldn't say that he regretted it.

"Go to bed," Manny mumbled as he turned and exited the kitchen, leaving Killian alone to deal with the consequences of his actions.

CHAPTER 26

KILLIAN

The sun was just rising as Killian left his small bedroom in the clinic and ventured outside. He tucked his map into his pocket, the one that showed magic usage around the kingdom. He no longer needed it, of course, since he had already located Elyse. Still, it brought him some comfort to look it over, like a habit that soothed him. And after the night he'd had, he desperately needed soothing.

He still couldn't believe he'd been reckless enough to kiss Elyse—and more. She was like a poison that he couldn't rid from his body, no matter how hard he tried. Yet every time he closed his eyes, he pictured her gasping his name, her subtle curves showing beneath the thin chemise...

Get a hold of yourself.

He didn't have time for such distractions, especially not ones as vile as her.

It was early enough that the air was still tolerable, not yet smothered with heat. Killian strode out of the clinic, which was quiet with sleeping inhabitants, and made for the nearest tree. He only made it a few steps before he realized someone else had already beat him there.

"Nina," he called, catching her attention.

The young woman smiled up at him. She sat with her back against the base of the tree, enjoying the shade just as Killian had planned to do. A mug of tea was nestled in between her hands, and she looked exceptionally cozy.

"Come to take over my spot?" she jested.

Killian shook his head. "No, I'll find my own spot." He couldn't help but stare at Nina, hypnotized by her transformation. Her skin was bright, her smile bold, and she had just teased him—actually teased him. She had made so much progress in only a few months while he had been... Well, depressed and vengeful.

"Join me," she offered, patting the patch of grass beside her. "Mornings like this should be shared with good company."

Killian couldn't say no to that, so he sat beside her in the shade.

"Are you always up this early?" she asked once he had settled in.

Killian sighed. "I can't sleep late, even if I try. I may not be a soldier anymore, but the habit remains." He tried to say it jokingly, but the words still cut him. He didn't know if he would ever get over leaving the Guard. "What about you?" he asked, quickly changing the subject.

Nina sipped her tea as a flock of birds soared overhead. "In the beginning I didn't sleep much. I used to come out here and feel better. I'd never really tasted fresh air before."

She was of course referring to when she first arrived at Privya's clinic, after Killian and Elyse offered her a life free from selling her body. Elyse had used her magic to restore Nina's teeth, which were rotted to the gums. They then brought her to Privya, where she was welcome to live and strengthen herself emotionally, in exchange for helping out at the clinic. It seemed that Nina had done more than just the bare minimum, though, when it came to pitching in.

"So what's next, now that you found a healing spring?" Killian asked.

Nina nestled herself further among the roots of the tree. "I'm not sure," she mused aloud. "Thanks to Elyse, we're far ahead of schedule."

Killian turned to look at her, one eyebrow arched. "Thanks to Elyse?"

"You didn't know?" she asked, surprise in her voice. "Elyse gave Corin a special compass. She connected it to a vial of the spring water so that the compass would point in the direction of the nearest spring. It probably saved us months of searching."

Killian was at a loss for words. Elyse had done that? She'd never told him about it. It sounded like a truly unique and helpful innovation, and an incredibly thoughtful gesture.

His surprise must have shown on his face because Nina laughed. "Why do you seem shocked?"

"I just—She..." She was what? Despicable? Heartless? The most frustratingly wretched person he'd ever had the pleasure of meeting?

"Is it hard to think of her doing nice things because she's a wanted criminal?" Nina smiled, but her question was serious.

"Sort of... Yes," Killian answered. He had seen Elyse do plenty of kind things. She had freed Nina, had contributed countless funds to Privya's clinic, and even trained Nina and Corin in her free time so that they could properly defend themselves. Somehow, though, he had convinced himself that these good deeds had all been part of her act to make Killian believe she was righteous.

But helping Corin with finding the springs... That was something she had kept to herself.

Nina sat up straighter, demanding Killian's attention with her posture. "I was a prostitute," she began pragmatically. "Does that make me a whore?"

"No!" Killian protested immediately. "Of course not."

"Why not?"

Killian considered this for a moment, taking in Nina's countenance. Something about her soft features and kind eyes projected such virtue. Even knowing everything she had been through, she still held an air of naivete—unlike Elyse, who seemed jaded and ruthless.

"Well," he began, "because it wasn't really your choice to sell your body. I assume it was something you did out of necessity, based on your circumstances."

Nina smiled knowingly. "Have you ever thought that maybe killing King Cyril wasn't Elyse's first choice either? That it was something she saw as necessary?"

No, I didn't think of that, Killian huffed to himself. "It's not the same," he said, exasperated.

"No, it's not," Nina agreed. "No two lives will ever be the same. But you have to listen to have a chance at understanding."

Killian didn't say anything else. He couldn't think straight. Was Nina really insinuating that perhaps Elyse had a good reason to kill King Cyril? What explanation could she possibly give that would justify her actions—and her lies?

The sun was starting to make its presence known as heat infiltrated the air. Nina continued to sip calmly on her tea, but Killian just sat there, rigid and simmering.

If Elyse did have a good reason for her actions—which he sincerely doubted—then she'd had plenty of time to come clean. Then again, would he have listened? Or would he have arrested her on the spot? She had tried explaining many times, but he had refused to hear it, assuming she would feed him more lies.

His attention was torn away from his convoluted thoughts as the clinic door opened. He prayed that it would be Manny or Privya or even Jaime that walked out, though he already knew that he wouldn't be so lucky. Fair hair and fairer skin glistened in the sunlight as Elyse stepped outside, and Killian stifled a groan.

Her expression morphed into an awkward grimace as she spotted Killian and Nina beneath the tree, an uncharacteristic look for the stoic witch. Good. At least she was as perturbed as he was.

He waited for her to approach them, gritting his teeth in anticipation of the encounter. Instead, she walked along the side of the building and disappeared around the corner, avoiding them completely.

Killian sighed with genuine relief. He wanted to pretend like last night never happened, and to go back to ignoring each other unless it was something pertinent to their investigation.

When he looked back at Nina, she was giving him a curious side eye—one that he disregarded. There might be some truth to her advice in regards to listening to Elyse's story. But that was not something he was ready to confront.

Not yet.

CHAPTER 27

— · —

ELYSE

I t was difficult for Elyse to say goodbye to Privya, Corin, and Nina. The clinic had become a safe haven for her, just as it was for so many others, and during her time there, she'd hardly thought about Lazarus or the blood pact or anything devious. In fact, with the help of a few glasses of wine, she'd been able to relax and enjoy her friends' company. That is, up until her tryst with Killian in the kitchen.

Devil's forked tongue, it had been so stupid of her. It was stupid and passionate and... incredible. Killian had always been a talented and attentive lover, but last night surpassed all their other engagements.

She'd hoped that something had changed between them, that perhaps he was beginning to soften toward her. That hope was immediately diminished when she found him beneath the tree that morning, glaring at her as if she was the source of all his problems. Because she was.

And so, all good things must come to an end.

They departed the clinic on three borrowed stallions, buddying up together for the journey. Elyse didn't deign to believe that Killian would even consider partnering with her atop a horse, so she asked Jaime to share her saddle. Manny and Sera paired up together, leaving Killian free to ride alone.

The heat was nearly unbearable as they rode, and each of them—even Sera—were swiftly drenched in sweat. For the hundredth time, Elyse found herself grateful to be rid of the widow's decay; sweat had made the rash completely intolerable.

She was determined to avoid meeting Manny's eyes, and it seemed he felt the same way. Eventually, though, after miles of riding through forests, the awkwardness seemed to dissipate, and they began to quiz each other about their backstory, in case anyone asked them too many questions. Elyse was grateful for the distraction. Anything that kept her mind off her troubles was a welcome reprieve. When it became clear that they both had a firm grasp on their fake identities, Manny grew tired of the conversation, letting the group fall back into silence.

"Shall we play a game?" Elyse asked, eager for something else to pass the time. "I spy with my witch's eye..."

"Elyse," Killian grumbled, shooting her an indignant look. "We are not playing a game."

No, nothing had changed between them at all.

They arrived at De Vesalis in the early evening, just as the city was starting to stir. Sunlight still covered the city, so at odds with the women who roamed the streets in lingerie and heavy makeup. Groups of men stumbled to and from various taverns and gambling halls, rejoicing in their winnings or lamenting their losses. Soldiers wandered the streets, but they didn't seem concerned with any of the drunken tourists. In fact, some of the soldiers were drunk as well. The one saving grace of the city was the ocean breeze rolling off the Staerion Sea. It wove in and out of the buildings, bringing sweet relief to Elyse's sweltering skin.

Sera seemed to enjoy it as well. She lifted her face to the sky, letting the wind tousle her hair. "You know," she began. "The city would be remarkable if it weren't for the—"

A boy no older than ten and six doubled over in front of Killian's horse and proceeded to spill his guts.

"...well, if it weren't for that," Sera finished her thought.

Manny roared with laughter, then hollered to the boy, "Water with hemberry! You'll thank me later!"

The boy, now seated beside his own pile of vomit, gave Manny a weak thumbs-up.

"You're incorrigible," Killian sighed, glancing sideways at his friend.

"Oh, don't be a curmudgeon," Manny replied. "We're in the City of Vice!"

Killian rolled his eyes and mumbled under his breath, something about "curmudgeon" and "ridiculous."

Elyse smiled to herself, but Jaime appeared unamused. "There's an inn up the road," he said in a stony voice, pointing to a sign post that read "Traveler's Rest" in a beautiful script.

Sera had been right in her assessment; De Vesalis was remarkable. A fountain blossomed in the center of the city, adding to the bustle of excitement. Each building's architecture was breathtaking, with exquisite woodwork painted in bright colors. The inside of the Traveler's Rest was no exception, its floors lined with plush carpets and ornate wallpapers. The innkeeper, a middle-aged woman with painted lips and a tight corset, was kind as she showed them to their rooms.

They'd barely set down their luggage when Killian announced he was going to get dinner for everyone and excused himself. Jaime said something about needing to rest and disappeared to another room, leaving Manny, Sera, and Elyse alone.

"I suppose we should take the potion now," Elyse suggested. She riffled through her bags until she procured a vial of deep purple liquid. Manny made a face, and Elyse didn't blame him. It looked like the blood of some obscene creature.

"Ladies first," Manny said as he eyed the concoction.

Trying not to look too closely at the liquid, Elyse uncorked the vial and drank half of it. It tasted unexpectedly sweet—almost disgustingly so. She passed the vial to Manny, who finished it off in one swig. He blinked a few times, looking back and forth between Elyse and Sera.

"Did it work?" he asked. "Do I look different?"

"Not yet," Sera replied.

"You should feel it when it starts to work," Elyse explained.

Right on cue, her own face started to tingle. Her skin grew hot, like she was sitting in direct sunlight, but it didn't hurt. Her scalp itched, and she watched the ends of her silvery hair turn to chestnut curls. And then—much to her surprise—her breasts began to swell.

Fortunately, Manny was too busy worrying about his own appearance to notice that Elyse's tits were practically popping out of her tunic. She watched with fascination as his hair darkened and his nose grew broader. Even his muscles started to wither away until his sleeves sagged around his arms.

"How do I look?" he asked, bolting for the nearest mirror. As he inspected himself, he touched his face, marveling at the transformation.

Sera giggled and looked excitedly back and forth between the two of them.

"I like the chin, but I could do without the eyebrows," Manny said, combing his fingers through the caterpillars that lined his brow. Then his eyes shifted toward Elyse. "That's quite the schnoz."

Elyse instinctively touched her hand to her nose, feeling the foreign shape of it. She wanted to rush to the mirror and shove Manny aside, but she walked coolly across the room until she stood before her reflection. Sure enough, her nose was quite large, shaped like a beak in the center of her face. Her cheeks and jawline were sharp and angular, only serving to emphasize the nose even more.

"I quite like it," Sera commented. "It's very vogue."

Elyse sighed. "Well, it's only for one night."

"How long did you say this will last?" Manny asked. "About six hours?"

Elyse nodded. "We should be good through the auction."

Manny left the room to get changed, allowing Elyse privacy to do the same. The dress she'd chosen was much more complicated than anything she would have normally selected, but Sera was there to help her navigate through the layers of bustling and tie up the back. The corset bodice squeezed tight around her ribs, and the sweetheart neckline did little to cover her newly acquired assets, but the dress did have a secret pocket hidden among the layers of silk that bunched at her hips—a pocket deep enough to hide a replica of the eternal rose.

"The navy really complements your new color palette," Sera remarked, twisting a strand of Elyse's rich chestnut hair between her fingers.

Elyse glanced in the mirror to see that Sera was right. The deep blue of the silk made her hair and skin seem brighter, more elegant. She didn't look like a princess—the dress was much too bold for that—but she did look stunning.

"The queen of the witches," Sera whispered in her ear. Elyse refrained from smiling, though she did like the sound of the title.

Manny returned, looking striking in his suit. The jacket had a long tailcoat, and he'd donned a navy vest that matched Elyse's dress precisely.

"Mr. Nottingfeld," Sera crooned, fanning herself for dramatic effect. She sauntered over to him and drew in close, placing a hand on his chest. "You look dashing."

"Sorry, darling," he smirked, "but I'm a married man."

Sera gave him a light shove before returning to Elyse to work on her hair and makeup. She twisted Elyse's long hair up into a loose chignon, then lined her eyes with kohl and painted her lips a deep red.

A knock sounded at the door, followed by Killian's voice. "Is everyone decent?"

Despite herself, Elyse's cheeks burned. She and Killian had been far from *decent* in the kitchen last night.

"Yes," Sera replied, and the door to the room swung open.

Killian strode in, his arms full with a basket of bread, meat, and potatoes. He took two steps then stopped abruptly, his gaze darting between Elyse and Manny. He studied Elyse's face, and then quickly, so quickly it was almost imperceptible, he glanced down at her chest.

"I see the potions worked," he rasped out. He seemed to come back to his senses as he strode to the table and set the basket atop it. "Eat up. You'll need to leave soon."

CHAPTER 28

— ⦁ —

ELYSE

Thirty minutes later, Elyse and Manny departed the inn, dressed in their finery and dodging drunken revelers.

The night air was warm, suffocating Elyse beneath her layers of silk. Fortunately, the mansion was only a short distance away, and walking allowed her to feel the breeze. Still, her movements were stiff, restricted by the tight gown.

Her nerves were frantic, sending jitters through her body. She tried to steel them by going over the details of the night. Jaime had said it was a private auction with only a handful of guests, and that there would be three items for sale. She tried to speculate what the other items might be, but her mind was too agitated to focus. Thoughts of Killian's hand gripping the hair at the nape of her neck kept stealing her attention, and though part of her ached to live in that moment, she knew it was the last thing she needed to entertain. Turning to Manny, she decided a conversation was the best form of distraction.

"So," Elyse began with a smirk, "since I'm likely going to die soon, why don't you entertain me with a story about one of your spy adventures?"

Manny turned on her, a whirl of dark hair and green eyes. "Let's get one thing straight," he snarled. "I'm cordial to you out of respect for Sera, but I do not like you." His face was mere inches from hers, ire radiating

OF BLOOD AND ROSES

from his whole body. "You murdered my king, and you broke my best friend's heart. Not to mention you let Sera lie for you."

Elyse froze. It might've hurt less if he had just choked her, since her throat seemed to close anyway, and his words stabbed into her chest. She was stunned by his sudden intensity, the fire in his eyes. She had never seen him so furious before, and now all his hatred was directed at her. She hadn't thought he liked her. Of course he wouldn't. Not with everything she'd done. But she had never expected him to ambush her like this.

She wanted to beg for his forgiveness, to explain that she had never meant to hurt him or Sera or Killian, but what was the point? He was clearly heated, his face red and eyes narrowed on her, sizing her up like the criminal she was. So instead, she lifted her chin an inch higher and said, as coolly as she could muster, "I would expect you, of all people, to understand the difficult decisions we make under duress."

Manny's brow lowered ever so slightly, his eyes softening a tad. He stared at her, and she let him search her face as he tried to understand her words. She knew Manny had spent time as a thief and a conman. When his mother died, he'd been forced to steal and cheat to get by, up until he was arrested at sixteen and Killian's father had offered him a position in the Royal Guard.

But his life could have very easily gone in a different direction. If he'd turned down Commander Southwick's offer, he would have gone to prison. Most prisoners either died or forfeited any remaining morals just to see another day. It wasn't the same, of course—his being a petty thief and her murdering the king on behalf of a demon—but if it made him think twice about telling her off, then she would take it as a victory.

Manny's throat bobbed, but he didn't say anything. Elyse took the opportunity to move past him.

They made the rest of the trek in silence until they finally reached the mansion. An iron fence surrounded the property, but Elyse could still see the enormous residence beyond. A man in all black stood guard outside the gate, watching them as they approached.

"Charles Nottingfeld," Manny declared once they reached the gate.

The guard nodded. "Mr. and Mrs. Nottingfeld, we've been expecting you." He ceremoniously opened the gate and held it ajar for them. "Enjoy your evening," he called as they stepped into the vast courtyard.

Fountains and flowers dazzled around them, lining the stone walkway to the front doors. Elyse fought to keep her nerves at bay as she let out a slow exhale. They had a plan. It would work.

To her surprise, Manny stepped closer and hooked his arm through hers. He must despise touching her, especially given the hateful words he'd just spewed, but he kept his expression neutral. Surprisingly, the simple gesture helped calm Elyse, and she held her head high as they strolled to the door.

As they approached, a servant clad in white pulled the door open for them, gracefully inviting them inside with a bow and an extended arm.

"Good evening," he proclaimed as he stood upright. "Welcome to the estate of Professor Belledieux."

Elyse looked around, expecting to find Professor Belledieux there to greet them, but the large marble foyer was empty. A grand staircase twisted its way up to the second story while expensive-looking paintings and artifacts lined nearly every inch of free space. Elyse had worried that she'd be overdressed in her extravagant gown, but she breathed a sigh of relief. This was a man of decadence.

"Professor Belledieux and the other guests are in the Sapphire Hall," the servant announced. "Luis will show you there."

Another servant dressed in white appeared seemingly from nowhere and sauntered toward them. He held a silver tray with two fluted glasses of pale liquid, which he delicately handed to them. "After me," he beckoned.

They followed Luis through a set of double doors on the right side of the foyer, and Elyse immediately understood why the room was deemed the Sapphire Hall. Every wall was painted a rich blue, made even more vivid against the white tile floors. The ceilings were adorned with chandeliers that glittered with dangling sapphires. Columns decorated in ornate mosaics stood throughout the hall, and in the center of each mosaic was a sapphire the size of Elyse's fist.

"Gods above," Manny breathed as his eyes roamed over the room. Elyse couldn't even think of the words to voice her astonishment.

"Mr. and Mrs. Nottingfeld!" called a man's voice from across the room. A tall gentleman dressed in a black velvet jerkin excused himself from the small group he'd been conversing with and headed their direction. He walked with the sort of grace that came with extreme wealth, his perfectly groomed black hair flowing behind him. "It is an honor to make your acquaintance," he trilled.

"Professor Belledieux, I presume?" Manny asked, a slight pretension in his voice. He extended his hand, which the man clasped with enthusiasm.

"Guilty as charged," Professor Belledieux declared with a wink. Then he turned his attention to Elyse. "Mrs. Nottingfeld, I must say you look absolutely regal. Your dress is exquisite—you fit in perfectly with the room."

"Thank you, Professor," Elyse said as she curtsied. It was true—the rich blue silk of her gown matched the deeper shades of the sapphires. "You have a lovely home."

"I'm glad that Jaime could arrange an invitation for you," Belledieux replied. "Come, meet the other guests."

Belledieux gently took Elyse by the elbow and guided her farther into the room. She put on her warmest smile in anticipation of meeting the other attendees, but as soon as she realized who she was to meet, that smile vanished.

Green eyes stared back at her—green eyes that belonged to none other than Niall Royce.

As she forced herself not to take in a sharp breath of air, Elyse reminded herself that Royce didn't know who she was, that she was disguised. It didn't, however, stop her throat from going dry and her heart from racing. Thanks to her, Royce had spent several days in prison after she framed him for assassinating King Cyril. That wasn't something he was likely to forgive.

He coolly ran a hand through his white hair before extending it to Elyse. "Niall Royce," he introduced himself as he dipped low and planted a kiss on Elyse's hand.

"Clarice Nottingfeld," Elyse answered, forcing herself to keep from cringing.

Manny was somehow managing to stay calm. He extended his hand coolly toward Royce, a bored expression on his unfamiliar face. "Charles Nottingfeld," he declared in a pompous voice. "Pleasure to meet you, Niall."

They shook hands while Elyse tried to relax. No one knew who she was. She was safe.

"Royce is a trader out of Sevhella," Belledieux explained. "He's rumored to own the Blade of Hanael."

Elyse knew the rumor to be true. She had seen the blade during a private tour Royce had given her—when she had distracted him as part of her scheme to plant evidence against him.

"It's not a rumor," Royce stated with some irritation.

"Very impressive," Elyse crooned. She placed a hand on Manny's arm. "Forgive my husband if he doesn't share my enthusiasm. I'm the artifact connoisseur; he's merely the financier."

Manny let out a haughty chuckle and placed his hand atop hers. "She's lucky I have deep pockets."

"Hear, hear!" Professor Belledieux agreed, clinking his own glass against Manny's. Then he gestured toward the next guest. "Allow me to introduce Mr. Grayson."

Elyse nearly gawked as her eyes landed on the ancient man standing next to her. She'd been so focused on Royce, she hadn't even noticed her beloved former customer.

"Please, call me Alfred," Mr. Grayson said, his eyes bright. He stood out from the other guests, not just because he was over one hundred years old, but because he wore a simple jerkin and trousers. Elyse supposed that at his age, he was given a pass when it came to dress code.

She curtsied and offered him a genuine smile. "It's a pleasure, Alfred." Truly it was. She missed his playful energy during his monthly visits, and seeing him here brought her a sort of contentment.

"Alfred also hails from Sevhella," Belledieux disclosed. "He's quite the... experimenter."

"Oh, and what do you experiment in?" Manny asked, sounding intrigued.

"Necromancy!" Mr. Grayson announced, just as enthusiastically as he always did.

Manny looked confused, his furry brows knitting together. Elyse leaned in and whispered, "He's trying to raise the dead."

"Ah," Manny said awkwardly, shuffling his feet. "Well, best of luck to you."

"Thank you," Mr. Grayson replied, beaming up at Manny. "But if all goes right tonight, I won't need luck." It was a wonder how he managed to hold so much vigor in such a frail body.

Belledieux smiled politely before moving on to the final guest. "This is Ymaritis," he said, motioning to a man with dark hair and the most striking eyes—one blue and one silver. His skin was a rich shade of umber, not far from Killian's, and his suit was impeccable.

"Lovely to meet you," Elyse purred. "And what do you do?"

"My family owns all the mines in the Asterial Mountains," he said in a deep voice, much like a growl.

Elyse had to keep herself from whistling. The Asterial Mountains covered most of the western half of Rhodan, and their mines were full of gold, silver, and nearly every gem known to man.

Manny looked around the room. "It's likely your family's sapphires that decorate this room," he joked.

Ymaritis gave Manny an almost predatory grin. "That's how Belledieux and I met, actually."

Belledieux clapped Ymaritis on the back. "I wouldn't settle for anything less than the best," he remarked with cheer. His eyes lit up as he caught sight of something at the front of the room. "Ah, it appears our final guest has arrived."

Elyse turned, curious to see who the last attendant was, and had to stifle a curse.

Jaime strode toward her, grinning wildly. "Sorry I'm late."

CHAPTER 29

— : —

KILLIAN

Killian sat inside the gaudy room in the inn, his knee bouncing without his realization. He knew it would be hours before Elyse and Manny were expected back, but he couldn't help looking out the window every few minutes. What if something went wrong at the auction, and their true identities were revealed? Would Elyse protect Manny? The blood pact prohibited her from hurting him, but that didn't mean she was obliged to keep him safe.

Of course she'll keep him safe, Killian chastened himself. For all her faults, Elyse cared about Manny. She would do everything in her power to make sure they were all safe.

Sera came bustling into the room and pointed to the washbasin. "Get cleaned up," she ordered. "We're going out for drinks."

She had changed into another dress, one much more scandalous than the delicate pink thing she'd been wearing before. This dress was black and low cut, hugging her every curve. A slit in the skirt emphasized her long, pale legs, which peaked out from the fabric.

Killian gave her a deadpan stare. "Does Manny know about this dress?"

Sera scoffed and put her hands on her hips. "Of course he does. His exact words were, 'Now *that* is the kind of dress you wear in the City of Vice.'"

He let out a huff and returned his gaze to the window. "It doesn't matter anyway. I'm waiting right here until they get back."

"No, you're not," Sera retorted. "You're driving me crazy, sitting there worrying. Take your mind off them for a while." She picked up Killian's bag and hurled it at him

Killian caught the bag and set it at his feet. "If I'm driving you crazy, you can go by yourself," he said, letting his impatience show.

"And what would Manny say if anything happened to me while I was out on my own?"

Killian grimaced, knowing she was right. Manny would be furious. "Take Jaime," he suggested, not ready to give up.

"He's still resting."

With a sigh, Killian turned to face her again. "You're going to pester me until I agree, aren't you?"

Sera crossed her arms over her chest and smirked. "Obviously."

"All right," he agreed. Groaning, he rose from the chair and trudged to the washbasin. "Just one drink, though."

"We'll see about that," Sera crooned as she sauntered out of the room.

Ten minutes later, Killian found himself roaming the streets of De Vesalis with Sera.

"See?" she cried, spreading her arms wide. "Isn't this wonderful?"

Killian grunted a reply. It was far from wonderful in his opinion, with the drunk and rowdy tourists stumbling around. The roads smelled of vomit and ale, and the heat only made it worse.

"Oh, cheer up," Sera urged him. "This might be your only chance to party in the City of Vice."

Killian hoped she was right.

"This place looks fun!" Sera exclaimed, pointing to a tavern painted in black and red. A voluptuous woman stood outside in little more than lingerie, inviting patrons in.

"I don't think—"

But before Killian could voice his disinterest, Sera had taken him by the hand and whisked him down the street.

"You're just in time," the lingerie-clad woman purred as they approached. "The dancers start soon."

Oh, gods. Not dancers.

Sera looked absolutely delighted. She practically squealed as she pulled Killian into the dark tavern. It was difficult to see as they made their way to a table, but Killian couldn't miss the women parading around serving drinks. They all wore corsets and undergarments, and there was a woman for every taste and fetish. Tall, thin, curvy, dark, pale—he even spotted a woman with a shaved head.

They settled down at a table in the corner, and Killian tried desperately to find a place to direct his attention that didn't involve half-naked women. He feigned interest in the decor of the tavern, his eyes wandering from the black walls to the fine woodwork of the bar to the high ceilings. Long silken ropes dangled from the ceiling, but he couldn't pinpoint their purpose.

"What'll you have to drink, darling?"

A waitress with fiery-red hair had approached the table while Killian was busy studying the room. Her lips were painted to match her hair, and her scarlet corset was stark against her pale skin.

"Honey mead for me," Sera ordered sweetly.

Killian cleared his throat and made sure to look directly in the waitress's eyes as he said, "An ale."

"Coming right up," she replied with a wink and a toss of her hair.

As soon as she walked away, a handful of musicians began playing a seductive melody, and a commotion stirred above them. Killian looked up to see several lithe bodies strutting across a catwalk that ran the length of the ceiling—bodies that were entirely covered in paint. Each woman was painted a different color, and upon closer inspection...

Of course they're nude.

Sera clapped excitedly as the women hoisted themselves onto the ropes hanging from the ceiling and began twisting their bodies in a choreographed rhythm. They moved with a precision and athleticism that rivaled that of Killian's former soldiers, and he couldn't help but be impressed. It might have been beautiful had they not been suspended directly over the patrons.

"Do you think I could learn to do that?" Sera asked, her eyes wide as she tracked the dancers' movements.

Killian smiled wryly. "Well, you got me to come here, so I'd say you're capable of doing just about anything."

Sera glanced at him long enough to shoot him a smile before reverting her attention back to the dancers.

"One honey mead, and one house ale," the waitress announced as she returned to their table. She set their drinks down and sashayed back into the crowd before Killian could ask to settle the bill.

Sera raised her chalice and indicated for Killian to do the same. He lifted his stein, and Sera clinked their drinks together. "To Elyse," she said somberly, "whose sacrifice shall not be taken lightly."

Killian shifted uncomfortably—likely Sera's intention—but he drank to the toast. As much as he hated to admit it, Elyse's decision to turn herself in was noble. It could never undo the damage that she'd done, the lives that she'd taken and the hurt she'd caused him, but it was the best possible outcome of the whole mess.

Still, as he took in Sera's solemn expression, he couldn't help but feel swallowed by empathy. For all her faults, Elyse had brought happiness to Sera, and others—Corin, Nina, and Privya to name a few. He wondered what a world without Elyse would be like.

It would be empty, his heart screamed at him, but he pushed the thought away.

He forced himself to relax, reclining slightly in his chair. The ale helped, its hearty flavor more delicious than he had expected. He was just starting to feel at ease when across the tavern, a silver-haired beauty caught his attention.

CHAPTER 30

— • —

ELYSE

"What the hell were you thinking?" Elyse hissed at Jaime the first chance she got to pull him aside.

Manny was there with her, equally as vexed. Jaime had explained to everyone upon his arrival that his evening had "suddenly freed up" and that he was "sincerely apologetic for the last-minute notice." Belledieux graciously welcomed him and told him he was happy to have his company regardless of how much warning was given, while Manny and Elyse had quietly simmered.

"I was thinking," Jaime answered in a hushed tone, "that it would be better for three of us to be here instead of two."

"And you didn't think to run that by us?" Manny asked, plastering on a fake smile so that no one would suspect any tension between them.

"I believe I am free to attend whatever parties I am invited to without consulting you or that brooding lieutenant you keep around."

Elyse was fuming, but she had to keep appearances up. She cackled loudly and placed a hand on Jaime's arm. "Oh, Jaime. You are too funny."

Jaime subtly rolled his eyes. Message received.

Manny took a step closer and lowered his voice, but the agitation he held was clear. "If you even think about—"

"Pardon me," interrupted a sultry male voice as Royce made his way to their little circle, looking especially smug. "Are you the same Jaime Lindgren that courted Elyse Crenshaw?"

Elyse nearly dropped her drink. She should have realized that Royce would have known about her and Jaime, but she hadn't been mentally prepared for him to speak her name. A shiver rattled up her spine, but she forced herself to merely act intrigued.

Jaime made a face similar to a grimace. "Unfortunately, I am."

Holding her breath, Elyse waited for Royce's reaction—and was stunned when he laughed and clapped Jaime on the back. "You could do much worse than her."

Jaime looked at Royce with one brow raised, his blue eyes curious. "I expected a much more hostile reaction," he said tentatively, mirroring Elyse's own surprise.

Royce's smug look multiplied. "Oh I was certainly angry when she framed me for the king's murder—though I will say it was quite fun toying with that magistrate. What was his name? Longshire? Lowfellow? It doesn't matter..." He waved his hand and sipped casually from his drink, as if merely discussing the weather.

Meanwhile, Elyse felt like she was going to be sick. In another circumstance, she might have enjoyed listening to people speak about her so candidly. But to hear Royce talk about how she had framed him, to hear him bring up Longfellow after she'd been forced to end his life—it was too much for her. She tried to keep her expression neutral as she swayed slightly on her feet.

"So what changed?" Manny asked, sounding genuinely bored.

Royce's smirk was rapacious. "Let's just say her absence has created a demand in the marketplace—a demand that I have been able to capitalize on."

Elyse squeezed her glass so tight it nearly broke. He had taken over her customers? Her fingers itched to hex him, to shut him right up, but she knew she couldn't.

"Excuse me, gentlemen, but I need to powder my nose." She could hardly get away from them fast enough.

As she hurried off, she heard Royce say, "I'd give away half my fortune to spend a night with both her and Madame Sera."

It took everything in her not to turn back and curse his manhood right off, but she kept walking. She had no doubt Manny would find a way to get back at Royce for that comment.

She dipped into the corridor and leaned her back against the wall, letting it steady her. With her eyes closed, she took several deep breaths in and out and focused on the plan.

Before the eternal rose could be auctioned off, there would be some sort of verification of its authenticity, which meant Manny had to wait until after that to make the swap. It would be too difficult to take the rose off whoever won it, so they would have a short window to replace it. Elyse and Manny would have to work during the actual bidding—likely only a minute or two.

She told herself that one or two minutes would be plenty of time to take down the wards and make the exchange. She was a damn good witch, and she had never failed before. After Elyse took down the wards, she would have to turn Manny invisible while simultaneously maintaining a magical illusion that he was standing beside her. She'd done plenty of illusions before, and she'd even turned herself invisible a handful of times, but she'd never attempted to make someone else invisible. It was extraordinarily complex magic that took immense focus, but she was certain she could do it.

The hardest part would be the timing. At the exact moment that Manny swapped out the real rose for the fake one, she would have to make one invisible while revealing the other. There could only be a fraction of a second in between the two, the span of a blink of an eye, while they prayed that no one was watching too closely. She'd never seen Manny's sleight of hand before, but if Killian trusted him, then that was good enough for her.

They would be all right. They were an unstoppable duo—the most powerful witch in the kingdom paired with the best spy. Even if something did go wrong, they could maneuver their way out of it.

Feeling more collected, Elyse returned to the Sapphire Hall. Manny still stood with Royce and Jaime, wholeheartedly appearing to be interested in whatever they were discussing. He caught sight of her out of the corner of his eye and beamed back at her.

"Ah, there you are, darling," he serenaded her.

She barely made it to him when Belledieux announced, "Ladies and gentlemen, if you would please follow me to the Diamond Room—the auction is about to begin."

Manny quickly gathered Elyse's arm in his own and pulled her in close. "I can't believe you left me alone with them," he growled, though there was a playful tone to his voice.

"Sorry," Elyse said, trying to convey her sincerity. "Was it that bad?"

He shot her a look that said, "Yes, it was absolutely *that* bad."

They strode into the corridor and back into the foyer, Manny keeping her close, perhaps afraid she'd slip away again. She felt him tense, and then he whispered, "About earlier..."

Elyse swallowed down her discomfort. Devil's tail, she did not want to revisit this now. "Let's just focus on tonight," she whispered back. But she squeezed his hand, silently relaying that she understood.

Manny caught her eye as a soft, grateful smile warmed his features, and together, they entered the Diamond Room.

CHAPTER 31

—·—

KILLIAN

For a moment, Killian thought Elyse was sitting across the tavern from him, batting her lashes at unsuspecting patrons. He realized, with some relief, that the woman's eyes were blue, not dark like Elyse's, and that her hair was too long. They could have been sisters, though, for all their similarities. Her hair was the exact same shade of silvery-blonde, her lips the same soft pink. She even had a cunning smirk like Elyse, which she flashed at each man who glanced her way.

Still, his breath caught. The woman might not have been Elyse, but his body didn't know better. He was assaulted with memories of the night before: tangling his hands in that pale hair, watching those lips tremble with each shuddering breath. She'd looked so beautiful in the moonlight. Beautiful and wicked.

His hatred had fueled his passion. He'd wanted to punish her. He'd wanted to make her weak for him. But he'd also wanted to forget for one gods damned minute everything that had gone horribly wrong between them.

"Killian?" Sera asked, tapping his arm.

"Hm?" Killian replied reflexively. He blinked and turned toward Sera.

She gave him a taunting look. "I was asking if you wanted to dance," she said, pointing to the very back of the tavern where a crowd of patrons swayed to the music. They seemed to be enjoying themselves immensely, though it looked more like a heap of bodies gyrating together than any sort of dance Killian had ever seen.

He quickly shook his head. "Oh, no. I don't dance. In fact, I think the last time I danced was with you at Royce's."

Sera had dragged him onto the floor then, and he had only obliged her as a way to keep her distracted while Manny searched Royce's home for evidence. Perhaps that was what she was doing again—distracting herself while Manny was away.

"Can I tell you a secret about that night?" she asked, her purple eyes full of mischief.

Killian glanced at the silver-haired woman across the bar. A man approached her, sending a sickly feeling through Killian. He cleared his throat and gave his attention wholly to Sera. "As long as it doesn't involve something you and Manny did privately after the party."

She giggled but waved him off. "No, it's much juicier than that." She looked deviously over both shoulders, then leaned closer. "I switched our glasses on purpose."

Killian's jaw fell open. "You what?" He remembered how after dancing, they had returned to their table and sipped from their drinks. He also remembered how Sera had handed him the honeysuckle wine instead of his own pear wine. He'd thought it had been a mere accident, especially since he'd claimed to have an allergy to honeysuckle. Apparently, he'd been wrong.

"But," Killian stammered, "but what if I really had been allergic?"

Sera brushed him off with a shrug. "Oh please, you were clearly lying."

"Really? You were confident enough to risk my life with that theory?"

She opened her eyes wide, conveying her point. "Well, you didn't die, now did you?" She lifted her chalice and playfully swirled her mead in circles. "I'm very good at reading people, and you, sir, were hiding something."

Killian leveled his gaze on her. He couldn't deny it—he had been hiding several things. The fact that he had feelings for Elyse, and that he had taken an emotion-suppressing potion to smother those feelings. Had she known that honeysuckle was the one antidote that would break the potion and send his feelings for Elyse flooding back to him?

"This ability to read people," he began skeptically, "is it tied to your clairvoyance?"

Sera tilted her head, considering. "Partially, yes. I do have some innate ability to discern people's emotional states, even without using tea leaves or tarot cards. But it's also from studying my clients over the years, and learning the patterns of human behavior. I'm sure you have similar skills from being a lieutenant."

Killian knew exactly what she meant. As a lieutenant, and often a lead investigator, he had carefully honed his ability to tell when someone was lying or hiding something, when they were a naturally nervous person, or nervous because they were guilty. Perhaps that was why being tricked by Elyse felt especially demoralizing—because it was undeniable proof that he was a poor detective.

The waitress brought them another round of drinks, and Killian sipped from his stein, garnering strength from the brew. There was something he'd wanted to ask Sera for months, and since they were being candid, perhaps now was the time.

He waited until the waitress left, then lowered his voice and asked, "How much did you know about Elyse's involvement in King Cyril's murder?"

Sera's throat bobbed, her fingers tracing the rim of her chalice. She seemed to steady herself, forcing her eyes to meet Killian's.

"I had my suspicions. She asked me years ago if I would be willing to lie for her, should anyone come around wondering where she was on nights with a full moon."

"And you agreed?" Killian asked, hoping it didn't come off as judgmental.

Sera nodded. "Of course. She's my best friend. And," she said, taking a deep breath, "I could see that she faced some sort of turmoil, but beneath that was an inherent desire to be good."

Turmoil—yes, it was clear that Elyse had her demons. She tried to hide it behind snarky jokes or snide comments, but it was there, simmering below the surface. Killian had hoped that one day she would open up to him about it, but he could see now how impossible that would have been.

"Do you know why she killed King Cyril?" he asked.

"Yes," Sera said plainly.

Killian held his breath before asking, "Why?"

Sera looked at him, pain and empathy, caring and concern all shining in her eyes. "It is not my place to tell."

Killian's chest tightened, but he nodded. Sera was right; Elyse deserved to tell her own story.

"Now I have a question for you," Sera said, securing his focus before his mind could wander. She took a sip from her chalice, then set it on the table and gave Killian a hard stare. "What was it that made you fall in love with her in the first place?"

Killian cocked his head to the side, surprised by the blunt question. The first thing that came to mind was the memory of watching her fight at Lex's safehouse, and the fascination that had ensued. He had never known a woman so powerful, so bold and fierce, and she had captivated him completely.

"Her strength," Killian answered, his voice subtly saccharine. "Not just the strength of her power, but her personality too. She had discipline. It showed in her magic, in the way she ran her store, in the way people looked at her. And with that discipline came values—values that we shared. Or at least, that I thought we shared."

Because his values would never include murdering a kind-hearted ruler in cold blood.

Sera's expression was deadly serious, all playfulness gone as she nodded along to his words. "And what if I told you that there was a reality where the two versions of Elyse that you hold in your mind—the version with discipline and strength, and the version who killed King Cyril... What if I told you that they could coexist?"

Killian shook his head. "That can't be—"

"But what if it did?" Sera asked, interrupting his argument.

He blinked a few times, letting the gravity of the possibility wash over him. He couldn't fathom it, being able to reconcile these two ideas that were so at odds with each other. But if, hypothetically, they were both true...

"I don't know," he breathed, because it was the truth. He had no idea how he would feel. Would it wipe out all the anger he had wallowed in these past months? Would he forgive her so easily? "I don't know," he repeated.

Sera looked away, giving him the privacy he desperately wanted at that moment. The tavern was too crowded, the ale too strong, the music too loud for him to even think properly.

Despite himself, he glanced up at the bar. The woman with silvery blonde hair and blue eyes still sat there, chatting with her companion. She reached out and laid a pale hand on the man's arm, sliding narrow fingers down his bicep. Killian shivered, remembering the way Elyse's hands felt on his body.

There was one other question that plagued him, one that he'd been far too afraid to ask Sera. Perhaps it was the ale giving him courage, or Elyse's twin across the bar unnerving him, but he gripped the handle of his stein and downed the rest of the drink before turning toward Sera, his question on his tongue.

CHAPTER 32

ELYSE

T he Diamond Room was exactly like the Sapphire Hall except for two things. The first was, of course, the incorporation of diamonds. They glittered, nearly blinding, across every wall and column, their decadence overpowering any sort of elegance. The second difference was that a dais stood at the far end of the room with three chests atop pedestals, and a stout man with a ruddy face. He was dressed in a simple suit, his expression all business as he watched Elyse and the other attendees file into the room.

A murmur swept over their small group as anticipation set in, spreading from one party-goer to another. Elyse was not immune to the excitement as a mixture of curiosity and apprehension mingled in her stomach.

"What are the other two items?" she asked Jaime, who had joined her and Manny. She had been so absorbed with plans to steal the rose that she hadn't bothered to ask sooner.

"The first is a necklace that will keep the wearer from being cursed," Jaime explained. "And the second is a pair of gloves said to be worn by Death."

Elyse nodded, her eyes fixed on the dais. That explained Mr. Grayson's interest in being there. He would probably use the gloves as some sort of bargaining tool with Death. Perhaps the gloves were the final piece he needed in his eighty-year quest to bring his wife back to life.

"And the third is the rose," Manny said. A statement, not a question. He too, stared up at the chests atop their pedestals, a sort of determination in his eyes.

Elyse used the moment to sense the wards, getting a feel for what she would be up against. Her magic brushed against a protective wall that surrounded the dais, safeguarding the artifacts and the man accompanying them. The wall was complex, like layered bricks, but not impossible to tear down.

"Are you ready?" she asked, turning her gaze on Manny.

His answering smile was roguish. "I feel like I've been preparing for this my whole life."

Elyse couldn't help but smile back at him, her anxiety transforming into excitement.

The stout man on the dais raised his arms, signaling for everyone's attention. "Thank you all for coming to this auction, and thank you Professor Belledieux for hosting," he called out to the room.

Belledieux waved his hand as the attendees politely applauded him.

When everyone quieted down again, the man continued. "I will be auctioning off these items on behalf of my employer, who has decided to part ways with them in exchange for your generous offerings."

"Who is his employer?" Manny asked Jaime in a low voice.

Jaime just shrugged. "He's selling them anonymously."

That was curious—but fortunate for them that this mysterious person had decided to sell the rose.

"Funds will be collected at the end of the evening, and you will be given your purchased artifacts along with letters of authenticity," the man added. "If you wish to bid on an item, simply raise your hand."

Seemed easy enough. Elyse glanced around at the others, noting their eager looks. She guessed that Mr. Grayson planned to bid on the gloves, but she wondered what everyone else was after. Who was interested in the rose?

"Without further ado, we shall begin!" the auctioneer announced.

Elyse felt goose pimples shiver across her skin. Her magic was clawing at her, ready to act, but she kept it at bay. According to Jaime, there were still two other items to be auctioned off before the rose.

The auctioneer waddled over to the first chest, and the small crowd fell intensely silent as he unlocked it and opened the lid. "The first item is a rare beauty," he proclaimed. "A gold necklace encrusted with enchanted rubies that will protect the wearer from curses."

He displayed it proudly, letting the pendant dangle from his hands. The enormous ruby sparkled in the candlelight, its brilliance undeniable. Elyse gasped, her eyes transfixed on the gem. She wasn't one for jewelry, but this necklace... It was mesmerizing.

"May I see it?" she asked, taking a step closer to the dais.

"Of course, milady," the auctioneer crooned, beckoning her forward.

As if summoned by its beauty, Elyse marched toward the necklace. She ventured closer, as close as the wards would allow her, and nearly forgot how to breathe. The necklace was even more stunning up close, the gold exquisite, the ruby pristine. She could barely bring herself to step away from it, but she forced herself to walk back to the others as the auctioneer gave her a simpering smile.

"The starting bid will begin at one hundred thousand gold coins," he declared.

Reality backhanded Elyse across the face. *One hundred thousand gold coins?* She couldn't fathom paying that much for any piece of jewelry—not even one that broke curses. And yet...

Ymaritis raised his hand.

"That's one hundred thousand, do I have one-twenty?" the auctioneer bellowed.

Elyse glanced back at the breathtaking jewel. It would be absurd if they didn't bid on anything, and she wouldn't risk taking the gloves away from Mr. Grayson...

Before she could fully think it through, she raised her hand.

"One hundred twenty thousand! Can I get one-forty?"

Manny and Jaime both gave her looks of subtle surprise, but neither said anything. She took that as affirmation to continue.

Belledieux raised his hand next, and the auctioneer shouted, "One hundred and forty thousand! One hundred forty, can I get one hundred and fifty?"

Elyse immediately raised her hand.

"Two hundred," Ymaritis called out in his deep voice, gesturing toward the auctioneer.

"We have two hundred from the gentleman in the back—can I get two-fifty?"

Elyse glanced at Ymaritis, his mismatched eyes bright with arrogance. She was out of her damn mind and she knew it, but still she raised her hand.

"Three hundred," she called, locking eyes with the auctioneer.

"Three hundred from the lady," he crooned. "Can I get three-fifty? Three-fifty?"

Neither Ymaritis nor Belledieux made any motion to counter.

"Three hundred going once... Three hundred going twice..."

Elyse held her breath.

"Sold to the lady in blue!"

She couldn't tell if she felt more ridiculous or excited as Manny pulled her in for a celebratory hug. Jaime patted her shoulder and wished her congratulations, and even Ymaritis and Belledieux gave her approving nods.

"A beautiful jewel for a beautiful lady!" Mr. Grayson declared.

She had no idea what she would do with the necklace—would she wear it? All the time? Or only on special occasions? It didn't matter, she supposed. At the moment, she was absolutely euphoric.

The auctioneer captured her attention again as he moved toward the second pedestal. "Now, this next item is a pair of gloves that have been worn by Death," he said as he unlocked the second chest.

The party had gone silent again as they waited impatiently for the reveal. Slowly, the auctioneer tilted back the lid and produced a pair of black leather gloves. They seemed ordinary-looking, but a strange force emanated from them. Everyone glanced around at each other, sizing up who their competition might be.

"Death's gloves," the auctioneer stated in a grave tone. "We'll start the bidding at five hundred thousand gold. Do I have five hundred?"

Mr. Grayson immediately raised a feeble hand.

The auctioneer pointed at him, acknowledging the bid. "I have five hundred, can I get six?"

Royce raised his hand.

"Six hundred thousand, can I get seven?"

"Seven," Belledieux offered, casually raising his hand.

"Eight!" Mr. Grayson countered.

"Nine," Jaime called.

Elyse snapped her head toward him, her eyes wide. *Don't*, she tried to convey silently. But Jaime didn't seem to understand.

"One million," Royce declared.

"One point five!"

"Two million."

"Three million."

Even Ymaritis had chimed in now, the bids coming in so quickly that Elyse could hardly keep up with them. Her stomach twisted, frightened for Mr. Grayson. He had worked so tirelessly to be reunited with his late wife, and she hated to see that torn away from him. Every time someone bid, he was right there to counter with a higher offer. Still, how far could he go?

Jaime was the first to back out, much to Elyse's relief. Had he won, she would have made him hand the gloves right over to Mr. Grayson. She watched with trepidation as the price rose higher and higher.

Finally, it seemed to come down to Belledieux and Mr. Grayson.

"I have thirteen million, can I get fourteen?" the auctioneer called.

Belledieux raised his hand, stealing the upperhand. Elyse clenched her teeth, waiting for the counter.

"That's fourteen, can I get fifteen?"

"Twenty-five million!" Mr. Grayson shouted, his ancient voice trembling.

Everyone in the room turned to him, stunned. Even the auctioneer seemed amazed.

"Twenty-five million, do I hear thirty?" he called after he regained his composure.

Belledieux just shook his head.

"Going once... Going twice... Sold to the centenarian!"

Mr. Grayson beamed as everyone broke into breathless applause. He certainly knew how to captivate a room, despite his many years.

"Congratulations, sir. You can collect your prize shortly. For now, we will move on to the most-anticipated item of the evening..." The auctioneer paused and slowly made his way to the final chest. He unlocked it and opened the lid, taking his time. Elyse thought her heart might explode as she waited. She wasn't breathing as the auctioneer donned a pair of crisp white gloves and reached into the chest.

With careful hands, he raised the eternal rose, displaying it for all to see.

Chapter 33

Killian

Killian set his stein on the table and spoke the question that had been burning in his chest.

"How does this all turn out?"

He stared Sera down, crossing his arms over his chest, trying to steady himself as he awaited the answer.

Sera's brows furrowed slightly as she blinked at him. "Pardon?" she asked, reaching for her chalice.

"You can see the future, right?" Killian answered, sounding more indignant than he meant. "So how does this turn out? Do we get the rose? Do we stop whoever is trying to raise a demon?"

Do I make peace with Elyse? That was the part that he was truly afraid to know. Even if he did somehow learn to forgive her, it would only end in heartbreak. There was no way of severing their blood pact, which meant she was destined to turn herself in to the Guard.

Sera laid her hand flat on the table, abandoning her chalice. She stared down at her pale fingers, avoiding Killian's earnest gaze. "I don't know," she uttered in a barren voice.

"You don't know?" Killian repeated. He had braced himself for the worst, for Sera to reveal to him that they would fail, but he hadn't expected this answer. "How can you not know?"

She didn't move for a moment. Killian couldn't read her expression beneath her lowered lashes, so he waited, holding his breath.

"I can't see everything," she replied in a low voice. "Only bits and pieces, and sometimes it's difficult to put them together."

There was something about her tone that made Killian uneasy. "So what do you see?" he pressed. "Do you see you and Manny growing old together? Do you see our kingdom burning?"

Do you see Elyse and I together? Or do you see her execution?

Sera's throat bobbed slowly. "I don't know," she repeated. She finally lifted her gaze to his, and there was nothing but cruel uncertainty in her eyes. "I know that it won't be easy, that we have a long, painful road ahead of us. But I don't know how it ends."

The tavern, which had been stuffy and loud, now seemed deathly quiet. All noise faded away as the intensity of Sera's words crashed into him.

"But surely you see—" he began, but she cut him off sharply.

"I don't." Her eyes bore into him, a finality in her voice. Killian didn't know what to say.

All at once, he wanted to be away from this place. He wanted to be back in the inn, waiting for Manny and Elyse to return. He wanted the night to be over.

Sera dropped her gaze to her lap, all liveliness gone from her posture.

"Come on," Killian said, touching her shoulder lightly. "Let's head back."

She nodded and looked up at him, a pitiful smile on her lips. She might have been trying to comfort him, but her eyes told another story. A story of the anguish that was to come.

He dropped a few silvers on the table—courtesy of Elyse—and reached for Sera's elbow. She let him guide her out of the crowded tavern, her posture devoid of its usual vivacity.

"Tell me about your family," Killian requested quietly as they stepped into the street. He wanted to cheer her up, though admittedly he didn't know much about her. He hoped that her family wasn't a sore choice of topic.

She sidled closer to him, avoiding a couple that groped each other openly.

"My family isn't nearly as exciting as you might think," she said casually, though her eyes gleamed with pride. "They're still in Otsuk, where I was born."

Killian had assumed Sera was from Otsuk but had never confirmed it. The lesser kingdom was known for its beautiful women with hooded eyes and hair the color of ink, features that Sera wore well. "Is your mother also a seer?" he asked. "I heard the gift is passed predominantly through women, for whatever reason." He didn't mention that it had been Elyse who told him.

"She is," Sera affirmed, nodding with a small smile.

"So she tells fortunes, like you?"

"Not exactly," Sera answered, her smile growing. "She uses her talents a bit differently. She's a political advisor to the Duke of Shenwil."

"Oh." Killian looked at her with eyes full of surprise, and Sera laughed at his candor. It was difficult for him to imagine her mother in a position of power, when Sera seemed far too free-spirited to give a damn about bureaucracy.

"Otsuk is more accepting of magic than Rhodan," Sera explained. "The Duke is happy to have her assistance."

"I'm sure he is. And your father? What does he do?"

Sera bit her lip, suppressing a grin. She looked at him sideways before admitting, "He *is* the Duke of Shenwil."

Killian let his jaw fall open. "What? How have I not known this?" Beneath his shock was a surge of guilt. He hardly knew anything about the woman his best friend had been seeing for months. He'd hardly made an effort to learn.

Sera shrugged. "It hasn't come up in conversation."

Because I never make conversation, Killian thought. Aloud, he said, "How did you wind up in Rhodan? You could have followed your mother's path."

Sera shook her head adamantly, as if repulsed by the thought. "Oh no, I would never." She looked around with awe at the numerous drunkards stumbling around them, gesturing her free hand toward them. "I enjoy this far too much. Interacting with different people, reading them and sharing in their joys." She smiled wistfully at a cheery group of young men. "My purpose is to give people hope and direction. I can't imagine doing anything else."

"I could use some hope and direction right about now," Killian mused quietly.

Sera gave him a warm smile, and together, they made their way back.

CHAPTER 34

— • —

ELYSE

The rose was immaculate, its petals the richest red, its stem a vibrant green. It shimmered, enchanted by the sparkling light of the chandeliers.

No one spoke. No one even breathed. The room was violently still as all stared at the artifact.

"It's beautiful."

Mr. Grayson was the one to break the silence, his words echoing into Elyse's soul.

"Indeed, it is," breathed Professor Belledieux.

"But—is it real?" came Royce's voice.

Elyse was certain it was real. If it wasn't, it was the best damn reproduction she'd ever seen. There was just something about it, something ethereal, that declared its veracity.

Even so, she was curious. She wanted a taste of its power.

"It is the true eternal rose," the auctioneer promised. "But my employer anticipated your need for assurance and has suggested that each of you take a turn touching the rose."

"Touching it?" Ymaritis questioned.

"What will that do?" Bellediuex iterated.

The auctioneer smiled. "See for yourself." Still holding the rose, he stepped down from the dais and passed through the wards.

Manny's eyes shot to Elyse, a silent question in his gaze. "Now?" his wide eyes wondered.

Elyse gave a tiny shake of her head. They would need to wait until after the rose was authenticated. Based on the power she felt rippling through the room, though, she was certain it was the real thing.

"Mr. Royce, why don't you go first?" the auctioneer suggested.

The offer seemed to stroke Royce's ego. He sauntered toward the rose, shoulders back and chin held high. With a cavalier smirk, he stopped before the auctioneer and placed one hand on the rose.

All pomp and circumstance came to a halt as Royce let out a sharp gasp, his eyes going wide. He stared directly ahead, mouth slightly ajar, captivated by something that no one else could see. Envy shook Elyse like nothing she'd felt before. She watched Royce closely, his awestruck expression only stoking her curiosity.

Manny looked to Elyse, his gaze seeking answers, but she gave him a shrug. She had no idea what was happening.

Royce's hand stayed planted atop the stem of the rose for a moment longer before the auctioneer pulled away, breaking contact. As soon as he did, Royce began panting heavily. He blinked several times, looking utterly stupefied.

"What was it?" Belledieux asked. "What happened?"

Royce shook his head, his white hair coming loose from its slick hold. "It's... ineffable," was all he could manage to say.

"Perhaps the lady next?" the auctioneer suggested, raising his eyebrows at Elyse.

She wanted very much to know what Royce had just experienced, and yet the thought of everyone seeing her like that, vulnerable and rattled, made her stomach churn. Still, it was not an opportunity she was going to pass up.

She swallowed down her qualms as she pulled away from Manny's arm and stepped toward the auctioneer. As she neared, she could see just how velvety smooth the rose petals were, and the sharp point of each thorn.

"Go on," the auctioneer coaxed.

Slowly, Elyse lifted her hand and lay it atop the soft petals.

The room disappeared, throwing her into what could only be described as a sunset. Oranges, pinks, and yellows surrounded her, their wispy shades interlacing and melting together. She was floating and yet grounded, weightless yet firm-footed. She saw her mother, Killian, Sera, Jaime, Manny. She saw everyone she had ever known, even in passing. She saw herself bathed in power, her future clear and bright and pure. Everything came in flashes, one image after another, yet somehow all at the same time. It felt so tangible, even as it existed only in her mind.

And then it was gone. She was back in the Diamond Room, its dull colors dimmed in shadow and dust. Power still thrummed in her veins, begging her for more, more, *more*. Yet she had never felt weaker than in the absence of the rose.

Her heart pounding, she turned to face Manny. Beneath his bushy brows, his eyes were wide with both intrigue and concern. She nodded to him, an affirmation that she was all right, then beckoned him forward. "Come, try," she gently urged him.

Manny hurried to join her, skepticism battling excitement in his expression. He placed his hand on the rose, and just as Royce had been, he became transfixed. Elyse could almost see his true self shining through beneath his disguise, that whimsy flowing from his body like it was his own form of magic.

When he returned to them, his face was bright, his grin wide. "I've never..." he began, though he couldn't seem to form the rest of the sentence.

One by one, the remaining guests took their turns with the rose, each of them just as hypnotized as the others. Elyse watched them all eagerly, as if reliving her own fantasy through them.

Finally, the auctioneer returned to the dais and set the rose on the pedestal. He clapped his hands, excitedly announcing, "The bidding will begin at fifty million gold coins."

It was time.

Elyse spared one glance over her shoulder at Jaime, who gave her an encouraging nod, before she threw her magic at the wards. She moved her fingers in tiny, nearly imperceptible movements, manipulating the spellwork. It was like forging a key—feeling the wards for invisible ridges and dips that made up the lock, then manifesting a spell that would fit precisely into place.

Someone raised their hand, and the auctioneer bellowed, "Fifty million, do I have fifty-five?"

Elyse tried to keep her face relaxed, but her brows naturally wanted to furrow with concentration.

"That's fifty-five million, can I get sixty?"

As quickly as she could, Elyse felt her way through the layers, listening with her mind and her magic for hints at how to navigate the labyrinth of the wards.

"Do I have seventy million?"

"Seventy-five," Ymaritis called out.

Elyse's heart beat faster as she plunged deeper into the wards. She didn't know how much longer the bidding would go on, and every second seemed to scream at her that she wasn't working quick enough.

"Eighty!" Royce shouted.

"Ninety!" Belledieux declared.

She was almost through to the other side, her magic key nearly complete.

"One-hundred million," Ymaritis countered, just as the wards came crashing down.

"One-hundred million," the auctioneer confirmed. "Do I have one-ten?"

Elyse squeezed Manny's hand, the signal that she was ready for him to make his move.

"One-ten," came Royce's response.

Elyse flicked her fingers, turning Manny invisible to everyone else. She created the illusion that he was standing next to her, hand in hand. With quick, adept movements, Manny seemed to stride out of his own body. He plunged his hand into Elyse's pocket and pulled out the fake rose, then darted toward the dais.

"Do I have one-twenty?"

Manny was on the dais, taking careful steps toward the pedestal that held the eternal rose. He pulled a handkerchief from his pocket and held it delicately as he neared the artifact.

But no one was bidding.

"One-twenty? Can I get one-twenty?" asked the auctioneer. He waited. No answer. "One-hundred and ten million going once..."

Manny stood just before the pedestal, his hands raised.

"One-hundred and ten million going twice..."

Shit. Elyse had taken too long on the wards. Manny's hands were steady as he prepared to make the switch, but he wouldn't have enough time to run off stage before Elyse had to start putting the wards back up.

"One-twenty!" called a voice from the crowd.

Elyse would've let out a sigh of relief if it weren't for the voice who said it. That was Jaime's voice. Jaime had just bid on the rose—for an amount of money he did not have.

Manny's free hand dove for the true rose just as the other hand dropped the fake rose into place, and Elyse twitched her fingers, making the proper changes of invisibility.

The trade was done.

Manny held the real rose in his hand, protected by the thin layer of handkerchief, as he raced off the dais.

"One-thirty!" Royce proclaimed.

Devil's taint, that was a relief. At least Jaime wouldn't end up on the hook for the gold.

She felt the weight of the rose as it slipped into her pocket, and then Manny's hand was back in her own, squeezing her assuredly.

"One-hundred-thirty million going once…"

Elyse worked to put the wards back into place, grateful it was easier than taking them down.

"One-hundred-thirty million going twice…"

The wards slammed closed, snapping each layer of protection precisely where it had been before.

"Sold to the merchant in black!"

Everyone applauded Royce and his new purchase, and Elyse exhaled. Her heart was slamming against her ribs so forcefully that she was certain everyone would hear it.

But they had done it. They had made the exchange and no one had seemed to notice.

Elyse nodded to Jaime, letting him know that the true rose was safely in her pocket, then she bit her lip, glancing at Royce. He would find out sooner or later that the rose he had just bought for a small fortune was not the real thing, but hopefully they would be long gone by then.

"Jaime," she said quietly, "can I use one of your checks to pay for the necklace?" She could feel the blood rising to her face, her head ringing with embarrassment. She'd acted impulsively, without a plan for how she would actually *buy* the necklace. "I promise I have the funds to pay you back." Jaime smiled and reached a hand into his breast pocket. He pulled out a slender piece of paper and handed it to Elyse. "I can't imagine another woman more suited for such a beautiful piece," he murmured. Now Elyse's cheeks heated for a different reason, and she swiftly looked away. That was not a door she wished to open.

"Mrs. Nottingfeld, if you would like to claim your necklace," called the auctioneer. He waved his hands, magicking away the wards that Elyse had just put back up, and invited her onto the dais.

"Of course," Elyse said, smiling as she went to claim her prize.

CHAPTER 35

— • —

ELYSE

The night air was much more crisp as Elyse and Manny exited the mansion, the salty breeze floating from the ocean congratulating them. Elyse no longer felt weighed down by the heavy layers of silk. Her gown now felt like a fitting choice, complementing her victorious spirit.

Jaime had left a few minutes earlier, promising to see them back at the inn shortly. She supposed she couldn't stay mad at him for attending the auction. After all, it was his bidding on the rose that had bought them crucial extra seconds. Regardless, she was glad for Manny's sole company as they made their way through the streets.

De Vesalis had come alive, well and truly. The streets were so crowded with revelers that Elyse and Manny had to weave through them. Once again, Elyse was grateful for the short walk as she kept one hand in her pocket, ensuring the safety of the rose.

"I wish we could stay here and celebrate," Manny said, bliss echoing through his voice. He smirked as he watched the tourists clamoring down the street.

Elyse couldn't have disagreed more. She hated crowds, especially ones full of drunk and reckless men. "The sooner we get out of the city, the better," she grunted.

"You're right," Manny ceded. "But a drink will still be in order when we get back."

Now that was something Elyse could get on board with. She fantasized about their celebration as they wound through the streets, imagining Killian giving her an especially appreciative look. Perhaps this would be the first step toward reconciliation. Maybe now he would be willing to listen to her.

They were only a few blocks from the inn when something shifted in the air. A shiver whispered down Elyse's spine, proclaiming a sinister presence.

"I believe you have something that doesn't belong to you," came a deep voice.

She whirled to see a tall man with dark hair and mismatched eyes. Ymaritis stood mere feet away, a sneer on his face.

"Did you think I wouldn't see?" he asked, his sneer turning to a taunting smile. He raised one hand and pointed to his silver eye. "I see everything." He gave Elyse a knowing look as he appraised her, his gaze seeming to penetrate her disguise.

Beside her, Manny tensed. Any lingering joy at their victory vanished as sweat gathered on Elyse's neck. They needed to get out of there—now. With one hand, she grasped Manny's wrist, and with the other she reached toward her pocket—the one that held a vial of transportation potion.

Ymaritis was quicker. He clenched his hand into a fist, and by the time Elyse's hand plunged into her pocket, there was nothing but broken glass and spilled liquid.

They wouldn't be getting away by magic.

She could feel Manny's eyes on her, waiting for her lead. Without taking her eyes off Ymaritis, she ordered, "Go back to the inn."

Manny's reply was firm. "I won't leave you."

Ymaritis continued to smile at them, violent energy radiating from him.

"Yes, you will," she commanded Manny. "You're a liability. I've got this."

She flicked her wrists and erected a massive shield, one that spanned nearly the width of the street. People all around her gasped, some even applauding, as if it were some party trick. But there was nothing playful about the vile look in Ymaritis's blue and silver eyes.

"Go!" she shouted.

From the corner of her vision, she saw Manny nod, and then dash away.

Hopefully she had made the right decision, keeping the eternal rose with her instead of sending it with Manny. But if she had given it to him, she would have put a target on his back. The best chance of keeping the rose safe lay with her.

"You don't want to do this." Elyse bent her knees and readied her hands, preparing for a fight. "Someone might get hurt."

Indeed, everyone on the street had stopped and was now staring at the two of them. A few people murmured, maybe even placing bets, but most were silent.

Ymaritis held out his hand before him and produced a shimmering dagger of light. "I'm counting on it," he growled, right before he pounced.

CHAPTER 36

—∙—

KILLIAN

K illian paced the small bedroom of the inn, his boots hammering on the wooden planks. The sun had set fully, casting no light through the lone window. He could hear the debauchery on the streets below, which only served to add to the noise crowding his mind.

Sera lay stretched across the bed, inspecting her nails. "Would you stop that already?" she asked, sounding aggravated.

Killian ignored her. Admittedly, he'd enjoyed parts of their outing, especially their walk back to the inn. It had been pleasant getting to know Sera better, something he ought to have done weeks ago. Yet as soon as they'd returned to the inn, his impatience had returned. Jaime wasn't in his room, which didn't bode well for anyone. On top of that, Sera's troubling words about their future haunted him. She'd had no words of comfort, instead conveying with a raw sense of dread that she knew nothing. The harrowing look in her eyes festered in his mind, growing into a demanding restlessness, which only worsened the longer he waited for Elyse and Manny.

"Working yourself into a frenzy won't do them any good," Sera uttered. She narrowed her violet eyes on him.

He was too worked up to care. Soon they would know if their plan had failed or succeeded, and he couldn't rest until he knew which one.

As a lieutenant, he had always been involved in missions. Lounging on the sidelines was a foreign feeling.

The door to the room swung open, breaking Killian's train of thought. He looked up, expecting to see Elyse or Manny. Instead, Jaime beamed at them.

"We did it," Jaime said, coolly running a hand through his hair.

Relief flooded Killian's ribcage, but it was suppressed by his anger. "We?" His brows furrowed as he took in Jaime's attire—the dark, lavish suit. "Did you go to the auction?"

Jaime opened his mouth to answer, but a commotion out in the hallway caught all of their attention. Killian shoved past him and into the corridor.

Manny, his appearance still altered, was sprinting up the stairs. "Killian!" he shouted. Sweat dripped from his dark hair and clung to his temple. His lanky body hurled him down the hallway. "We have to go," he ordered as he barreled into the bedroom. "Where are the potions?"

Sera leapt from the bed and rushed to him. Her hands roved against his chest, her wide eyes searching him for injury but finding none.

"Where's Elyse?" everyone asked at the same time.

"She's in trouble," Manny sputtered. "No time. Where are the potions?"

Killian snapped into lieutenant mode, his head clearing instantly, even as his lungs seemed to clear of air. He grasped his friend by the shoulder and forced him to meet his gaze.

"Manny, slow down. Where is she?"

"Someone followed us," he panted, his eyes crazed. "She's fighting him off, but we have to help her." He broke off and scanned the room. "Where are the *fucking potions?*"

Shit.

Shit.

Shit.

His stomach clenched as fear for Elyse shook him. Someone had followed them? Who? Judging by Manny's state of distress, it had to be someone bad—someone powerful. But Elyse wasn't just some two-bit witch. She was a gods-damned warrior. She would be all right.

"What potions?" Sera asked, her voice trembling slightly.

"The blue ones!" Manny said, waving his hands frantically.

It clicked, then, what Manny was trying to do. Killian reached into his pocket and pulled out a vial of transportation potion, then offered it to Manny.

"Take us to her."

Manny stared at the vial, all color draining from his face. "Me?"

Killian nodded. "It has to be you. You know where she is." He forced the vial into Manny's hand. "Just close your eyes and picture where she is, and then smash this bottle. I'll handle the rest."

Manny's chest was still rising and falling rapidly, but he nodded and clenched his fist around the vial. Killian tried not to dwell on the way his friend's knuckles turned white as he gripped the vial, or the terror that seized his own heart.

"Everyone hold on to Manny, and don't let go until I say so," he commanded.

Sera wrapped her arm around Manny's elbow while Killian gripped Manny's wrist. He met Jaime's eyes. Elyse's safety was the one thing they could agree on. Then two men exchanged a look of understanding, and Jaime clasped onto Manny's jacket, holding the fabric tight.

"Three, two, one," Killian counted down.

Manny thrust the vial at the floor, and they were gone.

CHAPTER 37

— • —

ELYSE

Screams erupted all around Elyse as tourists ran for cover. She was still safe behind her shield, but she hadn't been able to stop Ymaritis from hurting others. Three bodies lay dead in the street—three people Elyse had failed.

She'd tried to stop Ymaritis's attacks, but he was too fast. He rattled off hex after hex with ease, barely flicking his fingers. Elyse couldn't counter them all. She'd never seen anyone cast spells with precision and power that rivaled her own. Now utter panic took hold of her as she wondered if she'd met her match. She tried to shove down the fear, but the sweat soaking her dress and the roaring of her heart felt like a mockery.

Hysteria continued to rage around her. Most people had ducked into nearby taverns and inns, where Elyse prayed they would be safe. A few still fumbled around the streets, screaming for their friends and loved ones. Still others just gawked at Elyse and Ymaritis, either too drunk or too stupid to realize the danger they were in.

"Give me the rose or they will continue to die!" Ymaritis shouted from where he stood in the center of the street.

"I can't do that," Elyse snarled back, though it pained her. She was desperate for a way to keep the others safe, but giving him the rose would only wreak more havoc.

She lowered her shield for just long enough to send a stunning spell flying toward him, but he easily dissolved the white light. Her shield snapped back into place in time to block an incoming death hex.

Ymaritis wasn't pulling his punches. He grinned wildly as he sent out nothing but death hexes with no care for whom they hit. Elyse couldn't do the same. She would only use stunning spells as long as innocent people cowered around them.

"Then you leave me no choice," Ymaritis growled. His mismatched eyes were doom incarnate as he extended his left hand with sinister purpose.

A woman began to scream—louder and harsher than the other screams—and Elyse scoured the scattered crowd for the source.

Horror struck her, dark and unrelenting. The woman hovered just above the ground, terror on her face. She rose higher and higher, her shrill screams intensifying as she continued to rise.

Ymaritis watched with delight as he levitated the woman higher, her legs kicking frantically to no avail. She crested the rooftops, and Elyse's blood ran cold with dread. She knew what Ymaritis planned to do. He was going to drop her, and the woman would become nothing more than bloody pulps splattered on the street.

Elyse wouldn't let that happen—but she couldn't give him the rose. She shot from the ground, levitating herself up and over the buildings. She flew toward the woman, but Ymaritis kept going. Wind slapped her face as she climbed higher, clawing tears from her eyes. Below her stretched the deep blue expanse of the Staerion Sea and the vast buildings of De Vesalis, but she kept her sights trained on the woman.

The voices below began to fade as Elyse propelled herself higher, lured by the woman's screams. She soared toward her, fighting to close the space between them and suppressing the bile-infused fear that clotted her throat.

The woman's ascent slowed. Elyse could see how horribly pale she was, panic having drained her of all blood. She stopped rising altogether, hovering in the air for the briefest moment. It might have been beautiful, the way she floated in the air above a backdrop of ocean and stars, were it not for what came next.

The fabrics of her dress flew up around her, smothering her cries for help as she plummeted toward the ground. Elyse sped toward her, readying herself to grab the woman. She would have to lower her shield for a fraction of a second so she could take hold of her, and then they would be safe.

Elyse flicked her fingers, dropping her shield, and reached to grab the woman's waist. Just as she made contact, a white light pelted Elyse in her chest, knocking her backwards in the air. She hovered for just a moment, her hair flowing around her, the world seeming to stop altogether.

And then she was falling.

Numbness encapsulated her. She couldn't even feel the rush of air that assaulted her as she descended with harrowing speed. She could feel nothing except visceral, aching dread.

Ymaritis had hit her with a stunning spell. He'd timed it perfectly, waiting for the precise moment her shield would be down. It had knocked the wind from her, evacuating her lungs with the force of a thunderbolt. And now she was frozen, her limbs unable to move, her head reeling.

The wind in her ears was deafening as she toppled toward the ground. She was somersaulting, her legs tangling and untangling in the silk of her dress. She caught glimpses of the stars, the sea, the lights of De Vesalis. The rooftops grew closer with terrifying speed.

Move, dammit! she demanded of her fingers. They felt stiff and icy cold, unresponsive to any of her commands. Her blood was rushing to and from her head with such dizzying speed that she could hardly think, but she refused to die. Not with Sera and Manny and Jaime counting on her.

Not without one last apology to Killian.

Move! she cried at her fingers. She was nearly level with the rooftops now. She could see Killian's face in her mind, a blur of all the wonderful and terrible moments they'd shared together.

The surprise on his face the first time he produced a shield.

The pain in his eyes as he arrested her.

The tremble of his lips as he told her he was falling in love with her.

Move! she bellowed internally, tears clouding her eyes.

The woman's screams stopped abruptly. Elyse refused to acknowledge what that meant.

MOVE! she roared. And finally, her fingers listened.

The tiniest twitch was all she needed to slow her descent, and she prayed that it would be enough before—

WHAM.

Her knees hit the dirt first. She splayed out, face down on the street, every muscle and bone howling in agony. Her head crashed into the ground, blinding her with pain. She lay there, unable to move. Her body still refused to heed her commands, though she didn't know if that was from the pain or the stunning spell.

She was barely aware of anything except the hard dirt beneath her and the faint reverberation of footsteps coming toward her. They echoed through her whole body, a formidable symphony.

Far in the distance, someone might have been screaming her name.

"Thank you for this," a cold voice purred in her ear.

Ymaritis reached into her pocket and pulled out the rose, still wrapped in the handkerchief. She tried to fight him off, but all she could muster was a feeble jerk of her leg.

She heard him laugh before he disappeared, not a wisp of blue smoke to be seen.

"Elyse!"

Someone was pleading her name, and then strong hands were on her. Callused, umber hands. Killian's hands.

"I've got you," he said, and the darkness embraced her.

CHAPTER 38

— • —

KILLIAN

E lyse had been asleep for hours.

Killian sat by the side of her bed in the country estate, waiting for her to awake. Sera had done her best to heal Elyse, despite Jaime's frantic pestering. She'd eventually sent him on a fool's errand just to get rid of him. With Sera's blessing, Killian cleaned the scrapes on Elyse's knees and head. Sera tried to mend her other injuries, but she admitted she had little talent in the area. Between the two of them, they'd diagnosed her with several broken ribs, a dislocated shoulder, and a fractured knee. That was only what they could see and feel. She likely had a head injury as well, and maybe internal bleeding.

Sera had said the best thing they could do was give her something for the pain and let her rest, that Elyse would be able to properly heal herself when she awoke. If she awoke.

Her breathing was steady, a rhythmic reminder that she was still fighting. Every now and then, she would murmur in her sleep.

"He took it... He took it."

The man—Ymaritis—had stolen the rose. They'd been too late. They had failed her.

Killian dropped his face into his hands and rested his elbows on the mattress. It was bad enough that Elyse was hurt. But they had also lost the rose. If Ymaritis was the one trying to summon the demon, which seemed likely given the carnage he'd reaped on De Vesalis, then they were fucked—especially if Elyse wasn't able to help them.

He'd only caught a glimpse of Ymaritis, a lanky man with tan skin and dark hair. They'd arrived just in time to see him standing over Elyse, rose in hand—and then he'd just disappeared. There had been no vial, no blue smoke. He was there, and then he wasn't.

Killian knew enough about magic now to know that simply vanishing wasn't normal. If Ymaritis could do that, if he could leave Elyse in this condition, what couldn't he do? Summer solstice was in two days, and Killian felt completely, hopelessly adrift.

Footsteps padded down the hallway, and Manny appeared in the open doorway. The potion had worn off, his appearance returned to normal. "Still sleeping?" he asked.

Killian merely nodded.

Manny stepped into the bedroom and sank into one of the chairs. His eyes were red-rimmed, and he rubbed his face as he looked at Elyse with a mixture of compassion and regret. "I think she's sleeping for all of us."

For the last few hours, they'd mulled around the country house, talking in quiet voices about what their next move would be, and taking turns checking on Elyse. Killian had barely left her side, which had irritated Jaime to no end. He'd glared at Killian from across the bed until Sera demanded that he retire to his bedroom.

Manny was right though. No one was getting any sleep.

All Killian could do was stare at Elyse, at her pale face and silvery hair. She might have died last night. She might have died, and he never would have heard her side of the story.

"What if she's not the villain I made her out to be?" he uttered, his voice raw.

Manny sighed, low and heavy. His broad shoulders sagged, as he lifted his gaze. "You had every right to be angry with her, brother. You trusted her and she shattered that."

Killian met his friend's eyes and saw the same tangled emotions he felt reflected there.

"What do you think?" he asked.

Manny shook his head. "I think that Sera seems naive sometimes, but she's not. She's a good judge of character." He looked at Elyse, his brows furrowing. "There must be something."

Killian was determined to find out what that something was, but he needed Elyse to get better first. He needed her for so many reasons.

"You should get some rest," Manny suggested.

Killian scoffed. "There's no way I'm sleeping."

"Go outside then. Get some fresh air."

The sun was cresting, its rays illuminating the lake that shimmered down the hill from Elyse's bedroom window.

"Go," Manny encouraged. "Clear your head."

Killian glanced at Elyse. Her chest rose and fell steadily beneath the covers, just as it had for the whole night.

It might do him some good to get some fresh air, as Manny suggested. His joints creaked as he stood from the chair and strode to the doorway, pausing to look at Elyse again, the peaceful expression on her face.

"Go," Manny urged.

Killian obliged his oldest friend. He meandered outside and found himself a spot on the hill where he could look out over the lake. Its surface was calm, the blue waters sharpening into a fiery yellow where the sun's reflection shone. It was beautiful, yet oddly artificial. He had once seen a mural painted on the side of a building in Sevhella. The artist had used perspective and tremendous detail to create the illusion of a passageway. The bricks of the building had disappeared completely, instead becoming the branches of trees, the petals of wildflowers, and a winding dirt path. Passersby had stopped to gawk, some of them even pausing to touch the mural, as if in disbelief. As if hoping to step through the wall and into the fairy-tale forest that seemed to bloom before them. But of course, it was nothing more than painted brick.

That was how Killian felt as he stared at the lake: like its beauty was nothing more than a trick of the eyes. Like it was out of his grasp, no matter how much he yearned for its serenity.

He remembered being so angry the first time he'd come to the estate. The decadent rooms and manicured lawn had been fodder for his fury. To him, Elyse was living in luxurious disregard for the rest of the world. To him, she had somehow upgraded her life, leaving him alone to bear the weight of his actions.

There had been so many clues to her despair, and yet he had chosen to ignore them. If this life and this estate were such grandiose "upgrades," then why would she have chosen to give it all up by turning herself in? Why would she give a damn about Prestowne? And why would she have ever let Jaime become such a territorial bastard?

He had known, and he had denied it. Because it was easier for him to justify it all in his mind, painting her as a wicked witch instead of exactly what she was—what he'd always known she was. A human woman, broken and fighting.

Out of habit, he took his map from where it always stayed in his pocket. He unfolded the parchment and watched the blues, greens, and ambers sparkle across Rhodan. His eyes drifted to Sevhella first, as they always did, before gazing at the rest of the kingdom. The jewel tones shimmered from the Asterial Mountains in the west to the Staerion Sea in the south.

One of these dots is Ymaritis, he thought with a bitterness.

It was a shame they couldn't pinpoint which one. If anyone could do it, it was Elyse. She had done so many incredible things, like growing Nina's teeth back or giving Corin that compass. If only they had a compass, or even a map, that pointed them to the eternal rose. If only...

He leaned back, resting his elbows in the dew-soaked grass as an idea bombarded him. He'd only just begun to piece his thoughts together when a shout interrupted him.

"Killian!"

Manny's voice echoed down the hill. Killian turned to see Manny waving at him from the doorway of the cottage, beckoning him back inside.

"She's awake!" he called down.

Killian grinned. Elyse was awake, and right in time to hear his plan.

CHAPTER 39

— · —

ELYSE

Sera, Manny, and Jaime all stood in Elyse's bedroom, staring at her. She wanted to tell them that she was fine and insist that they stop giving her pitying looks—especially Jaime. He hovered by her side, fluffing her pillows and forcing water in her face, making her feel like an invalid.

The truth was she felt like hell. Every joint seemed to have been torn apart and crammed back together, and the little bit of sunlight trickling in through the window made her head pound. Worse than all of that, though, was the realization that she had failed.

Her memory was blurry, but she recalled enough. She remembered how Ymaritis had reveled in the havoc he reaped. She remembered the woman's screams as she plummeted to her death. And she remembered Ymaritis stealing the rose from her pocket as she lay there, helpless.

She had always known that there was someone out there, stronger and more powerful than her, but she had never imagined she would face that person with such dire consequences.

Killian finally hurried into the room, his eyes darting straight to Elyse. They were stunning, his amber irises glimmering as his warrior frame crowded the doorway. His clothes—the same clothes he'd worn the day before—were wrinkled and blood stained. Her blood, likely. Had he helped care for her? Had he been too distraught to change his clothes? The thought made her heart swell painfully against her ribs.

She remembered him calling her name as she lay in the street, waiting for death to take her. His callused hands had lifted her from the ground and held her in a safe yet gentle embrace. Was it so hard to think that he actually might have been worried for her?

Killian smiled, but only for an instant as concern overtook his expression. "How do you feel?"

Elyse leveled a gaze on him that said, "Did you really just ask me that?"

"I'm sorry," Sera said, smiling weakly. "I tried my best."

Elyse tried moving her hand to wave away Sera's apology, but a sharp pain in her wrist changed her mind. "I'm sure I'd be hurting a lot more if it weren't for you," she decided to stay instead.

"I'm glad you're awake," Killian said, staring directly at Elyse with an intensity that made her cheeks heat. It was nothing like the fervor he'd shown two nights ago in Privya's kitchen, all simmering hatred mingled with lust. He looked... Well, he looked incongruously happy given the circumstances. "I have an idea to run by you," he announced as he stepped toward the bed.

The room filled with hope and skepticism as all eyes eagerly turned to Killian, everyone awaiting his next words.

"So we know that Ymaritis has the rose, and that he's most likely the one going to conduct the ritual at sundown tomorrow," Killian posited. "And we know that the ritual requires both the rose and angel's blood. Exactly how rare is angel's blood?"

Jaime shrugged while Sera deferred to Elyse.

"It's pretty rare," Elyse said, wondering what he was implying.

"Do you know how we can acquire some?" he asked.

Elyse nodded, grimacing at the pain. "I do, but it's a bit of a hike."

Killian's face lit up, his hope seeming to flourish. "So if we acquired some angel's blood, would you be able to make us a compass, like you did for Corin? Or better yet—a map?"

Elyse's own face now mirrored Killian's excitement as she realized his plan. Before she could speak, though, Manny cut in.

"Wait, what compass? What's all this?"

Killian turned to his friend, something like pride in his expression. "Remember Corin, from Privya's clinic? She left to go find more hot springs like the one in the caves by the clinic so they can heal people all across the kingdom." He flashed a quick grin at Elyse. "Elyse took a sample of the spring water and bottled it up, then made a magic compass that would point them in the direction of the nearest source of that water."

"That's bloody brilliant," Manny uttered.

"So you're saying," Sera began, a tinge of aspiration in her voice, "that if we get a sample of angel's blood, Elyse can make a compass that points toward other vials? And help us find Ymaritis?"

"Yes—well, no," Killian corrected quickly.

He pulled a piece of parchment from his pocket and unfolded it. The edges were softened and worn, as if it had been folded and unfolded many times. Elyse sat up straighter, trying to get a better look at the bright colors scattered across the paper.

Killian continued eagerly. "I have this map, and it shows all uses of magic across the kingdom, with different colors for different intensities. So I was thinking," he paused, looking wishfully toward Elyse, "that you could use a similar magic to help pinpoint where the other angel's blood might be."

Elyse considered his idea. She could make a compass no problem. A map would be slightly more difficult, but the essential spell work was the same. "I think I can do it," she said, beaming at him.

"Of course you can," Killian said, as if he'd never doubted her.

"Who do you know that sells angel blood?" Jaime asked. He sounded skeptical as he stepped an inch closer to Elyse's bed.

"It's a long story," Elyse sighed. "His name is Zubir. He's... a bit of a loner."

Calling Zubir a loner was a bit like calling a shark a fish. It was technically correct, but didn't truly encompass the severity of the creature. Still, she didn't feel like divulging all of Zubir's oddities—especially when she'd been sworn to keep a particular one secret.

"A loner like you?" Killian asked.

Elyse made a noise somewhere between a laugh and a scoff. "Devil's horns, no. His property is surrounded by wards, and you can't use any magic there at all."

"Your shoppe was surrounded by wards," Sera pointed out, "as are many homes."

"Yes," Elyse agreed. "My wards extended about a hundred yards from the shoppe. The quickest way through his wards is a five mile hike."

Manny let out a low whistle. "Sounds like a right loon."

"He's definitely odd. But he owes me a favor, so he'll help us out," Elyse explained as succinctly as she could.

"Great." Killian was grinning at her again, his excitement contagious. "Now what do you need to get better?"

"Nothing—I'm fine now." Elyse tried to hide her agony as she made to pull her covers off. She didn't want to waste a second lying around, not when the summer solstice was only a day away.

Killian raised a hand, stopping her movement. "No. If we're going to have any chance at defeating Ymaritis, we need you at full strength—or close to it," he said, using his lieutenant's voice. "So tell us, what do you need?"

His gaze was unrelenting, so Elyse glanced toward Sera for support.

"Don't look at me!" Sera laughed. "I agree with him."

Elyse looked toward Jaime, who nodded his agreement as well.

"Fine," she sighed. "A few potions and a couple hours of rest ought to do it. But—" She held up her finger and immediately regretted it, stifling a grunt. "Only if you agree to get some rest as well. You all look like hell."

Manny grinned. "I won't argue with you on that."

"Three hours then—will that be enough?" Killian asked. Not harsh, just sincere.

Elyse nodded, then looked toward Jaime. "I think you should have most of the ingredients I need here."

"Sure, I'll get you whatever you need," Jaime answered. He paused, then looked around the room. "Actually, I'd like to have a word with you—privately."

"Okay," Elyse said tentatively, noticing the look exchanged between Killian and Manny.

Everyone else filed out of the room, wishing Elyse to feel better soon, and leaving Jaime standing alone by her bedside. He settled onto the mattress and stared intently at her, as if he couldn't believe she was really there. His overly sympathetic gaze made her uncomfortable, and she shifted on the bed.

"I'm just so glad you're okay," he breathed.

A lump formed in Elyse's throat, preventing her from replying. She was, of course, glad to be okay as well, but not without a certain amount of guilt. The woman's screams replayed over and over in her mind, and though she hadn't seen her hit the ground, she knew without a doubt that she had not survived.

Jaime didn't seem to need a response from her though. He shook his head, his blond hair falling into his eyes. "I should have walked you back to the inn. I'll never forgive myself. I—" His voice wavered, and he reached for her hand. "It was all I could do to pick you up and get you back to safety."

Elyse tensed, straining her sore muscles. "You carried me?" Everything that happened after she hit the ground was hazy, but it had been tan hands that had embraced her—Killian's hands.

Jaime tilted his head, his blue eyes blinking in an almost condescending manner. "You don't remember? You did hit your head rather hard." He reached out and tapped her forehead with his finger.

Elyse narrowed her eyes, trying to see past the haziness of the memory. Then a river of sadness seemed to burst past, mixing with her confusion. Had she really imagined it? Had she been so desperate to see him that she had muddled reality and desire? The pounding in her head intensified.

Jaime tucked a strand of hair behind her ear. "We'll stop Ymaritis, and then when this is all over, I'll take care of you," he continued. "I'll live here with you, and we can build a life together."

Elyse's lips parted slightly, but no words came to her. What was he talking about? When this was all over, she was going to turn herself in to the Royal Guard—to face execution. Even if she did somehow escape the blood oath, living here with Jaime wasn't exactly her first choice.

Killian's face flashed in her mind, replaying the way he had smiled at her when he first entered the room. Something had shifted between them. She'd thought she was imagining it, but then he had seemed so proud of her, speaking about her with so much enthusiasm, and it had stirred something within her. She didn't want to let go of that feeling.

For a moment, she let herself imagine a future with Killian. One where he forgave her, and where they fought the blood oath together. She pictured them walking hand-in-hand through the forest—Elyse barefoot and Killian in his polished boots. She pictured them training together, reading together, shopping together. She dreamed of them making love to one another, with all the intensity of their last tryst, but none of the hatred.

But even as she imagined it, something churned in her core, as if the magic of their pact was fighting her, telling her it was forbidden.

"You don't need to say anything now," Jaime assured her. "Just think about it."

"Okay," Elyse replied, eager to end the conversation. Guilt ate at her. She had needed Jaime. She still did. Yet it seemed like she couldn't repay his generosity—not in the way he wanted.

"Can you help me with the potions?" she asked, eager for the change of subject.

Jaime's gaze lingered on her for a moment longer, that charming smile flashing across his face. "Of course. Whatever you need."

CHAPTER 40

— ❖ —

KILLIAN

Killian only managed to sleep for two hours before he awoke, his mind whirling. He stretched his aching muscles, sore from cramping himself onto a settee, and rubbed his hands over his tired eyes and down his stubbled jaw.

They had a plan—get a vial of angel's blood, connect it to a map, find Ymaritis, and stop him before he could resurrect the demon. But there were so many variables. What if this person, Zubir, didn't have any angel's blood? What if the map showed forty different places across the kingdom, all little specks that could potentially be Ymaritis? They knew he had several residences in the Asterial Mountains, but he could be anywhere.

And the biggest question of all—how were they going to stop him? Elyse was by far the most powerful and cunning sorceress he'd ever met. He'd seen her take on five men at once and barely break a sweat. She'd cut off her own damn hand and magicked it back on to evade arrest. And yet, Ymaritis had been able to crush her in a matter of minutes.

He wanted to ask her about it. In the Guard, he'd conducted countless debriefings, all in the hope of finding ways to better understand their opponents, to run his unit more effectively. He wanted to do the same with Elyse so they could formulate a plan of attack. But he also wanted to give her a chance to face what had happened. There'd been a despondence in her eyes, one that went beyond her physical pain. He knew that look—he had seen it in the mirror many times over the past few months.

More than anything, though, he wanted to ask her about King Cyril. He wanted to break down the final barrier between them—for good, if possible. But he knew it wasn't the right moment. They had more important things to focus on.

He paced the sitting room where he had found Elyse two mornings ago, all of these thoughts bombarding him at once. He wished he could manipulate time, moving it ahead to when Elyse was feeling better and all their worries were at bay. Or perhaps he would turn time backwards, to find a way to protect Elyse and the rose.

But he couldn't do any of that. All he could do was wait and pace and think, none of which was helping him.

His fingers slipped into his pocket, twiddling the small blue vial there. There was one person who always helped put his mind at ease. Someone whom he had neglected lately.

He made up his mind and left silently through the front door. It was a quick walk past the wards, and then the blue smoke carried him off to the alleyway behind his mother's house.

It had only been a few days since he'd been home, yet it felt like years. He was exhausted, and he felt older but no wiser. Somehow it was sunnier there, as if this place was immune to all the evil Killian was wrapped up in. He could hear children playing out in the street, their laughter a reminder of what was at stake.

He opened the back door to his home and cocked his head at what he heard. His mother's laughter, boisterous and sincere, reverberated through the house. He took a step inside, glanced around the kitchen, and froze.

There, sitting beside his mother at the kitchen table, was Siamus.

He hardly recognized the leader of the mercenaries, who leaned an elbow on the table, presenting himself as a familiar house guest. His face, though, was inharmonious with the laughter lingering in the air. An eyepatch covered his left eye, and the surrounding skin was bruised a heinous purple, from the corners of his brow to the edge of his rough beard.

"Oh, Killian!" Mrs. Southwick crooned when she saw her son. She rose and immediately shuffled over to him, her apron swishing with her hips. Standing on her tiptoes, she planted a kiss on his cheek.

Killian didn't move. His eyes were still glued on Siamus, who gave him a sly grin and a casual wave.

"What are you doing here?" Killian growled, his voice low. He stepped in front of his mother, but she pushed him aside.

"Killian, is that any way to treat a guest?" she demanded, hands on her hips. "He came by to ask you why you weren't interested in the job anymore, and to see if he could make you a better offer." She shot him a look that said, "Be on your best behavior."

Darkness seemed to slither around Siamus, or maybe it was Killian's lack of sleep. "Yes," the mercenary affirmed. "I came to see you, but your lovely mother said you weren't home. She offered me a cup of tea and we have been chatting ever since." He lifted his porcelain mug and beamed at Mrs. Southwick. "I couldn't refuse such a kind woman." His voice was polite, disgustingly so—not gruff like the last time they'd met.

A protectiveness rooted itself in Killian's core, growing like ivy, clawing through his ribs. "Get out of my house," he snarled.

"Killian!" Mrs. Southwick cried.

But Siamus merely lifted his hands, palms forward, in a display of surrender. "If that is what you wish, I will be on my way." He sat up a little straighter, then added, "I just want to know why you turned me down."

"Change of heart," Killian grumbled, still staring Siamus down.

"That simple?"

"That simple."

"I see," Siamus said, standing and twisting the hairs of his beard. "I'll be holding on to your *application* in case you change your mind again."

He stressed the word "application," and Killian understood what he meant. He'd be keeping the money he already gave him.

"Fine," Killian groused. He supposed now that he and Elyse were on better terms, he'd have to explain the missing coin to her. That didn't matter right now, though. All that mattered was getting Siamus away from his mother.

To Killian's surprise, Siamus took a step toward him and extended his scarred hand. Up close, the bruising around his eyepatch was even more sickly, the skin swollen. Siamus didn't seem affected by it as he stood with his broad shoulders back, an air of swagger around him. "No hard feelings," he said.

Killian hesitated, but extended his hand in return. Siamus clasped it, shaking firmly, then pulled Killian in closer.

Killian's left hand flew to the dagger at his hip, but all Siamus did was clap him on the back of the shoulder before turning and striding toward the door.

"Take care now," he called, leaving Killian reeling.

Siamus shut the door behind him, and Killian immediately crossed the room to look out the window.

"Killian—what on earth?" Mrs. Southwick began, but he shushed her as he watched Siamus stroll to the end of the street.

Once he was out of sight, Killian whirled to his mother.

"That man is very dangerous," he explained, his voice firm. He fished in his pocket and dug out a vial of blue liquid. "If you ever see him again, no matter where you are or what you are doing—" He shoved the vial into her hand. "—I want you to throw this vial on the ground and picture yourself outside the palace gates. Demand for Manny—demand for the king if you have to—but do not leave the palace until I come for you."

Mrs. Southwick glanced between the vial and her son's face, her eyes wide. There was no fear in her eyes, only stunned confusion. As the wife of a prominent captain of the Royal Guard, she'd faced countless threats. It had been a sort of normalcy throughout Killian's childhood, knowing that there were criminals who wanted revenge on Captain Southwick.

She didn't argue with Killian's assessment of Siamus. Instead, she peered down at the little blue vial. "What? I don't—"

"It's a transportation potion, Mum. It'll get you someplace safe," he explained, a bit calmer. "Just promise me."

She looked closer at the vial, her brows furrowed, but she nodded her head. "I promise."

Killian let out a sigh of relief as those vines seemed to slacken their hold on his chest.

"What is all this about?" she asked, one hand on her hip. "Is this why you've been gone so much?"

Killian sighed again and moved to sit at the kitchen table. His mother followed him, bracing her hand on her thigh as she sank into the chair beside him—one of the subtle signs that she was growing older, along with the strands of gray that threaded her black curls.

He fiddled with the tea cup that still lingered on the table before pushing it aside. "I hired that man to help me track down Elyse, but then..." He trailed off, unsure of how to continue.

His mother's gaze was full of understanding. "But then you had a change of heart," she said, far too knowingly.

Killian nodded. He ran a hand through his hair and settled deeper into the chair as an aching exhaustion overtook him.

Mrs. Southwick's voice was much softer as she said, "I'll put on a fresh kettle."

"I don't have much time," Killian began to protest, but his mother held up a hand.

"You always have time for a cup of tea with your mother." Without another word, she filled the kettle and hung it on the hearth.

Killian didn't speak as he waited for the water to boil. His heart was still racing from the encounter with Siamus. Something about seeing that man in his own home, chumming it up with his mother, had deeply unsettled him. Why had Siamus made a special trip just to talk to him? Was their business really so important to him? Or was there more to the meeting than he realized?

The sharp whistle of the kettle interrupted his thoughts. As his mother poured the boiling water, the scent of lemon and sacred basil wafted toward him, instantly calming him. He didn't know if it was the effects of the herbs or a sort of nostalgia from so many nights sitting at that very table and drinking that very tea, that steadied his heart.

Mrs. Southwick set the two cups on the table. She rested her chin on her fisted hand and gave Killian an encouraging look. "Now, tell me what's on your mind."

Killian's shoulders fell as he absentmindedly stirred his tea. Where to even begin?

"I found Elyse," he said quietly, bracing for his mother's reaction.

To his surprise, she merely nodded. "I suspected as much."

He blinked. "Oh, did you now?" he asked, a hint of jest in his voice.

His mother's reply was simple yet cryptic: "Bonded souls have a way of finding each other."

Killian cocked his head. *Bonded souls?* What sort of bullshit was that?

At the look on his face, her smile widened. "I just mean that... When two people have been through a lot together, the universe has a way of bringing them together."

Killian stared at his tea, considering his mother's words. It sounded ridiculous. The universe hadn't forced their paths to cross—their connections and Killian's hard work had.

Yet he couldn't shake the feeling that something larger was playing out.

"So, are you going to turn her in?" Mrs. Southwick asked. There was no judgment in her voice, only a sort of prodding, as if she were walking him through the situation yet allowing him to make his own conclusion.

"I don't have a choice," Killian uttered. He quickly explained everything that had happened—about Prestowne, the blood oath, Ymaritis. As his mother listened, sorrow grew on her face, crinkling the faint crow's feet that surrounded her dark eyes.

"Oh, honey," she sighed when he finished. The pain in her features only affirmed his own agony.

"What am I going to do, Mum?" he asked, his voice cracking.

He wished he was still a young boy, that his mum could tell him everything would be all right, and he would believe her. Looking at his mother's saddened expression, he knew she felt the same way.

"Well, hon," she breathed, "if Elyse made her decision, you might have to let her face that."

At her words, a darkness entered his heart, eclipsing its light. He knew some part of his mother's sentiment was correct. Elyse had made up her mind, and when she was set on something, she didn't let anyone get in her way. She was adamant that she needed to make things right. But to die for it? This couldn't actually be what she wanted, was it? It wasn't like Elyse to give up so easily.

But he couldn't sit back and let the blood oath win. Letting Elyse turn herself in—that wasn't an option.

"I don't know that I can do that," Killian rasped, shaking his head and looking away. He still didn't know Elyse's story, and it would have to be a damn good explanation. Yet deep in his chest, in every muscle and bone, he knew that she didn't deserve to die.

"I know you can't," his mother said, smiling weakly. "So you'll have to find a way to break this oath."

Killian nodded as his thoughts traveled. He hadn't looked into breaking the oath. Until yesterday, he'd been more concerned with ensuring Elyse had no way of worming out of it. But if anyone could find a way, it was her.

"If I've learned anything from raising you for nine and twenty years," Mrs. Southwick said, beaming, "it's that you, Killian, can do anything."

"I think you overestimate me, Mum," he said, though a smile tugged at his lips.

"I think you underestimate yourself," she chided. "You were the youngest lieutenant in the history of the Guard. You solved the king's murder. And," she said, cupping his cheek in her hands, "you have grown so much. You inspire me with your strength."

Killian's heart lifted ever so slightly as he leaned into her warm touch. Maybe he was still a boy, yearning for his mother to tell him everything would be okay. And for a moment, he believed it would.

"Thanks, Mum." He leaned over and kissed her on the cheek. "I have to go. I'll be gone for a day or two. I just need to grab one thing from my room."

Mrs. Southwick smiled, but there was undeniable worry in her eyes. Killian pulled her into a tight hug and closed his eyes, allowing himself to breathe in her scent.

"I love you, Mum," he said, squeezing a little tighter.

"I love you too, Killy Bean."

Killy Bean. He smiled at the nickname that she hadn't used for years, not since before he'd joined the Guard.

Everything would be all right—he just had to believe it.

CHAPTER 41

— ◦ —

ELYSE

O ne moment, Elyse and the others stood hand-in-hand on the lawn of Jaime's country estate. The next moment, Elyse closed her eyes and let the blue smoke whisk her away. Before she opened her eyes, she could smell the salt in the air and feel the wind whipping at her back.

Sera was the first to gasp.

The group stood on a dock surrounded by water. The dock was small, so they crowded together to keep from falling into the sea. But it wasn't the vast waters that caused them all to gape at their surroundings.

At the end of the dock was a massive iron door built into the side of a towering cliff. The door was a menacing dark gray, heat radiating from it as it absorbed the sunlight that poured down on them. Scrawling designs were etched into its face, adding to its formidability. The cliffs formed a dominating wall of sienna spotted with mossy greens, a fortress in the middle of the sea. Beyond the dock was nothing but water that reached, unrelenting, to the distant horizon.

"What is this place?" Manny breathed.

Each of them craned their necks toward the crest of the cliff. Elyse could hardly make out the tops of the trees high above them.

"It's an island," Elyse answered as the waves crashed against the rocks. Despite the sun beating down on her, a chill snaked up her spine. "The only way to enter is through that door." She lifted a finger toward the iron monstrosity before them.

Killian stepped forward and tugged at the door's ornate handle. It didn't budge.

"It's locked," he said, turning back to the group.

Elyse snorted. "Well, what did you expect? That the eccentric hermit with a door built into the side of a cliff would just leave it open?"

All eyes turned toward her as she pulled a knife from the belt at her waist and sauntered toward the door. Ceremoniously, she sliced the knife across her palm and pressed her bloody hand to the warm metal. She couldn't see her friends, but she could imagine their eyes widening as a shimmer of light blazed across the door.

"Is this some sort of blood sacrifice?" Manny asked, sounding hesitant as Elyse pivoted toward them.

Jaime scoffed, though his eyes were still glued to the door, just like the others.

"Not exactly," Elyse said as she handed the knife to Manny. "Go on," she urged, a bit of challenge in her tone. "It's the only way to get through." She stepped back and used her uninjured hand to heal the cut across her palm as she waited for him to act.

Manny glanced between the knife and Sera, who gave him an encouraging nod.

Just as Elyse had, Manny stepped to the door and sliced his palm open. He laid his hand flat on the door, which replied with a shimmer of light.

Killian took a step toward the door, as if entranced. "What is all this?" he asked, his brows furrowed.

"This," Elyse said, jerking her chin toward the door, "is what I designed for Zubir. The door is bewitched. It uses your blood to read your intentions. If you plan to harm Zubir in any way, then you cannot enter."

Killian stared down at Elyse as the sun glowed behind him, casting a halo around his face. "You did this?" he asked, a hint of amazement in his voice.

Elyse shrugged, though Killian's fervent gaze made her heart stutter. "It's nothing."

"Give me your hand, Manny," Sera called. Still looking a bit bewildered, Manny maneuvered across the small dock toward Sera, who began healing his hand.

Killian took the knife from Manny and strode confidently toward the door. One by one, they sliced their hands and pressed them to the door, marveling at its glimmering magic. When everyone's hands were healed, they gathered in front of the door, waiting as Elyse reached for the handle.

It opened like the maw of a great beast, revealing nothing but darkness. Even the waves around them seemed to cease their crashing as they all stared into the void.

"This looks..." Manny began.

"Foreboding?" Killian finished for him.

Elyse suppressed her own anxieties, as she knew they were all looking to her for assurance. She'd walked this passage before. It was harmless. But the way the tunnel seemed to swallow the sunlight was, indeed, foreboding.

"Where exactly does this go?" Sera asked.

Elyse's eyes traveled to the top of the cliff.

"Isn't it obvious?" Jaime drawled. "Up."

He was right. On the other side of the door was a daunting staircase.

"See that?" Elyse asked, taking a step back and pointing to the side of the cliff.

Everyone joined her in lifting their gazes, shading their eyes from the sun as they peered up at the cliff. A staircase carved into the rocks switchbacked its way to the very top of the cliff.

"There are stairs in the tunnel," Elyse explained. "It's about ten flights before the tunnel opens up, and the rest of the hike is outside."

Her already sore body screamed at her in protest, knowing the pain that was about to follow as she trudged up the countless stairs. She shoved that nagging down; she couldn't afford any weakness.

"Well," Killian said decidedly, "let's get on with it."

And he stepped into the void.

Elyse followed behind him, Jaime at her heels.

The tunnel was stifling, the rocks trapping the humid air. They grasped at the walls to guide themselves, until they finally reached the stairs. Sweat formed on Elyse's brow, on her back, her thighs, between her breasts. It might have been distressing if she weren't more concerned with her footing.

No one spoke, but the staircase echoed with their panting breaths. Elyse couldn't reach the open air soon enough.

Every step she took, all she thought of was getting that damned angel's blood. It was her only chance at redemption. It was the only way to make things right—for the people she had let down in De Vesalis. For the woman that had fallen to her death, all because Elyse had been bested.

Her friends had at least halted their pitying looks, no longer treating her as an invalid. She wondered how much they had seen before rescuing her. Had they spotted the bodies in the street? Had they seen Ymaritis's speed and power? Did any of them *truly* know what they were facing?

Finally, after what felt like hours, the staircase opened up, and sunshine replaced the rocky ceiling of the tunnel. The group let out a collective breath, followed by a deep inhale of fresh air.

They still had a long way to go. Elyse tied her hair up to keep it off her neck. Ahead of her, the sweat seeped through Killian's shirt. It clung to his back, accentuating his muscles. Just two nights ago, Elyse had raked her nails down that back. She wondered if she left scratches.

No—she couldn't think about that. It had been wrong to be with Killian. It was certainly what he had wanted in that moment, but she knew it had been a masochistic decision—for both of them. She should have been strong enough to deny him, to walk away before he made such a regrettable choice, but she had been selfish. Their anger with one another had been underscored with such passion, made sharper by the words hissed at one another, and the words still unspoken. She had given in to it, and now she couldn't help but worry that she was only hurting him more.

She tore her eyes away from Killian's powerful back to check on the rest of the group, and nearly jumped when she saw how close Jaime was to her. He smiled up at her earnestly.

Ignoring Jaime, Elyse called down to Sera and Manny. "It's just a bit farther!"

Manny used the back of his hand to wipe sweat from his forehead while Sera paused to remove her jacket and tie it around her waist.

"I know back at Jaime's, you said it would be a hike," Sera called back, "but you didn't say anything about stairs."

Elyse smirked. "Aren't you glad I talked you into borrowing a pair of my boots?"

Sera had almost worn a pair of what she called "sensible heels" until Elyse badgered her into choosing something more reasonable. She wondered how long it would be until Sera caved and tied up her long, dark hair.

They continued up the stairs, the wind beating them relentlessly. It was little relief; more of a nuisance that kept blowing Elyse's hair in her mouth and eyes. Still, she didn't complain. She would walk a thousand flights of stairs if it led her to the angel's blood.

After nearly an hour, the stairs finally ended, and they crested the top of the cliff. Everyone stopped, doubling over and panting.

"Sera," Manny said between heaving breaths. "When we get back... to Sevhella... you're moving." He stood up straight, his hands knotted behind his neck. "I never want to climb another flight of stairs."

"Seconded," Sera wheezed as she flopped onto the ground. She didn't even seem to care about the reddish clay dirt that caked her bare arms.

Elyse straightened up. "Let's go."

Manny gave her a death glare while Sera silently pleaded with her eyes.

"Elyse," Killian said, stretching his back. "One minute won't kill us."

But it might. It might just kill Elyse. Every moment that they didn't have the angel's blood in their possession, she felt like she was going mad. Once they had the angel's blood, there was still so much to be done. They had to find Ymaritis—there might be dozens of places to search. How long would it take to track them down, eliminating them one by one? The summer solstice was tomorrow and—

"Elyse," Killian repeated, his voice gentler. "We'll get the angel's blood. We'll get Ymaritis."

He held her gaze, his chest still rising and falling with ragged breaths. But there was strength in his eyes, and for a moment, Elyse believed him.

"Okay," she breathed. "One more minute."

"I'm ready now," Jaime announced, readjusting the pack on his back.

Manny muttered something indiscernible under his breath, but Jaime didn't seem to notice it.

One minute later, they were off, lumbering down a path through the forest that covered the entire island. The trees were so different from those surrounding Sevhella. Their leaves were a myriad of different shapes, and they were all the richest shade of green. Vines wrapped the trunks of every tree, encircling their branches. Yet their beauty went unacknowledged by Elyse, whose attention was focused on driving them forward.

Jaime stayed by her side, walking in sync with her. If she slowed her pace, he slowed as well. If she stopped to tell the group something, he stopped too. He was always there, just within arm's reach.

It infuriated her.

Manny and Sera chatted with each other most of the way, leaving Killian on his own to bring up the rear. Occasionally, Elyse found herself glancing back at him. Each time, she found his eyes were already on her, before he hurriedly looked away.

"It's just a bit farther," she hollered over her shoulder.

When she wasn't thinking about Jaime's overbearing company, or the angel's blood, or her tryst with Killian, her mind slipped back to one thing. Ymaritis. How had he managed to disappear like that in De Vesalis? No one had seen him use a transportation potion, and there had been no blue smoke. He had just... vanished.

It wasn't supposed to be possible, and yet it was.

"Elyse," Manny called out, his voice coated in uncertainty.

"Yeah?"

"Where exactly are we?"

Still walking, she shrugged. "I'm not sure. Zubir always magicked me straight to the dock."

"It's just..." Manny began.

"It's the sun," Killian stated. "It's setting too fast."

At that, Elyse paused. She tilted her head up, peering through the thick canopy of leaves.

Killian came to stand beside her, pointing toward a ray of light that beamed low through the trees. "When we got here, the sun was still high. It shouldn't be this low already," he explained.

"What are you saying?" Elyse asked, her brows furrowed.

"I'm saying that we have to be very, *very* far south in order for the days to be this much shorter," Killian said, his voice flat.

Another shiver snaked up Elyse's spine. Sera wrapped her arms around herself. It wasn't just the sun that was eerie, though. There was something else. She could sense it now that her attention had shifted. The forest was calm—too calm. She hadn't seen a single bird or insect or any other creature. There wasn't even a breeze, as if even the wind was leery of the island.

"Let's keep going," Manny said, marching onward. "I don't want to hike back in the dark, not if we can avoid it."

They all followed after Manny, their silence an uneasy agreement.

Elyse's feet began to ache. Truthfully, her whole body still ached from her fall in De Vesalis, but she'd put on a brave face for the group, insisting that she was fine. If anyone noticed her exhaustion, they said nothing. They all seemed fatigued themselves, anyway.

After another hour of walking, she knew they were getting close. "It's just a bit—"

"Elyse," Killian growled, interrupting her. "If you say 'It's just a bit farther' one more time, I'll…"

Elyse turned to see Killian staring at her. His eyes were narrowed, but a hint of a smile touched his full lips.

"You'll what?" she asked with a smirk. "Need I remind you, the blood pact prevents you from harming me."

Killian's nostrils flared, but then his eyes grew devious. "Ah, but need I remind you—the blood pact also forces you to answer all questions truthfully."

Elyse's body went rigid, but she kept walking.

Killian's voice was light as he continued. "There are so many things I've always wanted to know. Where to begin?" he sang, mischief ringing clear. "Hmm… I could ask you why you hate your surname so much."

Elyse turned and glared at him. "You made your point," she spat as she marched ahead.

She knew he was merely teasing her, but he'd broached a sensitive subject. Talking about her surname would lead to more questions, and that was not a door she wanted to open.

Zubir's house was, in truth, only a bit farther. It wasn't long before the tall, wooden fence surrounding his property began to peek through the line of trees.

"Thank the gods," Manny huffed as they approached the gate.

"Aren't you a soldier?" Jaime asked incredulously. Elyse couldn't help but laugh.

Manny tucked a loose strand of his blond hair behind his ear. "Just because I'm a soldier doesn't mean I love traipsing through a hot, humid forest for hours after climbing a million stairs," he grumbled.

"Elyse," Sera said softly. Her gaze was fixed on the spikes lining the top of the fence. "Is Zubir... friendly?"

"The friendliest," Elyse replied. "But odd. Definitely odd."

Everyone nodded as Elyse approached the wooden gate and knocked.

It was a long moment before the gate creaked open—just a hair. A tan face with pale eyes peered through the crack in the gate.

"Who goes there?" came a man's voice.

"Zubir, it's me," Elyse answered, stepping closer and waving. "I brought a few friends. We need your help."

"Elyse!" Zubir hollered as he flung the gate open. Jaime had to jump out of the way to avoid getting hit.

Zubir took Elyse's hand, but his eyes roved nervously over the others.

"It's okay," she assured him. "We're sort of... on a mission."

Zubir nodded excitedly, though his eyes remained skeptical. "Well, come in then. Come in," he said, waving for them to step through the gate. He took off toward the house, babbling animatedly about something or another.

Manny, Sera, and Jaime followed him. As Elyse was about to walk through the gate, she felt a tug at her elbow.

"Hey," Killian said, pulling her aside. His body towered over her as he stood so close. His muscles rippled through his sweat-soaked tunic, and Elyse had to suppress the memory of those muscles pressed against her. "I just wanted to say that I'm sorry. I was only joking about the surname thing. I didn't realize it would upset you like that."

Elyse gazed up at him, at the tight line of his lips. She wasn't sure what to say.

"I know that we have other things on our plate right now," he continued, "but whenever you're ready to talk... I'm ready to listen." His voice was quiet and compassionate, yet firm.

Elyse's toes curled in her boots as she took in the raw expression in his golden eyes, yet her brows furrowed slightly. What was he saying? That he wanted to hear her side of the story? Or was he referring to what had happened with Ymaritis? Heat blazed in her cheeks as she realized he might have been talking about their tryst in Privya's kitchen.

She moved a half-step closer to him, a test to see what he would do. He stood firm, not backing away, his gaze holding hers. Her lips parted to reply, to tell Killian that she would make time for him no matter what, even if the world was burning. But before she could speak, her words were cut off by another's.

"Shut the gate!" Zubir hollered back, and Elyse nearly jumped out of her boots. For a second it had felt as though it was only her and Killian.

"Sorry!" Killian called back. He ushered Elyse through the gate before shutting it behind both of them.

As they strode toward the house, Killian gave her one last look, but Elyse couldn't read his expression. Was that longing? Encouragement? Something else altogether?

She shook her head, forcing all thoughts of Killian to flee her mind. There was no time to decipher his looks or his cryptic words. They had work to do.

CHAPTER 42

— • —

KILLIAN

J ust as Elyse had said, Zubir was odd. Definitely odd.

He zoomed around his small house, preparing tea and setting out dried fruits, all while trying to tidy up. Emphasis on *trying*. The cramped cottage was so full of haphazard trinkets and junk, it made the Emporium look like a high-end boutique. There wasn't much the small man could do in terms of decluttering.

Killian watched Zubir with faint amusement. He was short with tan skin and pale gray eyes, and his thick black hair was pulled back into three buns—one on top of his head, one at the back of his head, and one at the nape of his neck. He wore what appeared to be a woman's housecoat in faded lavender.

But Zubir's appearance and chaotic house weren't even the strangest things about him. He talked with lightning speed, jabbering on and switching topics so quickly, Killian thought he would suffer verbal whiplash. Manny and Sera both smiled at Zubir, nodding their heads enthusiastically at the words spewing from his mouth. The only one who didn't seem entertained by Zubir was Jaime, who simply looked put out. He stood with his arms crossed, a bored expression on his pale face.

"Elyse dear, how is your mother?" Zubir asked as he tittered about. "I haven't seen her in so long, I hope she's doing well. Will you tell her I said hello? How is Sevhella? Still as crowded as ever? I don't miss that place one bit. Although, I do miss the snow. And the tea—there was this one place, oh what was it called? Peterman's Tea House? Plymouth House of Tea? Oh, I don't remember, but they had the best tea in all of Rhodan. Nay! In all of the kingdoms. You know, I once saw King Cyril there."

Zubir let out a gasp, stumbling backward and nearly toppling over a stack of books.

"Are you all right?" Manny asked as he reached a hand to help steady Zubir.

"Yes," the hermit continued quickly. "But you heard about King Cyril, right? Dreadful, dreadful death."

Killian's eyes shot to Elyse, and he watched her throat bob.

"It was the vampires, of course," Zubir declared with absolute certainty. "You best be prepared. The vampires will take over Sevhella, and then all of Rhodan. The Guard *must* stop them—or else you'll all be sucking each other's blood by year's end!"

It was beginning to make more sense why Zubir lived all the way out here on a secluded island guarded by an absurd amount of wards.

"Zubir," Elyse said. She strode toward him and took his hands, which were busy stacking and restacking piles of books. "We don't have much time, but we need your help."

"Anything—you only have to ask."

To Killian's surprise, Zubir actually stopped talking long enough to listen.

"We need angel's blood," Elyse sighed. "We can—"

But Zubir had already taken off across the room, hurdling furniture and boxes of knickknacks. He made for a shelf in the corner of the room. Standing on the tips of his toes, he hefted down a small chest from the top shelf.

"Don't you even think about offering to pay, Elyse, not after everything you did for me," he babbled as he carried the chest over to the table. Everyone circled around as Zubir flung piles of paper off the table and plunked the chest down with a thud.

He lifted the lid of the chest, and Killian and Manny immediately exchanged a look.

The small chest was filled with vials of various-colored liquids. Most of them were dark red, but some were deep shades of blue, purple, and black. Glass clinked together as Zubir riffled through his bizarre collection, pulling out vials one after another.

Finally, he selected a vial of shimmering gold liquid and squealed with delight. "Ah! Here it is!"

Killian breathed a sigh of relief as the grip on his chest loosened. They were one step closer. Sera shot Manny a gleeful smile, and even Jaime's shoulders seemed to relax as he took a step closer to peer at the vial.

"Thank you, Zubir," Elyse murmured. "Honestly, we don't mind paying—"

Zubir held up a hand. "I will not accept any payment from you." He pointed to the vial in Elyse's hand. "Will that be enough? I have more. This here was from the angel Ramielle. Once every hundred years, her blood flows through the springs of Apolita. There are many fakes out there, but not this one, no! In fact, a month ago I proved to a gentleman that this was, in fact, true angel's blood."

Everyone's eyes narrowed on Zubir.

"Who?" Killian demanded. "Who was the man?"

Dread curdled in his core. He feared he already knew the answer, but he needed to hear it.

"I don't know his name," Zubir pondered aloud, holding his chin in his hand. "But he had mismatched eyes. One blue, one a sort of silver." He shook his head. "Very off-putting."

Killian swallowed. *This is a good thing*, he reminded himself. If Ymaritis had the angel's blood, it meant they could find him. The thought was little comfort, though. Hearing their suspicions confirmed aloud only made Killian's blood icy. Some part of him had been hoping Ymaritis wanted the eternal rose for a different reason—that he wasn't their ultimate foe. But that had been too much to ask for.

Elyse was ashen, Jaime glowering, but Zubir didn't seem to notice the change in their countenances.

"But I told him same as I told you," he continued. "It's the real thing, straight from—"

"I'm sorry, Zubir," Elyse interrupted, "but we really are in a hurry. We need to be going right away."

Zubir stared at Elyse, his head tilted curiously. "That's not possible."

Killian tensed, his hand moving to the hilt of his knife tucked securely in his belt. He could sense Manny doing the same as the tension in the room thickened.

"What do you mean?" Sera asked tentatively.

"Well, you'll never make it to the dock in time," Zubir stated plainly. "Sunset is only an hour from now, and the hike is much longer than that. You'll have to stay here for the night, until it's safe to leave."

Killian and Manny exchanged another glance.

"Why isn't it safe?" Manny asked.

"Because there is a creature that lurks in the dark—a nalusa falaya."

Killian had no idea what the creature was, but Elyse swore, and he knew it couldn't be good.

"You're joking, right?" she asked, eyes dark with anger.

"How on earth is there a nalusa falaya here?" Jaime asked with a haughty amount of disbelief. "They can't possibly be native."

Zubir shook his head. "I would never joke about something so lethal. And no, they're not native. I had one brought in."

"You had one brought in?" Sera asked incredulously.

Manny took a step toward the center of the group. "What is this thing—this nalala faloogie."

"Nalusa falaya," Sera corrected. "But you were very close."

"It's a being that haunts the dark," Jaime explained, his agitation plain. "Most people know them as shadow walkers."

Elyse, Jaime, and Sera had all gone pale. Killian watched them, their sudden fear unsettling, but he kept his voice strong as he asked, "What does it do?"

"No one really knows," Elyse answered, her voice chilling. "It drags its victims into the heart of the forest, and no one ever sees them again."

Sera shuddered and stepped closer to Manny. Killian had to repress his own shudder.

"You'll need to stay here until dawn," Zubir said. "I surround my property with enchanted fire before sunset, so it's impossible for the creature to enter the premises. I have a tent you can put up, and several blankets—"

"Absolutely not," Elyse cut him off sharply. "I'm grateful for the offer, but we can't waste any time. We'll take our chances with the walker."

Manny gaped at her, and though nobody else showed their concern as drastically as him, it was clear that no one liked that idea.

Killian understood where Elyse was coming from. They were running short on time, and it would be another ten hours until dawn—at least. But they had no magic, no weapons aside from a few small knives. Leaving was a terrible idea.

"Elyse," Sera breathed, her voice careful. "I know we're all eager to find Ymaritis, but we can't take on a walker—especially not without magic."

"We don't have a choice," Elyse growled back. Her shoulders were tight, her hands flexed by her sides, as if she were ready for a fight. "There's no way we're wasting any more time here than necessary."

Manny's voice was equally as sharp. "We can't stop Ymaritis if we're dead."

"Then we'll have to make sure we live, won't we?" Elyse hissed back.

The room burst into argument, Elyse vehemently defending her decision while Sera, Manny, and Zubir tried to make her see reason. Killian's attention was on Jaime, though. He knew if there was any chance that they could make it past the walker and to the dock, Jaime would side with Elyse. Instead he sat there, silent and tense.

"Enough," Killian commanded, and silence fell over the room.

Elyse's eyes were a mixture of pleading and anger as she stared up at him, waiting for him to speak. Her back was straight, her chin high. She looked beautiful—that fierce woman he knew her to be, who always did what she wanted and never cared what anyone thought. Killian felt a pull toward her, like something in his chest was reaching for her, but he pushed it down as he turned to face Sera. "How dangerous is this creature?"

"Extremely," she replied immediately. "It's fast, it's strong—it's deadly."

"But we're strong too, even without magic," Elyse argued. "We have two highly trained soldiers, and me."

"You can't fight against a creature that slithers through shadows!" Sera shouted. Killian had never heard her raise her voice before. "You're strong, but you're not invincible." She gave Elyse an unyielding look, one that Elyse returned.

Elyse didn't blink, didn't cringe or cower, but Killian could still see the betrayal seeping through her expression. A fatal cold emanated from her, chilling the crowded room.

"If that's how you feel," she spoke through gritted teeth, her brows lowered over her dark eyes, "then I'll go by myself." She pivoted and stalked toward the door.

"Absolutely not!" Killian and Jaime said at the same time.

"Are you crazy?" Manny shouted. "If you die or get injured or lost, we don't stand a damn chance against Ymaritis."

Elyse reached the door and laid a hand on the knob without turning toward them. As she twisted the brass fixture, Killian freed his knife from his belt and hurled it toward her. It lodged itself into the wall, not two inches from Elyse's face.

Slowly, Elyse turned. Her chin was lowered, her teeth bared. She looked absolutely predatory as she glowered at Killian through her fair lashes, her onyx eyes burning. They all stared at her, waiting for her to explode. Zubir let out a whimper.

"*Wake up*," Killian commanded. His voice was low, but it tore through the fraught silence. He marched toward Elyse, unfazed by her glaring. "Get a hold of yourself. If you walk out that door, you let Ymaritis win."

He ripped the knife from the door jamb and calmly slid it back into his belt, maintaining eye contact with Elyse the entire time. She didn't flinch at his gaze, but the resolution on her face had cracked, letting an ounce of fear show.

Despite himself, Killian's heart ached for her. He knew she wanted nothing more than to avenge herself, and those she hadn't been able to protect. That was something he could understand well. But she wasn't thinking rationally, and she was going to get herself killed.

"We'll get him. Okay?" Killian said softly. They stood so close, he could feel the heat radiating from her. "We'll leave at dawn. We'll have time. But we can't afford to lose anyone—especially not you."

She didn't say anything as she looked toward Jaime, a final plea for help.

He looked away.

"Fine," she ceded, crossing her arms.

Killian could have sworn he saw tears blooming in her eyes, but she didn't say another word.

CHAPTER 43

— • —

ELYSE

E lyse watched as the last rays of sunlight disappeared beyond the trees.

Killian, Manny, and Jaime had spent the last thirty minutes replenishing the oil supplies around the property. It seemed Zubir had set up a gutter system along the top of his fence to hold the oil for the enchanted flames. With a simple flick of a match, he'd set the oil ablaze, and fire had encircled the entire property.

"Zubir, what if it rains?" Manny had asked with a concerned look at the sky. There wasn't a cloud in sight, but of course Manny still found something to whine about.

"Oh, not to worry. The fire is enchanted against everything—water, wind, you name it. It can't even be smothered. The only way to put it out is with a special solvent." Zubir proudly pointed toward a jug sitting near his small house.

Manny simply stared at the jug for a few moments before shaking his head and returning to work.

Elyse had watched silently as the men worked. She was still furious. They were all cowards. Didn't they understand what was at stake? They needed every damn second possible to track down Ymaritis—if the spell to locate angel's blood even worked.

She sat alone in a rickety chair, simmering and shooting glares at anyone who glanced at her. Luckily, everyone seemed content to leave her be.

"I guess we should set up the tent," she heard Killian say.

Elyse rolled her eyes. *Cowards.*

Zubir left them for the night, slipping away into his cabin. Elyse wasn't sad to see him go. She was, of course, grateful for the angel's blood, but it was Zubir's paranoia that had stalled their mission. He was lucky he was a friend, or else she would have flayed him.

They could be halfway through the forest by now. But no, everyone had sided against her. Killian had even taken the angel's blood from her, as insurance to make sure she didn't go out on her own.

Jaime lit a small bonfire using the enchanted oil while Manny and Killian erected the tent. They had it up in no time. No doubt as soldiers, they had spent their share of time building tents. However, their years of experience hadn't prepared them for what was inside.

"Holy gods!" Manny exclaimed as he disappeared through the flap. He immediately came back out, circled the tent, and dipped inside. Poking only his head out, he called to Sera, "You have to come see this."

Sera looked sideways at Jaime from where she sat before the fire. "He thinks I've never seen an enchanted tent before—how precious." Still, she got up and joined him, letting out a gasp as she entered the tent.

Even Killian seemed amused. He gave the tent a contemplative look, a hint of a satisfied smile on his lips.

Elyse didn't bother getting up. She could guess what the inside looked like. It probably had a plush rug on the floor, divided sleeping areas, and a table with chairs. And, of course, it was probably much larger than it appeared from the outside.

She caught Jaime looking at her, and she narrowed her eyes. He looked away immediately, turning his attention to the blazing fire.

Now that the sun was gone, the temperature had dropped considerably. Elyse thought the shiver that tickled her spine had nothing to do with the chilly night, though. She'd never seen a walker before. She'd been told they were very tall—towering seven or eight feet—and that they had pointed ears. And yes, the thought of seeing one terrified her, but not as much as the idea of Lazarus being brought to life.

And it would be her fault. Not only in letting Ymaritis succeed, but in helping Lazarus all those years. Even if she didn't know what she had been doing, it was still something she wasn't sure she could ever forgive herself for.

Killian, Manny, and Sera came out of the tent, each with a chair. They settled themselves around the fire, quiet among the rustling of grass and the crackle of the fire. Tension still lingered among them.

Finally, Manny broke the silence. "So, this Zubir fellow..."

Elyse glanced over at him.

"Does anyone else think it's absurd that he brought in this falaya creature... for protection?"

"It's bloody insane," Jaime muttered.

"I want to know how someone managed to trap the damn thing," Sera said, sounding impressed.

Killian stared at the fire. "It seems like a lot of trouble to go through, hiding away out here behind all these wards and protections."

Elyse knew that Zubir had his reasons for hiding, but she wasn't about to tell his secrets.

The group fell into conversation, except Elyse, who sat in her chair with her arms folded over her chest. She ignored them, her mind elsewhere.

After a few minutes, she stood and exited the circle.

"Where are you going?" Sera called after her.

Elyse stopped. "To relieve myself," she drawled. "Is that okay?"

No one replied, but she could feel their wary gazes on her as she stalked away.

There was an outhouse nearby, but Elyse didn't aim for it. Instead, the moment she was out of sight, she slipped around to the front of Zubir's house and quietly crept through the front door.

It was nearly pitch black inside, the blaze of the fire outside glowing faintly through the curtained windows. On silent feet, Elyse padded toward the shelf in the corner. She held her breath as she reached for the top shelf and pulled down the chest, the one with the vials of blood.

As quietly as she could, she combed through the vials, holding them up to the window to try and see their coloring. When she found one filled with shimmering gold liquid, she smiled, and slipped the vial down the front of her shirt, tucking it between her breasts.

She didn't bother with placing the chest back on the shelf. By the time anyone found it lying on the floor, she would be long gone.

CHAPTER 44

— • —

KILLIAN

The fire did little to warm Killian as he sat in one of Zubir's ragged chairs. A permanent shiver caressed his spine, urging him to be on guard. It wasn't only the nalusa falaya that unnerved him—though the idea of a monster lurking outside the gates was certainly dread-inducing. Elyse had watched them from afar, her dark eyes venomous, proclaiming her anger. With her brows drawn low and her teeth gritted, she was more formidable than any creature that stalked the shadows. Now she was out of sight, and something nagged at Killian to follow her.

He waited as long as he could, then stood and raised his arms over his head, letting out an exaggerated groan.

"I'm going to go stretch my legs," he announced.

No one bothered to protest the obvious lie. They all knew what he was doing. He was going to check on Elyse.

He rounded Zubir's house and leaned against the wall, keeping an eye on the outhouse. A minute passed, then another. He shifted awkwardly. Maybe waiting for her outside as she relieved herself wasn't the best idea, but it was the only one he'd had.

A few more minutes passed, and she still didn't emerge. He was about to give her privacy when he heard a sound toward the front of the house. He strode around the side, squinting his eyes to see. As he rounded the house, he saw a movement at the gate.

Elyse had opened the gate, disrupting the ring of fire that encircled the property. She stood with one hand on the fence, as if pondering what awaited her. She looked regal, the fire casting her in magnificent shades of gold and copper, the shadows dancing at her feet. Then she slipped silently through the opening, shutting the gate behind her and disappearing into certain peril.

Dammit, Elyse.

He took off toward the gate. Each slam of his boots against the ground reverberated with realization.

She hadn't gone to the outhouse at all.

She'd stolen a vial of angel's blood.

This had been her plan all along.

Fury empowered him as he tore open the gate and raced after her.

It was dark, but he could see Elyse's figure a dozen yards ahead. She was walking fast, her knife at the ready in her hand.

"Elyse," Killian hissed as he ran to catch up with her.

He was fuming. She'd lied to them, she'd snuck out, she was putting herself—and their mission—in jeopardy.

Elyse whirled, her face glowing by the light of the fire that rimmed Zubir's property. Killian swore he saw fear beneath the determination in her eyes.

But she turned around and resumed her pace without uttering a word.

He grumbled to himself as he hurried after her. She had to be the most incorrigible person he'd ever met, and it would be the death of both of them. He grabbed her arm and spun her to face him.

"What are you doing?" His eyes darted around the forest, searching for signs of the creature. Shadows loomed all around him, provoking goose pimples on his skin.

"I'm doing what needs to be done," Elyse snarled, wrenching her arm from his grip and continuing down the path.

"No, you're not," Killian growled. He ran before her, blocking her path. "This is suicide, Elyse."

With her back to the fire, he couldn't see her expression, but he could imagine her dark eyes brimming with fury.

"Get out of my way." She tried to push past him, but Killian stood firm.

He grabbed both of her shoulders, forcing her to look at him. "You can't do this, Elyse. Certainly not by yourself."

"I know how to protect myself."

Gods, there was no getting through to her.

He stared down at her, his jaw clenched, as he made his decision. With one easy movement, he grabbed her by the waist and hurled her over his shoulder.

"Put me down!" Elyse demanded, though she kept her voice low. Her fists collided with his back repeatedly, but thanks to the magic of the blood oath, her punches were no more than light pats.

Her legs flailed as she tried to kick him, but Killian kept walking toward the gate.

"Put. Me. Down!" she insisted. "I swear, if you don't—"

She stopped abruptly, her whole body going rigid. At the same time, the hair on the back of Killian's neck stood on end. The entire forest went gravely still, wickedness devouring it.

He knew he should run. He knew he should take off without looking behind him. But he couldn't fight it as he slowly turned, his eyes searching the path.

At first, he saw nothing but a forest enshrouded in darkness. He held his breath, icy shivers whispering through his body.

Then he noticed a shadow that was slightly darker than the surrounding landscape. As he focused his vision, the shadow started to take shape. The silhouette was humanoid, but far too tall. Its head was smooth and bald, flanked by two pointed ears. Its fingers were long and thin. They twitched unnaturally.

Killian froze in place. This was the walker.

The creature began to sink as if it were melting. The ground darkened into an inky black puddle as the creature descended. It was like a nightmare seeping into the forest floor. The shadow deepened into an unnatural, sickly shade of ebony. It coursed with a haunting power before it surged forward at a harrowing speed.

It was coming for them.

"Run," Elyse breathed in his ear.

Killian didn't need to be told twice. He turned back toward the gate and began to sprint, still carrying Elyse over his shoulder. They were only a short distance away, maybe fifty yards at most.

"It's coming!" Elyse cried.

Killian didn't look behind him, but he could feel the creature bearing down on them. The air grew colder as his heart pounded in his chest.

"We're not going to make it," Elyse shouted, utter panic in her voice.

Killian felt spindly fingers wrap around his ankle and pull. He crashed forward, landing atop Elyse as her knife flew from her hand. It landed several feet away, just out of reach.

Killian immediately spun to his back, but what he saw made him freeze. The creature was sprawled on the ground, half sunk into the shadows. This close up, he could make out its mangled face, its nose nothing more than two slits. The falaya's sharp teeth gnashed as it reached for Killian with its grotesque fingers.

Elyse's boot smashed into the creature's face, and it let out a howl that tore Killian from his trance. He struggled to his feet, pulling Elyse up along with him.

"Run!" she screamed again.

But Killian didn't run. Instead, he reached for the knife at his belt.

"What are you doing?" Elyse's voice was frantic.

The creature was taking shape before them, its body towering high.

"We can't outrun it," Killian panted. "We have to attack." He lunged at the walker, swiping his knife and following with a punch, but the creature dodged the attacks with fluid, unnatural movements.

"Fuck." Elyse scrambled for her knife, apparently resigned to agree with Killian.

The walker pounced, and Killian rolled away. Elyse charged, her attacks nearly as swift as the creature's as she thrust her knife. Before she could do any damage, the walker faded into the shadow of a tree.

"Move!" Killian commanded, grabbing Elyse's wrist and dragging her toward the fence.

They both sent panicked glances over their shoulders, waiting for the walker to appear. Killian had never known such terror as he pushed Elyse ahead of him, urging her to safety.

They were only twenty yards out when the walker attacked again, flying in front of them as a shadowy phantom. Killian and Elyse both toppled over it, their knees crashing into the hard dirt. Killian spun quickly, his knife ready.

But the walker was ready too. It pounced on Elyse, pinning her to the ground. She screamed—a cry of both terror and fury. The creature had her by the wrist, keeping her knife at bay. Her face was twisted with rage as she kicked and flailed, but to no avail.

Killian hurried to his feet and kicked the walker in the ribs again and again, trying to push it off Elyse. It barely noticed. Dark, shadowy strings of saliva dangled from its maw as it lowered its head toward Elyse's neck. Her staccato breaths echoed in Killian's ears, a cry for help.

Killian plunged his knife into the creature's back, and it let out a shrill screech, but it didn't relinquish its hold on Elyse. With renewed intensity, it snapped at her, gnashing its teeth together.

Killian didn't know what to do. All he knew was the sound of Elyse's screams, the terror in his own heart.

He dove for the creature, tackling it to the ground and freeing Elyse. Its skin was clammy atop its sinewy muscles, but Killian gripped it with all his might. They grappled together as the creature squeezed its gnarled fingers around Killian's arms and neck. Killian couldn't land a single blow. He could barely keep hold of the creature. It was cutting off his airway, his vision going dark at the edges.

Distantly, he could hear Elyse. She scrambled on the ground, her boots echoing through the soil. "*Run*," he tried to tell her, but it came out as nothing more than a gargled cry as the creature's fingers tightened around his throat, sealing his fate.

This was it. This was how he would die. And he would never get to hear Elyse's story—would never get to hold her again. Would never see her overcome her sorrows.

Suddenly, it let out a howl, loosening its grip slightly. Killian blinked as his vision cleared, and he saw Elyse standing over the walker, her knife bloodied in her grip. With a fierce cry, she stabbed the creature again and again and again.

Finally, it let go of Killian, its attention fully focused on Elyse. But Killian wasn't about to let the creature go. He wrapped his arm around the creature's throat and held on as tightly as he could as Elyse brought the knife down one last time—in its eye.

The walker writhed in Killian's grip, shrieking in agony. The sound reverberated through Killian with a sickening intensity.

Elyse's white-knuckled fingers grasped at his shirt. "Let's go!" she screamed.

With one final, heavy shove, Killian threw the creature off him. Elyse was practically dragging him as he scrambled to his feet. Fueled by desperation, they sprinted toward the fence.

He could still hear the creature screaming, but he didn't dare look back. He prayed it was injured enough to keep from coming after them.

The gate opened a crack, and a figure carrying a torch emerged.

"Get back!" Killian bellowed as he raced forward.

Manny's horrified face was illuminated by the torch. He moved aside to clear a path for them as he swiped the torch furiously from side to side, trying to deter the walker from coming any closer. Killian heard the creature howl again.

With only a few strides between them and the gate, Killian shoved Elyse ahead of him. She cleared the fence, Killian mere inches behind her. Sera and Jaime stood right inside the fence, their eyes wide and faces pale.

Killian turned to see the walker flying toward them. Manny gave the torch a final wave before chucking it toward the monster and backing through the gate.

"Shut it!" Elyse screamed at the same time Killian and Manny slammed the gate closed.

The walker shrieked one last time, its defeat echoing into the night.

Killian doubled over, panting hard as he rested his hands on his knees. *Gods above.* They had almost died. That thing had almost killed them. Somehow, be it fate or luck or something else altogether, they'd made it.

Elyse collapsed to the ground, looking as terrible as Killian felt. Her shirt was torn to pieces, blood and dirt smeared across the fabric.

"Are you okay?" He dropped to his knees, reaching a shaking hand toward her.

Elyse nodded. Her face was pale, her eyes distant, but she didn't seem to be hurt.

She was okay.

Sera and Jaime stood silently, apparently too stunned to speak. Zubir came stumbling out of his house. He stared at them like he was torn between chastising Elyse and running away.

Manny, though, stared dead at Elyse with a fury Killian had never seen before.

"Elyse—what the fuck?"

CHAPTER 45

— • —

KILLIAN

The moment Manny spoke, something snapped in Elyse. She leapt to her feet, snarling as she pointed her finger in Manny's face. He didn't back down, his expression challenging her, and they stood together, indignation rolling off them.

But before Elyse could even speak, tears streamed from her eyes.

"I had to!" she half screamed, half sobbed. "I couldn't just sit here and wait. I can't... I—" Her voice cut off suddenly as she hung her head.

All Manny could do was stare at her with furrowed brows. Killian had never seen Elyse so shaken—not even when he arrested her. Then, she'd at least been calm enough to formulate a plan, but now she seemed... destroyed. Her shoulders shook as she gasped for air—from both adrenaline and the quiet sobs that afflicted her.

Killian wanted to reach out and place a hand on her shoulder, but he knew better than that. She was already showing far too much vulnerability. Accepting someone else's comfort in front of others would be downright humiliating for her.

Evidently, Jaime didn't know that. He stepped toward her, his hand outstretched, and she batted it away with a growl.

"Don't," she barked. "I don't need pity—not from any of you. I *need* to stop Lazarus."

Her words dissipated into the night, leaving behind a chaotic tension. *Lazarus?* Who was Lazarus? Killian looked to Sera for answers, but she was busy avoiding anyone's gaze.

Elyse seemed to realize she'd said too much. She wrapped her arms around herself as tears continued to fall, her body trembling.

"Elyse," Killian said carefully, trying his best to sound encouraging. "Please, tell us whatever is troubling you."

All eyes were on her. She opened her mouth to speak, but only a small rasp escaped. She looked at Sera, pleading with her eyes for help.

Sera stepped toward her, removing her jacket from her waist. She laid the jacket on Elyse's shoulders, covering her exposed skin where the shirt was torn.

"It's time to tell them," she murmured.

Elyse looked up at Sera with watery eyes, holding her gaze for a long moment before nodding. Sera wrapped an arm around Elyse and guided her toward the campfire.

Everyone sidled after them, except Zubir, who disappeared back into his house. Killian's heart was still pounding from their fight with the walker. Now, it was coupled with anticipation and anxiety as he waited for Elyse's explanation.

Slowly, they settled themselves around the campfire as Zubir returned, carrying a jug.

"Palusan rum," he explained, lifting the jug. "I thought it might be needed."

He was surprisingly quiet, for which Killian was grateful. He wasn't sure how Elyse would react to his chatter at this moment.

Zubir extended the jug to Elyse. She accepted it with a trembling hand and took a hearty swig. Wiping her mouth with the back of her hand, she passed the jug to Sera.

The jug made its way around the circle. They were all silent, taking their turn at the rum as the fire crackled before them. When it came to

Killian, he took a long, deep pull. The rum was acrid and bitter, but it helped settle some of his lingering agitation.

Finally, Elyse knitted her hands in her lap, staring at them as she began.

"My whole life, I have been indebted to a demon named Lazarus."

Killian stared across the fire at her. Indebted? What did that even mean?

A silent tear fell to her lap. "That's why I'm so powerful—why I don't need a crystal to do magic. I was born with these powers, but at a cost."

She exhaled slowly and wiped another tear from her cheek. Killian ached to sit beside her—to hold her hand—but her body told him this was something she needed to confess, and she needed to do it alone.

"Every month, on the night of the full moon, Lazarus gave my mother and me a task to complete. Usually it was something simple, like sacrificing an animal or burning bones. But after my mother passed, the tasks became more difficult."

Killian was holding his breath. A chill breathed down his neck. He knew where this was going. Part of him wanted to run away, to never hear this story that he knew ended so badly, but he was rooted to the spot, paralyzed by a morbid curiosity.

"Lazarus started demanding that I kill people. At first, they were lowlifes. Rapists and such, people who no one would miss. But then... But then he ordered me to kill a girl. She was fifteen, and so innocent. She had the sweetest smile and the brightest eyes."

Killian's gut twisted. Gods above, a fifteen-year-old girl? Surely, Elyse would never.

A sob tore through her body. Her next words were nearly incomprehensible as grief overtook her. "I couldn't do it. I couldn't kill her. My mother had always told me that I had to follow Lazarus's orders—no matter what. I think once she disobeyed him. She disappeared for a few days, and when she came back, she was different. After that, she made me promise to do whatever Lazarus asked of me.

"But I still couldn't, so I took my own life instead. I killed myself—and yet, I woke up the next morning in my bed, as if nothing had happened. I killed myself nine more times, but I always came back. And then... Then Lazarus made a threat. He showed me what he would do to the girl if I didn't kill her myself. It was—awful." Her chin wobbled as she squeezed her eyes tight. "He told me it was a mercy for me to take her life. So..." she said, opening her eyes and staring at the fire. "I did."

She let the words sink in as she took a swig from the jug, and then another. No one spoke, out of a sort of reverence for her courage. Killian stared at her, studying the haunted look in her red-rimmed eyes. His heart was in his throat. He'd known all along that she was tormented by something, but he never dreamed it would be so terrible. To be forced to take a life like that—to take her own life so many times—it was unimaginable.

It was quiet for a long moment as Elyse regained her composure. When she finally continued, her voice was a touch stronger, like the worst was over. "After that, I stopped caring," she went on, passing along the jug. "Lazarus had won. There was no point in fighting him anymore, so I did whatever he asked."

Manny passed Killian the jug. He accepted it but didn't bring it to his lips.

"That's why you killed King Cyril," he uttered.

Elyse nodded, her face contorted as more tears flowed down her cheeks. "I never knew why he made me do it. I never asked. I just did whatever Lazarus said and tried not to think about it. But then Sera found the passage in the book, about bringing a demon to life. It was all for this. Killing the girl, murdering King Cyril—he made me do those things as part of the ritual to bring him to life."

A horrible numbness wrapped itself around Killian. It all made sense. Not only about King Cyril and the full moon. But how she had acted tonight, and why she needed so desperately to leave and stop Ymaritis.

She felt guilty.

She closed her eyes again, shaking her head. "I can't let Lazarus walk this earth. Because if he does... It will all be my fault."

Killian finally took a drink from the jug and passed it to Zubir. He stared at the fire, unable to speak. He could barely think. His mind was racing as so many pieces lined up together, fitting into place.

He finally had his explanation, and damned if it wasn't far more horrific than he'd imagined. He'd told himself that there could be no possible explanation that excused Elyse's behavior, but this... He didn't know what to make of it.

He understood it all now. The words she spoke that night at the clinic echoed in his mind.

You don't know me.

Manny let out a breath. "And I thought I had a tragic backstory."

A soft laugh escaped Elyse's lips as she wiped another tear away. When she finally looked up, her gaze pierced Killian, her dark eyes searching his face. She didn't look at anyone else. Just him.

But his face remained neutral. What was he supposed to do with this information? Forgive her? He had spent so much time hating her. He wasn't certain he could stop over the course of a few minutes.

And even if he did, there was still the blood pact. She was bound to turn herself in—for a crime she had been forced to commit.

Killian finally broke her gaze, glancing instead to Manny. Manny looked at him with such sympathy, his eyes asking the same question as Elyse's.

Is it enough?

The terror Killian had felt moments earlier surged through him again as he remembered the walker clawing at her. He had been desperate to save her, and not because they needed her to defeat Ymaritis. But because he needed her.

Elyse had gone back to fidgeting with her hands in her lap. Killian set his gaze on her and spoke in a soft voice.

"You don't have to bear this alone, Elyse."

She looked up at him, and a lone tear slid down her face. She said nothing, but the look in her eyes sang of gratitude.

The others offered their own words of encouragement, but Killian didn't hear them. He stared at Elyse, struck by her courage, her strength. She was enslaved to a demon, and had been her whole life. She'd been forced to do unspeakable things—to herself and to others. And yet here she sat, trying to make it right.

Half of her hair had fallen loose from its hold, and dirt caked her chin. Her eyes were swollen, her lids heavy. The fire cast her complexion in a glaring orange hue. And yet to Killian, she had never looked more beautiful. As he gazed at her across the fire, he didn't see a murderer or a liar or a coward.

After the Guard had issued a warrant for her arrest, she could have run away to another kingdom, started a new life. Even after Prestowne, she could have fled. But she had chosen again and again to do everything in her power to prevent any others from suffering. She was broken, and Killian now understood why. But she was strong—stronger than he ever even realized.

Sera took Elyse by the arm and helped her inside the tent. Killian watched them go, craving more answers, more explanation, but unable to ask for it. All the words he wished to voice were caught in his throat, clogged by emotion. His mind was still muddled as he tried to comprehend everything.

He knew one thing, though. He wasn't going to get any sleep until he spoke to Elyse—alone.

CHAPTER 46

— • —

ELYSE

E lyse's head throbbed from crying. She wished she had a warm rag to place over her swollen eyes, but she settled instead for pulling the covers over her face and enveloping herself in darkness.

The sleeping pad was surprisingly comfortable, and the linens were soft. She even had a curtain that she'd drawn to give herself an extra layer of privacy. Yet as she tried to lose herself in sleep, all she saw was the horrid silhouette of the walker. The crackle of the fire outside was the gnashing of its teeth, and the wind rustling the canvas of the tent was its snarls.

She yanked the covers off and sat up in bed, cradling her head in her hands. Her entire body throbbed from the disasters of the last four-and-twenty hours. She had almost died twice—first at Ymaritis's hands, then by the claws of the walker. But worst of all had been baring her soul for the others, blubbering like an infant in front of them. She'd nearly given herself hiccups from sobbing.

As she'd poured her heart out, she desperately wanted to cover her face and run inside the tent. Even being so vulnerable in front of Sera and Jaime, who already knew about Lazarus, was difficult enough. But telling Killian? She'd almost rather face the walker again.

And yet, it had been cathartic. Coming clean, all of it, without being shackled or attacked. They had listened politely, encouragingly even, and had not shown her any ill will.

Most of all, as she recounted her life story, she had craved Killian's approval. She'd forced herself not to stare at him and scrutinize his facial expressions, harrowingly lit by the campfire. But she hadn't been able to help stealing glances at him, searching for forgiveness.

Her stomach churned now as she thought of it. Surely, if he'd forgiven her, he would have said so. As much as she needed to hear him say that he no longer held a grudge against her, she tried to understand that it was something he might not let go of right away—if ever.

She heard the tent flap open, and the soft sound of footsteps against the carpeted floor. She expected to find Sera checking in on her and was surprised by Killian's face peering in at her as he tugged back the curtain.

"Elyse?" he asked softly—almost hesitatingly. "Do you need anything? Water or... company?"

Her heart leapt in her throat. At that moment, she wanted his company more than anything in the world. But if it was mere pity, or an obligation to help keep her head straight for the mission ahead, she knew that she wouldn't be able to bear it. Perhaps it was better to dismiss him and face her feelings on her own.

Killian, however, took her silence as an invitation. He moved swiftly into the sleeping area, shutting the curtain behind him, and eased himself onto the makeshift bed. He left several feet of space between them, but to Elyse, it felt like miles.

"Can I speak freely?" he asked.

Elyse only nodded, too afraid to open her mouth. She knew her voice would sound weak.

Killian sighed as he leaned his elbows onto his knees. "I'm sorry for not asking you sooner. I should have given you a chance to explain before I arrested you—or attempted to."

Though it was dark, she could see a crooked smile on his lips. She stared at that smile, unsure what to say. Those words took her breath away.

"I think you understand why I didn't want to hear any of it at the time... Why I wasn't ready," he continued. "But that doesn't mean it was right for me to do so, and I'm sorry."

Elyse closed her eyes as she felt tears welling to the surface. Dammit—how did she still have any tears left to cry?

She sniffled, and Killian's brow furrowed. He immediately shifted closer and wrapped his arm around her shoulders, pulling her in tight. "Hey," he breathed as she buried her face in his chest. "It's okay."

Her whole body shuddered as she failed to stifle a sob. Killian ran his hand over her back in soothing motions, and Elyse felt her anxieties begin to melt away.

This, being held by Killian, letting him comfort her... Why had she been so terrified of it? It felt so right. After her mother's death, she had borne this weight completely alone. And now, she had friends—friends who were willing to listen without judgment or condescension.

She lifted her gaze to meet Killian's. He looked down at her with open, attentive eyes. "What is it?" he asked gently.

Elyse swallowed. Before she could change her mind, she asked, "Do you think you'll ever be able to forgive me?"

Killian took a deep breath. He reached out and gingerly tucked a strand of hair behind her ear, stroking her cheek with his thumb. The touch electrified her, igniting her hope, but she held her breath and waited for his answer.

"Twice this week, I thought I was going to lose you," he began, his voice gravelly. "And both times, I knew I would do anything to save you."

Elyse tried not to look away as her chin trembled.

"I'm still hurting, Elyse. I don't know that I can simply forget that I was lied to, that you took away my king..."

She hung her head. She should have known. She should have realized that forgiveness was too much to ask for. Her hope diminished as anguish gripped her heart.

Killian let out a breath. "But I'd like to try."

Slowly, she lifted her head. His eyes were on her—calm and encouraging.

"You were right," he uttered. "There's something about us."

He took her trembling chin in his hand, staring at her for a long moment. And she let him. For the first time, she truly let him see all the torment, the shame, the regret. Everything she had deemed as weak for so long, marking her as unworthy.

He did not flinch. He leaned closer until his lips rested on her forehead.

Elyse let out an exhale that she had been holding for months.

They sat there like that for a long time, Killian with his head pressed to hers, Elyse holding onto his shirtfront as if she never wanted to let go. Because she didn't. At that moment, there was no Ymaritis, no Lazarus, no warrant for her arrest. There was only the soft cadence of the tent rustling in the breeze, and the distant crackle of the fire.

There was only him, and there was only her.

She looked up and found his eyes mere inches from hers, his lips closer. An eternity seemed to pass as they gazed at one another, and Elyse savored every moment of it. She held her breath, her lips parted slightly, and closed her tired eyes.

First, she felt Killian's kiss on one corner of her lips, then the other. He kissed her nose, her brow, then turned her head slightly to kiss her jaw. His thumb caressed the flesh of her bottom lip, and she exhaled. That simple touch had her core heating, her skin tingling.

Slowly, his hand migrated to the back of her neck, and his lips moved closer to hers until they were finally touching.

His kiss was gentle and slow, as if they had all the time in the world. He wove his fingers through her hair, and Elyse's lips parted, deepening their kiss. She released her hold on his shirt and let her hands rove over his strong chest.

At the movement, Killian growled against her lips, sending tantalizing shivers down her spine. With his free hand, he gripped her backside and pulled her onto his lap. Elyse obliged, wrapping her legs around his hips and pressing closer to his body.

Their last time together had been fueled by a confusing mixture of lust and hatred. But this was different. This was gentle yet powerful, slow yet unyielding. This was the first taste of a fine wine before melting into a drunken oblivion.

Her hands acted of their own accord, pulling off Killian's shirt, then her own. He immediately pressed a hand to her breast, massaging it in a way that coaxed a moan from her. She felt him grow hard against her, and she kissed him again, this time sliding her tongue against his mouth.

Killian pushed her on her back, pressing his full length against her. His hand moved up and down her body, as if he wanted to touch all of her at once. As if he couldn't get enough of her.

It was the same way her own hands traveled across his skin, taking in every curve of his muscles, even the scarred skin of his chest. She tangled her hand in his hair and pulled him closer, gasping at the sensation of her nipples grazing his chest.

They were both panting now as lust overtook them completely. One look from Killian, and Elyse lifted her hips to help him remove her pants. He sat up and threw his own trousers to the floor before touching Elyse's knee, spreading her legs, and climbing on top of her.

He lowered his lips to hers, then kissed his way to her neck, her ear, all while she felt him throbbing between her legs. The anticipation killed her. She needed him inside her. And yet, she would wait as long as he demanded. She would let him tease her for an eternity. Her body was his, now and forever.

Killian moved a hand down her stomach, pausing to caress her hip with the back of his fingers. She shuddered with pleasure, and she could feel him smile against her skin.

His hand moved to her thigh, and she held her breath as he dragged his finger closer to her center. As his fingers met their mark at the apex of her thighs, she gasped and pulled his face to hers.

"Don't hold back," she murmured against his ear. And she meant it. She wanted to experience everything they had missed out on over these past two months. She wanted nothing between them—no inhibitions, no insecurity, just raw intimacy and passion.

Killian didn't need her to explain. He turned his face to hers and nipped at her bottom lip as he plunged one finger inside her. Elyse groaned as a life's worth of pent-up aggression escaped her. He circled her most sensitive area with his thumb as he continued working his finger inside her, and Elyse writhed atop the bed. Then he slid a second finger inside, provoking a gasp from her, and began pumping furiously.

Elyse could feel her pleasure building with each flick of his fingers. She bit her lip to contain her cries as her hips bucked helplessly. Hell's gates, she never wanted him to stop. But right as she was about to reach her climax, he withdrew.

Elyse immediately grasped for him, needing him, wrapping her hand around the length of him. A shiver licked its way up her spine. Having his girthy member in her hands was equally as exhilarating as being touched by him. She reveled in the way his body seemed to both tense and relax against her as she stroked him in smooth motions.

As she dragged her fingers up and down just the way he liked, she savored every inch, fantasizing about how intoxicating it would feel to finally have him again. She was practically squirming with the heat of anticipation. Killian let out a noise somewhere between a moan and a snarl. It wasn't long before he reached down and removed her hand. He interlaced their fingers and pinned her hand beside her head as he ground himself against her.

"If I'm not going to hold back," he said, his voice low and guttural, "then you can't either."

Elyse's toes curled. Killian positioned himself at her entrance, but went no further.

"No hiding your face," he explained. "No holding in your screams—"

"Killian," Elyse gasped.

His answering growl at the sound of his name on her lips tumbled through her chest.

"But the others..." she protested feebly as her hips gyrated, aching for more of him.

Killian lifted his head. The curve of his lips was mischievous.

"The first thing Manny did was test the tent to see if it was soundproof."

Elyse's expression mirrored Killian's. She'd never been so grateful for Manny's perversion.

Killian planted his lips on hers, and slowly, he pushed inside her. Elyse gasped at the sensation, and she squeezed his hand tighter.

He started off slow, letting her remember the way he felt, the way he moved, until his entire member was buried inside her completely. Elyse did as she was commanded. As Killian thrust harder, penetrating deeper, she let her exhilaration be known. She whimpered with each surge of his hips, feeling blissful yet needing more. And Killian seemed to feed off it, empowered by every moan and gasp.

He hooked one of her knees around his elbow, then the other, lifting her rear from the bed. "Say my name," he roared as he pounded with animalistic vigor.

"Killian," Elyse cried out as pleasure washed over her. Her face contorted and she grasped the linens, clutching with all her might. She gave herself to him completely. Every vulnerable sound, every tremble of her body as he impaled her again and again. Her legs were shaking, her back arching, her release nearing.

"Killian," she practically screeched, a plea for ecstasy.

Killian understood. Sweat dripped down his chiseled abdomen as he brought her closer to that edge. He locked eyes with her, a feral hunger in his gaze. That look said everything. He was hers, and she was his.

Euphoria swept through Elyse, surging from her core, up her back, through her breasts, her neck, all the way to her fingers and toes. Her legs shook and her lips parted as a silent gasp escaped her throat.

Killian didn't relent. He drove harder, sending her over that edge again and again until his body shuddered and he let out a sigh.

Elyse immediately pulled him down to her, pressing their lips together. His salty kiss was the most delicious thing she'd ever tasted. Still inside her, he buried his face in her neck. Their chests moved together, searching for breath as they waited for their racing hearts to slow.

When she regained control of her trembling limbs, Elyse lifted a hand and stroked her nails along Killian's powerful back. She was utterly exhausted, and yet she knew she wouldn't sleep any time soon. She wanted every second with Killian.

He seemed to sense her thoughts. He lifted his head, a sweet smile playing at his lips as he took her in.

"I'm not going anywhere," he murmured. The sweetest words Elyse had ever heard.

CHAPTER 47

KILLIAN

They talked for hours, their heads sharing the same pillow, their bodies pressed close. Killian trailed his fingers up and down the length of Elyse's arm, a languid, protective movement. She tangled her feet around his legs as they murmured to one another, their voices nearly inaudible.

Eventually, Sera and Manny entered the tent, retiring to their own private space, and Jaime followed shortly after. Soft snores echoed through the tent, but Killian hardly noticed. He was too entranced by Elyse's whispers.

"I missed you," she breathed again and again. "I missed this."

"Me too," Killian uttered as he pulled her closer by the small of her back.

Elyse quietly explained everything, about how she had been struck by his arrow and transported herself to Jaime's doorstep. Killian pressed his head to her brow as shame overwhelmed him. He had fired an arrow at her, at his Elyse, without even listening to what she was trying to tell him. Out of everything that had happened, that was what he regretted the most.

Elyse lifted a delicate finger to his chin and tilted his face up to hers. "Right now," she demanded, "let's both promise to forgive ourselves."

Her finger grazed the line of his jaw, and he closed his eyes. In that moment, Elyse could have asked him to go back into the forest to face the walker, and he would have done it. But forgiving himself for not even attempting to hear her out, for shooting an arrow at her...

She gently took his hand and held it to her chest. He felt the soothing, rhythmic beat of her heart.

"Promise me, Killian."

There was no denying her. His eyes still closed, he pressed his lips to hers. "I promise."

"I promise, too."

She stroked his hair as they nestled together, and her breathing slowed. He thought she had drifted off to sleep when her voice rasped into the night.

"Ask me about my surname."

Killian opened his eyes to find Elyse staring at him. He could ask her anything, and the blood oath would force her to tell the truth. In the darkness, he studied her eyes, searching for certainty.

"Ask me about my surname," she repeated.

Killian stroked a hand along her back, and swallowed. "Why do you hate your surname?"

Elyse closed her eyes as if drawing strength from the power of the oath.

"It's my mother's surname," she began. "When she was sixteen, she became pregnant. She thought she was in love with the man, and that he loved her. But of course, when she told him the news, he avoided her and even moved away."

Killian's stomach turned. There were few things in this world that he hated more than cowardly men. But he listened, bearing witness to her pain.

She sighed and continued. "My mother tried to hide her pregnancy from her parents for as long as she could. She knew they wouldn't approve. They were old-fashioned. They believed in things like purity and discipline. But eventually they found out."

Her voice began to waver. "My grandfather dragged her to a healer. He demanded that she have the child removed."

Killian tensed. He tried not to show his surprise. He thought this was the story of how Elyse was conceived. Evidently, he was wrong. He held his breath as she went on.

"When the healer was finished, the assistant came in. She handed my mother a note from my grandfather. He'd enclosed a single gold coin and told her never to return home."

Killian kissed Elyse's cheek. He wasn't surprised to find it wet with tears.

"I'm sorry," he whispered. It was all he could think to say. He understood her hatred for her surname, and why she wouldn't want to be associated with such vile people.

"I'm not finished," Elyse rasped. "My mother worked odd jobs to get by. She was friendly and smart, and she made enough to afford a small apartment, but she mourned the loss of her child. She thought about that baby every day, and eventually, she did something desperate.

"She summoned a demon to make a bargain. She wanted her child back. The demon told her that he couldn't bring her child back to life, but that he could give her a new child, and that he could give her the means to make sure that child was well cared for. All he asked for in return was that she do one thing for him every month on the night of the full moon."

Killian realized he'd stopped stroking Elyse's back. This wasn't just about how her mother's family had abandoned her. It was about how that action had led her mother to make a terrible decision, enslaving herself and her child to a demon. He pulled Elyse's face to his chest and held her tight as she finished her story.

"My mother agreed immediately. The demon helped her get started with the shoppe, and just like he promised, it was a lucrative business. Nine months later, I was born."

They were quiet for a moment as her words sank in. Killian had researched Elyse and the Emporium before he had ever met her, noting how no man's name had been attached to the property. He'd often wondered about her father, but she'd never brought him up. Now he understood why.

Elyse tilted her head up to him, her eyes wide and watery. "What if I'm..." she began, but her voice trailed off.

She didn't need to finish for Killian to understand. What if she was part demon?

"Did your mother ever explain to you how the conception happened?" he asked, trying to ignore the mental picture of a demon impregnating a sixteen-year-old girl.

Elyse shook her head.

He was quiet for a moment as he chose his words carefully. It was certainly a possibility. It would explain Elyse's immense power. But it didn't seem right.

He cleared his throat and tucked a strand of hair behind her ear. "First of all, I don't think you are. I mean, I've never noticed horns or a tail or anything."

Elyse's body shook with a laugh, though she sniffled.

"Second of all," Killian continued, "even if you are part demon, does it matter? You're still you. And there is far more good in you than you realize, more than enough to outweigh any slight demonic traits you might have."

Elyse didn't say anything as she nestled her head against his chest. Killian wrapped his arms around her, holding tight.

"You are so much more beautiful, inside and out, than you give yourself credit for," he said, his voice strong. "That's why we're going to have to find a way to break this blood oath, so that you can live a long life."

Elyse peered up at him, her brows drawn. But there was hope in her eyes.

"I'm not letting you turn yourself in," he whispered. "I don't know how we'll do it, but I do know that the world needs more people like you, Elyse."

He held her chin as he gently kissed her lips. She felt as the tension in her muscles seemed to fade away. She curled her head against his chest, her breaths soft and warm against his skin. It wasn't long before he faded into sleep.

When he dreamt, it was of her, fierce and free.

CHAPTER 48

— ◆ —

ELYSE

W hen Elyse awoke in Killian's arms, she thought she was dreaming. The tent was still dark, and her muscles were sore. She didn't want to move.

Then she remembered everything. The angel's blood, the walker, making love with Killian. Her heart thundered with every recollection, forcing her to sit upright.

"What time is it? We need to get going." They needed every second of daylight to hike back to the dock and find Ymaritis. As much as she wanted to stay in bed with Killian, there was work to be done. A demon to destroy.

Her nerves on edge, she scrambled to find her clothes as Killian rubbed his eyes. He stretched his muscled arms over his head and sat up, reaching for his tunic on the ground. By then Elyse was already dressed and lacing up her boots. She was just about to stand and enter the main area of the tent when a hand yanked her back down to the bed.

"Just one thing," Killian said, and he pulled her close to kiss her.

And just like that, everything suddenly felt lighter.

"Thank you," she breathed against his lips. "I needed that."

"Go on," he said, tilting his head toward the curtain. "I'll be out in a moment."

Despite the heavy bags under his eyes, Killian was glowing. His golden eyes shone at her with pure admiration, and his smile gave her hope. Elyse stole one more kiss before leaving him on the bed.

No one was in the main area of the tent, so Elyse darted outside. Daylight grazed the property, skimming the edges of the trees. Sera, Manny, and Zubir were already gathered around the smoldering remnants of the fire, preparing a small breakfast in the dim light of dawn. They all looked tired, purple shading their eyes, though they seemed to be humming with the same frenzied energy as Elyse.

"Good morning!" Zubir said cheerily as he shoved a mug of tea at her. His ebony hair was arranged in a new style—a pair of buns on either side of his head. "Feeling better?"

Elyse felt her cheeks heat. Devil's horns, she'd acted like such a fool last night—first by endangering herself by trying to leave on her own, then by completely breaking down. She glanced at Sera, who was trying to hide a smirk. Of course—she was probably beside herself with excitement that Elyse and Killian had shared a bed.

"I am, thank you," Elyse mumbled as she cupped the mug in both hands. "Where's Jaime?"

"Washing up," Manny answered. When she looked at him, he gave her a tiny nod—so small, she almost thought it hadn't happened.

She thought that would be the worst of it, that they could go on about their business without making a fuss over their reconciliation. But Killian emerged from the tent a moment later, and Manny beamed at him.

"Get much sleep last night, mate?" he asked, his voice simpering, which earned him a smack on the arm from Sera.

"Shut up," Killian grumbled, but he came to stand by Elyse, placing a hand on the small of her back.

Elyse hid her smile behind her mug.

Jaime rounded the house and nearly stopped in his tracks. He stared at Elyse, tension brewing in his icy blue eyes. Then his gaze slowly moved to

Killian. His shoulders squared as he took in the way they stood together, his nostrils flaring subtly. Elyse shifted on her feet. Jaime had given Killian plenty of dirty looks, but this one was different. There was true malice in his eyes as his warning to stay away from Killian echoed in her mind.

Elyse cleared her throat. "Is everyone packed up?"

The group gave various affirmations that they were ready to leave. Sera handed Elyse a slice of bread slathered in jam. Her purple eyes were soft as she touched a hand to Elyse's shoulder.

"Are you ready?"

Elyse nodded, her heart in her throat. No, she was far from ready to face Ymaritis—to face Lazarus—but she had allies. She slipped her arm around Killian's waist.

She had him.

She scarfed down the slice of bread and threw on her pack, and they all made their way to the gate. The men offered Zubir handshakes and thanked him, and Sera wrapped the small man in a tight hug.

Zubir's gray eyes met Elyse's and she stepped toward him. "Thank you, old friend," she said, trying to sound firm. It didn't seem like enough, a simple thank you. But Zubir grinned back at her.

She closed the space between them and gave him a quick hug before turning away. The sun had just breached the horizon, brightening the tops of the exotic trees. She took a deep breath as Manny opened the gate, and prepared to leave.

"Wait," she said as she suddenly spun back to Zubir. "Come with us."

Zubir's eyes widened, and he shook his head, the hair on both sides wriggling. "I-I-I can't."

"Yes, you can," Elyse protested, taking his hand in hers. "You can't hide here forever, Zubir. We could use your talents."

Zubir continued to shake his head. "No—no, I'm not safe out there."

Elyse opened her mouth, about to vow to protect him, but she felt his hand trembling. His eyes were laced with genuine fear, and it tugged at her heart.

"Perhaps another time," she said instead.

Zubir nodded, gratitude shining in his face. "Another time," he ceded quietly, before Elyse slipped her hand from his and left through the gate.

The hike back seemed to pass faster, especially since the morning wasn't so blistering hot. Even as the sun rose higher, Elyse kept her eyes peeled, apprehensive of the walker. She noticed the others doing the same, their gazes darting about.

They hardly spoke as they trekked through the forest, as if conserving all their energy to propel themselves forward. Or at least, that's what Elyse was doing. Every thud of her footsteps against the dirt path seemed to mock her, ticking away the time until sunset. Every muscle ached, a reminder of how powerful Ymaritis was—and how destructive he could be.

When they reached the stairs, they practically sprinted down to the dock, eager to escape the island. The iron door opened for them, and the spray of sea air was a welcome feeling as they hurried out.

By the time the door shut, Elyse already had the vial of angel's blood in one hand and the map of Rhodan in the other.

"You're doing that here?" Manny asked. "You don't want to—"

"Shhh," Elyse commanded. She couldn't wait a second longer to find out where Ymaritis was.

Everyone immediately fell silent, allowing Elyse to work her magic. She tuned out the sound of the waves slapping against the dock and instead focused on the spell work, willing the map to obey her magic.

They crowded around, holding their breath as they stared down at the map, waiting. Ever so slowly, shimmering, gold dots glittered across the page—five of them in total.

"Only five—that's good, right?" Sera breathed.

Elyse would have preferred one, but she supposed five was manageable.

"Which one is us?" Manny asked.

"I don't think we're on the map," Killian answered. "We're too far south."

Elyse nodded in agreement as she studied the map. The dots were scattered throughout the kingdom, but one in particular caught her eye.

"There," she said, pointing to a sparkling dot in the Asterial Mountains. "His family owns property all along this mountain range. It's got to be here."

She looked up at Killian, who gave her a reassuring nod.

"Has anyone ever been there before?" Sera asked.

Jaime stepped closer. "Can I see that?" he asked, reaching for the map.

Elyse handed it to him, and Jaime's brows furrowed as he squinted at the parchment.

He turned the map around for them to see and pointed to a town not far from the glowing dot. "Cliffguard. I've been there before. It can't be more than ten, fifteen miles away from Ymaritis."

"It'll have to do," Elyse huffed as she shoved the vial of angel's blood into her pocket. "Keep that," she said to Jaime, offering him the map. "You'll be our guide."

As Jaime stowed the map into his sack, Elyse dug out a vial of transportation potion.

"We'll go back to the country house, grab supplies, and leave right away," she said as she slipped her hand into Killian's. "Ready?"

Everyone held onto each other, preparing to be whisked away.

Elyse's heart was roaring, but she ignored it as she pictured Jaime's estate in her mind. She closed her eyes and hurled the vial at the wooden slats of the dock. The salty sea air was replaced by the scent of grass and rain, and when she opened her eyes, she was once again on the lawn of the estate, staring at the ornate cottage.

Before anyone could move, before they even let go of one another, a man's voice crooned behind them.

"Well hello, Killian."

CHAPTER 49

—◦—

ELYSE

F ear and confusion overcame Elyse as she whirled toward the voice.

Two dozen men commandeered the lawn. They all wore the same brown leather vests, the fabric torn where the sleeves used to be. The men were various heights, builds, and skin tones, yet they were unanimously vile. It wasn't their tattooed knuckles or countless scars that had Elyse's heart in her throat. It wasn't their crude muscles or sheer numbers. It was the sadistic look in each of their eyes, a promise of violence.

Their leader stood at the front of the cadre, a rugged-looking man with shoulder-length hair and a wiry beard. He stared Elyse through one dark eye, for the other was covered by a patch.

Killian immediately stepped in front of her. "Siamus," he growled. "What are you doing here?"

Elyse's jaw slackened as she stared at the leader. She knew that name. This couldn't be—was Killian working with Rhodan's Bastards?

She'd heard of the crew—had even sold to them before—but she'd never met Siamus. Now he stood before her, a brutal lust for power in his expression. He looked as she would have guessed: gruff and hardened. The eye patch only added to his menacing appearance, the bruised and swollen skin giving him a crazed look. Despite the sun that heated her skin, she shivered. She could feel her friends tensing beside her, sizing up the men just as she was.

"I found it curious that you would renege on our agreement." Siamus began. He sauntered forward, a casual yet threatening air to his gait. His voice was taunting, a lion playing with its food. "What would make you change your mind about having us capture Elyse Crenshaw? The answer was obvious: you found her yourself."

A sickening feeling clamored its way into Elyse's stomach as she made sense of Siamus's words. Killian had sought out the Bastards to help hunt her down. It shouldn't have mattered—even Siamus admitted that Killian had called them off. Yet she couldn't help feeling as if a wedge were creeping between them, driving away the trust they had rekindled.

Killian took another protective step in front of Elyse. "You have no business here," he answered, his voice deep and commanding. "Leave now." He glanced at Manny, and Elyse knew they were holding another silent conversation—a strategy among soldiers.

"Our business is over," Siamus affirmed, a sly smile cracking his grim features, "though I do owe you my gratitude."

Elyse observed the Bastards as her heart thundered against her ribs. They were each smiling, their expressions a macabre mirror of their leader. One of them cracked his knuckles, and another pulled a dagger from his belt to slide it between his thumb and forefinger.

Manny stepped closer to Sera as he shot a questioning look at Killian, waiting for his command. Jaime's chest was rising and falling rapidly as he glared between Killian and Siamus.

"Get in the house," Killian ordered over his shoulder at Elyse. There was a hostility in his eyes, aimed at Siamus. Beneath that, though, was an apology—and fear.

Siamus's answering laugh was haughty. "You're going to lead us here only to send her away?"

Jaime advanced on Killian, his finger pointed as he trembled with rage. "I knew you couldn't be trusted!" He spat the words at Killian and flung his hands out, shooting blue sparks in his direction.

Elyse tackled Killian to the ground right as the sparks soared by.

Chaos erupted on the lawn as the Bastards took the opportunity to attack. Sera threw up a shield, protecting herself and Manny, as three men shot hexes their way. Elyse leapt to her feet and began firing off spells, Killian just behind her.

She was murderous. She was exhausted, she was angry, and she didn't have time for this shit. They picked the wrong fight.

She didn't hold back as she thrust her hands forward, knocking three men off their feet. Killian advanced on one while she took the other two, her knife making quick work of both of them.

Killian, a true warrior, moved with conviction and precision. His spells were powerful, his knifework elegant and merciless, but the Bastards had decades of magical training on him. Two of them cornered him, their barrage of hexes slamming against Killian's shield. They taunted him, making a game of it, until Elyse's knife found their hearts, ceasing their laughter.

Her eyes searched the havoc, scouring the faces to find her friends. Sera and Manny were at the far end of the brawl, Sera's shield still intact as they backed away from an advancing man. Jaime was trying to fend off a Bastard, his brows drawn tight in concentration.

Elyse raced through the center of the fight, hexes flying from her fingers. It might have been easier if it were her against two dozen Bastards. She would have been able to suck the air from their lungs, to send fire to obliterate them. But with her friends there, she was distracted. They could barely defend themselves, let alone coordinate any sort of offensive attack. And if they were caught in the crossfire of one of her spells—she would never forgive herself.

Her heart flurried as she took down one Bastard, then another, all the while keeping an eye out for her friends. A mental checklist for each of their safety.

Killian, Sera, Manny, Jaime.

Elyse started toward Sera and Manny. A Bastard sent a stunning spell at her. She waved her hand to send it back toward him, the spell barreling into his chest.

Killian, Sera—

Another Bastard shot black ropes at her, their threads reaching like vines to entangle her. She blasted them to pieces before sending a death hex his way.

—Manny, Jaime.

Two more Bastards stepped before her, their smiles drenched in bloodlust. She hurled her knife at one as she shot a ball of fire at the other. Sera and Manny were behind her, enshrouded by Sera's glimmering shield.

"Get inside," she shouted, pointing toward Jaime's house.

Sera's lips parted. She looked like she would object, but Manny grabbed her waist and pushed her toward the house. Relief filled Elyse as she watched them weave through the mayhem. If she could get everyone inside, she could turn her full attention on making the Bastards suffer.

A torrent of black smoke bombarded her shield, and Elyse whirled. Through the smoke, she could make out the silhouette of a barrel of a man. She zapped him with a stunning spell before turning to find her friends.

Jaime. She spotted him first, sparring with a lanky thug. With one flick of her wrist, she sent the man spiraling backwards, his feet flying over his head.

"Get inside!" she screamed at Jaime over the chaos. But he ignored her, instead setting his sights on another Bastard. Frantic, Elyse continued her mission.

Killian.

She searched the havoc but saw no sign of him. A stunning spell blasted her shield, and she turned to put an end to whoever had sent it.

Where is Killian?

Sera and Manny neared the house. Jaime's shield was intact as he fought from the edge of the brawl. They were relatively safe, for now. But she couldn't find Killian. Her breathing hitched as she searched the faces of the lifeless bodies scattered across the lawn, praying she wouldn't find him there.

Killian?

Siamus's voice cleaved the morning air, drowning out the sounds of combat and last breaths.

"Elyse!" he roared.

She spun to face him, heart pounding.

No.

Her chest seized as she took in Siamus. He stood poised behind Killian with his knife to his throat. A single drop of blood trickled down Killian's neck.

Killian's mouth was a tight line, sewn with fury.

"Do anything stupid, and I'll slice his throat right open," Siamus snarled.

Elyse could feel everyone's eyes on her. She froze, sweat beading on her brow as she tried to calm her thundering heart.

"Drop the knife," Siamus ordered.

Without hesitation, Elyse let her knife fall to the grass. She lifted her hands slowly in surrender.

Killian stared at her with pleading eyes. "Don't do this, Elyse," he begged.

She couldn't look at him, yet she couldn't tear her eyes away. Didn't he realize? She would do anything to save him—even if it meant sacrificing herself.

Siamus grinned over Killian's shoulder. He knew the only thing stopping her from massacring every last one of them was fear for her friends.

"Let him go," Elyse demanded. "It's me you want. Take me, and no one else has to get hurt."

Siamus's eyes glimmered with satisfaction. "I'm so glad you were able to come to your senses."

A man with dark skin and a scar across his cheek approached her. He wrenched her arms behind her back, then she felt the cold touch of metal as he cuffed her wrists.

"Let him go," she repeated, her demand ringing clear.

Killian was shaking with anger. His throat bobbed as he stared at her, begging her not to go. Begging her forgiveness.

In that moment, everything coursed between them. All the heartache, the betrayal, the whispered confessions and encouraging words. Every moment she had shared with him, the ones she cherished, and the ones that made her stomach turn to stone. *This* was what Killian had become after her treachery: a scorned soldier and lover, desperate for revenge. So desperate that he would seek the help of savages. This was what she had forced him to become.

His eyes were wide, shame and fear swimming in those golden irises. Not fear for himself, though. Fear for her, and her alone.

"Finish the job," Elyse told him. She held his gaze as she silently added, "Then come find me."

Killian seemed to understand her message. He nodded, almost imperceptibly. *I will find you,* his expression promised.

Elyse glanced toward Sera and Manny. Sera had tears in her eyes, and Manny had his arm wrapped around her waist. Beside them, Jaime was panting as he sent death glares at both Siamus and Killian.

"I'll be okay," Elyse told them, sounding braver than she felt.

The dozen or so Bastards who were still alive all reached into their pockets and fished out blue vials.

"It's been a pleasure," Siamus sneered as he shoved Killian to the ground.

With one last look at Killian on his hands and knees, Elyse took a deep breath and let the blue smoke take her.

CHAPTER 50

— ◆ —

KILLIAN

K illian sprang to his feet and ran to where Elyse had been standing, but she was already gone.

"No!" he cried out, his fists clenched so tightly his knuckles were white. He pounded at the ground, as if doing so would bring her back to him. He didn't know what else to do—his mind was a cloud of rage and guilt.

A body pummeled him from behind, slamming him to the earth.

"You did this!" Jaime screamed as his fist collided with Killian's face.

Killian didn't even fight back. He deserved every punch, every blow. He felt as the tender skin beneath his eye split open, his blood spilling. He felt his nose break, the bone cracking and the cartilage shifting unnaturally. Still, he did nothing as he let Jaime punish him relentlessly.

He had failed her. Somehow, he had led the Bastards right to her. He didn't know how to find her, or what they were going to do to her.

They'd only just reconciled. He feared their newly healed relationship couldn't handle this—that the thread between them was too fragile, the wound reopening. Despite the promises they'd whispered to each other. Despite the intimacy they'd shared.

Jaime's weight lessened. Through swollen eyes, Killian watched as Manny yanked Jaime by the collar. He pulled him to his feet and pressed his blade against Jaime's chest. Jaime might have been several inches taller than Manny, but Manny had at least twenty pounds of muscle on him—and countless years of training.

"That is my lieutenant," Manny snarled as he gripped Jaime's throat. "If you so much as look at him, I swear to the gods, I will kill you right now."

"Don't," Killian rasped. Didn't Manny understand? The physical pain was nothing compared to the regret that assaulted him.

Sera rushed in, hovering over Killian. She helped him sit up, which only intensified the pounding in his head. He held a hand to his face; he could feel bruises sprouting on his cheek.

Manny glared at Jaime with pure contempt, but Killian spoke softly.

"We need him," he said, a hint of desperation in his voice. "We need all the help we can get."

Manny looked from Jaime to Killian and back again before releasing Jaime's neck and kicking him away. "Fine—but if you breathe wrong, you're a dead man." He tucked his knife back into his bandolier before extending his hand to Killian.

With Manny and Sera's help, Killian rose to his feet. He could feel Sera's hands trembling as she braced him. She was terrified, that much was clear. Her lilac eyes were full of sympathy, but he looked away. He didn't deserve her encouragement.

Jaime's eyes were glued to Killian. For a moment, he looked like he was going to attack again. Killian braced himself, though he had no doubt Manny would make good on his promise.

"What did you do?" Jaime demanded instead, his voice gravelly. "You brought them here. You let them take her away."

Killian opened his mouth, unsure how to answer. He was spared from answering, at least momentarily, by the stamp of Sera's foot.

"In the house—now," she commanded, her alabaster hand pointed toward the cottage.

"He's not welcome in my home," Jaime hissed, his blue eyes dark with hatred.

"Oh, get a hold of yourself, Jaime," Sera shouted, whirling on him. She stepped closer and pointed a finger in his chest. "If I thought for one second that Killian was a danger to Elyse, I would have killed him myself. By the goddess, stop attacking him for one damned second so we can sort this out."

Killian exchanged tentative glances with Manny and Jaime. Sera's commanding voice didn't leave much room for argument, though the thought of all of them crammed together indoors felt like the last thing he wanted.

Eyes still narrowed at Killian, his chest rising and falling with each angered breath, Jaime nodded, ceding to Sera's wishes. Hesitantly, they followed her inside, Manny a step behind Jaime to keep him in line.

Sera led them to the kitchen and ordered the men to sit at the table. She pulled up a chair beside Killian and leaned in close, inspecting his face. He was grateful that she blocked Jaime from his view. His own self-hatred was plenty at the moment, without piling on the simmering glares from Jaime.

"I should be able to heal you," Sera murmured, and she laid both hands across his face. A mixture of heat and cooling emanated from her hands, soothing Killian's swollen skin. After a moment, she let go of his cheeks.

"Feel better?" she asked.

Killian nodded. Physically, he felt better, but his mind was still racing, soaring through all the horrid possibilities of what the Bastards were doing to Elyse.

Sera slid her chair away from Killian and rested her forearm against the table. The sympathy was gone from her eyes, replaced by a stern focus. "Now, tell us everything," she said calmly.

Killian glanced toward Jaime, who was still radiating fury. He didn't blame him. Killian would have done the same—or worse—if their roles were switched.

He sighed and looked toward Manny, gathering strength from his friend. "A few weeks ago, before Prestowne, I met with Siamus. I hired Rhodan's Bastards to find Elyse and bring her to me—alive." Guilt rose in his throat, forming a lump that made it hard to breathe. Somehow, admitting it out loud made it feel even more despicable.

Jaime folded his arms across his chest. "Go on," he said through gritted teeth.

"After the blood oath," Killian continued, "I sent Siamus a letter telling him his services were no longer needed. I didn't hear from him, and I thought that was the end of it. Then yesterday, he showed up at my mother's house."

Sera's brows pulled together as concern laced her features. "Is she all right?"

"She's fine," Killian breathed. "It was strange, actually. Siamus was chatting and laughing with her when I arrived. He said he wanted to discuss our deal in person, and see if there was any way he could change my mind."

"What did you do?" Manny asked quietly.

"I told him to get the hell out and never come back." Killian rubbed his hand on the back of his neck as he tried to discern how things had escalated. "I guess he came by to follow me, but I don't know how. I transported back here afterward, so there's no way he could know where I was going... Right?" He looked to Sera, pleading with her for an explanation. He prayed that somehow this wasn't his fault, though he already knew, deep down, there was no one else to blame.

Sera bit her lip, thinking. "Did he touch you at all?" she asked hesitantly.

Killian shrugged. "He shook my hand before he left." He tilted his head as he added, "And he clapped me on the shoulder."

Jaime rose from his chair and cursed under his breath. He paced the kitchen, each step reverberating his anger.

"What?" Killian asked, dread growing in his stomach.

Sera gave him a sympathetic look. "He likely put a tracking spell on you," she said quietly. "Is this the shirt you were wearing when you went home?"

Killian nodded, unable to speak. Sera rose, towering over him. He felt like a child who'd disappointed a parent as Sera looked down at him pityingly.

She hovered her hand over his shoulder, and Killian twisted his head to watch. For a moment, all he saw was the dirt caked into his shirt, the dried sweat and blood. Then, something began to shimmer in a bluish hue. It vaguely resembled the shape of a hand.

Sera sighed as Killian's stomach clenched. "It's a tracking spell."

He dropped his face in his hands. How could he have been so stupid? In all his research trying to find spells to track down Elyse, he'd never come across anything like this—yet he felt like he should have known. He should have been more careful.

"Killian," Sera breathed, placing a hand on his back. "You couldn't have known. It's dark magic, and incredibly rare. The spell requires a powerful warlock, and some... unseemly ingredients." Her voice was compassionate, but it did little to soothe Killian's regret.

He lowered his hands and looked up at her, not bothering to hide the raw guilt on his face. "What kind of ingredients?"

Sera shifted but she held his gaze. She never shied away from telling him the truth, but she waited to speak, as if needing Killian's full consent.

"What?" Killian demanded. "Tell me."

She took a deep breath. "To keep people from using it lightly, they must..." She paused, glancing from Killian to Jaime.

"He cut out his own eye," Jaime finished for her. "That's why he was wearing the eye patch."

Killian shook his head, trying to clear the nauseating shame that clouded his mind. If he wanted to find Elyse so badly that he would cut out his own eye... This did not bode well for Elyse. He stood from his chair so fast that it clattered to the floor behind him. "We have to find her—now."

"And we will," Sera said calmly. "But we can't rush off without a plan. We don't even know where they are."

Despondence settled over them as Sera's words sank in. She was right. Elyse could be anywhere in the kingdom—in the continent, even. It was hopeless.

"Does Elyse still have the angel's blood?" Manny asked.

Killian furrowed his brows. "Does it matter? We're not going to face Ymaritis without—" He cut himself off as he realized what Manny was getting at. His eyes shot to Jaime. "You have the map, right?"

Jaime looked like he might throw a punch at Killian as opposed to answering him.

"Just give him the fucking map," Manny demanded.

With a huff, Jaime pulled the map from his pocket. Killian, Manny, and Sera crowded around him as he unfolded it.

Killian held his breath as he scoured the map. The same five dots from before were there, spread across the kingdom. His eyes widened as he spotted a new, sixth dot, right in the center of Sevhella.

"There," he said, tapping the dot. "That's got to be her." He turned to Manny and smiled at his friend. "Manny, you genius, I could kiss you."

"Sorry, brother. I'm taken," Manny said, flashing a grin at Sera.

Jaime rolled his eyes and leaned in closer to the map. "I'm not familiar with the area."

Killian looked more closely. The Bastards were keeping Elyse in the northwestern sector of the city. He'd been there several times during investigations with the guard. It was mostly abandoned and rundown—the perfect place to hide out.

"We've been there before," Manny said, gesturing to Killian. "It's probably an old apartment building or something."

"I guarantee it's heavily warded," Sera sighed. "Elyse is the best with wards."

"Yeah," Jaime agreed. "It's too bad she can't break herself out."

Killian sat back down and dropped his face in his hands. If that wasn't the damned, ironic truth. Their best shot at breaking someone out of a building guarded by wards and warlocks was the one who needed rescuing.

He rubbed at his face, trying to coax the worry from his mind.

"What if..." Sera said quietly.

Killian looked up at her. Something in her voice gave him hope.

Sera caught his eye. "What if Elyse *could* break herself out?"

Jaime scoffed, but Killian held Sera's gaze. "What do you mean?"

Sera began to pace, her excitement ringing through the kitchen. "It's a difficult spell, but we've done it before... Once... When we were a little under the influence." She gave Manny a quirky glance but kept talking. "You see, we'd had quite a bit of wine, and we got the idea that we should switch bodies. So we flipped through some spell books, had some more wine, and found a way to do it. We only switched for about ten minutes, and we only did silly things like dance—and Elyse was fascinated by my double jointed thumb—" She held up her pale hand and displayed how her thumb popped in and out of place. "—but we did it. And we could do it again."

Killian crossed the room and touched Sera's elbow, stopping her pacing. "Are you suggesting what I think you're suggesting?"

Her lilac eyes were wide, her hands wringing together, as if she could manifest the plan between her palms. "We could try and switch bodies. That way she can take down the wards herself from outside, and she can break in and unleash hell on the Bastards. It'll be harder without her being in the same room, but—I think we can do it. We just need a couple things—"

She stopped short, dropping her hands to her side. Heartache tore through her features as she turned toward Killian. "I need to have something that belongs to her. And she needs to have something of mine."

Killian dropped his gaze to the floor, his shoulders dropping as well. His chest burned, like it was incinerating in Elyse's absence. He could feel the distance between them, tearing at the bond they'd worked so hard to repair.

Manny sighed, and Sera began pacing again, her boots tapping against the wood floor.

Her boots.

"Sera." Killian's head snapped up to her. "You're wearing her boots."

Sera's lips parted, a gasp of hope escaping from her lips. It was half of the equation—but it wasn't enough.

Every memory from the past four-and-twenty hours flooded him as he grasped at the possibility. Elyse tying her silvery hair back to keep it off her neck. Elyse's red-rimmed eyes as she confessed about Lazarus. Elyse plunging her knife into the walker's eye.

"She has my jacket," Sera whispered. She sounded as if she were in disbelief at her own revelation. But it was true. Sera had given Elyse her jacket after they escaped the walker.

Killian grabbed Sera by the shoulder as excitement poured through him. "Can we do this?"

She blinked a few times as her lips curled into a hopeful smile. "I think so," she said softly. "I need a few more things—they should all be at my apartment."

Killian was already grabbing his short sword from the table and strapping it around his hips.

"Where do you think you're going?" Jaime asked, darkness in his voice.

Killian froze, his eyes shifting toward Jaime. But it was Manny who answered first.

"You don't get it, mate," he said, quiet but indignant. He stood and took a menacing step toward Jaime. "*We're* going, with or without you. And if you promise to behave, we'll let you tag along."

Killian placed a hand on Manny's shoulder, a silent order to step down. "I made a mistake," he said as he looked toward Jaime, letting some of his pain ring through. "A dire one. Now it's time for me to make it right. I'd appreciate all the help I can get."

He extended his hand toward Jaime, who stared at it with contempt.

"Fine," Jaime answered. He turned away without shaking Killian's hand.

Killian couldn't be bothered to care about Jaime's insult. He whirled toward Sera and Manny, giving them a confident grin. "Let's go get our girl."

CHAPTER 51

— · —

KILLIAN

The sun was high, casting few shadows for Killian and the others to hide in. They gathered in an alley not far from the Bastards' hideout. Manny had been right; the mercenaries ran their operation out of an old, abandoned apartment building.

They'd taken turns scurrying past the building, pretending to be passersby on errands, and gathering whatever information they could. Killian's heart pounded violently as he eyed the building. Elyse was in there, going through gods knew what. It had taken all his strength to keep himself from kicking down the front door. But he could sense the wards that surrounded the building. He was starting to get a feel for these things.

Back in the alley, Jaime confirmed his thoughts. "There's definitely wards, and they're strong," he said as he pulled the hood of his cloak further over his face.

Normally, wearing a cloak in such heat would draw unwanted attention. But the few people who meandered through the area seemed just as eager to keep their identities hidden beneath cloaks as Killian and the others did. Still, he could feel sweat dripping down the center of his back. He moved his hand to the hilt of his sword, gathering strength from the cool metal.

"Nothing Elyse can't handle, I'm sure," he said, willing truth into his words. He took a deep breath, and hoped beyond hope that this plan would work.

"Are you sure you want to do this yourself?" Manny asked Sera, his expression earnest. "You don't know what you're getting into. Let one of us do it instead."

Sera gave him a small, reassuring smile, though her bobbing throat betrayed her fear. "I'm certain," she said. "Besides, I'm the only one who can do it."

Manny nodded. Anxiety still marred his face, but he wouldn't question Sera's decision further.

"And you're sure the wards won't interfere?" Killian asked her.

"Yes," she said confidently. "The spell is rooted in clairvoyance, which can't be contained by physical magic like wards. We're essentially going to be interacting with each other on a metaphysical level."

Killian's brows furrowed. "Clairvoyance? I didn't think Elyse was predisposed to clairvoyant magic."

Sera raised an eyebrow at him. "Who told you that?"

"She did," Killian said, shifting on his feet. "Back when she first explained magic to me."

She had briefly told him on their first day of combat training that certain people were more naturally adept at certain types of magic. Clairvoyance was often passed genetically and seemed to favor females. Elyse had stated that she was more inclined toward physical magic, like spellwork.

"Then she was being uncharacteristically humble," Sera said, a sly smile playing at her lips. "Elyse has unrivaled power in all forms of magic. If she set her mind to it, she could be as strong of a seer as me, and as talented of a healer as Privya. She merely chooses to focus on physical magic."

Killian blinked a few times. Elyse's power never ceased to amaze him. He recalled their conversation the night before, when she had explained the source of her magic, confiding in him that she feared she was part-demon. Her uncommon powers only seemed to prove her theory.

"Let's get started," Jaime said with a glance up at the sun. There was still about six hours of daylight left, but they didn't know how long they would need to track down Ymaritis.

Sera settled onto the dirty floor of the alley, criss-crossing her legs, and began rifling through her pack. She pulled out a long wooden pipe and began packing it with a damp, pungent herb.

"Is that...?" Jaime began, skepticism coating his question.

Sera gave Manny a hesitant glance as she nodded. "It's al-afhun."

"What's al-afhun?" Manny asked, one eyebrow quirked.

"It's a hallucinogen," Jaime spat.

"Only in high doses," Sera retorted as she finished packing the herb. "In small doses, it has sedative qualities." She held the pipe in both hands, staring down at it in her lap. Her voice was softer as she added, "I don't normally keep it in my apartment, but after the visions of Prestowne, it helped me sleep better."

"Sera," Manny said softly as he knelt on the ground beside her. "That's nothing to be ashamed of."

Killian moved closer and rested a hand on Sera's shoulder, conveying his agreement. He and Manny had both seen the devastation at Prestowne, and he didn't blame her for seeking a way to ease her mind. He looked up at Jaime, half-expecting some pathetic apology, but Jaime only turned away.

"It'll help put me in a relaxed state of mind, so I can enter the ethereal realm better, and talk with Elyse there," Sera explained, her voice a tinge stronger. "Let's just hope Elyse is able to communicate back." Her gaze lifted to Killian as she spoke, and they exchanged a silent look of strained optimism before she raised the pipe to her lips.

She pointed a finger at the end of the pipe, where the al-afhun was packed tightly into the bowl, and a wisp of smoke rose from the dank herb. Sera inhaled deeply and held in the smoke for a long moment before blowing it out. A tangy scent filled the alleyway, and Sera closed her eyes as she took another considerable drag from the pipe.

Finally, she set the pipe on the ground beside her and rested her palms face-up on her knees. All Killian could do was watch and wait.

Chapter 52

— · —

Elyse

It felt like Elyse had been in the warm, windowless room for days. She was forced to stand, her arms outstretched as chains pulled her wrists in opposite directions. Chains that were too short to allow her any rest on the grimy floor. Chains that disabled her magic.

She was drenched in sweat from the stagnant air of the room, and Sera's jacket wasn't helping. Her shoulders were sore from being stretched out for however long she'd been there, and her legs were screaming at her after hiking nearly ten miles the day before. She hadn't bothered screaming for help; even if her throat wasn't bone dry, no one would hear her.

They'd dragged her up two flights of stairs before throwing her into a room with no furniture. A single candle affixed to the wall by the door was all she had to examine the scope of her captivity.

At first, her mind had raced through all the possibilities of escape. She'd scoured the room for any tools, had searched the man who chained her up for any weaknesses, but there was nothing. Hope had quickly deserted her and been replaced by an all-consuming numbness.

So she stood. And she waited.

She prayed that Killian would go after Ymaritis first. She could withstand whatever the Bastards put her through. What she couldn't stomach was the thought of her friends wasting precious moments to rescue her. Yet at the same time, she knew if their roles were reversed, she would burn down the world to save them.

Her tired mind pondered what sort of lashing Jaime had given Killian. She'd seen the look in Jaime's eyes, the pure hatred. He'd truly believed, on some irrational level, that Killian was still against her—that he'd led the Bastards there on purpose. When had Jaime become so daft?

Elyse knew without a doubt that Killian had been tricked. Shame and guilt had battled for dominance in his expression as he realized what he'd inadvertently done. Her captivity was not a victory for him, but a defeat.

She also knew, with every fiber of her being, that Killian would have let Siamus slit his throat if it meant saving her. She shuddered, the chains rattling, as she replayed that moment. She never wanted to see a knife pressed to Killian's throat again.

Finally, the door opened. Elyse wasn't surprised to see Siamus himself sauntering in. He stroked his scraggly beard as he took her in, the slightest hint of a smile on his lips.

"Comfortable?" he asked calmly, cruelly.

Elyse spat on the floor.

Siamus's petty smile grew to a full smirk. "Glad to see you're not so easily tamed."

She watched him as he pulled a dagger from his hip, palming it with ease. He pricked his thumb with the dagger's edge, taunting Elyse. She looked on with disdain. She wouldn't give him the satisfaction of seeing her squirm.

"I've always been curious about you, Elyse." He purred her name, letting it slip over his tongue like an aged mead. "Such power, such grace... It's almost unnatural."

He took a step closer, then another, until he rested the dagger against her chest. Elyse kept her breathing steady, despite the way his words evoked a shiver.

"Where does your power come from?" he asked in a lilt as he caressed the dagger against her jacket.

Elyse met his gaze and forced a snarl into her lips. "While you were out raping and pillaging, I was practicing my ass off."

Siamus let out a low chuckle. "I do not think so. I think there's more to you than meets the eye."

Elyse tried not to cringe as he gently grazed the dagger down her arm. His eyes, cool and unrelenting, never left hers. Slowly, he began to roll up her sleeve.

"What if it's in your blood?" he asked. It sounded more like he was thinking aloud rather than actually asking her. "I wonder, could you share your power with others?"

Elyse's heart raced as Siamus pressed the dagger to the flesh of her wrist. He cut a long, clean line across the width of her arm. Elyse gritted her teeth but refused to cry out.

"No need to be brave," he crooned as the blood seeped from her arm. "It's just you and me here."

Without warning, he lowered his mouth to her wound and began sucking. The intimacy of his lips on her skin was revolting. Elyse tried to pull away, but her shackles held. Siamus drank deeply, squelching sounds echoing loudly through the stone room.

She began to feel queasy. Her knees buckled, threatening to give out. She tried to take deep breaths, but her head was spinning, her vision blurring. When she thought she was about to pass out, Siamus lifted his head.

Blood was smeared across the lower half of his face, dripping down his beard. He gave her a feral grin and wiped his mouth with the back of his hand.

"That should be enough," he sneered. "For now."

He laid his hand across the cut, and she felt the itching warmth as her skin stitched back together.

Even with the wound healed, she still felt weak. She'd hardly eaten, and Siamus had drunk nearly a pint of her blood. Pushing away the dizziness, she managed to rasp, "If you think that will give you some of my power, you're even more stupid than I thought."

With every ounce of strength she could muster, she kept her fear from showing on her face. Truthfully, Siamus might have been on to something. If Lazarus had procreated with her mother to make her, then it was possible that her magic ran through her blood. But she wasn't about to let the Bastard think there was any validity to what he'd done.

Siamus smirked, showing blood-stained teeth. "We'll see."

Elyse watched with blurred vision as he took slow, deliberate steps to the center of the room. He turned back toward Elyse, lifting his hand and flexing his fingers dramatically. She might have scoffed if she had the energy.

"I've never been very good with fire," he recited, staring at Elyse intensely. Then he turned his gaze to his hand, his expression evolving into one of concentration.

Elyse's eyelids were heavy, but she forced them open, watching Siamus as he summoned a flame. She schooled her features into boredom, though curiosity and dread churned within her.

He smiled as he watched the flame grow larger, consuming his hand and forearm. Elyse held her breath as he opened his other hand and called fire to it as well. He bent his fingers and twirled his wrists, testing the limits of his powers. But the flame grew no more, and his smile faded, replaced by knitted brows.

Elyse huffed an aching laugh. "Pathetic. Let me out of these chains and I'll show you true power."

Siamus clenched his fists, extinguishing the fire. He glared at Elyse, and she tried to flash him her characteristic grin, but it felt more like a grimace.

"I guess we'll just have to proceed with more experiments, won't we?" he crooned as he stepped to the door. "Be a darling and stay put," he added before he exited the room.

The moment he was gone, Elyse closed her eyes and focused on taking slow, deep breaths. *It could be worse,* she told herself. They were keeping her alive. They weren't torturing her—yet. She would survive until Killian came to find her.

Killian. As she blinked, trying to ignore the aching that thundered through her body, she cursed him for leading the Bastards to her. She hated him. But of course, she didn't. Not at all.

If he could forgive her for lying and killing King Cyril, she could forgive him for this.

Elyse.

A whisper echoed through the room, tapping the edge of her senses. She closed her eyes, took a deep breath in through her nose and pushed the air out through her mouth. She was dizzier than she thought if she was hearing things.

Elyse.

The whisper caressed her spine. It nudged at her mind, as if asking to be let in. But whispers didn't nudge, and they certainly didn't caress. Was this some sort of trick? Had Siamus drugged her without her realizing it?

She opened her eyes, expecting to see some sort of hallucination, but there was nothing except the soft flicker of the candle across the room.

Please. Elyse, please.

Again, the whisper dragged its delicate finger across her mind. There was something familiar about it. Something comforting. Goose pimples rippled across her body as she tried to understand.

Elyse. Elyse. Elyse.

The whisper was relentless now. It grew from a soft tapping to a steady, unapologetic knocking.

"Go away," Elyse commanded weakly as she closed her eyes. "You're not real."

Elyse.

She was too tired to fight it. She didn't know what it was, or how it was happening. Somehow, it felt like home. It felt like a lullaby, inviting her to escape. Yet it felt like a trick all the same.

Please, the whisper called, one final petition. Something stirred in Elyse's gut, coaxing her to give in. She took a final deep breath and prayed that she was doing the right thing as she welcomed the whisper into her mind.

When she opened her eyes, she found herself face-to-face with Sera.

Sera wore one of her usual flowy gowns, the silk fabric stirring around her. Her long black hair floated in the air like ink spilling into the night.

Elyse blinked. Sera was floating in the air, and so was Elyse. A starry night sky surrounded them with a rich gradient of magentas and violets. The ground was nowhere in sight—just twinkling stars as far as Elyse could see.

"We're in the ethereal realm," she breathed as she looked back up at Sera.

Sera's lilac eyes matched the shimmering canvas of sky behind her. She looked just as beautiful and celestial as the night around her. "Are you okay? Are they hurting you?"

Elyse looked down to her arm, where moments earlier, Siamus drank blood straight from her vein. But there was no freshly healed cut. She still felt dizzy, though, as she touched her hand to her arm.

"I'm fine—for now."

Sera nodded as tendrils of dark hair swirled around her. Somehow, she looked even more elegant, as if she were made for this place—as if this was her true form, and her beauty couldn't be wholly expressed in an earthly body.

"Do you remember that night we stole a few bottles of vintage wine and smoked al-ahfun?" Sera asked with a strange urgency.

Elyse's brows furrowed even as a smile twisted her lips. What an odd memory to bring up at such a desperate time. "I don't remember much about that night," she laughed. "Except that we—" Her eyes widened as she floated toward Sera, hope igniting within her as she realized what Sera was planning. "You want to switch bodies."

"Yes, and we need to do it quickly. Do you think you'll be able to?"

Elyse nodded. In a deranged twist of fate, the blood loss had lulled her into the perfect, placid state of mind to perform the spell.

"Good," Sera continued, her expression serious. "We'll make the switch, and then you can break in and free yourself."

"Sera," Elyse interjected. The thought of her friend taking her place in that dark room, being subjected to whatever torture Siamus was surely coming up with... She wouldn't allow it. "I can't ask you to do that. They have me chained in there—"

But Sera lifted her hand. "You're not asking. I'm offering, and we're not arguing about this." She floated closer and laid her hand on Elyse's shoulder.

Elyse looked down at her friend's pale hand. The starlight seemed to reflect off her skin in shimmering waves. "I'll be quick," Elyse promised. "I'll get you out before they can hurt you."

Sera smiled. "I know you will." She took both of Elyse's hands in her own and closed her eyes. "Now let's do this."

Elyse took one last admiring look at her friend before she closed her eyes. She rarely used any sort of clairvoyant powers, but she reached deep inside herself and called upon them. Her heart beat faster and the air seemed to stir as she recalled the spell, willing her mind to enter Sera's body, and allowing Sera's mind into her own. Everything began to tingle, from her toes to her lips to the ends of her hair. She squeezed Sera's hands tighter, even as she felt her slipping away.

With one final push, she felt her mind disassemble. It fell apart like the petals of a flower, only to be reconstructed again, one at a time.

When she opened her eyes, the starry backdrop was gone, replaced by a dirty alleyway. Killian stared eagerly down at her.

A smirk grew on his full lips, a fire igniting in his eyes. "You did it."

CHAPTER 53

— • —

KILLIAN

The moment Sera opened her eyes, Killian knew it wasn't the seer looking back at him, but Elyse. Her soft countenance shifted into something fierce as her lilac eyes darkened.

"You did it," he said, unable to help the smile that spread across his lips. He offered a hand to Elyse and helped her up from where she sat in the alleyway.

Elyse stumbled a little as she stood, and Manny touched her elbow to steady her. He stared at Elyse—at Sera's face—no doubt studying the same change Killian had noticed.

"How do you feel?" Killian asked.

Manny took a step back and let her stand on her own while Jaime stood watching, brows knitted with concern.

Elyse blinked and shook her head. "Strange," she said as she lifted a hand and examined it. "I forgot how much longer Sera's limbs are than mine. Devil's dick, she's a giant!"

She flexed her fingers, curling and uncurling her hands into fists, and walked around the alleyway.

"What are they doing to you in there?" Manny asked with a thick coating of concern.

"It's nothing," Elyse said quickly—too quickly. "They have me chained in a room. Sera will be fine." She glanced at Killian for the briefest moment before averting her gaze.

She was lying. Whatever they were doing to her, she didn't want Manny to know.

Manny either didn't catch on to the lie or was too eager to get Sera out to bother discovering the truth. "Here," he said, thrusting a tiny vial at Elyse. "It's a smelling salt. Sera said it would help if you're still feeling groggy."

She took the vial from him and clumsily uncorked it, then held it beneath her nose. She sniffed briskly and turned her head to the side, scowling at the scent.

"That's foul, but it'll work," she rasped.

Whatever was in the vial seemed to do the trick with only one whiff. When Elyse faced Killian again, her eyes were wide and fiery, and she stood taller.

"Is everyone ready?" she asked, glancing at each of the men. She looked as if she might bolt into the Bastards' hideout without warning.

"One moment," Killian said as he dug his hand in his pocket. He pulled out a small vial—the one item he had retrieved from his mother's house. He handed the vial to Manny, who quirked one eyebrow at him.

Manny accepted the vial and studied the words on the label: ANTI-HEX POTION. A curious Elyse peered over his shoulder before her eyes shot to Killian.

"You kept it?" she asked, breathless.

Killian smiled. He'd wondered if she would recognize it—the potion he'd bought from her the day they'd met.

"Of course I kept it," he said softly.

She smiled back at him, holding his gaze, a thousand unspoken words exchanged between them. Yes, he had kept it. Just as he'd always held hope for her, for them, even when he hadn't acknowledged it.

"Enough making eyes with my woman," Manny quipped, breaking the tender moment. "Why are you giving this to me?"

Killian turned to his friend. "I'll do my best to shield both of us, but just in case, I think you should drink this."

Elyse nodded her agreement. Manny didn't argue. He hadn't exactly been helpful during the skirmish at Jaime's estate. He was probably grateful for the added protection.

Once Manny had downed the potion, they all looked to Elyse. Her expression was cold, her brows drawn nefariously. A part of Killian reveled in that look, eager to watch her take revenge. He had once pondered the extent of her powers, believing that she was capable of burning the world down but that she would never dare to. Now he understood the folly in that theory. Elyse would turn the world to ash for Sera, and for him.

Her gaze met his, heat radiating incongruously from soft lilac eyes. She nodded at him—a plea to stay safe, to not bring her any more pain. Killian nodded back, silently promising to stay vigilant, and they marched out of the alley together.

CHAPTER 54

—— • ——

KILLIAN

E lyse surged like a forest fire, fierce and unrelenting.

One moment she had her eyes closed, her mouth drawn tight as she focused on ripping down the Bastards' wards. The next she was off, kicking in their door and sending three men to their deaths before they could even fire off one spell.

Commotion roared through the rundown building. Killian heard voices shouting, boots crashing into the floor above them. Elyse hardly seemed to notice as she tore onward, hurrying down the hall.

Her friends followed, allowing her space to unleash her magic. She'd given them one command: Stay behind me. So they obeyed, watching in awe as she eviscerated her enemies with mere thrusts of her hands.

The third floor was their target, where Elyse said her body was being held captive. They found a staircase at the back of the house and climbed it, but a menacing Bastard waited for them at the top of the first flight, his shield at the ready.

Elyse simply clenched her fist, and a gust of air sent the man tumbling headfirst down the stairs. She sidestepped him with ease while Killian had to leap over the man as he hurried to keep up with her. He spared a glance back to make sure that Manny and Jaime were still behind him as he mounted the landing.

The second floor was the same—another half dozen cocky Bastards who all underestimated Elyse. Though she fought with cold intensity, Killian could see that something was off. The exhaustion in her shoulders, the subtle gracelessness of fighting in a body foreign to her. Still, vengeful fire burned in Sera's features as Elyse hurled everything she had at them—fire, stunning spells, and death hexes.

Killian kept his shield intact, protecting both himself and Manny. As Elyse bludgeoned a man's head against the wall, they exchanged wide-eyed looks. "Stay on her good side," Manny's stunned expression seemed to convey.

It was difficult to watch Elyse without aiding her. She didn't need their assistance as she ducked and spun, hitting her enemies with exhilarating precision, yet Killian's hands flinched of their own accord, desperate to help. He balled his hands into fists, forcing himself to watch, to learn the beauty and nuances of magical combat.

And beautiful it was. She seemed to know her opponents' moves even before they did. She caught a man's wrist right as he was about to bring his dagger down on her chest. Ice curled from her fingers, encapsulating the man's entire arm in the blink of an eye. He screamed and stumbled backward, and Elyse finished him off with a blast of magic to the chest. He crashed to the ground, his frozen arm shattering.

No, she didn't need their help at all. In fact, given the amount of pent-up anguish she held, it was likely therapeutic.

When Elyse was finished, nearly a dozen bodies lay scattered in the hall. Several of them appeared to be sleeping, slouched against the walls, their bodies unmarked by the death hexes that had ended them. A few of them still sputtered blood from fatal wounds, but their open, foggy eyes were unseeing. Elyse didn't glimpse at any of them as she headed toward the staircase at the end of the hallway.

This time, no one was there to block their way as they bound up the stairs. Only a narrow corridor met them, empty and desolate. Elyse stopped before a door on the left and blasted it off its hinges. She charged into the room, Killian hastening after her.

What he saw made his heart ratchet in his throat.

Elyse—or rather, Elyse's body—was pinned against the far wall. Chains pulled her arms in opposite directions. Chains that bit into her wrists, bruising them. And on the bare skin of her left arm, a freshly healed cut, caked in dried blood. Sera lifted her head, a weary smile on her lips at the sight of her rescuers.

Killian looked to Elyse—the one who inhabited Sera's body—and saw the darkness in her eyes. Something had changed in her the moment she entered this smothering, dimly lit room. Anger had exploded to rage, laced with fear.

Her gaze was not on herself, but on Siamus, who stood smirking, flanked by three other Bastards. They didn't bother with any formalities this time as they lifted their hands and set off a barrage of spells.

A green arrow flew across the room, zipping past Killian's shoulder. Manny took a step toward Sera, but Killian caught him by the wrist as he threw his shield into place. "Getting yourself killed won't save her," he barked at his friend, though he understood his pain. Seeing Elyse chained like that, the blood on her arm—it made him feral.

Elyse and Jaime took three of the Bastards for themselves, and Manny stood watch at the door, leaving Killian to face Siamus. His vision blurred red, his anger threatening to make him snap, but he knew this was what he'd trained for. Siamus stood for everything he hated. Dark magic, wicked intentions, immoral actions—things he'd associated with all magic-wielders. Things he'd wrongly associated with Elyse.

As he raised and lowered his shield, shooting precise yet powerful spells at Siamus, he made sure to keep Elyse—both versions of her—in his sights. Siamus met him spell-for-spell, hex-for-hex. He laughed as Killian let his hatred show.

Across the room, he heard screams as Elyse and Jaime cornered the last Bastard. Killian's rage was centered on Siamus, though. Unable to find the means to advance, he kept his shield up as Siamus pelted smoke and curses at him. Siamus only grew more confident, more aggressive, as his vicious smile slithered wider across his face.

Violet, emerald, fiery red—spells of every color assaulted Killian's shield as he shuffled around the floor, biding his time to attack. He glanced over his shoulder to see Elyse stooped over a body, pulling her dagger from the man's chest. Just as he looked back at Siamus, a ball of white light came hurtling at him.

The light bounced off the side of his shield, reflecting at a hard angle. Killian realized with horror what was about to happen, but it was too late to stop it. The light slammed into Elyse just as she stood up, her shield still down, and she went soaring backward.

CHAPTER 55

— • —

ELYSE

Everything went dark as Elyse collided with the wall and then crashed to the ground. Pain seared through her ankle as it twisted beneath her weight, and she gasped sharply.

She was a fool for letting her guard down, even though Siamus seemed thoroughly preoccupied with Killian. Fighting off the Bastards below had been easy; they were idiots, and she hadn't been distracted by her friends' safety. The melee in the cold, stony room was far more chaotic, and she'd gotten cocky.

Her vision returned, cloudy and distorted, but she couldn't bring herself to look at her ankle. She would no doubt see her foot jutting out from her leg at an unnatural angle. The pain rattled her completely, her stomach in her throat, trying to force its way through her mouth.

"Elyse!"

"Sera!"

Killian and Manny shouted for her at the same time, agony in both their voices.

Manny was at her side instantly, his eyes scanning her for injury. "Don't move," he demanded as she tried to sit up. He'd gone ghostly pale, his skin's golden hue retreating as he stared down at her mangled joint.

Killian, though—Killian gave Siamus a murderous look.

He lifted his chin and squared his shoulders as he lowered his shield. No—he didn't lower it, not completely. The shimmering air grew smaller, enveloping his left forearm in a circle, the way a soldier bears a shield of metal. His right hand unsheathed the short sword at his hip, twirling it with a dark elegance. A sneer played at his lips. "You will regret that," he uttered in the most sinister voice Elyse had ever heard him use.

Killian didn't wait for Siamus's reply as he advanced toward him, swinging his sword. Siamus moved aside but shot a flare of blue light at Killian, then another. Killian barely flinched as he let the light deflect off his shield, his golden eyes burning with ire.

Pain still racked Elyse's body, and she stifled her trembling. But she couldn't tear her eyes off Killian—couldn't breathe as she watched him move with precision fueled by fury.

Everyone else was just as captivated. Elyse could feel the tension rippling off Manny as he watched his brother at battle. Sera looked on through heavy-lidded eyes, and even Jaime seemed impressed from where he stood across the room.

Siamus backpedaled around the room, sending hex after hex at Killian. But no matter where the mercenary went, Killian was there, easily parrying the spells and furiously thrusting his sword. He was a torrent of vengeance, wrath incarnate. Elyse spotted a hint of fear in Siamus's lone eye.

The room echoed with the sound of Killian's sword cleaving the air, and Siamus's rapid breaths. Elyse knew with complete certainty as she tracked their movements that Killian's sheer determination would win out. It was only a matter of waiting for Siamus to tire or slip up.

She held her breath as Killian stood up straight, lifting his shield higher and leaving his legs wholly unprotected. She saw the conniving gleam in his eyes, and she knew what he was doing.

Siamus sprang for the trap. A massive ball of fire flew at Killian's legs, but he was already two steps ahead. He spun out of the way and brought his sword down on Siamus's shoulder.

Blood sprayed and Siamus screamed as his flesh tore apart. Killian offered no mercy. He thrust the sword at Siamus's gut, then ripped it clean out. Siamus fell to the floor, clutching his wounded stomach. Killian's chest heaved as he stared down at Siamus, and for a moment, Elyse's pain vanished as she beheld her hero.

Killian took one step, then another, and reached for Siamus's scruffy hair. He grabbed a handful and thrust backward, exposing Siamus's neck. Siamus held his stomach tighter as he grimaced in pain, but he couldn't fight.

Killian shoved his sword straight through Siamus's throat.

CHAPTER 56

— ❦ —

KILLIAN

K illian towered over an impaled Siamus. Fury still rang in his ears, along with the sound of his own heaving breaths. He did not move. He was frozen there, trapped by his own rage.

Siamus had hurt Elyse. He might have killed her. Killian had never known such wrath. It terrified him, paralyzing him.

Elyse's pained murmur carried to his ears, coaxing him out of his trance.

"The key—it's in his pocket."

She spoke so quietly, her ferocity dampened by her pain. He'd seen the way her foot jutted out from her leg at a sickly angle. His silver-haired witch was acting brave, but he knew she was in agony. He also knew that he should go to her, but he couldn't pull himself away from Siamus.

The Bastard had hurt her. He had paid for it with his life.

Yet it didn't seem like enough.

A firm hand landed on his shoulder. "It's over, brother," he heard Manny say.

The touch seemed to awaken him. He blinked, then blinked again, before staring down at the blood that coated him.

It was over.

He slid the sword from Siamus's throat, and the body crumpled to the floor. Manny knelt beside him and riffled through Siamus's pockets as Killian turned to Elyse.

As soon as he saw her, staring up at him through Sera's purple eyes, his heart swelled. "Elyse," he cried, dropping his sword and running to her. He fell to his knees beside her and tenderly wrapped his arms around her. She whimpered but nestled her body against his.

They didn't speak. Even though she wore Sera's skin, she was undoubtedly his. He held her tighter, grateful that she hadn't been hurt worse.

Distantly, he heard the clatter of chains as Manny freed Sera. They came to stand before them, Sera rubbing the chafed skin on her wrists where the shackles had been.

"Are you okay?" Killian asked her.

She nodded, her dark eyes distant. "Just a little dizzy is all." Then she shifted her gaze to Elyse. "Are you ready?"

Elyse lifted her head an inch from Killian's chest. "Are you?"

Sera glanced down at the mangled ankle, and her lips tightened. "I'll manage," she said quietly.

Sera knelt before them, and Killian helped Elyse sit up. The two women held each other's hands—their own hands—and both closed their eyes.

The moment their minds re-entered their own bodies, Sera gasped and clutched her ankle.

"Fuck," she groaned—the least lady-like thing Killian had ever seen her do.

Manny was instantly at her side, replacing Killian. "We'll heal it—right?"

Killian looked up at Elyse, wondering why she hadn't already healed the broken ankle. Her expression was grim.

"I can heal it," she said tentatively. "But..."

"It'll take too long," Sera finished for her through gritted teeth. "And we'll need potions."

"And even then, she should rest for a few hours at least," Elyse added. Her mouth drew into a taut line, and the shadows beneath her tired eyes seemed to darken.

Manny's hand stroked Sera's back in a soothing motion, but the seer's face was resolute. She'd already known this would be the end of the mission for her.

"I'm going with you," Manny declared, drawing closer to Sera.

Killian opened his mouth to protest, but Manny cut him off with a sharp look.

"I'm not leaving her," he said with stony determination. "Besides, I'm more harm than help. You'll be better off not having to worry about me."

Killian knew there was no changing Manny's mind. He would have done the same for Elyse. Still, fear turned in his stomach. Part of him knew Manny was right, that his inability to properly defend himself was a hindrance. Yet he didn't know if he could face Ymaritis without his second, his best friend, by his side.

Elyse slipped her fingers into his, and warmth immediately spread up his arm, filling his chest. She turned to Manny. "Take her to Privya's," she commanded softly. "Stay there, and we'll meet you after—with the rose," she added, a hint of bravery in her voice.

Killian handed Manny a transportation potion from his pocket as Elyse knelt before Sera. She slid her hand across Sera's face and blinked a tear from her eyes.

"Thank you," she uttered.

Sera forced a pained smile onto her lips. "You would have done the same for me."

They stayed like that for a moment before Elyse let out a ragged sigh. "Okay," she breathed. "We should get going." She rose and stared down at Manny, giving him a fierce look. "Take care of her," she said, equal parts demand and request.

Manny nodded as he slipped his hand into Sera's. "We'll see you soon," he said, and threw the transportation potion to the ground.

Killian waved his hand in front of him, clearing the blue smoke from his vision. He turned to face Elyse but jumped when he saw Jaime standing behind her.

Gods above, he'd completely forgotten Jaime was there. He was surprised the buffoon hadn't been fawning over Elyse's injury.

"I'm glad you're okay," he said to her, glaring sidelong at Killian. He pulled a transportation potion from his pocket, but Killian held out his hand.

"Wait," he urged. "I think we should take a look around. Maybe there's something here that will be helpful."

Jaime looked like he might argue, his eyes narrowing as his lips parted, but Elyse spoke before he could.

"Okay," she uttered, nodding her head. "That could be a good idea."

He held out his hand and waited for Elyse to take it. "I'm sorry," he said.

"I know," she answered calmly as she took his hand. There was no bitterness in her features, no distrust or hostility. Killian let out a sigh of relief—though he silently vowed to spend the rest of his life making it up to her.

Together, they ventured out the door, leaving Jaime to follow behind.

CHAPTER 57

— • —

ELYSE

Cliffguard was a placid town, its only fierceness in the wind that tore through the streets. The buildings were all the bland color of tree trunks—a murky mixture between gray and brown—and the denizens were just as lackluster.

Elyse couldn't leave the damn place fast enough.

She pulled her jacket tighter as she, Jaime, and Killian all huddled around the map. A few passersby gave them inquiring looks, no doubt curious about the mysterious strangers in tattered clothes. It was unlikely the town had visitors very often, especially ones with large bows slung over their shoulders, as Killian had. He'd spotted the massive weapon at the Bastards' hideout and immediately pilfered it. Elyse had witnessed firsthand his proficiency with the bow and arrow; it had been a smart move to take it.

They'd also snatched a few other items that might come in handy: magic-suppressing shackles, potions for speed and accuracy, and a generous vial of poison that prevented injuries from being healed magically. Killian had also quickly rummaged through the kitchen to find bread and water, and forced Elyse to take a moment to eat something. She had absolutely no appetite, and initially she resisted, but Killian insisted—in his stern lieutenant's voice—that she had to keep her strength up.

Admittedly, she did feel better after eating. Her body still ached, but her mind felt clearer as she focused on the map before her. Her eyes narrowed in on the neat, gothic letters that notated CLIFFGUARD, and the shimmering gold dot just northwest.

"That way," Jaime said, nodding toward the mountains that spanned the western landscape. They appeared endless, a formidable expanse of evergreen trees and craggy peaks.

Elyse brushed a strand of hair from her face and looked to the east. Somewhere out there, her friends were together—counting on her. Counting on them.

She inhaled, nodding her head, gathering her momentum. "Okay," she breathed. "Let's go."

A narrow dirt path led them into the forest, away from the small town bustle. Elyse normally savored the feel of packed dirt beneath her boots, the soft cadence of marching feet, but she found no joy in it now. Not when worries pillaged her mind and anxieties swarmed her chest.

The path wove around trees, a scenic sort of labyrinth with no clear agenda or destination. It wasn't long before they abandoned it, instead taking a more direct route, cutting through the forest.

It was endless.

Thousands of trees, millions of rocks, all while climbing a subtle yet taxing slope. But at least she had Killian.

His presence brought her a sense of calm. Not completely—no, there was nothing that would wholly soothe the panic that ravaged her. But with Killian by her side, she felt as if they were journeying toward possible victory instead of certain death.

Jaime marched ahead of them, as if unable to bear seeing her and Killian together. He kept a steady pace, one that Elyse's short legs and aching muscles struggled to maintain. She rotated her shoulders every few minutes, trying and failing to alleviate the stiffness from being chained for hours. Distantly, she wondered how Sera was doing.

Most of her thoughts, though, were on what lay ahead. She was torn between checking the map religiously to monitor their progress, and continuing on, trudging ahead without interruption.

One thing was for certain, though. Ymaritis was here.

She knew it, somehow. Or rather, her magic did. It thrummed through her veins, snarling yet anxious, like a scared dog that bared its teeth at a stranger. Elyse didn't understand how her magic could sense something dark lurking among the wildflowers and vibrant trees. It wasn't something she cared to think about at that moment.

Her magic stirred more as the miles and hours passed, coupling dangerously with her anxiety. Killian and Jaime might not have been able to sense Ymaritis's presence as she could, but they could see the sun hovering lower in the sky. The trio increased their pace, an unspoken understanding between them, until they were practically jogging up hill after hill.

Tension grew as the sun descended. The eastern sky was now a deep violet, while the western horizon brewed with the pink-and-orange gradient of dusk. The cicadas hummed their song, a fervent anticipation of nightfall. A buzzing manifestation of Elyse's dread.

She could hardly keep herself from shaking. Even Killian, who had kept his expression neutral, his posture confident, now seemed to sway with worry.

"I'm going to climb one of these trees," he declared, tugging Elyse's wrist. "Maybe I can see something."

She nodded, her stomach clenching as she noted the way his throat bobbed. His chest rose and fell along with his shallow breaths, and sweat coated his brow. He stalked toward the nearest tree and heaved himself onto the lowest branch.

"We should leave him," came a low snarl in Elyse's ear.

She turned to find Jaime standing directly behind her, so near that her face nearly brushed against his chest. She took a hurried step back, a branch cracking beneath her boots like the sound of a bone snapping.

"What?" she breathed, too stunned to say anything else. She blinked, and the reality of his demand slammed into her. "Are you *mad*?"

"We should leave him," Jaime repeated, vehemence drenching his voice. He took a step toward her. "We'll face Ymaritis on our own, and then we'll run away together—somewhere far from *him*." His eyes shot toward where Killian had disappeared into the branches.

"I'm not leaving him," Elyse answered firmly as fury heated her blood. "And you are not in charge of me."

She turned away from him, but Jaime caught her shoulder. There was nothing but loathing in his blue eyes as he spun her back to face him.

"You're not thinking straight," Jaime said. "Killian will be the death of you—literally. This blood pact will kill you."

"And you think you can fix it?"

"I think you stand a better chance fixing it by coming with me than you do by fucking him!"

He spat the words at her, like they were filthy. Like she had defiled herself.

Elyse cringed and shook Jaime's hand from her shoulder. She didn't take her eyes off him as she backed toward the tree, inching away from him and toward Killian.

"Let me make one thing clear," she said, her voice low but emphatic. "Wherever I go, Killian goes. And wherever he goes, I go as well." She lifted her chin an inch higher. "There will be no negotiating that."

A rustling above announced Killian's return before he dropped from the lowest branch. He landed, knees bent, eyes drilling into Jaime.

"Is everything all right?" he asked, glancing toward Elyse.

She raised an eyebrow at Jaime, signaling him to answer.

Jaime looked from Elyse to Killian, then back to Elyse. His nostrils flared, and he gritted his teeth so hard that Elyse could practically hear them grinding together. But he nodded, slow and cool.

Elyse knew that Killian could sense their tension, had probably heard Jaime's disgusting accusations. He would let Elyse fight her own battles, though. He took a step closer to her and gently touched a hand to her back, and she lifted her face toward him.

"There's a ridge not far from here," he said, jerking his chin to the north. "We might be able to see something from there."

Elyse gave Jaime one last seething look before she slid her hand into Killian's. "Lead the way."

CHAPTER 58

— • —

ELYSE

Elyse clenched her fists as she followed Killian up a steep, rocky slope. Her magic was only agitated more by Jaime's outburst. It hissed to be let out, to unleash itself on him and make him pay for his words. She couldn't do anything about it though—or wouldn't. Not when there was too much at stake.

By the time they crested the hill, dusk was nearly upon them. The sun's rays seemed to reach out to Elyse, a hand pleading for aid. She wanted nothing more than to reach back, to grab hold of the sun and keep it from disappearing beyond the horizon. She steadied herself by folding her arms over her chest and gripping the sleeves of her jacket.

Below them, the forest spanned out in a sea of leaves and shadows. And there, nestled among the towering evergreens, was a clearing. It was easy to spot, not only from the absence of trees, but by the dozen or so lit candles that littered the ground. A figure stood among the candles, someone tall and dark.

Elyse fell to her knees immediately, hiding from anyone who might see them. Her heart thundered as the rocks bit into her shins. Killian and Jaime dropped to a crouch beside her, their whispers frantic.

"Did you see that?"

"It must be him."

Elyse felt a cold sweat trickle down her temple as they exchanged frenzied glances. Slowly, the three of them crawled to the edge of the ridge and looked out over the forest.

She spotted the candlelight immediately, their tiny flames a beacon in the quickly darkening forest. It took a moment for her eyes to adjust to the dimming light. As soon as she caught sight of him, her magic roiled.

"Ymaritis," she breathed, a declaration and a threat. Her magic pulsed in her veins as she spoke his name.

"I can take him out from here," Killian said from beside her. His voice was soft but sharp.

Jaime let out a scoff.

Elyse glanced toward the bow, still slung over Killian's back.

"I can take him," he said again. He stared into Elyse's eyes with a vengeful intensity.

Holding his gaze, she nodded. Ymaritis had to be nearly a hundred yards out, but Killian's expression was confident. If he said he could do it, she believed him.

She turned her sights back toward the clearing, and a movement caught her eye. Figures lurked among the trees. The longer she looked, the more figures she spotted stalking through the forest encircling the clearing.

"Henchmen," Killian uttered, voicing Elyse's thoughts.

"At least a dozen of them," Jaime iterated. He shifted, stirring the rocks. "What's your plan for them?" he asked, voice haughty, directing his question at Killian.

Elyse shot him a scathing look. "I'll handle them," she hissed. "And you'll help."

She slid from the edge of the cliff and rocked back onto her heels. To the west, the sun dipped dangerously low, kissing the tops of the trees.

"Ymaritis doesn't have a shield," she said, thinking aloud. "And I don't sense any wards."

Killian and Jaime both shuffled closer to her. They huddled together, their faces gravely serious.

"What if it's a trap?" Killian asked.

Elyse had been wondering the same thing.

"I don't know," she said, shaking her head. "Maybe it is. Maybe he can't use shields or wards for the spell. But I don't see any other way."

Both men nodded. Sunset was nearing too quickly; they were out of options.

"Okay," Killian sighed as he pulled an arrow from the quiver on his back. "Give me the poison."

Elyse fished in her pocket and pulled out the vial of glittering green liquid. It looked like a toxin as the luminous liquid swirled in its tiny glass vessel. She uncorked it and held the vial carefully as Killian dipped the tip of the arrow in the venom.

"I hope this works," Jaime muttered.

Elyse hoped so too. If they could kill Ymaritis from afar, or at least injure him badly enough, then they stood a chance.

Crouching low, she moved toward the edge of the ridge. The wind picked up, its wild movement mirroring Elyse's anxieties. She realized she was breathing heavily, her chest rising and falling rapidly. Clutching a nearby rock, she tried to steady her nerves. She couldn't afford to be rattled, not when so much was at stake.

Beside her, Killian kneeled on the rocky ledge. He held the bow in both hands, the arrow nocked and ready. His golden eyes reflected the waning sunlight, beautiful yet perilous.

"Get the rose and get out," he said. "Then come back to me."

It was a plea in its sweetest form.

Elyse reached out and laid a hand on his cheek. Killian leaned into it, his eyes half closing as he stared back at her.

"I will," she promised.

She let her hand linger there for a moment before turning to Jaime. Behind him, the sun had crested the distant trees.

318

"As soon as Ymaritis is down, we go in," she said, forcing strength into her voice. "Watch my back, and I'll watch yours."

Jaime nodded, though his eyes flickered toward Killian.

Elyse pivoted, fully facing Ymaritis once again. This was it. They would either fail, or they would succeed. Either way, they had to act fast.

She heard the groan of the bow string as Killian pulled the arrow back. The forest seemed to quiet, intensifying the sound of Elyse's racing heart. Ahead of her, Ymaritis knelt in the clearing, tending to something on the ground.

An exhale.

An echoing *thrum* as the bow released.

A whistle as the arrow soared through the air.

She couldn't hear the arrow strike, couldn't see it, but she saw Ymaritis's silhouette as he collapsed to the ground.

"Now," she growled, grabbing Jaime's hand and yanking him to his feet.

She leapt from the edge of the cliff, dragging Jaime behind her. A wave of her hand had them floating, a powerful wind propelling them toward the clearing.

Shouts sounded from below as Ymaritis's soldiers barked orders to each other. Elyse flicked her wrist to summon her shield around herself and Jaime, who held tight to her hand.

One blast, then another, pelted into the shield, but Elyse kept her eyes trained on Ymaritis's writhing body. He still lay on the ground, one hand clutched to his chest. As Elyse soared closer, her toes nearly skimming the tops of the trees, she could see the dark pool of blood that surrounded him.

"I'm going to have to lower the shield to grab the rose," Elyse shouted, barely audible over the cries of the men below and their endless barrage of spells.

Jaime nodded, his body tensing in preparation.

They reached the edge of the clearing, and Elyse held her hand parallel to the ground, guiding their descent. Three men waited for them on the ground while two more crowded over Ymaritis.

"I can't heal him!" one screamed.

That gave Elyse a surge of confidence as they sank lower, branches hurtling past them. Killian had done his part, and now victory was within reach. All she had to do was take out a few men and grab the rose. Adrenaline overran her, setting her magic ablaze.

One last look toward the sun, which was now halved by the horizon, before Elyse's boots met the grass.

Her hands moved with fierce speed, no longer hindered by exhaustion. With one swift motion, she lowered the shield and sent a blast of hard air at the surrounding men, driving them onto their backs. Another henchman emerged from the treeline, but Jaime hurled a stunning spell at him before the man could even raise his hands.

Spinning around, Elyse scanned the small area for the rose. The dim light of dusk cast shadows across the ground, but her senses remained sharp, heightened by purpose. The rose lay on a small blanket across the clearing, its crisp colors vibrant against the pale fabric.

The two men who had been tending to Ymaritis stood and whirled toward them, hands ready for casting.

Elyse raised her shield just in time to deflect their spells, then sent her own hexes barreling into their chests. As they fell to the ground, she raced toward the rose, her boots driving into the ground. Behind her, she heard the clash of magic as Jaime held off the others.

She dove, her knees sliding in the grass as she wrapped the magical rose in the blanket, careful not to touch it. A shadow emerged from the treeline, taking the form of a snarling man. Elyse's hands fumbled with the rose as she tried to snap her shield into place.

The man's brows knitted together, his hands lifting with wicked intent. A fierce *whoosh* met Elyse's ears before the man dropped to the ground. Stunned, her breathing rapid, she stared at where he lay.

320

An arrow protruded from his stomach, blood curdling around it.

She would have to thank Killian later.

Turning on her heels, she spun to see Jaime with his shield intact, fending off a flurry of attacks. Elyse tucked the rose under her arm and used her free hand to cast a trio of spells at the henchmen.

Between her and Jaime, Ymaritis lay on the ground. His body twitched, his hands spasming, but no shield protected him. His magic had likely been drained, just like the blood that spilled from his chest and lips.

Elyse stood, frozen in place as she watched him. Her fingers flinched toward her knife, still sheathed at her hip. She could end Ymaritis, could slice his throat and watch the light fade from his mismatched eyes. It seemed pointless—reckless even. His waxy skin and violent breaths spoke of an inevitable end, one that didn't require her to put herself at risk by getting any closer to him. Who knew what he was capable of, even as death gripped him?

"Let's go!" Jaime bellowed, snapping Elyse from her thoughts.

Ymaritis's soldiers were scrambling back onto their feet. She raced forward, her free hand digging into her pocket to secure a transportation vial.

As she passed Ymaritis, she gave him one last look. She expected to see him gasping, trembling as life fled his body.

Instead, he smiled at her, blood leaking from the corner of his mouth.

Elyse surged faster, crashing into Jaime. He gripped her forearm in a tight hold at the exact moment that she slammed the vial against the ground. Blue smoke erupted, vanquishing everything around them.

An instant later, dirt replaced grass. Tendrils of blue smoke dissipated into the darkness as Elyse clutched the rose to her chest. Beside her, Jaime dropped his hands to his knees, breathing heavily. Ahead of her stood the clinic, its windows alight with the flicker of candles.

It was only a few seconds, but it felt like an hour as she waited.

Another puff of blue smoke, and Killian's silhouette appeared beside her. He was instantly upon her, wrapping his strong arms around her shaking body.

"We did it," he breathed. "*You* did it."

She closed her eyes and leaned further into him as her heart migrated back into her chest. She allowed herself a moment. One moment of rest, of being with Killian, before she would check on Sera. Before she would figure out what to do about the blood pact. Before she would sleep for an entire day.

"You did it," Killian whispered again in her ear. All of the anxiety and self-loathing she'd felt faded with those words as she sank deeper into his arms.

She lifted her head, finding strength and awe in his gaze. His lips were so close to hers, and she rose to her tiptoes to close the space between them. Their mouths met, a tender yet passion-filled kiss that melted everything else away.

And then—

CHAPTER 59

— • —

ELYSE

Elyse crouched low, the wind whipping her hair as she lingered near the edge of the ridge. In the distance, the setting sun crested the treeline.

"As soon as Ymaritis is down, we go in," she said, forcing strength into her voice. "Watch my back, and I'll watch yours."

Jaime nodded, though his eyes flickered toward Killian.

Elyse pivoted, fully facing Ymaritis once again. This was it. They would either fail, or they would succeed. Either way, they had to act fast.

She heard the groan of the bow string as Killian pulled the arrow back. The forest seemed to quiet, intensifying the sound of Elyse's racing heart. Ahead of her, Ymaritis knelt in the clearing, tending to something on the ground.

An exhale.

An echoing *thrum* as the bow released.

A whistle as the arrow flew through the air.

Ymaritis's silhouette disappeared.

He was gone—not dead. Not injured. Simply... gone.

"You didn't actually think that would work twice, did you?"

Elyse whirled and nearly tumbled backward off the ridge.

Ymaritis stood on the rocks behind them, his silver eye iridescent in the fading sunlight. A menacing smile slid across his lips as he stared down at them.

Elyse's mind raced to catch up. He had transported himself from the clearing to the ridge using that inexplicable magic. But how had he even known they were there? And what did he mean—about thinking it would work twice?

Her teeth gnashed together as fear overtook her confusion. On pure instinct, she flicked her hands toward him, summoning her magic. Ymaritis gracefully waved his hand, bringing his shield up in time to deflect her death hex.

"Have you learned nothing?" His voice was a laugh that hissed with arrogance.

Before she could comprehend his words, the world darkened—so quickly it might have been a blink. Yet when reality returned, it was in a different setting. She stood, her hands behind her back, bound by rope. Silhouettes of trees surrounded her, their towering branches haunting in the light of dusk. In the distance was the ridge where she'd been perched moments earlier, its jagged edge jutting against the sky. Confusion clutched at Elyse's lungs, making her breaths serrated.

Ymaritis ran a hand through his dark hair as a confident sneer tore at his lips. His mismatched eyes gleamed with triumph. Behind him, Killian and Jaime both knelt on the grass. Their arms were pulled behind their backs just as hers were, but while Elyse struggled against her binds, they were both rigid, every muscle taut. Daggers hovering menacingly in the air, their points pressed to both Killian's and Jaime's hearts.

Elyse's fingers twitched, evoking her magic, but Killian grimaced as the dagger kissed his skin, drawing a single drop of blood.

"I wouldn't dare," Ymaritis drawled.

She halted all movement immediately. The glimmer in Ymaritis's blue and silver eyes grew brighter as resignation befell Elyse. She wouldn't dare use her magic, not when one flick of Ymaritis's fingers would cost her the lives of both Killian and Jaime. He could have used shackles or wards to stifle her magic, but he hadn't. This was a game to him, a sick test of her control. Her power both rioted and lulled within her, a desperate battle that brought a pounding to her temples.

"And just to be safe," Ymaritis crooned as he stepped toward her. He slipped his hand into her pockets, retrieving the two vials of transportation potion she had stashed away. Ymaritis crushed them in his hands, letting the blue liquid spill to the grass.

He strode away, and Elyse's eyes followed his movements, each swaggering step. With his back turned, she considered taking her chances, her muscles tensing as she debated which spell to cast. But the daggers were like sentient things, sensing her intentions. She heard Jaime's wince as his dagger broke skin, a twin slice to Killian's.

"I told you," Ymaritis sighed. He turned around and glared at the blood that bloomed across Jaime's shirt. "You're only hurting them."

Elyse's eyes burned as she took in Killian's brave facade, Jaime's chaotic fear. This wasn't how this was supposed to go. She was supposed to save everyone, was supposed to avenge the people of Prestowne. Helplessness roiled in her stomach, making her knees quake.

Ymaritis glanced toward the west. The setting sun was to Elyse's back, but she could tell it was low by the shadows that drenched the clearing. Then Ymaritis let his gaze drop to a spot beside him.

Even in the dusk, the rose was unmistakable. Its brilliance was incongruous with the tattered fabric it lay on. She stared at it, her magic pleading with her to take it and run.

"You almost had me," Ymaritis declared. Something sinister in his voice demanded Elyse's attention. "An arrow tipped in poison—what a clever idea." His eyes flickered knowingly toward Killian, whose face was drained of color. "It pierced me right through the heart, you know?" Ymaritis tapped his chest, and Elyse's brows furrowed.

What did he mean, it "pierced" him? He'd disappeared before the arrow had hit him, like he'd known it was coming—known exactly when and where it would strike.

Her heart dropped to her stomach. Understanding was a powerful, sickening wave that threatened to send her to her knees.

"You—" she breathed, her voice weak. "You went back in time?"

His answering smile corroded the air from her lungs.

She fell to the ground, gasping. She hadn't realized she'd been clinging to the faintest ember of hope until it was doused completely, smothered by Ymaritis's incomprehensible strength. He had *turned back time*. He had been on the verge of dying, an arrow through his heart, and he had still managed to cast a powerful spell—one she hadn't believed was possible.

"You're lying," she rasped, fighting the bile that rose in her throat. But she knew he wasn't. She knew this was the end, that she was utterly helpless, that she had finally, undoubtedly been bested.

"Elyse." Killian's voice—followed by a hiss as the dagger bit deeper. "Don't you dare give up. You hear me?"

He sounded so far away, like he was already lost. She faintly heard his ragged breaths, his knees shifting against the grass. "Fight, Elyse. You're just as strong as he is. You know it's true."

He groaned, and she lifted her gaze to meet his. The tip of the dagger protruded into his skin, tearing wider with each ragged breath he took. But it wasn't the blood seeping from the wound that broke her heart. It was the unshakeable faith he held in his eyes as he pleaded with her to fight.

But she couldn't. She could try, and she would fail, and Lazarus would win anyway. She wouldn't be the reason for Killian's death.

"How touching," Ymaritis sang, an ingenuine sweetness to his voice. Then, in a more sinister tone: "It's time."

He pulled a vial from his pocket—one that glittered with gold liquid, one that Elyse immediately recognized. The angel's blood shimmered, despite the darkness around them. Ymaritis knelt before the blanket and unsheathed a bejeweled knife from his hip. As he sliced the knife across his palm, he didn't grimace or wince. His eyes widened as if he relished the pain.

Blood poured from the cut, which he held over the eternal rose. The rose's brilliance slowly diminished as blood spilled across its petals, its radiant leaves. Rich gold joined the deep red hues as Ymaritis coated the rose in angel's blood, mixing it with his own.

Elyse watched, breathless, helpless, just as the last rays of sunlight ebbed away. All the warmth was stolen from the air, and she shivered as she waited, cold and afraid.

The clearing was still, until suddenly, violently, it wasn't.

Shadows coursed among the trees, darker than the surrounding air. They flew and spun, obsidian blurs all congregating in a whirlwind. The earth shook and the trees groaned, and Ymaritis disappeared behind a cloud of festering shadows.

His scream tore through her ears, a bellow of both pain and victory. The air seemed thicker, rife with vile magic that burned her lungs. She thought of ending it, of unleashing her own magic and getting the three of them far, far away, but each time she did, she could hear Killian and Jaime both straining to breathe against the dagger's deepening claim. Every muscle was frantic, every inch of her skin sweating, as she racked her brain, her heart, for what to do.

The shadows surrounding Ymaritis slowed, the whirlwind growing thinner. She caught glimpses between the spinning shapes as he writhed. His figure grew clearer, sharper, as the shadows faded to wisps, then dissipated altogether.

A silent prayer floated from Elyse's lips as she waited, hoping by some inconceivable chance that it hadn't worked. Ymaritis kept his head bowed, his chest heaving, his hands planted on the grass.

It was when he lifted his head, his mismatched eyes meeting hers, that she knew he had succeeded.

He grinned at her, and the memory of a skull's lipless smile clawed at the back of her mind.

When Ymaritis spoke, it was not the haughty voice of a well-mannered merchant that met her ears, but the inhuman growl of a demon.

"Hello, Daughter."

CHAPTER 60

— • —

ELYSE

T hose words.

They were the words that haunted her nightmares, that made her want to tear her own flesh from her body. And Lazarus knew it.

He was taunting her, as he had done so many times. Yet hearing him call her *daughter*, seeing the words roll off human lips instead of the hollow jaws of a skull... She trembled with both rage and fear as she waited for whatever was to come.

Lazarus rose to his feet slowly, as if savoring the taste of the earth, the wind, the despair around him. His chest expanded, shoulders rolling back as he inhaled the crisp forest air. He let out a blissful sigh, a smirk tickling his lips.

Elyse watched, trembling. Though Lazarus wore Ymaritis's body, there was a hellish aura to him. He appeared taller, as eminent and ancient as the trees surrounding him. His movements were sharper, made vivid by the contrast of darkness that seemed to swallow the air around him.

Her eyes flickered to Killian and Jaime. They still knelt, arms bound, the daggers now half an inch into each of their chests. But they were still alive, which counted for something. If she could find a way to outsmart Lazarus, maybe she could save them.

Lazarus followed her gaze to her friends, eyes narrowed with distaste, before he slowly turned back to her.

"Thank you for all of your help, Daughter. So many years of service. It has not gone unnoticed. As a display of my gratitude, my ability to show mercy, I will make you an offer."

She blinked, and he was gone. She couldn't see him behind her, but his presence was undeniable, confirmed by icy hands that caressed her wrists. Her body went rigid, fear ricocheting through her, immobilizing her.

Using his hands instead of magic, Lazarus began untying her bindings. As the rope slackened, the grip on her lungs tightened. The ropes fell to the ground, a whisper against the grass, and Elyse turned to look up at her enslaver.

"Join me," he commanded, extending his hand. His voice was low, yet it still bellowed through the forest. "Join me in wreaking havoc on this land. All will know our names, and all will fear us. I will show you power you could never imagine." His eyes—Ymaritis's blue and silver eyes—sparkled with insatiable bloodlust. "Join me, and I will let them live."

Her head snapped toward Killian, to the dagger drawing a slow river of blood. He didn't need to speak for her to know what he was thinking. His expression begged her—*Please, Elyse. Do not do this.*

Even Jaime, panting and coated in sweat, silently pleaded with her not to give in.

Her mouth opened, and she almost said, "Yes." She almost agreed—would have agreed to anything if it meant saving Killian. Yet her throat refused to emit a sound as images of charred corpses lying in the street touched her mind. The hundreds of ruined bodies of Prestowne, lives ended tragically. Her own hands coated in blood, evidence of the deaths she'd caused. A smiling, curly-haired girl with a future ahead of her, gone in an act of violence.

If that was what Lazarus was capable of as a demon confined to Hell, what worse devastation would he inflict now that he was on earth? She would not stand beside him, enabling him to terrorize the kingdom.

Yet Killian deserved more. He deserved life, and happiness, and salvation. Jaime, who had stood beside her at her darkest time, deserved more. They deserved to live.

"I'll do it," she uttered, voice limned in calamity. She would join Lazarus, she would bide her time, and she would betray him.

"Elyse!" Killian's cry cleaved the forest in two, echoing off the distant ridge and reverberating back to her in haunting waves.

She looked to him, subtly lifting her chin. *I love you*, she tried to say. *I would do anything for you.*

Lazarus's smile brightened—so different from Ymaritis's, and yet born of the same wickedness. "You have lied to these men so much," he said, taking a step closer to her. "You have hidden your true self from them again and again, betraying their faith."

He now stood mere inches from her. Elyse had to crane her neck to look up at him, her heart hammering with determination and regret. He lifted a hand, tucking a strand of tangled hair behind her ear, and leaned closer.

"But you could never hide your true intentions from me."

Before the words could even penetrate her mind, shouts shattered the small clearing. Killian and Jaime both knelt on the ground, though their hands were freed, and the daggers were gone. Their faces were pale, fright making their movements staccato, though Elyse didn't know *why*.

She realized it then, in a moment of panic. They weren't kneeling, the earth had swallowed their feet and calves and was now slowly devouring their knees. Killian's fingers dug into the dirt as he tried to keep himself anchored aboveground, his face contorted with the effort. Slowly, he and Jaime sank deeper into the soil.

Elyse sent a blast of green light at them, a spell meant to clear away the ground that enveloped their legs. The green light hit an invisible wall and disseminated upward and outward, unable to reach them.

"No!" She hurled her hands forward, again and again, but each time that invisible wall arrested her spells.

The earth was now as far as their thighs, creeping closer to their hips. Both men clawed at the ground with panicked hands. Desperately, Elyse ran toward them but slammed into the wall of hard air. She pounded her fists against it, willing the wall to shatter and let her in.

Lazarus let out a low laugh at her useless pounding, and she turned on him, unleashing a new type of hell upon him. The veins in her hands were stark against her white skin as she flexed her muscles, pouring her hatred into each spell she cast. White light, black smoke, red fire—none of it seemed to affect him. He stood, his laughter juxtaposed against the intense aching in Elyse's chest. Yet each and every shot was useless. She couldn't hurt him.

She turned her focus back to Killian and Jaime, who were now up to their chests in dirt. She raked her fingertips down the wall, her nails bleeding as they tore.

"No, no! *Please!*"

She said it again and again, but her friends sank deeper into the ground, no matter how hard she slammed her palms against the wall.

"Elyse," Killian called. He'd stopped struggling, his expression grave. Every part of him beneath his shoulders was lost below the surface. He met her eyes, so much emotion conveyed in one desperate look.

He had resigned himself to his fate. He was trying to tell her goodbye. But she refused to hear it, refused to let him sink beneath the ground and out of her reach forever. Tears streaked her cheeks, but she wouldn't acknowledge them. She wouldn't grieve for Killian because he would make it.

There had to be *something* she could do. Lazarus was powerful, but she wasn't completely weak. She fell to her knees, hands cradling her stomach as if reaching for something inside of her that would save them. She felt the tiniest splinter of hope buried deep in her core, and she clung to it, latching on with whatever chaotic magic she could muster. It was fierce and violent and desperate, but Elyse wouldn't let go, even as it tried to shake her off.

For Killian, she would hold fast. For Killian, who had held out hope for her after everything they'd been through. For Killian, who had come for her when she was in chains. For Killian, who had taught her grace and forgiveness, and awakened her soul. For Killian, whom she loved.

She let that love consume her, burning her insides in a white-hot rage until her magic erupted, tunneling through her like oblivion.

A hand, tan and callused, clasped within her own.

Another, pale and soft, fingers tightening around her grip.

And the clearing was gone.

CHAPTER 61

— · —

ELYSE

C old water splashed around Elyse's feet as she landed, clutching Killian and Jaime. Heavy breaths reverberated through the surrounding forest, clamoring against Elyse's fragile mind. Darkness encircled them, the trees mere shadows in a sea of night.

"Elyse."

Killian's breathless voice thrummed through her as he pulled her tight against his chest. "Are you okay?" he rasped against her hair.

Unable to speak, she pressed herself closer to him. Tears still streaked her cheeks, tears that now mingled with the dirt and sweat drenching Killian's tunic. She was not okay. Her body shook against Killian's, waiting, waiting, *waiting* for Lazarus. Ymaritis had been able to turn back time. Surely Lazarus could do the same, or worse.

Behind her, she heard Jaime splashing through the water. She couldn't see him, but she could hear the tension in his footsteps. "Fuck," he panted. "Where are we?"

She'd brought them to the one place she could think of. The place where she always went when her world was upended: the creek by her cottage.

No, she was definitely not okay.

Her trembling was ceaseless, even as Killian held her in his strong arms. She could feel his heart thundering in his chest, in sync with hers. Still she waited, still she breathed heavily against Killian's shirt, as if these might be her last moments.

But Lazarus did not come.

Killian pulled away, just enough to look her in the eyes. His usual umber skin was ashen, marred by fear and failure. But he was alive. Elyse touched a hand to his face, still not fully believing it.

"How did you do that?" Killian stared at her, amazement glowing beneath everything else. "How did you magick us out of there?"

Elyse opened her mouth, but only a small, hoarse sound came out. She shook her head, stunned by her lack of an answer. "I don't know," she croaked.

The truth. She had no idea how she had managed to transport them away. Desperation had taken hold of her, unleashing some part of her magic she hadn't known existed. Somewhere deep inside her, she knew it was the same power Ymaritis used to transport himself. The thought that they shared any sort of magic made her stomach churn, but she would do it again if it meant saving Killian.

"I just—I couldn't lose you," she added, the words raw.

Her chin trembled, and Killian enveloped her. He stroked soothing lines against her back, every caress a reminder that he was alive. He was with her.

They had failed, utterly and completely. Lazarus was alive, inhabiting a human body. But she had gotten Killian and Jaime out. And they would face this together.

She wrapped her arms tighter around Killian, letting his strong body take more of her weight.

"I've got you," he murmured, lulling her anxieties.

Elyse closed her eyes and focused on the rise and fall of his chest. Even through his tunic, she could feel the scar beneath. Jaime was pacing, his boots crunching violently against the rocky creek bottom, until he stopped suddenly.

Elyse barely paid him any mind. She wished it was just her and Killian at that moment. She wished the two of them could run away and pretend none of this had happened.

"Look at me," Killian said, his fingers grazing Elyse's chin to lift her face toward his. "This isn't over. We'll go to Privya's and meet with the others and—"

He stopped abruptly, his mouth hanging open, his next words lost on his tongue. His body trembled, and Elyse trembled with him, unsure what was happening.

"Killian?" she asked, barely above a whisper.

He dropped to his knees, crashing into the water. He fell against her, practically knocking her into the creek, and she grasped at him as a sickly fear tore through her body.

"Killian!" She could barely say his name, her throat rough with terror. They collapsed together, plunging into the frigid waters as Elyse grappled at Killian's shirt.

She saw it then—the blood spilling into the water. "Killian," she cried again. Her eyes landed on the knife protruding from his back, the blood surrounding it. Without a second thought, she reached for the knife and tore it free. Blood cascaded from the wound, but Elyse plunged her hands atop the gash, pouring her magic into it.

"Stay with me, Killian," she begged. His breathing was ragged and shallow.

"Don't bother," came Jaime's voice, low and sadistic.

Elyse's head snapped toward him, confusion clouding her thoughts. His face was contorted with hatred as he stared down at Killian. She looked between him and the knife in in hand, stunned by the revelation. "*You* did this?"

Terror and denial blinded her as she heaved every ounce of her magic into healing Killian, but the blood was endless.

"You can't save him, Elyse," Jaime drawled.

She ignored him, refusing to accept his taunting. For now, she had to save Killian—but her damned magic wasn't working.

A horrid realization filled Elyse. She felt as if she were being dragged down into the creek, drowning in the icy waters.

She couldn't heal Killian.

She couldn't heal him because Jaime had used poison—the poison they'd stolen from the Bastards' lair.

"No. No, no, no, no, *no*." She said the word again and again, commanding her magic to save him. She couldn't see for the tears that spilled endlessly, couldn't think for the agony that ravaged her. She was barely aware of Killian's hand cupping her cheek.

"Elyse," he rasped, stealing her attention. Those two syllables on his lips were her undoing as her heart exploded. She forced herself to look at him, despite the inevitability she would find there.

His eyes were heavy, as if it took the last of his waning energy to keep them open. But he stared at her, his lips a tight, pained line. When they parted, blood trickled from the corner of his mouth. A morbid clarity shone in his eyes.

"It is not the end."

A sob tore through her as his words shredded her heart. There was a haunting acceptance in his voice—acceptance that his life would soon be over. Even through his dying breaths, he was consoling her, insisting that she had a future, though he did not. She blinked away her tears, needing desperately to bear witness to Killian in his last moments.

"I love you," she said, the words pouring from her lips as more blood spilled from Killian's. She needed to tell him. She needed him to know that she loved him more deeply than she'd ever loved anyone, that he had brought her out of her despair and loneliness.

But Killian just stroked her cheek, a soft smile on his lips as if they were in her bed, whispering to one another across the pillows. "Bonded souls have a way of finding each other."

He said it with finality, a decision that this would be his parting gift to her. And it was a gift, perhaps. A splinter of hope. But as he took his last, rasping breath, and his eyes glazed over, it felt more like a cruel mockery than a promise.

She held him, letting the waters of the creek dispel around them, numb to everything but Killian's weight in her arms. Guttural, incoherent sounds quivered from her throat, a cacophony of the agony and anger she felt.

He could not leave her.

He could not leave her when she needed him most.

It might have been minutes, it might have been hours. Slowly, the world returned to her. First with the pounding of her own heart, hammering in her ears. Then the icy waters that flowed into her boots, soaking her trousers. The rustling of leaves that surrounded her, the faint scent of bark and wildflowers. And finally, the calm, resolute breaths of another.

Jaime.

She'd somehow forgotten about him, so entrenched in trying to save Killian that she'd blocked out the source of her devastation. All that fury assaulted her at once.

As she lifted her head toward Jaime, she trembled with that rage. She smoldered in it, welcoming it, bathing in it as if her ire could cleanse her pain.

Jaime stared back at her with pity and determination. "It had to be done." He said it low yet firm, as firm as the trees that surrounded them.

Still holding Killian, Elyse gritted her teeth. *Not yet*, whispered something deep within her as more hatred stoked the hysteria within her.

"You're angry," he continued, shaking his head. His eyes were wide as if pleading for her to understand. "But you'll understand. He never loved you. He shot you with an arrow. He sent mercenaries after you. He was going to turn you in."

He spoke as if blind to Elyse's fervor, the power stirring within her.

Not yet, came the whisper again, paralyzing her.

"You don't belong with him, and you never did," Jaime went on, his voice growing more bold. "I am the one who healed you when you arrived at my doorstep, bloodied from his arrow. I am the one who fed you and housed you and protected you. I am the one who deserves your love."

A shiver wracked Elyse's body as the meaning beneath his words dragged a cold finger up her spine. He said nothing of his love for her, only the devotion he felt he was owed. He didn't care for her, he cared for the idea of her—the idea that she was his to claim.

Not yet. Her power coursed through her, a hungry dog biting at a steak that dangled before it. *Not yet*, it purred as the fire within her grew.

"You should be thanking me," he uttered, a hint of condescension in his voice. "I broke the blood oath."

Now.

Her magic seethed. It writhed within her, a fire that blocked out the cold waters of the creek, a power that made her feel weightless despite the heaviness of Killian's body slumped against hers. It vibrated through her, until it was bursting from her skin.

Between clenched teeth, she growled, "You. Are. *Nothing.*"

Jaime stood in the creek, pride and anger and confusion furrowing his brows, and then he was gone.

Blood rained across the forest.

It speckled the trees, tainting their perfect, verdant leaves. It sprayed across the grass, droplets intermingling with the creek's clear waters. It covered Elyse's face, blinding her senses with a coppery tang.

That was all that was left of Jaime, aside from a few shreds of fabric that floated away, tangling in nearby branches. That, and the anger boiling in Elyse's veins.

It wasn't enough. It would never be enough. Even as she savored the taste of his blood on her lips, she knew that wiping Jaime off this earth would never erase her pain.

Her gaze slowly dropped to Killian's face. He was splattered with blood—the blood of his murderer. With a trembling hand, she tried to wipe it away. A sob eviscerated her body.

Killian was gone.

Her Killian.

The only one who made her feel safe, and seen. He had found it in his heart to forgive her, and now he was gone.

His last words echoed through her mind, torturing her.

Bonded souls have a way of finding each other.

As if they would see each other again. One day, perhaps soon, her death would come. On that day, she would be reunited with him, and they could have the future she hadn't allowed herself to dream of.

She ran a hand through Killian's curls and closed her eyes. The world seemed so cold without him. She couldn't wait for death to claim her before seeing him again.

Hope was determined to steal its way into her heart. It started small, an ember fanned by frantic thoughts as a plan began to develop. There was one person who could help her, if help was even attainable.

Still kneeling in the creek, she clutched Killian tighter, pulling his limp body to her chest. She closed her eyes and tried desperately to draw from the same power as before.

Please, she begged of her magic. *Please.*

She gripped Killian's body with everything she had as she willed her magic to navigate away from this place, to flow through time and space and deliver her at her savior's door.

As the cold waters of the creek disappeared, she repeated one name over and over again in her mind.

Mr. Grayson.

ABOUT THE AUTHOR

Thank you for reading Of Blood and Roses.
You can learn more about Samantha Ziegler, including her other works,
by heading to her Link Tree.
Reviews on Amazon and Goodreads are always appreciated.

ACKNOWLEDGEMENTS

First and foremost, thank you to Jade Austin. I value your friendship, critique, and support so much. I can't wait until we're both rich and famous and can take writing retreats together.

Thank you, Ced, for the beautiful covers. Your art was the start of everything.

Thank you to Karina for the amazing playlists and for all of your support. You are a wonderful friend, and I cherish you.

Evie, your maps and drawings are awesome. Thank you for bringing Rhodan to life, despite my subpar sketches.

Nicole, you're a phenomenal proofreader, and this book would be a hot mess without you!

Shannon, you're incredible. I'm continually impressed by your trailers, and I am so glad to call you my friend.

To my street team members, especially Gracie, Carmella, Cassie, Carrie, Frankie, Hailey, Dominque, and Riniya. Without being too cheesy, you're the wind beneath my wings. And to Holly as well, for all your support and input.

Printed in Great Britain
by Amazon